ENEMIES

Facing ENEMIES

A Historical Novel of 1803

By

Mary Ann Trail

ISBN: 9781983864704 (paperback)

I want to acknowledge the support of a number of people, but especially Elaine Ingulli, who patiently read several versions of *Uniting Enemies,* and now *Facing Enemies.* Her suggestions and encouragement have been unmatched in helping me bring my stories to life. I also want to let my beta readers know their contributions made *Facing Enemies* a better book and helped bring depth and reality to Jeffrey and Georgina's story.

I doubt I would have succeeded, in realizing my dream of becoming a novelist, without the backing of my daughters, Marion and Maura and my sister Carol, who have been unfailing in their encouragement and support.

Thank you all!

Contents

Chapter One: Dublin 1803 Spring

Georgina stepped from the door of the dress maker on Sackville Street and quickly looked both ways trying to find her coach. Drat that coachman! Tom had said he would be waiting where she could see him. She should be able to find that garish, over-done carriage anywhere, even on this bustling street. Despite teeming with shoppers and vehicles, Sackville Street was one of the few places in Dublin that had an island of trees and shrubs running down the middle of the wide avenue giving the area an interesting combination of city bustle mixed with the greenery of a park.

"Humph!" she huffed. Tom wasn't anywhere in sight! She gave another quick look around to make certain she didn't recognize anyone she might offend and then muttered, "Damn and blast" under her breath. Another annoyance to add to the seemingly endless list of today's irritants and frustrations.

A glance over her shoulder assured her that her maid, Mary, was in close attendance and carrying several of the smaller packages of items purchased today.

"Mary," she snapped peevishly, "keep up. Tom is not where he said he would be, so I assume we have to go search for him. Probably around the corner."

She joined the foot traffic moving rapidly to the right and the closest corner. Spring had brought an unusual amount of daily rain. Today was no exception, and more rain seemed in the offing if the dark clouds were any sign of warning. Anyone caught on the sidewalk edge was sure of a splash from the muck thrown by the traffic moving up and down the street. Why had he moved? She hadn't been in the shop that long. Now her hem and maybe her whole skirt was really going to be splattered.

What a frustrating day! She had made a special trip to Sackville Street's shopping district to pick up the hat. This had required another argument with her brother when he insisted she take the carriage. She had wanted to walk from her home on Mount Joy Square, only a few blocks away. She knew the carriage would be a problem and it would be faster to negotiate the area on foot. But Walter insisted on the coach. She probably should be grateful for his thoughtfulness, but life in Dublin could be so confining. She had too much energy to sit patiently in a coach that was usually stuck in traffic. She wanted to be out and moving.

She was beginning to dislike intensely the restrictions of Dublin. Even life in boarding school seemed to have more freedom. At least, during her last year at school the headmistress, had treated her as more of a staff member than a school girl, allowing her walks to the lending library, and to the market street with only a maid as a companion. In Dublin, Walter assured her that being on the streets alone, just would not do. Georgina tried to admit to herself that since Walter was at least ten years older and had been in society so much longer, he probably did know more about how she should go on. She just did not like someone always organizing her life for her, even if it was for her own good. Since her mother had died, she had spent the time away at school, and only now realized how much freedom she had enjoyed. She was not confident she liked being home all that much.

And now, those wretched people were not finished with her hat. "They told me two weeks," she grumbled to herself. Now it would not be ready to wear to Frances' garden party tomorrow. She seethed with indignation and a sense of injustice. If they had not promised the new headgear in two weeks, she would not have counted on wearing it. Reaching the corner, she turned right on Prince Street and her indignation reached new heights. No coach.

Sighing mightily, she turned to face Mary, "Where do…" and stopped.

Mary was not standing in her usual spot, three steps behind. Instead, a large bearded man, two heads taller and dressed in stained working clothes, stood blocking her way. She noticed a scar over one eye that and reached his hair line. He reached out and gripped her arm. "This way, missy," he ordered. "Your coach is along here." He gestured up the street with his head.

Georgina stepped back, trying to look around him and pull her arm out of his grasp. She could barely peer around him and to see Mary kneeling on the ground trying to retrieve the packages she had obviously dropped. "Mar -!" she started to call.

The stranger pushed her along the street. "This way miss. The maid will catch up."

Still being pulled by her arm, Georgina began to protest. "No, take your hands off me. I will wait for Mary." She tried to place her feet to stop him moving her away from the crowd of shoppers on High Street.

"The carriage is just down here, lady," he snarled. "Not far now."

* * *

Dublin Castle

Captain Jeffrey Chadwick, late of the Third Regiment of Foot, one of the oldest infantry regiments in His Majesty's service. Currently he was a member of the select group assigned to the Alien Office, and now, recently arrived from London, he stood in the archway leading to the parade ground at Dublin Castle. He paused a moment to get his bearings and to identify which door would take him to his new workplace.

Any stranger passing by would have noticed the Captain, who stood almost six feet tall and was usually tallest among the groups he found himself in. The stranger, especially if it was a woman, would also noticed his classic good looks, thick dark blonde hair, and bright inquiring eyes. Even in his traveling clothes, he stood out as a pleasing specimen of British manhood.

The buildings that formed the square of the parade ground were imposing. They were mostly three stories and made of brick and stone. *Made to impress the locals*, he thought, *and easily defended against rioters*. He knew well that Dublin had its fair share of rioters, rebels, and, as his office officially referred to various upheavals in the peace, disturbances. An ironic term, he thought, that did not do justice to the murder and mayhem some of the 'disturbances' wrought.

His directions told him to cross the parade field and look for a tower on the left. Looking like something out of the Middle Ages, stuck between beautiful Georgian buildings, the tower was slightly taller than the buildings around it. Chadwick walked the perimeter of the square, angling towards the tower but still closely observing his surroundings. Although no longer in the military, his army training and then his field work with the Alien Office had made studying his environment not only compulsory but natural. It also gave him time to collect himself before he faced Wickham.

* * *

A short while earlier, his ferry was still being tied up at the pier and Chadwick was on the deck of the ferry talking to the boat captain when a messenger from his superior, William Wickham, had found him and bid him come immediately to the Alien Office in Dublin Castle. The lad, who must have been waiting at the docks for the boat to land, would take Chadwick's valet, David Thomas, and his bags to the lodgings Wickham had organized. Chadwick would have liked to follow that luggage and clean up after what had been a pretty rocky ride over the Irish Sea. The note, however, had left no doubt that Wickham wanted him immediately, if not sooner.

Chadwick spent the short hackney ride from the docks mulling over what crisis might have caused his superior to act so uncharacteristically but so far he had come up with nothing. He had not worked directly under Wickham when he had been attached to the London Alien Office, but for Lord Samuels. Wickham had been in charge of the office, reporting directly to Lord Grenville, a member of Prime Minister Pitt's cabinet. But whenever Captain Chadwick had interacted with Wickham, he had always found him to be a man who faced emergencies with composure. Nothing for it but to show up in his travel clothes and find out what had put Wickham in such a tizzy.

Chadwick was approaching the tower to the left of the imposing parade field, when the doors were suddenly thrown open and an older gentleman rushed out. Although the man was almost a head shorter than Chadwick, he was moving so forcefully that if the Captain had not jumped aside, he might have been bowled over. Although the older man moved with purpose, Chadwick noticed he was extremely pale and seemed under stress. Without so much as an 'Excuse me,' the man strode across the parade field heading for the archway leading to the street. A younger man charged out the door, practically running in his haste to catch up with the older man.

"Father, wait!"

Chadwick stood aside and watched as both men practically ran across the open space and disappeared through the arch. They did not look like hackney riders, so he assumed their carriage was waiting somewhere on the main thoroughfare. Ireland must be pretty tumultuous if Wickham and these men were any example of the normal state of affairs. The Captain turned in some bemusement to the doorman – whose presence had been totally ignored by the exiting gentlemen – but who was stiffly standing and holding the door open for Chadwick. He looked at Chadwick inquiringly: "Sir?"

At his height, Chadwick was used to looking down on his fellow man. This chap met his eyes without so much as a tilt of his head. If anything, he was a bit taller than Chadwick. And he noticed, the man had the shoulders to match. What was he doing, just manning the doors? At his size, he could be doing a number of other, better-paying jobs.

But the Captain just nodded his thanks for the open door and asked, "Which way is Mr. Wickham's office?"

"Upstairs, sir," the man responded, nodding to the stairs in question. "Up one set and then follow the corridor to the last door at the end."

"Right," Chadwick responded. Although he no could longer see the two hurried gentlemen, his eyes were drawn to their rapid exit through the arch. "People always that rushed around here?" he asked.

"No sir, Mr. Yelverton usually is a lot more reserved in himself." His eyes also went to the arch the men had gone through. "He has been here a lot lately, though." He stopped abruptly so Chadwick assumed he had just remembered he shouldn't be chatting about visitors, especially to strangers. "But since he is just come from Mr. Wickham's office, Mr. Wickham is sure to know what upset him," he added helpfully.

Chadwick nodded thoughtfully to the man, passed into the building and started up the stairs. The stairs followed the walls of the tower and curved upwards forming an open space in the center of the tower. Chadwick leaned over the balustrade to look up. He could see the roof from the first floor. The tower seemed to consist solely of stairs. Where were the offices if not in the tower? He soon found that each floor had a door opening into the building that abutted the tower. He pushed open the door in question to find himself facing a fairly short hallway that was flooded with natural light coming from several doors opened on the right side and windows overlooking the parade field on the left.

"Chadwick! Just the man I need." Wickham stood in the door of the last office. He seemed to have been waiting for him. He walked forward to shake the Captain's hand with more enthusiasm than Chadwick was used to.

"Good Afternoon, Mr. Wickham," Chadwick returned. He was startled by Wickham's eagerness. His presence had never evoked such enthusiasm before. He couldn't quite find a name for the energy that seemed to be coming from his superior.

"I came from the ferry as soon as I got your message," he said cautiously.

Before Chadwick could apologize for his appearance or make any other remarks, Wickham took his arm and pulled him into the office. He motioned for the Captain to close the door. He then plucked two glasses and a bottle of claret from his desk. Chadwick couldn't remember an interview he had ever had with Wickham with a closed door. He had never been offered drinks of any kind. He had not been in the upper echelons of Alien House nor in on any planning sessions, except, of course, that involving the very recent situation concerning the Madra Dubh and the kidnapping of Miss Coxe's nephews. He sighed. Whatever was going on, he doubted his skill as a translator was needed.

"Sit, sit," Wickham ordered. He poured two generous portions of claret and pushed one to Chadwick. Wickham remained silent, tapping his fingers on the desk, obviously thinking about how to begin.

The Captain looked around for a chair. Both desk chairs were pushed far from the desk as if someone had stood in haste, shoving the chair away as they did. He wondered if Yelverton had been here with Wickham. He took one chair, obviously designed for a smaller man, and positioned it in front of the desk. Then he took the glass. "To your health, sir," he toasted. He would have preferred tea and some sandwiches but this was more than he was usually offered.

"What?" Wickham seemed startled. "Oh, right." He saluted Chadwick and took his glass and sipped. "I am having trouble trying to decide where to begin," he said to Chadwick's amazement.

"Begin with what, sir? My orders were to take over the translation desk and to work with you in all matters of intelligence. Has something changed?" Chadwick took another sip and wondered if it would go to his head too fast. He was starved. He always lost his appetite on boats, especially rocky ones and the trip from Holyhead had seemed unnecessarily rough in his opinion. But he found that appetite again when he had reached land.

"Yes, oh, my God yes, *something* has changed," Wickham exploded. "I have a very delicate situation on my hands and no trained agents to deal with it."

"A delicate situation, sir?" Chadwick rolled the glass between his hands while he observed Wickham quietly. His superior was acting very unlike himself.

Wickham had his glass in his hands but after his first sip had not taken another. He seemed to be in a fog of thought.

"As I said, I have a delicate, very delicate, situation," he reiterated, "and no trained agents. You have more experience than anyone else I have available and the situation is too urgent for London to send someone more skilled in time."

Chadwick began to get a very bad feeling that he was about to be pushed into deeper waters than he was comfortable swimming in. He said cautiously, "As you know, sir, I am not a real field agent. I am a translator. I have done some small jobs, usually with Nathan Donnay. But I have done very little on my own."

"I know that, Chadwick," Wickham said flatly. "But not much choice, is there?"

"I guess you had better tell me what all this is about."

Wickham slumped in his chair, took a sip of his wine and then said flatly, "I have a missing daughter of a very highly placed diplomat. This gently bred miss disappeared about a week ago. Father, a man named Yelverton, has been up and down the Castle from Cornwallis to the Lord Lieutenant trying to get someone to investigate. Now it's landed in my lap."

The Captain frowned. "Why is a missing girl a matter for the Alien Office?" he asked. "We investigate the activities of insurrectionists and trouble-makers from outside the kingdom." He took another sip and realized he had finished the claret. He placed the glass on the desk. The way this conversation was going had caused a knot to form in his stomach. He could feel his hopes for the calm work of translating newspapers and reports slipping away.

He had asked for this transfer from London for a very specific reason. He had finally met a woman that interested him and challenged him, but his best friend had already claimed her heart. Marion Coxe had been nothing like he imagined his perfect mate would be. She had courage, wit, and was interested in politics, as well as the usual womanly concerns. But Nathan Donnay had met her first and their love had lasted despite a separation. He couldn't stay in London and see their happiness every day. He did not want to spend the rest of his life depressed and jealous.

He felt a twinge of guilt thinking of his sister. To get out of London before his transfer was approved, he had arranged a walking tour of some historic sites in the South-west with his favorite uncle Festus and his old tutor, Thomas Grant. Chadwick had planned to take Frederica with them, as a way of getting her away from her step-mother, Hermione's influence, at least for a little while. He gathered from her letters that living with Hermione was, at times, trying for the young woman. But his transfer had come through unexpectedly suddenly and he was ordered to report as soon as possible to Wickham in Dublin. Since he was forced to leave his traveling companions in the lurch, he had done the best he could by leaving money with Festus and getting his promise to take Frederica. His tutor was a wonderful soul but not in the first blush of youth. How would he deal with a young woman? The situation had all the makings of a disaster, but he had promised Frederica and he hated to break his word.

Chadwick tried to push his personal affairs aside and focus on what his superior was saying.

Wickham paused to refresh their glasses and then said, "Chadwick, let me bring you up to date on what has been happening here in Dublin and to a lesser extent, in Ireland."

"Well, sir, if you remember, I was part of the planning after the threats to kidnap Ralph Coxe's sons." Chadwick tried to jog Wickham's memory gently and save himself a long recital of the Irish 'disturbances'. Although, usually a calm and controlled man, Wickham could talk. Sometimes his meetings with underlings took on the aspect of Chadwick's old lecturers at Oxford, long and at times very tedious. He tried again to forestall a repeat of information he was well aware of.

"I am not positive you know, sir, but I was stationed here in Dublin in '98. Once I joined the Alien Office, I made several trips here with Donnay, usually to 'bring resources' for the vote on unification."

"As you know…" Wickham started, then stopped. "You seem more knowledgeable than I thought. Maybe it would be easier if you told me what you do know."

Chadwick smiled to himself, relieved that his strategy had worked. "I was still in the army in '98, so my experience of Dublin and of Ireland is from the military standpoint. I can't say I enjoyed the experience much. My own mother was from the Colonies and she was pretty fiery about the rights of man and so forth. Anyway, when we finally got the riots put down, I had had enough and sold up. But I was here long enough to get the lay of the land and find my way about. I did not have much to do with information-gathering when I was stationed here or when I made trips to deliver cash used by the government to make certain the vote for unification went the way they wanted.

"I did rather enjoy those trips here with the money. It was almost like being let out of school; easy trip to Holyhead ferry to Dublin and then drop off the bags here at the Castle. But I have never been in this section of the Castle before," he said.

"Until the unification, we, the Alien Office, didn't have a presence here," Wickham answered. "When the unification didn't pass the Irish Parliament the first time, Prime Minister Pitt decided that we needed to focus more on the effort. We started to replicate the London Alien Office over here to identify the French agents and then expanded out to collect information on the members of Parliament who were sympathetic or could be 'helped' to be sympathetic to the cause of unification with England. I only just recently got sent here to take over."

"Yes, sir, I remember when you left London. It's what gave me the idea that Dublin might be a good place to work."

Wickham nodded in agreement. "Well, Dublin has its own set of issues. There seem to be French spies everywhere," he sighed. But back to the unification, I cannot help but wonder if it doesn't have some bearing on the missing girl. Her father was a vocal proponent of the unification and a recipient of our government's largess. Maybe this has something to do with retribution on the part of factions who didn't like the way he voted?"

Chadwick raised his eyebrows inquiringly and placed his empty glass on the corner of the desk. It looked like the lecture was coming anyway. He sat back, trying to get more comfortable in the uncomfortable chair.

"Mr. Pitt felt that the best way to calm the unrest in Ireland and keep France from using Ireland as a launching point for an invasion of England was to make Ireland part of England by an official act approved by both the Irish and English Parliaments. As you know the original vote on that resolution went down in magnificent defeat. So Pitt increased the amount of money the government was willing to spend and tried again for another vote. According to our sources, most of the anti-unionists were concerned for their personal income and had no real opinion on unification. Most of them used the Irish Parliament has a source of income or personal influence. Mr. Pitt wanted to offer them incentives to change their vote."

"I was pretty confident the cash Nathan and I delivered here was for bribes. Pretty obvious when on the first trip our saddlebags were only filled with half bills. After the vote, I heard the second halves were sent over." Nathan and he had always assumed that was what the money was for, but Chadwick was glad to have his theory substantiated.

"Correct," Wickham agreed. "They got the second half after the final vote. But as you know, the vote was not without controversy. Especially from a faction of the Catholics who want total independence from England. You remember the threats and then the kidnapping of the Coxe boys?"

Oh, yes indeed did Chadwick know about the Coxe affair. As far as he knew, Wickham had delegated handling the matter to Lord Samuels so Wickham might not be aware how deeply Chadwick had been involved with the family's attempt to keep Ralph Coxe's sons safe. When that had failed and the twins had been spirited away by a faction of the United Irishmen called Madra Dubh, he, Chadwick, had led the mission to rescue the twins in Southampton.

Chadwick's thoughts returned to the lovely and feisty Marion, and how he had ended up in Dublin hoping a change of scenery and the challenge of opening a new office might help him better face his loss of Marion to his best friend. Now, something in Wickham's voice caught his attention and brought him back to the present.

"Yelverton accepted a lot of money for his vote," he was saying.

"I still don't see the connection, sir."

"I don't either," snapped Wickham. "I am just trying to give you all the information I have."

Chadwick stood up to stretch his legs. He was still stiff from the cramped conditions on the ferry. Even Wickham's spacious office was a bit low for a man of his height. He listened carefully while Wickham went on about the current conditions in Ireland and the troubles he was having finding reliable sources of information. Chadwick felt persuaded that Wickham was winding himself up to tell him to go find the girl, if she was still alive, and bring her home. Why this was a duty of the Alien Office and not someone else was still not clear to him. Did Dublin have anything equivalent to the Bow Street Runners back in London? He wandered to the window at the back of the office and saw the view was of the stables and part of a garden.

Finally he interrupted the flow of words, "Sir?"

Wickham stopped in mid-sentence and looked up at him. From his position at the desk, he had to tilt his head back. "What?"

"Why us?" Chadwick asked. "As I said earlier, we usually just deal in information. This seems something the Irish equivalent of the Runners would be asked to do. As you said, we don't have the manpower or the resources to take on such an assignment."

Wickham did not answer immediately. He stood and joined Chadwick at the window. There was a small group of men by one of the stable doors. He recognized the young chap with the broad shoulders standing with his back to the stable wall, smoking a cigarillo and obviously joking with the other men.

"Well, now that you are here, we might have the manpower."

Chadwick started to argue, "But sir, I don't..."

"Let me finish. You asked, didn't you?" At Chadwick's nod he continued, "Cornwallis is deeply disturbed by the situation. The young woman's father, as I said, is Mr. William Yelverton, very rich, very powerful and related to the King. Distant, but still related. Her brother is Walter Yelverton, very rich, going to be powerful and is even now something of a powermonger.

"Cornwallis has done a yeoman's job settling Ireland down after the last riots. He managed to do it without wholesale slaughter of the Irish but peace is hanging over a precipice. The whole unification thing was a botched job in my opinion. In spite of Coxe's efforts, they had to bribe half the members of the Irish Parliament to get it to pass.

"Cornwallis met with me this morning. He is very worried that the Madra Dubh will fire up the locals and cause instability in Dublin. This might be especially true since it is now obvious that the Catholics will not get the emancipation they were promised by Pitt."

Chadwick nodded in agreement. "Yes, I heard the King was adamantly against anything that gave the Catholics the vote, and that caused Pitt to resign over the issue. Right pretty mess."

"True," Wickham agreed. "I don't think Addison will be as strong a prime minister as Pitt was. I think we are in for a rough time of it, especially with France." He paused and sat down in his chair again although he now turned it to face Chadwick, who was still by the window. "There is something else," he said.

"Do you remember some reports we received in London concerning ship building in northern France? I think you were the one who translated them." He paused and waited for Chadwick's nod of agreement.

Chadwick turned from the window and looked at Wickham, crossing his arms and leaning against the window frame. Wickham had his total attention now; ships and Normandy could only mean Napoleon and invasion.

"I remember the report, but it was vague and full of rumors. It did not have many real facts, just things the writer had gleaned from other people," he said.

"You know as well as I do, Chadwick, that the same information from multiple sources means something is happening even if the writer's interpretation is not spot on."

"Yes," Chadwick agreed reluctantly. "He did mention that he had heard the same from at least two different sources, that there was a lot of lumber heading for the ports but not being shipped out. Obviously not being shipped, as nothing is leaving those ports, thanks to our navy. But that is still quite a leap to a massive ship-building effort." Chadwick had been taught to question and question again the information in the reports he translated. Even the wrong translation of a word could change the meaning of the information presented and cause a political mess.

"I agree and it has been next to impossible to verify his findings." Wickham paused and took a deep breath. "What I am about to say is partly my own supposition. I have been hearing things here in Dublin and I am trying to see if these puzzle pieces might not fit together."

"What do you mean? What have you been hearing?"

"If, in fact, Napoleon is building ships on the coast of France, it can only be for an invasion of England, correct?" At Chadwick's nod, he continued. "Who would be the logical ally in such an invasion? Not the Welsh or the Scots, they are too integrated with England. The Irish would be the logical allies and Ireland would be an excellent place to launch an invasion from. Maybe even use it as a second front. And I don't think the recent unification will make a damn bit of difference." Wickham practically snarled the last few words. To Chadwick, he seemed pretty steamed up. Again, he was startled that Wickham was showing such an emotional side. He must be pretty concerned about recent events.

"What are you basing this theory on?" Chadwick asked.

"Glasse seems to be behind this."

"Glasse is dead. I saw the body myself," he said.

"Yes, I know. I used that name so you would know who I was speaking of. I mean the husband, Hastings. James or Jimmy is his first name.

"He is the one who sent her to London in the first place and planned that whole atrocious scheme. He is still alive," Wickham announced. "He is still active, still running the Madra Dubh and is planning his next move, according to the little intelligence I can gather. The missing Miss Yelverton may be part of it."

Chadwick sighed, seeing his dream of peaceful translations cast aside in the face of Napoleon's plan to conquer Europe. "What does she look like?" he asked.

Chapter Two: Mount Joy Square, Dublin

To Captain Chadwick, Mount Joy Square did not look remarkably different from any of the famous residential squares in London. Façades of each building forming the square were identical, and in the middle of the square stood the ubiquitous city park with a few trees and lots of nursemaids with small children. Broad streets ran in front of each building and were filled with vendors and tradespeople conducting late morning trade.

Upon closer study, he noticed several differences between Mount Joy and the grand squares of London. Here, only three sides had identical fronts; the fourth proved to be a large freestanding house, which, according to his map, was called Gardiner's Place. Unlike the three that completed the square, the structure facing Gardiner's Place did not run the full length of the park. Instead, it had small alleys on either side, cutting the building short but giving access to the mews in the back. The alleys also helped set off the L-shaped buildings on each corner, which appeared to be individual homes.

Evidently, the driver did not know exactly where the Yelvertons lived, as Chadwick could hear him ask one of the venders for directions. From the response, it seemed they would need to circle the park again and stop at one of those freestanding corner houses.

The Yelverton house turned out to be a handsome building, large and well-kept. Even a visitor to Dublin could tell by the way the houses were maintained and the lack of horse manure in the street that the occupants of Mount Joy Square were flush in the pockets. The residents were no doubt not the type to take seriously someone who was not of their social class. Even a legitimate Bow Street Runner would probably not be let in the front door, but would have to make do with the servants' entrance. Chadwick was grateful he had stopped at his new lodgings to change clothes and make himself more presentable. His experience in active investigation was somewhat limited, but he had learned enough to know the Yelvertons would have to trust him first. That he was of their class, although a good deal poorer, should help.

The carriage stopped. The Captain paid the driver and asked him to return in two hours. That should give him enough time to talk to the people he needed to talk to and still get back to meet with Wickham before the end of the day.

The house seemed unoccupied, with the shades drawn and the knocker swathed in cloth. As far as he knew, the girl had not been found dead. What was going on? Maybe he should have sent a note ahead, but there hadn't seemed enough time for such niceties.

To Chadwick's surprise, a quick tap on the door with his cane almost immediately brought a very proper butler, complete with white gloves, to the door.

"I am sorry, sir, Mr. Yelverton is not receiving visitors," he intoned.

"No, I'm assured he's not," agreed Chadwick. "But I am not here socially. Please tell Mr. Yelverton that Captain Chadwick from Mr. Wickham's office is here to see him on a matter of urgency." Chadwick handed him the note Wickham had given him. "Give him this; it will explain my visit."

Now he did have to wait while the butler took his name and Wickham's note up to Mr. Yelverton, but he returned shortly.

"Mr. Yelverton will meet you in his library, sir. Please come this way."

He led the Captain upstairs and down the hall. Opening a door on the right of the hall, he announced, "Captain Chadwick, sir."

Behind the desk was the man Chadwick had seen earlier in the day at the Castle. But this man lacked the energy of the one he had last seen striding across the parade grounds. He seemed deflated; he guessed the word he wanted was 'sad.' A large glass stood on the desk but was almost empty.

"Do you have news?" he asked anxiously.

"No, sir, but Mr. Wickham has sent me to help," Chadwick responded.

Yelverton stood to shake Chadwick's hand but seemed to lean on his own hand, still resting on the desk. Was the man drunk and having trouble with his balance?

At Chadwick's response, Yelverton sighed, gesturing to the chairs in front of the fireplace. He glanced at the butler. "More brandy, unless the Captain wishes something different."

Chadwick sighed again internally. Tea and food would have been more welcome, but if his host was drinking brandy, then he should, too. They settled in front of the fireplace while the butler poured drinks. The host managed the trip across the room without mishap, so maybe he had not been imbibing for long.

Almost as soon as Yelverton sat down, he stood again, gesturing for Chadwick to remain sitting. He began pacing. Chadwick noticed he seemed secure on his feet. He must hold his liquor well, and he certainly wasn't slurring any words.

"This sitting around waiting is killing me. That is the worst part, that I can't do anything. Georgina has been missing almost a week and all I can do is sit here!" he burst out. He turned suddenly and demanded, "And who are you anyway? Wickham said he did not have anyone to put on the case immediately."

"I just arrived from London today, Mr. Yelverton. I have been assigned to the Alien Office for some years."

Chadwick didn't think it wise to say that most of that time had been spent translating newspapers. However, he was not totally without experience.

"What does Wickham think you can do? After all, you've just arrived in Dublin."

"I understand your frustration..." Chadwick began.

"You do not begin…"

The Captain talked over Yelverton. "Please, hear me out," he said. "I have been a field agent for the government for some time. I have experience in tracking and retrieving kidnap victims." He thought briefly of Nathan in St. Petersburg and the Coxe twins last year in Southampton. "I know your daughter has been missing a week, but Mr. Wickham only received the assignment to find her this morning. So we are somewhat behind you in the search. You can be assured, Mr. Yelverton that we will be doing everything we can to arrive at a happy outcome and bring your daughter home."

Chadwick placed his untouched brandy on the table. "Mr. Wickham has already notified his contacts in Dublin. My visit with you today is to gather information. Mr. Wickham does not even have a description of your daughter. We'll need as complete a story as possible. So I want you to tell me everything you can, including every detail you know, no matter how minor you think it is. But I should start by asking if you have been contacted by anyone about your daughter."

Yelverton gave a started jerk. "What makes you think I have been contacted?" he demanded aggressively.

"Have you not, sir?" Chadwick asked calmly. "A kidnapping for money would be the normal route for such matters to follow."

He surveyed the man before him, who was obviously having trouble maintaining his composure.

"Do you think this is a runaway or an elopement situation? Mr. Wickham did not lead me to think so. If, however, it is a runaway, it is not a situation in which my office would normally be involved. We deal with political situations."

The Captain stood, making it obvious that he was preparing to leave.

"No, wait..." Yelverton began.

He seemed to be trying to control his temper when the door to the library opened and a younger man entered. He was the same man Chadwick had seen following Mr. Yelverton from Dublin Castle earlier in the day; the Captain had assumed he was Yelverton's son, Georgina's brother.

Closer inspection showed him to be a somewhat younger version of Yelverton, already losing his hair and filling out in the mid-section. If Georgina was in her early 20s, then this chap was an older brother by some years, maybe ten, Chadwick estimated. Here, too, was another example of aping London styles. The man's waistcoat was as loud and glaring as any Chadwick had seen on the fashionable dandies in London. Not his taste at all. He tore his gaze away from the garish combination of yellow and purple stripes to find a hand being offered as Yelverton made introductions.

"Chadwick, this is my son, Walter Yelverton. Walter, this is Captain Jeffrey Chadwick from Wickham's office; he has come to help us find Georgina."

They shook hands, Yelverton poured his son a drink, and they found their respective chairs before Chadwick had a chance to repeat his question. "Have you been contacted?"

Chadwick was surprised when the son answered.

"Well, yes," he said slowly. "We *have* been contacted."

When he paused, Chadwick prodded, "And what happened?"

"Well, that is why this is all so confusing. We met the demands," he answered.

Chadwick looked at Mr. Yelverton to see if he was going to contribute anything. He seemed to have turned the whole discussion over to his son and distanced himself from the discussion. He wasn't looking at either the Captain or his son, but at the wall over their heads. Chadwick glanced back over his shoulder to see what had caught the older man's attention. The portrait hanging there was of a beautiful woman. She was in a riding habit, standing next to a handsome horse. One hand rested gracefully on the horse's bridle, while the other held her hat with a long feather drooping from the brim. He hazarded a guess that the portrait was fairly recent, as her hair was not powdered and fell gracefully to her shoulders in a cascade of blond curls. She had dazzling blue eyes. She looked back at the artist with an aristocratic tilt to her chin and the absolute knowledge that she was an elite member of society. Chadwick wondered if she was the mother or the daughter. Whoever she was, she was breathtaking.

He turned back to the son. "I need to see the note," he said.

The younger Yelverton nodded, "Of course. I will have it sent around to the office."

"Why not now?" he asked.

"It is not here. It's at our businessman's office. He handled the money transaction."

Chadwick frowned, trying to understand. "Let me repeat so I am clear on events: Miss Yelverton goes missing, you receive a note. You then ask your man of business to drop off the ransom?"

Before he could continue, the son, nodding vigorously, replied, "Yes, exactly. We didn't know what to do. Kidnapping just isn't in our realm of experience, you know."

"I think we'd better start over. Begin at the beginning and tell me everything you can remember."

Neither man seemed to know where to start, so he asked, "How did you know she was kidnapped?"

"Dead maid in the street and a hysterical coachman was our first clue," Walter replied sardonically.

Chadwick took a sip of his drink, trying to extend the silence and hoping the other man would be uncomfortable enough to be more forthcoming. The younger Yelverton's attitude toward a serious and possibly life-threatening situation seemed unfortunately jocular, but maybe that was just his way of dealing with strain. Chadwick's patience won out.

"The coachman who was carting Georgina around showed up here with the maid's body and a story of how Georgina went missing in the middle of the shopping area just a few streets from here. Seems the traffic was heavy and he had to move down the street a bit. He could see the shop; he saw Georgina and her maid come out, and then he heard someone screaming that there had been a murder." He re-crossed his legs and slumped even more casually into his chair.

"Murder it was, all right. Someone had stuck a knife in the poor thing. Coachman, the maid, yes, but no Georgina. He brought her body back here with the news." Walter Yelverton sipped his brandy. "Not an idea what he thought we could do with the maid's body."

"Does the maid have any family?"

"Don't know. Father?" he asked the older man.

Mr. Yelverton seemed startled, as if he was miles away, thinking of something else. "Maid? Family? No, I do not believe so. Best ask Mrs. Smith. The housekeeper, you know?"

"How about a name?"

"That I do know," the younger Yelverton responded. "Mary. Georgina was always talking about 'Mary this' and 'Mary that.'"

Chadwick wrote the name in his otherwise empty notebook. He shook his head. This interview was as odd a conversation as he could ever remember having and as slow-going as the proverbial treacle going uphill.

"Now, has anyone been back to the shops to locate witnesses? And what was the address where the murder occurred?"

"You are supposed to be finding my daughter, not the murderer of some useless maid," Mr. Yelverton interjected.

"I believe, sir, they are connected. Don't you agree? Find the murderer, we would probably find the kidnapper," Chadwick responded. "It seems obvious to me that the killing of the maid was a distraction from the actual abduction.

Everyone was probably looking at the maid and no one noticed what was happening to Miss Yelverton. However," he continued, "I want to interview the shopkeepers and look for witnesses. Where exactly did this take place? Or do you think the coachman will have better information?"

"Somewhere on Sackville Street. I suppose the coachman would know better."

Chadwick was startled. He remembered Sackville Street from his previous stay in Dublin. It was a very popular shopping area, sure to have had people about.

"That is a brazen place for an attack," he said. "What time of day?"

"Fairly early in the day."

To Chadwick's surprise, it was the father who now answered. Chadwick wasn't even assured the elder Yelverton was following the conversation. He had topped off his glass at least once that Chadwick had noticed.

"I needed the carriage for some business later in the day. Georgina was happy about having to go shopping early."

"She wanted to walk," the son interrupted. "I insisted she take the carriage. We argued about that again. That boarding school you sent her to, Father, gave her some very independent ideas. She thought she could just walk around in public with only a maid. I tried to convince her it just was not safe, even in Dublin.

Chadwick studied the brother again. It sounded to him as though Walter and Georgina weren't the most congenial siblings, but obviously the man was right, given what had happened. "When did you get the ransom note?" he asked.

"That evening."

"How did it come?"

"Some chap knocked at the front door, just handed the note to the footman who answered the door."

The brother was back to answering the questions. Chadwick wondered if the elder Yelverton was too much in his cups to know the details of what had transpired. Maybe he just didn't talk much.

Chadwick stared at the younger Yelverton, again willing him to continue without prompting.

"We paid out the money, but no Georgina. That's why we went to Cornwallis, who I guess dumped this into Wickham's lap. Thought he might have some ideas."

The Captain got to his feet. Maybe more information could be had from the coachman. "I still need the note. But do you know where the money was dropped off? Did the note say how Miss Yelverton would be returned?" he asked.

"The note said if we paid the money, she would be returned to us, but not how. We assumed they would bring her here."

Chadwick nodded thoughtfully. He had a number of ideas about how the ransom should have been handled differently, but he couldn't fault the Yelvertons. They obviously didn't have experience dealing with criminals and other lowlifes. Their lawyer didn't seem much better. He stood up.

"I would like to talk to the coachman and, if you have one, I need a likeness of Miss Yelverton."

The younger Yelverton also rose. "I'll have Tom brought here for you," he said.

Chadwick tried to keep his expression neutral. He shook his head. "No need. I'll go to the stables. I assume he is there?"

"No, I will have someone bring him from the stables. That way we can all hear what he has to say."

Chadwick tried to keep his expression neutral. Wickham had assigned him this investigation and he was going to handle it his way. The brother was probably concerned he would turn up some family scandal. The father seemed concerned but was not really functioning; he was still in shock.

Again, Chadwick shook his head. "I am sorry, Mr. Yelverton, I must insist on doing my interviews in the way I feel most efficient. He will be more at ease where he's comfortable and can answer more easily. Also, it would be best if there is not an audience. If you could just direct me?"

The younger Yelverton rose slowly to his feet, his reluctance obvious. Nevertheless, he started to lead Chadwick out of the library.

"Excuse me, Mr. Yelverton, one other question," Chadwick turned to the older man. "I am sorry if this is intrusive, but why is the knocker on the front door muffled? Has there been a recent death in the family?"

Again surprisingly, it was the younger Yelverton who answered. "Father is still in mourning for his wife."

"Forgive me for asking," Chadwick responded. "I did not realize Mrs. Yelverton's death was so recent."

"It was not that recent; she died about a year ago. My father is still not himself. Makes this place very lively," Walter said sarcastically.

Chadwick was astonished at the younger man's insensitivity with Yelverton still in the room. As he moved to the door, the elder Mr. Yelverton put a hand on Chadwick's arm.

"You wanted this?" he asked. In his other hand was a small frame with the portrait of a lovely young woman. Chadwick noticed the same color hair and vivid blue eyes as the woman in the portrait.

He gestured to the portrait on the wall. "Is this Miss Yelverton's mother?" he asked.

The older man nodded. "I lost her only a year ago," he said quietly. "I do not want to lose my daughter, too. Take this. Please find her and bring her back."

Chadwick pocketed the small portrait to study later, following the son out of the library and through the house to the backyard leading to the mews.

At Walter Yelverton's shout of 'Tom," a dark-haired man emerged from stables. The man's age was impossible to tell. He could have been anywhere between 20 and 50. His stooped shoulders and weather-beaten face may have added years, but the strain in his face probably added more.

"Yes, sir?" The coachman continued to wipe his hands on a rag while he joined them in the door to the stable.

"This chap wants to talk to you about my sister's kidnapping." Yelverton gestured sharply in Chadwick's direction. "Tell him what you can."

He leaned against the doorway as if taking up a post for the duration of the interview.

The coachman looked at Chadwick, his face taking on an even more cautious aspect if possible. A closer look at the man made Chadwick think the coachman looked more scared than anything else. He doubted he would get any useful information out of him if Yelverton loomed in the doorway listening.

The Captain turned to Yelverton. "Thanks for the time with your man. I will not take him from his duties too long. You do not need to wait; I will find your father in the library before I leave and tell him what the next steps will be."

Yelverton hesitated, the dismissal obviously rankling. Then he nodded abruptly and headed back through the small garden to the house.

Chadwick continued, "Mr. Yelverton did not tell you who I am, Tom. I'm Captain Chadwick, recently attached to the Alien Office here in Dublin. Mr. Wickham, who heads the office, has directed me to look into the kidnapping of Miss Georgina Yelverton."

He looked closely at Tom to see if he understood. Instead of reassuring the man, somehow he had managed to make him look even more panicked. He had taken several steps back and was holding his hands up in a manner meant to protest his innocence.

"Not me, sir. I didn't hurt Miss Georgina. I didn't have anything to do with her disappearing…"

"Be at peace, Tom. I am not accusing you of anything. No one is accusing you of anything. I am not here to arrest you. I just need to talk to you. I need information." He nodded at the house. "They do not seem to know anything helpful. You're as close to a witness as I have."

Tom seemed to calm down a bit, but he still wore the look of a frightened man.

"Let's go into the stable and find someplace to sit," Chadwick said.

The man reminded him of young army recruits, afraid of everything. He wondered if the Yelvertons did indeed think he had had something to do with the kidnapping. The Captain walked into the building and looked around in the dim interior for someplace to sit. He spotted a couple of stools against the wall, presumably for sitting on while polishing tack; they would serve. He seated himself on one and gestured to Tom to take the other.

"Who did you say you worked for, sir?" Tom asked. He seemed to have gathered himself together somewhat.

"The Alien Office," Chadwick replied. "It's part of the government. We investigate anything that might be trouble for the government."

"Why would Miss Georgina's going missing be an issue for the government?" Tom asked.

That was a shrewd question, Chadwick thought. He replied, "Well, you know Mr. Yelverton has influence in the government, right?" Tom nodded, so he continued. "And I am assured you understand how we all have to obey orders? That is what I am doing. My boss told me to find Miss Yelverton, so that is what I am doing. I am not positive what it has to do with the government, but sometimes we have to act without knowing everything."

Tom nodded thoughtfully. "I can understand that. But what do you think you can find that the beadles couldn't find? It was like she disappeared into the mist," he said.

"I will not know until I try to put all the information I can find together. Also, the office I work for has a way of finding information that the beadles might not have."

Chadwick wished he had brought his cigarillos. Sometimes a mundane activity like smoking could calm a subject. He mentally shrugged; no luck there.

"Tom, what can you tell me about the day Miss Yelverton went missing? Would you walk me through the day with as much detail as you can remember?"

Tom did not have a lot to add to the story the Captain had already heard, and it sounded as though he had told his story a few times already. But Chadwick did pose a few questions.

"Did Miss Yelverton have a sudden desire to go shopping or had she set this up the night before?" he asked.

"Come to think on it, sir, it was kind of sudden," he answered thoughtfully. "Usually Miss Georgina liked to walk to the shops. They aren't far."

"Why take the carriage that day?"

"She said as how Mr. Walter insisted she take the carriage, saying it wasn't safe for her to be walking about. She was pretty put out about that; she liked her freedom, did Miss Georgina. She didn't want to be waiting about for me to find her all the time."

Looked like young Yelverton liked being in charge of everything, including his younger sister. He hadn't got the impression the father was much involved in anything but his grief.

"Did Miss Georgina go to an establishment that she usually frequented?" he asked.

"Now that you ask, no, sir, it wasn't one I remember going to before. It was a good part of town, though, not some havey-cavey section."

"But not a part she went regularly visited, so you would not know the area very well, either?"

Tom was shaking his head thoughtfully. "No, sir, I knew the area well enough. I had been there before. Mistress that passed away liked the shops there. This time, though, I had trouble finding a place to wait, and when I did, some chap yelled at me and told me to move on, he had a delivery coming in. I had to drive around the corner a few times," he replied.

"What did that man look like?" Chadwick asked. "Can you tell what shop he was from?"

"Yes, sir, I'd seen him before, from the wine merchant in the next block from the hat shop."

"And what did he look like?"

Tom frowned thoughtfully. "Rough, he looked rough. He seemed to be one of those chaps that empty wagons and carry the heavy stuff around."

"Could you tell hair color or see any scars?" Chadwick continued.

"He had a knit hat pulled down tight, but he did have a scar across the top of one eye, now that you ask. Old knife scar, I think."

"That's good, very good. See? You saw more than you thought," Chadwick said approvingly. "Now, tell me in detail about when and how you realized something was amiss."

"Like I said, I was coming up the street, as I couldn't find a waiting space near the shop. I saw Miss Georgina and Mary come out. Miss Georgina looked mad as fire. She has a temper, that one," he smiled a bit. "Before I could get up to her, I thought I saw Mary trip. All her packages went every which way. By the time I got up to them, Miss Georgina had vanished and Mary was dead; someone knifed the poor thing." He paused to take a shaky breath. "I was pretty fond of Mary, sir. She was a nice girl. Quiet and a hard worker. Wasn't right what they done to her."

"No, indeed," agreed Chadwick.

He gave the scenario Tom described more thought. He drew a rough map in his notebook. "Can you tell me the name of the streets where all of this took place?"

Tom did know his way around the area. After he named the streets and marked where he had been waiting and the shop Miss Yelverton had been in, Chadwick could understand why he didn't see where she had disappeared to.

"And you say the murder was committed on the corner of High and Feltson. So Miss Georgina could have turned and walked into Feltson, that being the side street?" he asked.

"Yes, sir, although there wasn't any reason for her to go there. There aren't any shops up there."

"I need to see the area," Chadwick decided. "We'll take a hackney; it'll be quicker."

"I can't just walk out, sir," Tom said with some fear in his voice.

"I will just step inside, fix it with Mr. Yelverton, and get my hat. I'll be back in a couple of minutes," Chadwick promised.

It proved to take more than a couple of minutes to convince Mr. Yelverton that he needed Tom, but finally he had everything arranged to his satisfaction, and he and Tom set off for the last place he knew Georgina Yelverton had been seen.

* * *

"I did not have time to talk to every shopkeeper on that street; there must be dozens," he said. "But I did talk to the hat maker Miss Yelverton visited. Seems her hat was not ready and she left in a huff. No one really remembered seeing her, but several of the people I talked to remember the chaos after her maid was found stabbed."

Wickham's office was now deep in shadows. Several candles were lit against the gloom, but they only lit the desk, leaving the rest of the room in dark shadows. It was full night, long past dinner, and Chadwick's stomach kept reminding him he had missed most meals today. "Have you heard anything from your sources, sir?" he asked Wickham.

Wickham leaned on one elbow, making notes while Chadwick gave his report. He stopped writing at Chadwick's question. He shook his head tiredly.

"Not enough time for any of my sources to get back to me, and honestly, I do not have many here yet anyway. I was hoping you would come up with some clue from the interviews today. But from what you've told me, Miss Yelverton seems to have disappeared into thin air."

"Whoever took her was not inexperienced, judging by the way they killed that poor maid to cause a distraction."

Wickham frowned thoughtfully. "There are too many coincidences in this scenario, too many in my opinion," he said.

The Captain nodded in agreement. "Someone had to know she was going to take the carriage and head to that hat shop."

"Someone also made positive the coachman was not where he should have been so that there was time to intercept the girl," Wickham added. "I think we are looking at a group of jackals working together."

"I was thinking along the same lines; some sort of organized gang. Someone in the household fed the kidnappers information. I do not think the coachman is involved. He seemed genuinely upset, particularly over the maid's death. And then there's the strange way the Yelvertons themselves handled the payout. Who sends a man of business to do something like that? You would think the son would have at least transferred the money if the old man was not up to it."

"When they came to see me, the son did all the talking. The father acted just like you described – there, but distant, not really involved."

"Have there been any other kidnappings like this that you know of, sir?" Chadwick asked. "If it is a gang, perhaps this is not their first abduction."

Wickham leaned back in his chair steepling his fingers as he thought over Chadwick's report. He shook his head tiredly. "I do not think we can do anything else tonight, Chadwick," he said. "Go along, get something to eat. In the morning we'll meet and I hope some new information will miraculously come to hand that will allow us to move forward."

"Do you think now this is a political kidnapping, sir?"

Wickham stood and moved to the coat rack to get his coat and hat. "Well, it is obviously a kidnapping, what with the ransom and all. Is it political? Yes, simply because of who her father is. The ransom demand changes everything. At first I thought if this was an elopement, it would not be so well-planned, and it's highly doubtful they would kill the maid, right? No bride would want her groom to kill her maid. Especially as, according to the brother, Miss

Yelverton and the maid were close. If she was just a runaway, again, she would not have killed the maid, but probably would have taken her," Wickham added thoughtfully.

"And, of course," Chadwick added, "there's the ransom note which neither of those scenarios would involve. I sincerely hope Yelverton remembers to send it to us."

"If not, I'll get it. Come on, I'll walk you out."

Chapter Three: Breadcrumbs

The next morning, Chadwick arrived at the Alien Office early. Wickham seemed to have a knack for selecting working and living environments that were practical and no-nonsense. In London, the Alien Office was housed in Whitehall. In Dublin, it was situated within the Castle, a structure that was not chronologically any older than Whitehall but was architecturally of an earlier age. The tower where the Office was located reminded him of a medieval castle set in the middle of a city. He appreciated that most of the offices were on the second floor, as he suspected the novelty of running up and down four or five floors in a turret all day would rapidly pale.

The rooms Wickham had found for him on Temple Street also fit the instinct to favor practical and no-nonsense things. They were located only a couple of blocks from the Castle – a quick and easy walk that did not require him to keep a livery in town, he noted with satisfaction. The Captain found the upkeep of a horse and carriage an unnecessary drain unless they were used regularly. If Wickham wanted him to run off somewhere, Chadwick intended him to pay for it from the Alien Office funds.

Temple was a small, quiet residential street just off Dame Street, the major throughway between the Castle and Trinity College. Although Wickham had said it was an area where many undergraduates had rooms, last night had been quiet, with no drunken students to keep him awake.

The three rooms were more than enough space for Chadwick and his valet, David Thomas, who had agreed to come to Dublin to serve as general factotum. He had been with Chadwick for a while now, the two having met during their army years when David had been a soldier in Chadwick's company. Disabled by a wound suffered during the Irish Rebellion (or Disturbances as some called them), David had become Chadwick's manservant, following him on several assignments.

David had done pretty well, Chadwick thought, organizing the lodgings in only one day. His bed had been satisfactory, as were the other furnishings that came with the rooms. Nothing too fancy, but then after his time with the army and the subsequent years traveling for the Alien Office, Chadwick was far from fussy. Clean and as few bugs as possible were at the top of his wish list these days. But to achieve that end, he had made sure David had packed his own sheets.

It was just as well there was no formal kitchen. Any cooking would have to be in the fireplace. This did not bother the Captain too much, as neither he nor David were competent to do more than just heat up items. He fully expected to eat most of his meals out, as he had done in London. He knew that as a good-looking bachelor he would soon have his choice of dinner invitations, as anxious mamas tried to interest him in their daughters. Until that happened, there were, of course, always chop houses. He had directed David to scour the neighborhood and locate those that served decent food. With a college and so many government offices close by, he assumed there would be plenty of places to dine. The only disappointment so far was that David had not found a source of coffee yet in the neighborhood and could only offer tea for breakfast. Tea was not Chadwick's preferred morning beverage.

Chadwick arrived at the office early in the hope that someone would know where to get coffee. But the few people around were all tea drinkers. Two things were obvious to him: Dubliners seemed to prefer their coffee in the afternoon, and they were not early risers. He scrounged another cup of tea from one of the transcribers and made himself comfortable in the hallway, waiting for Wickham to arrive, which thankfully he did a few minutes before eight.

Unlocking his office door, Wickham gestured for the Captain to enter. "Come in. Have a seat. I have some news for you," he said.

"Did you hear from your sources?" Chadwick asked.

Wickham sat at his desk and began to take papers out of the sack he used to transport items he took home. Chadwick took the chair in front of the desk, the only other one in the room. He noticed the office was almost identical to the one Wickham had occupied in London and just as severe. It contained a large, no-nonsense desk with lots of papers in neat piles, a few bookshelves, and little else. He remembered Wickham telling him once,

"I do not want too many chairs in the office. Chairs invite visitors who stay too long. I do not have time for long-winded colleagues." Chadwick grinned to himself. He could come up with a few names of people he knew Wickham had been thinking about when he said that.

"I have a name for you. I got a note this morning at my house that this person might have some information for us. But he is a careful chap, does not want to be seen with the likes of us, but he will not put anything in writing, either. He probably can't write, but the end result is that you have to see him face to face – quietly."

The Captain leaned forward and carefully put the empty tea-cup on the edge of the desk. "Do you think he'll talk to me?" he asked.

Wickham formed a moue. "Probably not," he replied.

"Well, who does he usually talk to then?"

"Usually he just drops a word with the local postmaster. That won't work in this case, as most people know by now that the postmaster forwards information to us and this is too sensitive." He sighed and said, "I cannot immediately think of anyone who can just walk up to this chap and get him to talk."

Chadwick replied thoughtfully, "If that's the case, we need help. A local chap not associated with information-gathering. I'll need someone who can gain his confidence. And someone who can help out in a tight situation if need be."

He looked at his tea-cup again and sadly found it still empty.

"How about that chap from downstairs who guards the door like it's..."

"Paddy?" Wickham asked quickly. "He is not too bright."

"Is he Irish?" Chadwick asked.

"Yes."

"Come from around here?"

"I do not know much about him except he has a problem with authority," Wickham responded.

"Really?" Chadwick was interested. "What do you mean?"

"He broke his sergeant's jaw. I never really did find out what for. But the Colonel was going to hang him for insubordination. Seemed a waste to me. I thought he would look good at the door."

Now Chadwick was bemused by Wickham's reasoning. "You save a man from hanging and put him on guard duty even when he's proven to be unreliable and possibly dangerous. Why? What did you see in him?" he asked.

Wickham sighed, "I was not completely convinced he wasn't in the right about that sergeant. I had heard some information that did not come out in the trial that the sergeant liked to beat women. Paddy might have had a legitimate reason for taking him on. Of course he did not do it the right way, but it did not seem a hanging offense to me."

"So you got him transferred?"

"It was not too hard. The judge is an acquaintance and I've done some favors for him," Wickham said cautiously.

"If I talk to him and he seems what I need, can I have him for this job? I do not think I can do a disguise here very effectively, and obviously your source would not be comfortable with the likes of me."

"If you can keep him under control, he is yours. But I have to say, since he has been here, there have not been any issues."

"Good, I think he will do nicely. But I need to be assured my first impression is the right one, as I will likely need to talk to him more than once." He leaned back in his chair. "Now, sir, about this source?"

* * *

Finished discussing the topic with Wickham, Chadwick trod the stairs to the ground floor reflecting on how to convince his chosen assistant to take the job. Things would go so much more smoothly if Paddy wanted to work with him. He hoped Paddy would not decide that opening the door to visitors was his dream come true or that being ordered about would become problematic. Chadwick had found that unwilling colleagues in this line of work were rarely useful and even less often trustworthy. But he did not have much time and at least Paddy had the physique for the position.

As Chadwick came off the last steps, he could see the doorman standing just to the side of the door. When Paddy saw him, he stood straighter and reached for the door handle.

"Hold up there," the Captain said. "I'd like a word."

"Sir?" He looked around to see who the Captain was talking to. When he realized Chadwick was addressing him, a look of surprise crossed his face and he blushed. His skin was the pale color that was often seen on red-haired people. Although Chadwick couldn't see his hair under his helmet, the skin tone and the freckles he could now see across his nose made the Captain sure this man was red-haired. Up close, with no wrinkles and clear blue eyes, he appeared to be very young.

"What can I do for you, sir?"

"A private word," Chadwick responded. "Is there someone who can cover for you for a bit?"

"Yes, sir," the doorman replied. "There's a chap who trades off the work with me."

"Here," the Captain held out a few coins. "Ask him to come up."

Paddy returned shortly with a man of nearly equal height, although he was older than the young guard and walked with a limp. He saluted Chadwick in a brisk manner and took up his station beside the door without a word.

Paddy looked cautiously at the Captain. "Not much around here as is private."

"We will walk then," Chadwick replied. It was hard to overhear a conversation that kept moving. The two men left the tower for the parade field that formed the large inner court of the Castle.

"Wickham and I thought you might be useful to me on one of my assignments. I need someone local to help me get around Dublin and understand people." He looked at Paddy to see his response. The doorman's face looked questioningly back.

"Why not just order me? I'm under his command."

"Honestly, the job might get dangerous. I do not want someone who is just obeying orders. I need someone who wants to be involved," Chadwick responded.

The young guard nodded, and the Captain went on, "Are you from Dublin?"

"Yes, sir. Born over on Skinner's Alley, past St. Patrick's Cathedral. You might not know the place since you're new in town, but it's southwest of here. Not a fancy place, but my mam saw I went to church regular and the priests saw we got a bit of learning."

Chadwick paced with his hands clasped behind his back. He looked thoughtfully at Paddy, who walked as if he were on parade, with his arms stiff at his sides and staring straight ahead.

"So you grew up in Dublin. That must mean you know your way around." He took a scrap of paper out of his pocket and glanced at the address written there again. "Do you know where St Michael's Church is?" he asked.

Paddy frowned a bit, shaking his head slowly.

"Sorry, sir, that one I do not know. There are so many churches in this town, it's hard to keep track of them all," Paddy said ruefully. "I still go to St Patrick's when I can. That's south of here," he added.

"St. Michael's is supposed to be off Church Street, somewhere north of here," Chadwick replied.

"I know where that is. Couldn't be that hard to find then."

The Captain glanced over at the young man beside him. He noted that he was looking over, not down, at him. Paddy had good height and strong-looking shoulders.

"How are you in a dustup?" he asked.

"I can hold my own," Paddy said proudly. "Did a bit of boxing when I first entered the army." He took a deep breath and turned to look Chadwick in the eye. "Mr. Wickham tell you of my troubles in the army?" he asked.

"He might have mentioned it," Chadwick said cautiously. "Tell me about it."

"Not much to tell," Paddy said shortly. "I lost my temper and slugged the sergeant. He had me up on charges and they came this close to hanging me. I owe my life to Mr. Wickham."

Chadwick studied Paddy, whose face was now closed and shuttered. He decided on another course of inquiry. "Do you know what the Alien Office does?" he asked.

"They review papers of people coming to Ireland. I see them emigrés coming and going," he offered promptly. Paddy was obviously glad the issue of his less-than-stellar army career seemed to be behind them.

"Anything else?"

"They do a lot with paper. I see them chaps that spend their day writing a lot, too. They talk to me, not about the work, you understand, but about how their hands might be cramping or how their back aches from sitting. That kind of talk, you twig. Nothing important, I guess."

Paddy seemed to grasp that there were secrets in the upstairs office that shouldn't be discussed. Good. He knew about keeping his mouth shut.

The men reached another turn in the parade. "Where can we get some coffee?" Chadwick asked suddenly.

"Coffee house on Dame Street right outside the gate," Paddy answered promptly.

"Patrick, my man!" the Captain said jovially. "We're going to get along very well. Let's get some coffee. I have a proposition for you."

* * *

Several hours later on Bow Lane, Chadwick propped one booted foot against the wall at his back. He wanted to rest just the barest part of his coat against the wreck of a building. The alley was dank and smelly and he worried for the condition of his coat. Waiting was part of the job he least liked and considering his surroundings – rotting garbage, human waste, and other disgusting matters – he was anxious for Paddy to complete his business so they could leave. He took a deep draw on his cigarillo, trying to cover the smells. They had decided the alley was the only place a man of his stature and dress might remain secluded.

Paddy had left him over an hour ago and headed toward St. Michael's Church to meet the informant. Well, before the meeting time, the two men had scouted the area with a casual walk around. St. Michael's was a small brown building around the corner from – and just out of sight of – Bow Lane where he now stood. It was not a big cathedral with multiple side chapels that would have made a secret meeting easy. Chadwick could only surmise the informant's permanent hiding place was close by and St. Michael's was a recognizable and convenient landmark.

He mulled over the steps needed to get to this point, hoping he had not overlooked anything. It had taken some time to get his assistant ready to meet Wickham's mysterious informant. He remembered with some amusement the look on Paddy's face when he had finally realized what Chadwick wanted him to do.

"You're going to pay me money to dress in regular clothes and talk to people?" he asked with some amazement. "Why? Can't you talk?"

"I'm too posh," Chadwick replied. "I need someone who these folks will trust. They do not know me and I do not have enough time to learn the local language well enough to disguise my accent so people will trust me. You're from Dublin. Even if they do not know you personally, they will know you're not English, and that's a start."

"Why can't I wear my uniform?"

Obviously, Paddy was proud of his uniform. Rather surprising since he had almost got killed in it. But the army evidently had been a turning point in his life and he did not blame it for what had followed.

Chadwick had taken some time to explain the responsibilities of the Alien Office and how it screened foreigners and watched that they did not ferment a revolution like the one in France, or even the short-lived rebellion like the one in Dublin a few years before. Paddy had caught on pretty quickly. After all, he had been opening the door for Wickham's associates for some time; he had ears, eyes, and evidently a brain to put all the clues together. He looked thoughtful and then asked some questions that showed he understood the need for discretion.

Of course Chadwick had glossed over the inner workings of the Alien Office, omitting details of the more sensitive 'special assignments' he had worked on recently. He especially omitted assignments such as ferrying cash to be used for bribes and trips to elicit information about English citizens suspected of fermenting disturbances.

Movement across the street caught Chadwick's attention. Glancing up, he saw Paddy striding across the square in front of the church. He was looking anxiously about. Tossing his cigarillo into the collection of garbage, Chadwick exited the alley. Paddy looked relieved as he crossed to meet him.

"Let's get out of here before we talk," the Captain said.

Paddy nodded and led the way to a busier thoroughfare. Shoppers bustled by and street traffic picked up. Of course, the Captain realized, there was no real place to talk.

Paddy pointed to a small pub on the corner. "Would that be all right, Captain," he asked, "if we keep our voices down?"

At Chadwick's nod, they entered the shabby pub and headed for the darkest tables at the back. Chadwick noticed Paddy's demeanor had changed from obsequious doorman to someone confident in his surroundings and in himself. Maybe there was more acting ability there than he had given him credit for.

Paddy looked at Chadwick and gestured to the bar. "Can't sit here without drinks."

"Obviously." He handed Paddy some coins. "I have not had anything to eat today and I bet you haven't either. See if he has any food."

Paddy returned shortly with two tankards of beer. He took a large swallow of beer.

"This stuff isn't too bad," he said. "I heard his wife brews it and she's a likely hand. They have some bread and cheese and will bring it out shortly."

Chadwick took his own quaff and nodded in agreement. "Not bad at all." He looked around the pub carefully and saw it was mostly empty. It must be too early for the tradesman crowd.

"How did the meeting go?" Chadwick asked.

"That was one strange chap you sent me to talk to," the doorman answered. "He was late and then when he did show up, he creeped in like a spider. Short of shuffled along the walls of the church, never went to the middle of the aisle, and made sure he wasn't in any light from the windows. Real skittish, he was."

"Did you have any trouble finding the meeting place?" Chadwick asked.

"No, sir. There was only one little side chapel to the Blessed Virgin in that church. It was off to the right side of the church, just like you said it should be. That chap probably liked it because there was no light there. Just a few of them tall candles. I was sure glad he finally showed up. I said two rosaries and my knees was killing me by then." He flashed a cheeky grin at Chadwick. "It was almost as bad as standing at the door all day with one break."

Before he could continue, the landlord arrived with a platter of bread, cheese, sliced ham, and boiled eggs. He plunked down knives and a crock of butter.

"Sorry, gents, but it's the best I can do on such short notice."

They assured him it was more than they deserved; it looked fine and no, there was nothing else they needed...well, maybe some more beer? When their tankards had been refilled and the landlord had gone back to his duties,

Chadwick loaded bread with cheese and ham before he noticed Paddy had not taken anything.

"Eat. No ceremony between us when we're on a case. No time for niceties, so eat while you tell me about the meet-up," he said.

Paddy crammed an egg whole into his mouth and took a slug of beer before he continued. "This chap I met was a real member of the group you mentioned before."

"Madra Dubh?" Chadwick asked. He slathered more bread with butter. For a dingy pub in the backwaters of Dublin, either the fare here was pretty good or he was really hungry. Paddy was doing fine making a dent in his side of the platter, too.

"Yes, that one. He's right ticked off with the head chap. Seems he decided to go to France and fight with Napoleon. He thinks Boney is going to invade England and will use Ireland as a jumping off point." He drank more beer. "This informant chap went on about that a long bit. Kept saying the fight for freedom was here in Ireland and running off to help Napoleon was not just useless."

"Did he give you a name for this head man?"

"Hmmm…wait, it's coming to me. Harrison or something like that. Jesus, I'm sorry, Captain, I was trying so hard to remember all he said."

"Never mind. I think I know what the man's name is. That he is leaving for France is big news. When?"

"Soon, Captain. For sure, he was so mad about it and he couldn't stop this chap, who I gather was taking all the money they had, and the girl…"

Chadwick cut him off quickly. "What girl?" he demanded.

"They had a girl they was supposed to use for ransom and to make some more cash."

"What's the address?" Chadwick snapped. He stood, draining his mug, and threw more coins on the table.

"We leaving, Captain?" Paddy looked up startled.

"Yes, come on! We may already be too late!"

Paddy stuffed bread and cheese into his pockets before following the Captain out the door.

* * *

Cuckoo Lane, the address the informant had finally given Paddy, proved to be remarkably close. Just as Chadwick thought, the informant was using St. Michael's as a meeting place because of its proximity to his headquarters, or more probably, former headquarters.

The urge to move on the information and try to find Georgina Yelverton made the Captain's long stride even faster than usual as they hurried up Little Mary's Street. Each street got progressively more dismal. The houses became more derelict and rundown. There was more trash and, from the smell, the streets were used as more of a cesspit. The people reflected their surroundings with poorer clothing and the hopeless demeanor of hunched shoulders. Chadwick marveled that in the matter of a few blocks, the neighborhoods went from working class to downright hopeless. He noticed a number of appraising glances and wondered what kind of trouble he and Paddy might be facing even before they found the Madra Dubh headquarters.

But speed seemed paramount, and who knew how old the information was? Chadwick did not think there was any time to alert Wickham to send reinforcements. He decided the two of them would reconnoiter and then, if he needed to, he would send Paddy rushing back for troops. He hoped the poor girl was there so he could return to his normal job of translating.

"Left here, sir," Paddy cut into his reverie. "The landlord said George's Lane leads right to Cuckoo."

And in a few steps it did, cutting across the middle of the lane.

"Which way do you think we should go?"

"Gaol's up there, sir," Paddy pointed to the right. "The house should be the fourth one from the gaol."

"We'll walk by the house and keep going as if we are going to the gaol." Chadwick paused before saying, "Actually, I have a better idea: let's go to the gaol and see if the jailer can give us any information."

They continued up Cuckoo Lane at about half the speed they had previously used but still quickly enough to seem only interested in reaching the gaol. They reached the building identified by the informant quickly. It opened directly onto the street without even a front step. To get to the door, one had to jump a gutter filled with brown muck. The front door was slightly ajar.

"It looks empty," the Captain said. In spite of his intention to go to the gaol, Chadwick stopped and surveyed the house. The shutters, such as there were, were closed. He could see none of the signs of life seen in the other houses, however decrepit they were. His shoulders sagged as he studied the building. They were too late.

"You come to arrest those buggers?" A shrill voice sounded behind them. Chadwick turned to face a miniature figure that reminded him of a picture of a gnome in a book of Irish folklore. He raised his hat respectfully. Information came in many guises.

"Ma'am?" he asked.

"You from the government? Those buggers up and left and they owe me money."

"You own this building?" Chadwick verified. At her brusque nod, he continued. "How long did they rent it?"

"They been in there a year or so, doing what all damage, and then they just up and run off. Ain't right, me being an old widow woman and all," she added piteously.

Chadwick couldn't help but notice the sly gleam in her eyes as she sought to exploit the situation. Obviously, he could not hide the fact he was interested in the house and its inhabitants. He had given himself away. But maybe there was information to be had from this wretch.

"Can we get off the street and discuss this?" he asked. It was the best way he could think of to get inside and search the premises.

The old woman led them inside and immediately started complaining about the condition of the house. "Look what they done. This place was fine when they took it over. They made a mess."

Chadwick doubted the Madra Dubh had destroyed the house as much as she made out. It was too dilapidated for that much damage to be made in one year. He gestured to Paddy to go upstairs.

"See if there's anything upstairs that can tell us where they have gone," he said. He looked at the landlady again.

"When did they leave?" he asked.

"Why do you want to know?" she responded.

"My business," he said and waited for her to name her price. It came promptly.

"Information ain't free around here," she returned.

"How much?"

"They owed me six months' rent."

"Bollocks, I'll give you one." The old woman was really going to try to gouge him, he thought with amusement. "And I want someone else to verify the information before I pay over."

"Ain't you the untrusting one?" she returned. "Because you such a handsome one, I'll talk for two months," she smiled, showing gums with only a tooth or two left.

Paddy came downstairs shaking his head. "Nothing upstairs to tell us where they've gone, sir. But I did find this." He held out his hand and dropped an earring into Chadwick's palm.

The old woman made a grab for it. "Anything in my house is mine," she screeched.

"Not likely!" Chadwick clenched the earring in his fist. "Paddy, would you go ask any of those people outside if they can tell us when the kidnappers left and anything else that might be of interest?" He was purposefully vague so the old woman couldn't make up answers to get the cash.

"Now, to business." He stared at the old woman with his best military face. "When did they leave?" he demanded.

Hastings had a head start of about a day and a half, and that was the extent of the old woman's knowledge. She knew a lot about what they had done while they were in her house, for sure. She must have kept quite a sharp eye out for them from her shack across the street. But she couldn't give Chadwick much about where they had gone, only that they had piled into a carriage two nights earlier and that was the last she had seen of them. He paid off the old witch and joined Paddy in the middle of the street, avoiding the open sewers. Paddy had a small boy by the collar.

"What did he do? Try to rob you?" he asked, looking inquiringly at the boy. Grimy from head to toe, he was glad Paddy was holding him. He wasn't eager to acquire any of the insects that were probably crawling all over his body.

"No, sir. You told me to find someone who'd seen them leave." He nodded at the boy. "Seems he sleeps in the streets."

Chadwick looked at the boy with interest. "Really? And he saw them leave?"

"So he says. But he won't talk for free."

"Just like the old crone in there." Chadwick nodded his head at the shack the old woman had disappeared into. He could see her peering at them now through the crack in the shutters.

"But I *saw* them," the waif protested. "Her just listens to people and repeats it to make money."

"I will pay for real information," the Captain promised. "What did you see?"

Once he had their attention, the boy had a real tale to tell. The sound of the carriage had woken him from the stoop down the street where he and some others in the homeless gang he belonged to were huddling. He had jumped out to hold the horses, hoping for a coin for his services. Getting nothing but a grunt, he'd been angry enough to want to see where they were going. He'd followed the carriage through the streets to the quay. Then he'd watched as they were rowed aboard a boat farther out in the river. When asked to describe the boat, he gave a good description of a small packet boat. It was not, however, flying any flag that the lad could see. "I wants to go on them ships someday," he finished.

After the boy described the mast head, Paddy murmured, "Free trader."

Chadwick practically moaned out loud. Could this case get any more complicated? And now smugglers!

He studied the lad. "What is your name, lad?" he asked. Wickham was always looking for new informants.

"Kit, Mister."

"Know where the Castle is, Kit?" he asked. At the boy's nod, he continued, "In a day or two, come around and ask for Mr. Wickham. He might have a job for you. I will tell him you might be around and that you're good at noticing things."

The boy nodded eagerly and the coins Chadwick slipped him disappeared rapidly. He gave a sharp salute and disappeared into the gathering gloom.

"What now, sir?"

"Back to Wickham and to find out how far he wants to take this chase," the Captain answered.

Chapter Four: Masquerade

"**I** cannot take him to France with me, sir," Chadwick protested. "He does not speak any French. He cannot make the whole trip without talking!"

"He's Irish, not English. Believe it or not, the French can tell the difference," Wickham responded.

"He still cannot speak French."

"He will not need to; he can pass as an Irish volunteer for Napoleon. The United Irishmen have been going to France for years. They see being in Napoleon's army as a way of fighting us. Hell, one of Napoleon's best generals is Irish. Have you heard of O'Hara?"

Chadwick paused to give Wickham's proposal some serious thought. They were back in Wickham's office, the desk between them, this time covered with sandwiches and tea cups. After the debacle yesterday, they were trying to put together an array of reasonable plans for Chadwick to follow the kidnappers in hopes of retrieving Miss Yelverton. All the plans involved going to France; they differed only in their mode of transport or disguise. The Captain rather wished Wickham would produce the brandy bottle, although he knew that for a clear head, tea was better but coffee was best. He sighed. He really could use Nathan Donnay's input and advice. Wickham had not been in the field for many years and never on such a mission as this. Chadwick knew Director Wickham had lived in Switzerland for a long time, overseeing the government's clandestine operations in France and Germany. Had he ever even been in Napoleon's France?

"You need backup," Wickham was saying.

"I totally agree. But Paddy was just for the one-time shot. I do not know him well enough to take him along on such a delicate mission," Chadwick protested.

"There *is* no one else," Wickham responded. "You told me he did well today, did you not?"

"Yes. Today. In Dublin, where he grew up and where he is comfortable. He has never traveled anywhere."

"I think you are selling him short. How do you know he never traveled anywhere? And after all, he enlisted in the army; he wasn't pressed. That shows a certain initiative, I think."

"I need someone like Donnay," Chadwick said out loud. "Someone who can think for himself when things go bad." Nathan did not stand around waiting for orders, he saw what needed to be done and did it. Would Paddy have those kinds of reactions? Chadwick didn't think so. He wasn't sure he could react so quickly himself when thrown into a dangerous and challenging situation. All of his field work had been with Nathan. But as Wickham had said, 'There was no one else.'

"All right, I will think about utilizing Paddy. Maybe there is a place for him. In the meantime, back to basics. When I said my French was good but I would never pass for a Parisian, I was not trying to be funny. I have met a number of emigrés over the past years and none of them thinks I originated in France. However, one chap thought I was from Louisiana. Maybe we could utilize that possibility."

"Go on," said Wickham. "Utilize how?"

"I could be some kind of a merchant or tradesman from New Orleans or a surrounding planation."

"A slave owner?"

"No, I could never sustain that façade. I do know that a lot of the owners, especially the French, send their sons to travel to Europe before settling down and marrying. Maybe a second son, one that could be expected to travel without an entourage of slaves."

Wickham was shaking his head. "No, you are too old for that role. You need some credible reason for traveling around and talking to lots of people. You need to be of a certain class so you have entrée into all levels of society. That is why you need Paddy to talk to servants."

"Mr. Wickham, that just doesn't make sense." Chadwick tried to keep the frustration out of his voice. "French servants do not speak English and, Paddy speaks no French. What good will he be except to polish my boots?"

"Wine merchant," Wickham said suddenly.

Chadwick stared at Wickham. Dear Lord, what was the man on about now?

"Wine merchant hired by several rising families in the Louisiana colony. You will be visiting various chateaus, buying up cases of wine to be shipped to the Americas. You will sample wine, wander about talking to local folks, listen to gossip. Paddy is an Irish lad you hired in Dublin, where you landed when you got to the old world. He is looking to join the United Irishmen in Napoleon's army and has been traveling with you." Wickham stopped speaking and looked at Chadwick inquiringly. "How is that for a cover story?" he asked. "It explains the accents and, why you traveled from Ireland and it gives you license to wander about." He grinned unexpectedly, obviously happy with his own idea.

Chadwick added more hot water to the tea-pot from the small pot that was kept over a candle for that purpose. He mulled over Wickham's cover story, searching for holes. He knew there must be holes big enough to drive a carriage through. But the more he pondered it, the more plausible it seemed. The one person he had met from New Orleans had talked about how small and closed French society was. Maybe he could pretend he had come from an island and had just started working as a wine buyer. The biggest problem he saw-and one he could not explain away-was that he knew nothing about the wine trade. He turned back to Wickham after pouring himself more tea, weaker but at least still hot.

"So I introduce myself as John Smith from New Orleans recently arrived via Dublin and then what? I know a lot about drinking wine, absolutely nothing about buying or shipping it. And, I might add, I have damn little time to learn the trade."

Wickham rose unexpectedly and went to the door. "Chambers!" He bellowed. "Be a good chap and run downstairs and get me Cavanaugh. I want to talk to him."

Faster than the Captain thought possible, Paddy was standing in the doorway. He was back in his red uniform.

"Mr. Wickham," he said respectfully. "Captain Chadwick." He grinned at the Captain conspiratorially. "You wanted to see me?"

Wickham replied, "Captain Chadwick here has said how much help you have been in this matter of the missing girl, Miss Yelverton."

"My pleasure to work with the Captain, sir," Paddy interrupted. "Captain is a sharp one and I was really glad to help out a bit. Have you got something else in the spying business I could do? It beats minding a door all day," he added ingenuously.

Chadwick saw Wickham cover a smile. "We might. Got a couple of questions for you first." Paddy brightened at the prospect of more exciting employment.

"Can you speak any French?"

Paddy's shoulders sagged. "Not much, sir" he said sadly. "I can order a beer, know the parts of a boat and some parts of a woman."

Now it was Captain Chadwick's turn to smother a grin. "Where did you learn that much?" he asked.

Paddy suddenly looked stricken. He stared at Chadwick without saying anything for a few moments.

Chadwick finally took pity on him. "Did some runs with the Free Traders?" he asked.

Paddy nodded unhappily. "Yes, sir. But I gave that up years ago," he said fervently. "Not since I took the King's shilling. I wouldn't do something like that as a soldier," he avowed.

Wickham was looking decidedly interested in these revelations about Paddy's past. "We might be able to put that experience to good use," he said. "Chadwick, the free traders might just be the best way to get to France rapidly. I would bet good money that is the way Hastings got out of here so fast."

He turned to Paddy. "Do you still have any contacts with the traders, Paddy?" he asked. "Someone who could help get the Captain here – and an associate – to France, specifically, to Calais, quickly?" he demanded.

Paddy's eyebrows rose in surprise. "You mean you want me to contact my um… old mates?" he asked in an astonished tone. "You are not going to throw me in the brig?"

Chadwick, who had been thinking over the free traders as a possible travel method, spoke up. "Yes, I think we do want you to contact them. I need to follow those kidnappers quickly and I do not have time to find and hire a ship. Besides, if Hastings made use of the free traders, someone might know where they are headed. France is a big place and even if we narrowed it down to the areas where Napoleon has armies, I might never track them down." He paused, considering how to phrase his next comments.

"This investigation is bigger than one person. I am going to need someone to go with me..."

Before he could continue, Paddy interrupted. "I am your man," he said proudly. "I know more of the language than I let on. I just wasn't sure why you were asking. First thing I learned in the army, Captain as I know you did, you shouldn't tell everything about yourself. Just gets you volunteered for more work. But I want to see this through. Wasn't right, snatching that girl and making off like that."

Chadwick switched to French and asked, "How soon can you contact your mates in the free traders?" he asked.

Paddy's accent was execrable; he would never pass for a true French native. But his answer was understandable. "If I start now, I should be able to reach them soon enough to find us a way to France in a few days, weather permitting."

Wickham dismissed Paddy so the lad could change out of his uniform and attempt to contact his old employers. He was given some coin to pave his way and told to report back in the morning.

"Rush isn't far, Mr. Wickham, but I am not certain I can get back by morning. Rush is a nearby town where most of those chaps hang about, Captain," Paddy said in an explanatory aside to Chadwick.

"Then take a horse from the stables. Mr. Chambers will set it up for you," Wickham replied.

Paddy nodded and took off.

"That lad is a real mixture of unsuspected experiences," Wickham said with some satisfaction. "I hope he will come up with a way for you to get to France quickly and without much paperwork. Speaking of which, we had better get started on some papers for you. You will need some, you know."

Chadwick sighed, "I still need to know something about the wine business. I cannot be a complete novice; real merchants will see through me immediately. Do you have any ideas where I can get up to snuff quickly?" He paused, giving himself time to consider a likely timeline.

"I think we have a couple of days until we get transport with the free traders and I want to spend it learning as much as possible about the wine trading business and about the United Irishman who are already overseas. I want to know who to avoid if I possibly can. By the way, do we have any maps of northern France?"

Wickham had cleared his tea things to the side of the desk and was making rapid notes in his spidery handwriting. He talked as he wrote. "It will take a few days to get the right documents, same amount of time to get some portable funds for you and to set up bills of credit with the appropriate banks. Early tomorrow, you and I will visit some local wine merchants and see what they can tell us about the trade. Hopefully, we can learn enough about the buying and shipping to give you some cover. But I suspect that Paddy's old mates may be the best source of information. I know they bring all sorts of things from France, but wine is by far their most lucrative import."

Chadwick had to admire Wickham's organization once he got going. He was really focused on the details of what needed to be done once the general plan had been outlined. The Captain had a few thoughts of his own that he wasn't going to lay before Wickham. He'd rather set them in motion on his own. Always good to have back-door plans in case something went awry. In what he thought of as his limited field experience, it usually did.

* * *

Chadwick's letter to Nathan Donnay took longer than he had expected. The number of staff in Dublin's Alien Office was small but they all tried to be helpful, supplying him with use of a desk and other supplies. The letter itself stretched to a few pages as Chadwick laid out the kidnapping, what he had done so far and his plan to head for France. He left space at the end to add in whatever information Paddy would bring back from his former colleagues, hoping it would include specifics that would give him an idea as to where in France he should begin searching.

He rubbed the cramp in his neck as he wondered what exactly he thought Nathan could do – ride, or rather boat, to his side? He knew that by going to France, he was going into a dangerous situation where the guillotine was the likely end if his cover was blown and he was identified as an agent of England. And, as his companion, he had a young Irish lad who had been a free trader and had been convicted of assaulting a superior. As charming and seemingly willing as Paddy was, he couldn't really rely on him. Paddy, too, would be headed for the guillotine if caught. Captain Chadwick sighed as he stood up and promptly hit his head on the low ceiling in the alcove where the writing desk stood. Food! He would go back to the rooms and see if Thomas had found a decent chop house. Maybe things would look better after he had a meal. He pocketed his letter and set off.

* * *

"I have a new idea about getting information on the wine trade," Wickham said as he and Chadwick met in the parade field the next morning.

"Good morning, sir," Chadwick responded. "And what is your idea?"

"I was thinking it might be difficult to get a merchant to talk to us in detail without divulging why we need to know. So I think we should approach someone who buys a substantial amount of wine and also knows what our office does. At least for a start. Then we can see how much more you need to learn."

Captain Chadwick nodded in agreement. "I was wondering about that myself. Why would a merchant want to train someone who might be competition? Who did you have in mind?"

"Lord Cornwallis."

"That is a surprising answer. Going to the top?"

"Well, I know we can trust him to keep a confidence and he has been in Dublin a lot longer than me, so he should know the merchants."

They had reached the door to the tower which was opened by a guard who Chadwick did not recognize. As they started up the stairs, Chadwick asked, "But does he buy his own wine? Would his butler not do that?"

"Probably. So Cornwallis can direct him to speak to us. I'll send a note over asking for a meeting as soon as possible."

Chambers, Wickham's office manager, met them in the hallway leading to Wickham's office.

"Cavanaugh is not here, sir," he reported. "He left a note I was just placing on your desk. Seems that he is still trying to make contact with the people you sent him to make contact with. He also said they were out of town but were expected back very shortly. He will keep in touch."

Chadwick remembered Chambers from the London office as a man whose efficiency was overlaid by a crusty personality. He hadn't changed since London. Chadwick hoped that meant he would be helpful over the next few days in the procurement of maps, letters of introduction, and credit.

Wickham must have been thinking the same as he said, "I have to write a note `to Lord Cornwallis and then I will need some other papers. Please give me a moment to settle and then join me."

The next half hour was a flurry of activity as Wickham wrote out a note asking for a meeting with Lord Cornwallis and then dictated to Chambers a list of documents Chadwick would need for France. He also remembered papers for Paddy.

"Are you taking your valet, Chadwick?" he asked.

The Captain remembered the terror on Thomas's face last night when he had mentioned the journey to France. "No, I do not think he is up to foreign parts. He is very good with boots and such but I think France at war would be too much for him. Sort of a weak Willy. I will leave him here," he said.

* * *

A week later, Chadwick stood on the deck of the Sweet Betsy holding the cameo of Georgina Yelverton and wondering what he had got himself into. Rescuing a maiden in distress was not a role he had ever seen himself in. Until he met Marion Coxe, he had not really figured out how he liked his maidens. Now he wondered how Miss Yelverton would match up against Miss Coxe.

Marion had been short in stature but made up for it in personality, making her appear so much larger in life. She took disasters in stride. He thought how the Madra Dubh had hunted her and her nephews and how she had coped with each crisis. She wasn't much older than Miss Yelverton but she wasn't the pampered miss he thought Miss Yelverton to be. He remembered how the shop keeper he had interviewed had talked about her ill temper when her hat wasn't ready. He had only seen Marion visibly angry once – and that had been over an attempted kidnapping not a silly hat.

Ironic wasn't it, that the Madra Dubh was involved again? When he and Donnay had taken down the London splinter group, he had assumed wrongly that that was the end of the group.

Now he looked around the boat. It wasn't the newest one he had ever been on – it had obviously seen a number of tours – and been built for speed. Except for not being well-painted, it seemed to have been kept pretty shipshape. Since most of the sails were hoisted he could see they were well mended and the deck was clean, with all tools, ropes, and other equipment stowed away. All the men, including Captain Byrne slept in hammocks that hung below-deck in the large storage areas. Before last night, Chadwick had never slept in a hammock. He had to admit it wasn't bad. The rocking of the boat proved to be rather relaxing and he had slept surprisingly well.

Chadwick saw Paddy with the boat captain at the rear of the boat. Byrne seemed to do most of his own steering. Chadwick had not seen anyone else, even the first mate, handling the tiller since he had come onboard.

"So, Mister Wine Merchant, change your mind yet about going to France?" Captain Byrne called as Chadwick joined him and Paddy. His tone was jovial, and Chadwick didn't take his question seriously.

"No, Captain, why would I change my mind?" he asked. "France is where the wine is."

"Not the healthiest place for an Englishman," the Byrne responded.

"You have that wrong, Captain," Chadwick corrected him. "I am from New Orleans."

"Then you shouldn't have a problem," Byrne replied. "But remember, I know Paddy here and the tale that he is joining the Frenchies is so much crap. But your story is safe with me, Paddy. I do not care for them Frenchies any more than I care for the English. Both just want to be in charge and tax you to death."

This topic of conversation seemed dangerous to Chadwick and he wanted to change the topic fast. "Do you have any better idea if you will be able to take us all the way to Calais?" he asked.

Byrne studied the sky for a few moments and focused on the horizon. "If this weather holds, and I see no reason why it shouldn't, I mean to uphold my end of the bargain and drop you off as near Calais as I can. If the weather turns bad, I will give a signal when we pass Boulogne for my contact to meet me at a different rendezvous point. We can switch you to their boat and then he lands you."

"Why will it not be just as unsafe for him on the coast as for you?" Chadwick asked.

"Nah, he knows all the nooks and crannies. He's French. I do not know that part of the coast all that well. Although my route is usually closer to Cherbourg, I've done a lot of business here and the locals know me. It's the English Navy that we need to be careful of. If the weather turns real bad, we just go home."

"Pray that doesn't happen. I am in a rush to get started."

"Really?" Captain Byrne smirked. "Then why did you stop off in Dublin?"

Chadwick shrugged. He had thought this was also weak part of their story. "The ship was supposed to go to Bordeaux, but we hit a bad storm – got blown off course and damaged. The captain headed for the nearest port once he got clear of the storm."

"You need a better story than that," Byrne returned. "It's not the time of year for storms bad enough to damage a ship on that route, and Dublin would never be the closest port. You would more likely end up at Gibraltar or Spain. And, in case you were wondering, this time of year I do not expect the weather to get that bad for us, either."

Chadwick noticed that the Captain's eyes never really stopped roving, from the horizon to the sky, to the sails, to what each of the sailors was doing. He was a man who really noticed what was going on in his world. And he was right: the part of their story about showing up in Dublin as a result of a storm was garbage.

"Here's what I would say," Byrne continued to Chadwick's surprise. "At the time you set out, Ireland wasn't really part of England. That unification business just happened. That made Dublin a safe place to visit on your way to France. Why not just be visiting some relatives or acquaintances from New Orleans? Maybe some relatives escaping from France ended up there. I know I brought some over from France during that chop-off-your-head phase. Maybe these same relatives would like to go to New Orleans and need your help. Keep it simple."

Chadwick looked with surprise and some dismay at Paddy, who had been totally mum during the whole exchange. Had Paddy already blown their cover with the boat captain? Paddy stared back with a slight grimace on his lips.

The observant Byrne noticed Chadwick's response and continued.

"Nah, he didn't say anything. But I know Paddy. He sailed with me a fair amount. Good worker. And I know a thing or two about ships so your story just didn't make sense. You paid me good money to take you to France, that's all I need to know. But I don't want you getting Paddy here in trouble or killed. I've always been hoping he would come back to work for me, and besides, I don't get the rest of the money if I don't pick you up and take you back to Dublin. Oh, and you probably should have some ships' names in mind if anyone asks you what you came over on."

Byrne stood up, clamping his pipe in his teeth. "Paddy, take over the tiller for me? I want a cup of tea." He ducked down to the stairs leading below decks.

"So besides speaking passable French, you can also navigate. You picked up quite a few skills as a free trader," Chadwick remarked.

"Not so much, sir," Paddy replied. "I can steer in calm weather, but a hint of wind and I'm not your man. Maybe if I had stayed, the Captain would have taught me more, but I get seasick a lot. Unlike most, I never got over it. Which is why I am up here and not below in my hammock."

"He saw through our story right off. That is not good. I wonder if the rest of our story will hold up." Chadwick glanced around to make sure they were not overheard. "What do you think?"

Paddy took some time before answering. "Captain Byrne is a smart man. He has been around a long time and heard a lot. To my knowledge, he doesn't usually get involved in politics but from the way he has been talking, that attitude seems to have changed. He seems to be developing a side line of running folks to and from France in addition to his regular runs." He paused again to consider his words. "I think he is right about the part of the story of why you were in Dublin. It is probably a good idea to talk up the French link between New Orleans, France and Dublin, but not too much. Too much detail will only cause problems."

"I agree," Chadwick said. "However, I am more concerned about the wine business and whether that will hold as a cover story. After all, most of the vineyards are in southern France and we are in the north."

"Well, I guess we are on our way to southern France. Got dropped off in the north by mistake as that was all the transport we could find and we are heading south."

Over the next two days they worked on their cover story, looking for gaps and repeating it enough that they sounded believable.

"So what's the story now, Mr. Couture?" Byrne asked as Chadwick joined him at the tiller one afternoon. Chadwick almost looked behind himself before he realized the Captain was speaking to him and using the name he and Wickham had devised for this mission. He really needed to get used to the new name: Jeffrey Couture. Thankfully, Jeffrey was a common French name, even if often spelled differently.

"You were right, Captain. I was in Dublin trying to find a relative for one of my clients in New Orleans who wants him to come to stay in Louisiana. Since I was already going to France to buy wine, he just asked me to make a short detour. The relative had escaped to Dublin after his parents were sent to the guillotine. The political climate of Dublin is unstable and I did not want to give myself away, which I am afraid I did the first time anyone with any knowledge of the sea asked me anything. That would be you."

"Better, Mr. Couture. Better. What's Paddy doing with you?" he asked.

"He's just a young man looking for some adventure and possibly to join the Irish regiment in Napoleon's army."

"Ah, Mr. Couture, you can do better than that. You don't want him to be pressed to actually join up, do you?" the Captain chaffed. "Why not just say he is someone you hired in Dublin and are training in the wine trade? I know you have been working on his French and yours is pretty good. Get him some better clothes and work on his manners. Frenchies won't notice his English isn't as posh as yours. Travel in France is dangerous. No one will mind that you have a hulking bodyguard with you."

Chadwick nodded thoughtfully. "You do not think being Irish will be a problem for him?"

"Nah, I've dropped off lots of Irish lads in France going to fight for freedom. Young idiots. I don't bring too many back," he added sadly.

Chadwick just stared thoughtfully at Byrne. Really, the man was almost too helpful.

Just then the Captain started to chuckle. "Worried I will turn you in?" he asked. "Didn't Paddy tell you I fancy his sister? She has been leading me quite a chase. Her brother gets into trouble in France and I had any hand in it, she will gut me with a fish hook. Ain't that right, Paddy?"

Paddy handed mugs of steaming tea to Captain Byrne and Chadwick. "Sure is true that you have been running after her for some time. I don't understand why you don't get anywhere." He grinned cheekily at the Captain.

"Could be the wife I already have has something to do with it," he replied. "Church doesn't like men having multiple wives."

Paddy had been taking a sip from his own mug and at the Captain's news, he spluttered hot tea and his eyes almost bugged out of his head. "Does my sister know?" he gasped.

"For sure. She's helping nurse her. Poor Betsy is pretty poorly. She's a good woman, but she's been off for some time and your sister is very comely."

Chadwick chuckled. It was his first laugh, he realized, in quite a few days. He must be beginning to feel a little more relaxed. At least Byrne had a legitimate reason for keeping Paddy alive: lust.

Byrne leaned towards Captain Chadwick and talked in a lower voice. "I don't have much love for the government, any government for that matter. And for all making my living the way I do, doesn't mean I want to see my own country over run with Frenchies. Not really positive that can be said of all my men. But I have been known to pass along a message or two about what I might see while I am at sea minding my own business."

A couple of connections started to come together in Chadwick's mind. "Messages that Paddy would relay to Wickham?" he asked.

Byrne and Paddy nodded simultaneously.

"So that is why Wickham seems to trust you, Paddy," he said.

Paddy grinned back. "I still broke that sergeant's jaw and almost got myself hanged. I still can act the stupid git when I lose my temper, sir," he added ruefully.

"Seems like it would have been easier to just tell me I could trust Captain Byrne." Chadwick said.

"Seemed best to let you get to know him first, Captain Couture," Paddy said.

"Trust is a hard thing to earn, don't you think?" Byrne noted.

"Yes, it is," Chadwick agreed.

"Anyway, we need to work together and since I want Wickham to pay me in full, that means I need to return for you and take you back to Dublin." Byrne added.

"And I too want to get back to Dublin. So about the pick up plans..." Chadwick started.

Byrne interrupted, "I am heading to Germany to see about a load of wood, for once a totally legal load. Don't need to be picked up by the custom men on this trip. That would be very inconvenient. That trip should take about two or three weeks. I am hoping that will be enough time for you to do whatever you have to do." When Chadwick nodded, he continued, "Keep in touch with my French contact. You will meet him when I drop you off. I will signal him when I return and arrange for you to get back on board."

Chadwick was thinking about how simple the arrangements sounded as he put his foot on the pier and a voice greeted him from the darkness. "*Arrêtez! Montrez-moi vos papiers!*"

Chapter Five: Calais

C hadwick sat back in his chair, crossed his legs and tried to appear relaxed. There was a window behind the man at the desk – he had not introduced himself – through which Chadwick could see that the sky was now gray, no longer black. They had been here all night. Well, *he* had been here. He hadn't seen Paddy since they met up with the port guards who had shuffled them hurriedly to the basement of the *hotel de ville* where the man now sitting behind the desk had started to question them. He could only hope that Captain Byrne's contact had disappeared and not got taken up in the sweep.

For what seemed like the hundredth time, he looked around the office and tried to find something to think about besides his situation. The office was sparsely furnished, with only a table in the center serving as a desk and two chairs, one on either side. Behind Chadwick's inquisitor was another table with piles of correspondence and papers in sorted stacks. There were several hooks on the walls for coats, two lanterns and several candles that illuminated the table and little else. No tea tray, coffee urn or even a brandy bottle was anywhere in sight. Chadwick would have welcomed any or all three of the beverages. Even a glass of water would have been nice. His throat was dry from talking and his eyes burned from being open too long and exposed to the smoke given off by the oil lanterns.

He tried to think how a totally innocent man would react.

"Monsieur," he said now leaning forward. When the man looked up from his writing, Chadwick met his eyes frostily. "You have kept me here all night." He kept his voice low as he had for the past few hours. But now, he gauged, was the time for an innocent man to be angry. "I am tired, hungry and running out of patience. You ask the same questions over and over, but my answers do not change. What do you want?"

"The truth!" the man snapped back. "You are not telling me the truth!"

"The truth!" Chadwick snapped back. "I have told you the truth. You just do not accept it because it doesn't fit into your assumptions of what the truth should be."

"Bah," the man said in disgust. "You expect me to believe a wine trader, from New Orleans no less, begins his journey in Calais? And with an Irish assistant? You think me a fool?"

Chadwick allowed his voice to rise in anger. "A wine trader who stopped in Dublin to do a client a favor, not realizing how hard it would be to get to France from Ireland. When I left New Orleans, Ireland was still somewhat neutral. Now it is crawling with British soldiers and there is no legal shipping going anywhere near France since the war restarted."

He paused in disgust. "But I have told you all this, over and over again. And you do not even have the courtesy to name yourself. Instead, you threaten me because you do not like what I have told you."

"You are right, I don't like your story. Too convenient. You could be a British spy with that accent."

Chadwick decided to be doubly offended. "What is wrong with my accent?" he demanded. "You understand me well enough."

"Well, you obviously aren't French."

"I never pretended to be French. I am from a land founded by the French, ruled for some time by the Spanish and now French again. The people now often speak their own dialect. I am not trying to pass myself off as other than who I am. After getting this kind of shit from the lackeys in Dublin, I was looking forward to France. I certainly didn't expect to be arrested by my own people because my *accent* is different.

"And who the hell are you anyway?" Chadwick rose to his feet and pounded his fist on the desk for emphasis. An innocent man probably would not have put up with this interrogation as long as he had, probably would have tried to walk out by now. "What kind of gentleman doesn't even offer a friendly visitor a cup of coffee?" he demanded. "I have had enough. I am leaving." He grabbed his hat from the desk and turned to face the door.

"Just a moment, monsieur," the man said sharply. "My men beyond that door are not going to be allowing you to leave so easily." He sat down and gestured for Chadwick to do the same. The Captain decided to remain standing.

"You are right, I should have introduced myself. I am Henri Jean Vilet, Agent in Charge of Northern France and Commissioner of Police. It is my duty to investigate all people coming into Calais who might be agents of our enemies."

Chadwick nodded stiffly that he understood. The organizational name rang all kinds of bells for him and now that he thought about it, the man's name did also. Just his bad luck that as soon as Byrne's men rowed him and Paddy ashore, he ended up facing the counterpart of Wickham in the French government. What was this man doing in Calais?

At that moment, there was a knock at the door.

"Enter," Vilet called. A young soldier entered, saluted and handed Vilet a scrap of paper. To Chadwick, he seemed to retreat faster than he came in. Vilet studied the scrap.

"Well," he said, "you have come in via the free trader Captain Byrne who is known to our port agents. I have been able to confirm that much of your story as they saw his ship tonight and they saw him drop you off."

"I told you," Chadwick protested, "I am not hiding anything."

"Yes, you have said that many times." Vilet stared at Chadwick thoughtfully. "But I am going to have to confirm the rest of your story," he said to Chadwick's surprise.

"I do not understand," Chadwick said cautiously.

"I am going to have to send messages. It will likely take some time."

Chadwick rolled his eyes. "This is ridiculous. I need to go south to do what I came here to do: buy wine for my clients. When can I do that?"

"Not yet."

"What do you mean? Are you planning to keep us in jail?" he asked in shock. "We have not done anything wrong."

Vilet's lips became even thinner in exasperation. "You might be surprised to find I don't really like jailing innocent people."

"Fine, I will just walk out of here and be on my way and you won't have to do that."

"Not so fast." Vilet leaned back in his chair and crossed his arms. "Until I verify your story, I cannot let you wander about France. You are to give me your word, that you will stay in Calais until I am satisfied that you are not an enemy agent. You will check in at this office once a day."

"This could take months if you are planning on writing to New Orleans," Chadwick protested. "I cannot stay here that long. I have work to do."

"Don't worry, it won't be that long. I am convinced you will find Calais to be an interesting place to visit for a few weeks." Vilet stood abruptly. "You are free to go. You will find your luggage and your Irish assistant in the hall."

He nodded at the door. Chadwick had been dismissed.

Chadwick leaned in and snatched up the letters of credit off Vilet's desk. He had been keeping an eye on those all night. Without them, he and Paddy would be begging on the streets penniless.

Vilet's hand came down with a plunk on a second pile, the letters of introduction. "I will be keeping these," he said.

"Fine," Chadwick responded, "but I will be keeping these." Putting the valuable papers in his inner pocket, he strode out of the office.

* * *

Because Paddy's English was so much better than his smuggler's French, Chadwick switched to that language once they were in the street. He kept his voice low so as not to attract too much attention.

"How are you?" he asked Paddy once they were a block or so away from the building where they had been held.

Paddy nodded. He also kept his voice low. "They didn't even ask me questions. Just left me in the hall with your trunk. And you, sir? What happened all night?"

Paddy shifted the small trunk from his right shoulder to his left so he didn't have to look around it to see Chadwick. His eyes searched Chadwick's face and then glanced over his figure.

"I am fine. Just questions. The same ones, over and over. He did not believe me but evidently your old Captain is known in these parts as a reliable bloke. It really helped that we came with him. If anyone else had dropped us off, we probably would be spending time in some wretched cells. But we did not get off totally free."

As they made their way through the streets and back to the port, Chadwick filled Paddy in on the questions Vilet had asked, his responses and the fact that Vilet had kept their letters of introduction and identification.

"Sir?" Paddy asked. When Chadwick paused and nodded, he continued, "My belly is eating itself. Can we get some food?"

Chadwick grinned. "Good idea. Where?" He paused in the middle of the street and turned slowly, studying the shop fronts that were opening with the new day. He didn't see any food vendors.

"Captain, over there." Paddy was gesturing with his head towards a corner where a sign *The Citizen* showed a man in his shirt sleeves drinking a pint.

Chadwick was impressed: Paddy did seem to have a knack for finding a pub when you needed one. That was a very useful skill.

The Citizen not only had food, although at this hour it was cold meat and cheese and yesterday's bread, but also a few rooms to let. Paddy might have dozed in the hall during the night, but Chadwick had not slept at all. As soon as he put some food into his system he realized sleep was imminent. The only thing he noticed about the room the landlord took them to, was that it contained one large bed. He took off his boots and jacket and lay down. He felt the other side of the bed sink as Paddy joined him. He knew nothing more until someone rocked his shoulder and he heard Paddy calling, "Captain Chadwick? Sir?"

Chadwick managed to crack open an eye to peer blearily at Paddy.

"What?" he croaked. His throat felt like a desert.

"It's dark out, sir," Paddy replied. "Landlord's been knocking at the door, wants to know if we are staying the night. I thought we might start looking for taverns where Irish hangout."

"Right," Chadwick managed. "What we came for. Blast, my head feels like it is full of cotton wool." He managed to sit up and swing his legs over the side of the bed.

"Would you see if you can get some water from the landlord? Oh, and tell him we are keeping the room for a couple of days," he said.

Paddy exited the room and Chadwick continued to try to wake up. He had pulled his boots back on and was trying to see how badly crumpled his shirt was when Paddy returned with a pitcher of water, followed by a maid with a tray of food.

"I wasn't positive if you wanted to sit in the common room downstairs, sir." Paddy's mangled French obviously identified him as a foreigner but the sense of his meaning was clear to Chadwick. Vilet probably had some fellows keeping an eye on them and Paddy thought it better if they ate quietly here before slipping out the back to search for Hastings' relative.

Paying no more mind to Paddy than if he had been invisible, the maid set the tray on the small table under the window, favoring Chadwick with a bright and rather charming smile. Charming, that is, except for some missing teeth. He thanked her in French and she left after assuring him that if he needed anything, anything at all, he was just to ask her.

Paddy closed the door quietly and stood rather indecisively.

"Paddy, go ahead and eat. I want to wash up a bit first and then eat, but you should go ahead and get started." That was all the encouragement Paddy needed to head straight for the table and start in. While he ate, he filled Chadwick in on his afternoon. He hadn't needed as much sleep as Chadwick and had gone out to check out the tavern and get the 'lay of the land', if you know what I mean, Captain."

He had indeed seen some fellows downstairs that looked like Vilet's minions. Paddy was convinced he recognized one of them from the night before.

"He is the one who actually went through your trunk. He's not the one who took the shirt though. That was another chap."

"I suppose he took the good one," Chadwick growled. "I didn't count on this being a long trip, so I didn't bring much. That probably was a mistake. Now I think on it, I am guessing a merchant travels with a lot more gear." He finished drying his face and headed for the table.

Paddy poured him coffee. "The coffee is pretty good, Captain. Not as good as tea, but not bad. Had to argue with the landlord a bit. He only wanted to send up wine."

"How are you doing arguing in French?" Chadwick asked, grinning. The idea of Paddy facing off with the landlord over coffee was amusing.

"Better than I would have thought. The lessons on the boat helped a lot, too. I am never going to be taken for a local, but I can make myself understood."

Chadwick helped himself to ham slices and cheese. He said thoughtfully, "I think you had better call me something besides 'Captain'. We would have to make up too much of a story to explain that. How about just calling me

Couture? And I will call you Cavanaugh? You are supposed to be my assistant, not a servant."

"Is that what you would call your assistant?" Paddy asked. "Just his surname?"

Chadwick nodded and said, "Yes, when Nathan and I first worked together, we called each other by our surnames. Actually, at first, he didn't call me anything. He was too feverish to know what was happening. Later on, we got to a first name basis, especially in private."

"And why was that, sir?" Paddy asked interestedly. "I mean, why was he feverish?"

"Oh, gaol fever," Chadwick answered after swallowing a large chunk of ham. He cut another large slice of cheese and bread. "His task had gone horribly wrong and he was in a prison, a Russian one at that. Wickham sent me to get him out. That was a mess."

"Come on, sir, tell me," Paddy pleaded. He knew a good story was in the offing.

"Not a lot to tell really. I got him out of the prison simply by bribing the guards."

"How did you get from Russia to England?" Paddy asked. "Aren't there some seas between?"

"There are seas. I made for the coast and got us on the first boat headed in the right direction. It took months to get him home." Chadwick finished his bread and cheese and cut the small fruit pie in half. He put half on his plate and pushed the other part to Paddy. He also split the rest of the coffee between them.

"Anyway, by the time we got home, we were using first names. I do not think Christian names would work in this situation. You are supposed to be my assistant, so I think surnames would be more appropriate."

"Surnames it is," Paddy said agreeably. "Here's to you, Mr. Couture." And he raised his coffee cup in a toast. "And to our success."

* * *

On their way out through the kitchen, Chadwick and Paddy were accosted by the landlord. He looked at them and the back door meaningfully.

Chadwick handed him some coins. "Playing a joke on our friends in the front room," he said. "How about giving them some extra brandy to keep them happy while they wait for us?"

The coins disappeared quickly.

"And what is it you do, sir, that warrants the likes of them sitting in my establishment and, I might add, demanding free drink?"

Chadwick handed over some more coins for causing the landlord to serve the freeloaders. "I am a wine merchant from New Orleans in the Americas."

"I know where New Orleans is," the landlord replied crisply. "I also know there are not many wineries around here." The later was said in a much more sarcastic tone.

Chadwick sighed deeply. He tried to portray a much put-upon man.

"I made an unfortunate side trip to Dublin to check on some relatives for a client. I found the relatives and then I found that Ireland is now part of England and there were no legitimate ships to France from there." He stopped, hoping the landlord would fill in the rest for himself. What he got was a raised eyebrow from the landlord, telling him to continue.

"With limited options, we took ship with a chap who frequents these parts. He set us down last night at the port. Your local police commissioner was not impressed with our arrival and seems to think we are English spies. He is, however, checking my story during which time we need to stay in Calais. I am eager to head south particularly to the Bordeaux region but without my identification papers, we are stuck here. Those chaps out front are his, come to make sure we do not slip out of town."

"And are you going to slip out of town?"

"Not without my papers. I need those letters in order to do business. However, while I am here, we do have another errand for a client that is a bit delicate." Chadwick stopped again, hoping he wouldn't have to fill out the story any more. The more lies, the easier to trip over them.

The landlord nodded as if coming to a decision. "Well, you have played fair with me and paid your bill, unlike those freeloaders in the front. Will you be wanting breakfast?"

"Yes," Chadwick responded, "and a little information, if you would."

More coins changed hands. He gestured at Paddy as he started on their previously agreed-upon story.

"My assistant's brother-in-law has overstayed his time here in Calais and his wife wants him home. Personally, I can't think why. He is Irish and a member of one of their many organizations. His wife has a feeling he has another woman over here. We promised her we would try to look him up if we got here. Do you have any idea where such a fellow might be spending his time?"

The landlord's eyes went to Paddy and surveyed him carefully. "What's wrong with him?" he asked. "Can't he talk?"

"Not that well. As you know, he has some French, but not a lot."

The landlord shrugged indifferently. "Couple of taverns come to mind. *The Green Isle* on…, damn it! What's the name of the road they renamed over by the green?" he yelled at the kitchen at large.

The pot boy answered, "Do you mean Rue de Bastille, Papa?"

"Yes, that's the one. They keep changing the names of the streets. Nothing royal allowed which is fine, but damn confusing," he grumbled. "Anyway, *The Green Isle* is there and there is another place near the docks. *Hibernia* is the name I think. You can't really call it a tavern. It's a dump, but I would check there first for a good-for-nothing like you describe."

He turned away to bark orders at the maid who had been avidly listening, to get back to work taking drink orders. Chadwick and Paddy left quietly out the back door.

Half way down the street, Paddy spoke using his broken French. "Not married, my sister," he grinned.

"Speak English, but make your accent as broad as possible. But quietly; let's not draw unwanted attention," Chadwick cautioned.

Amusement flavored Paddy's voice, "Mr. Couture, sir, my sister is not married and a right brawny woman. You don't want her to be finding out you are taking her name in vain and putting about she is married to a scoundrel. You could get hurt." Paddy chuckled.

"Do you think he believed me?" Chadwick asked.

"Not at all, but it would seem Mr. Wickham was right that the Irish are considered allies. I think he saw we are not spying for enemies but are French allies so he didn't question further. But we will find out soon enough if he runs out to the front room and alerts Vilet's spies."

"Well, we cannot do anything about that yet. Let's check out the tavern by the docks. The more dicey it is, the more likely they are keeping our victim there with no one the wiser or to ask any inconvenient questions."

They reached a broad street that seemed to be lined with shops, although in the dark it was hard to be certain. Chadwick cursed. "We should have brought a lantern."

"I think I can find the way. It has been a while since I've been here, but I did spend some time walking about the port for Byrne. Go left here," he directed. "This street heads to the port, eventually."

The streets were dark and fairly slippery with what Chadwick hoped was a recent rain, not effluent from the houses but the smell seemed a combination of both. Paddy didn't speak again, intent on finding their way through to the harbor. Chadwick sensed rather than saw a number of shadows slipping through the streets. There seemed to be a lot of people out tonight, probably sailors.

As they rounded a corner, the duo saw light from burning torches. Suddenly they were on the quay, with the masts of ships forming what appeared to be a forest. The torches were burning brightly about a ship that was being off-loaded.

"Isn't that unusual?" Chadwick murmured.

"Off-loading in the dark?" Paddy asked. "Very. Lots of things you can't see and then can go wrong. But look at this place! So many ships. I wonder what is going on?"

He paused and then continued, "Sir, you should ask someone where *The Hibernia* is."

"You do it," Chadwick decided. "It will seem more natural."

Paddy nodded dubiously and headed off to the area lit by the torches. He was back shortly.

"Got lucky and ran into a fellow countryman," he said. "The inn is just over there, maybe a hundred yards or so."

The Hibernia was every bit as decrepit as Chadwick had expected it to be. However, it was doing a lively trade and the door swung open every few minutes with men coming and going. From within, voices were raised in song, arguments or debate. Although he was pretty sure most were speaking English, the accents were thick and he had trouble understanding them. He looked at Paddy questioningly. "Got an idea what they are speaking?"

Paddy nodded. "Some English, some Gaelic. No French that I can hear. So how are we going to play this?" he asked.

"We go in and order drinks. If there is a maid, you see if you can charm some information out of her. I do not want to do much talking as I will probably stand out too much even if I do not."

Paddy surveyed Chadwick thoughtfully. Even having slept in his clothes, he was clean and more decently dressed than any of the men in the tavern. His height and looks would make him a center of attention. If he opened his mouth, they would probably kill him just on principle.

"May I make a suggestion, sir?"

Chadwick nodded. "Better idea?" he asked.

"This dump only has one floor and that looks like it is about to fall in. So, I am thinking no one could be kept upstairs. How about I go in there alone and see if I can chat up anyone about my 'brother-in-law'? You go around back and check out the out-buildings."

Chadwick groaned, reality just having set in.

"Damnation. Even if we find her, what do we do with her? We do not have any place to hide her until Byrne comes back. Without papers, we cannot just ride out of town, which was my preferred plan." His brain was working feverishly trying to come up with an alternative.

"She might not be here, sir," Paddy said.

"Right," Chadwick agreed. "Tonight is for reconnoitering. I think it wouldn't hurt if you told the truth about why you and the chap you work for are stuck in Calais without papers. See if you can get some sympathy, or at least get them used to seeing you around. If you can find out anything about the ass, Vilet, it would also be a good thing."

"How long before we meet?"

"You need at least two beers to seem acceptable. I will probably finish long before that, so I will make my way back to the inn."

"Can you do that, sir, without me?" Paddy looked dubious again.

"Well, I did not drop bread crumbs, but I did take note of the turns. Do not get yourself beat up on the way back. There seem to be a lot of soldiers and sailors about."

"You, either. They're more likely to want to take you on than me. I don't look so posh."

A thought occurred to Chadwick. "Here, take some coins for the drink. I got these in Dublin, so they should help get you in."

Paddy grasped the coins in his left hand, dropped his shoulders to appear smaller, and slouched towards the door. Chadwick watched as he slipped in the door and silently wished him luck. Paddy was proving to be a reliable associate, almost a friend, and he didn't want anything to happen to the young man. He sighed again as he surveyed the run-down tavern. How was he going to get to the back to see if there were any other buildings? He didn't see any obvious alleys.

Maybe he would not beat Paddy back to the inn. It seemed to take ages to find the disgusting opening between the buildings that led to the back of *The Hibernia*. Once there he almost wished he could change places with Paddy. The muck clung to his boots, making each step a fight to lift his leg out of the grasp of whatever the muck was made of. He really didn't want to know. Even in the army, he hadn't come across anything quite this repulsive. Suddenly, he was grateful for the dark so he really couldn't see what he was stepping in. He stopped by the corner of the tavern to see how the buildings were laid out and if any could be used to hold a young woman.

While Chadwick studied the area, the back door of the pub opened suddenly and a couple of sailors came out. They left the door open while they relieved themselves against the wall. The sailors went back into the tavern, not bothering to close the door. The dim light was enough to allow Chadwick to peer around the corner from his hiding place and identify several shacks or outbuildings. Then the door swung wide open again and another two men came out.

"Gar, Donald, don't you ever clean out this place?" one man snarled in disgust.

Chadwick could see they were headed towards a badly tilting shack in the corner. He could see that the second man – who hadn't bothered to answer

– was carrying a plate and a cup. The two came out shortly thereafter and returned to the tavern. Before they entered, Chadwick could hear one ask the other, "How much longer?" He didn't hear any answer.

The Captain waited for some time longer but the alley remained quiet. There were no more visitors. He thought there might have been other men coming out to relieve themselves but maybe they found the area too disgusting for even that activity.

Chadwick crept over to the door of the ramshackle shed and listened carefully. He could hear some straw rustling, but thought that could be mice. He realized the door was barred from the outside with a thick slab of wood holding the door closed. He carefully removed the bar so he could inch the door open.

"Hello?" he called softly. "Anyone here?" He repeated it in English and then again in French. No answer. Behind him, the tavern door opened, spilling dim light into the space between the buildings. Chadwick hurriedly moved into the shack and pulled the door closed behind him. He could peer through the slats and see another figure in the door of the tavern, a figure that stood just in the doorway and relieved himself not even going into the alley. In the very slim fragments of light, Chadwick surveyed the inside of the shack. He could just see the outline of a figure lying on the straw in the far corner.

As soon as the man went back into the tavern, Chadwick reached into his coat pocket and produced a small tinderbox that all agents attached to the Alien Office carried with them. It came with a small tub candle which he now attempted to light. After several strikes, he got the candle going and now had enough light to survey the shambles that made up the inside of the hut.

There was nothing in the hut but some straw in the far corner where he had seen the figure-no table, no chair, no nothing. The smell in the shed was not much better than in the alley.

"Oh, my God," he breathed.

Chapter Six: Calais Quayside

C hadwick didn't dare bring his candle closer to the cowering figure on the straw; he was afraid of setting the straw on fire or burning what he assumed was a 'her' from what he could see of a tattered dress. She huddled face down on the straw. All he could see of her head was a mass of long matted hair. Skinny arms were raised to protect her head and even in the gloom he could see they were badly bruised. He moved the candle to see her legs, they, too, appeared bruised with welts still seeping blood. He put a gentle hand on her shoulder only for her to flinch away, moaning in English about not hurting her.

"Georgina?" he asked softly.

No answer.

"Georgina Yelverton?" he repeated. "I am Captain Jeffrey Chadwick, sent to take you home." Chadwick crouched down, trying to see the young woman's face. Even if this wasn't Georgina Yelverton, he couldn't leave her in this condition. He did not want to think about how she got to be this way. Whoever did this to her was an animal, no matter who she was.

He tried again to rouse her. He put his hand on her shoulder to turn her to face him. She flinched and tried to pull away, but he gripped her shoulder tightly and succeeded in getting her to face him although with her eyes downcast. He repeated again, "Miss Yelverton? I am Captain Jeffrey Chadwick, sent to bring you home." And then a bit more forcefully, "Are you Georgina Yelverton?"

His voice seemed to finally get through to her as she gazed up fearfully at him, even as she shrank back as far as she could, given his grip. "Yes," she whispered.

"Where do you come from?" Chadwick asked. A woman might say anything to get out of this horrible situation.

"Dublin."

If this girl was at all related to the beautiful woman in the portrait, he didn't see it. Trying to identify her by candlelight was close to impossible especially with the layer of dirt and the stringy mass of filthy hair covering her face. In fact, everything about her seemed dirty. She was covered in straw as if she had burrowed down for warmth. From the smell, he was pretty certain that the straw had not been too clean.

As far as he could see, Hastings had not hit her in the face. The rest of her seemed to be a mass of bruises, but her face only showed where the tears had made crevices down her cheeks. He reached for her hands, only to hear her cry out in pain. It didn't take long to see why. One finger was at an odd angle, obviously broken. Hastings must have broken it dragging off a ring or some such bauble, he assumed. Chadwick realized Miss Yelverton was positively shaking. Of course she was; she was only wearing a shift. If he had a real light, he imagined he would see that her lips were blue with cold. Taking off his overcoat, he draped it around her shoulders.

God forgive me, he thought *but she's not only covered in filth. She probably has fleas! This is my only good coat and I doubt that Wickham pay for another one if this one is ruined.*

He blew out the candle stub. "What do we do now?" he whispered. "I have no safe place to take you. No decent landlord would take you in like this."

He sat back on his heels, still holding her other hand. He was almost afraid to let go in case he lost her in the dark. Although she seemed to be in shock – and not likely to go haring off – he wasn't sure enough of her condition to trust letting go.

There was no answer from the young woman, but he continued talking out loud.

"I can't leave you here, not like this," he murmured. "I need to get you someplace safe where we can take care of your ..." He paused while he tried to think of the right word.

Georgina whispered before he could finish, "I do not think that is possible. He said he would kill my father if I tried to get away, if I tried anything. He knows people in Dublin who would hurt my father."

Chadwick was surprised. At a time like this, she was thinking of her father? Hastings must be pretty convincing and terrifying. At some point, he now noticed, she had started rocking back and forth. Her whole body seemed to vibrate with tension and fear.

"Your father sent me to find you," Chadwick answered.

Now did not seem the occasion to give her the whole story of who he was and how he had found her. Time was passing, and he was anxious to at least get away from the shack and its filth. But he couldn't very well drag her through the streets if she was fighting him. He needed her to trust him and come willingly.

"No, no, I can't go back," she moaned.

"I am not leaving you here in this filth," Chadwick insisted. "We need to get away and hide out until morning, when I will find us some shelter."

He could feel her hand stretch as she tried to pull away.

"He is going to hurt my family. I cannot let him do that."

"He's *not* going to hurt your father," Chadwick said. "Hastings does not have anyone left in Dublin who is listening to him."

"You do not know that."

"I do know that," Chadwick said decisively. "I have been trying to track you for some time and there is no one left in Dublin who cares about Hastings. I promise you that I can protect you and your father." He knew he was not getting through to her.

The door to the tavern opened again casting shadows where there had only been pitch dark before. They both froze as they listened for footsteps.

"It's dark as a crypt out here," a familiar voice complained in English. "How do I know where to go?"

"Anywhere," the second replied.

The footsteps stopped. Chadwick could hear the man relieve himself. Then he heard Paddy say, "I'll be right along."

Chadwick had to let go of the girl so that he could peer out the cracked door. As he studied the space between the buildings, he could just make out Paddy's familiar outline in the entrance to the tavern. Seeing his assistant alone, Chadwick gave a soft whistle to get his attention and tried waving him over. He breathed a sigh of relief as Paddy slipped into the shack.

"Change of plans," Chadwick whispered. "Miss Yelverton is here and we must get her away. But she is not in any condition to go waltzing into a tavern, or to be seen at all, really."

"We not only need to go, we need to get right away. Those bastards are selling her favors around the bar right now," said Paddy. "First one will be coming out here soon. That's why I came out. To warn you if you were still here."

"Right, we are leaving now," Chadwick commanded. "I will carry her; you lead the way."

"No," she whispered. "I have to stay. He will hurt my father." She tried to pull away but between the two of them, they easily cornered her.

Chadwick was taken aback at the strength of her resistance. There seemed to be a lot of bravery, however misplaced, in that thin body. "Hold her," he ordered Paddy. He ripped off his cravat and gagged Georgina before she could respond. "I am so sorry, Miss Yelverton," he said as he worked. "We are in a hurry and I can't stay to convince you this is in your best interest. You have to be quiet and this is the only way I am convinced you will be." He wrapped his coat around her more tightly, which served the purpose of keeping her arms pinned to her body. Tossing her over his shoulder, he took a deep breath and followed the Irishman out into the open sewer of a yard.

Paddy surprised him by turning towards the quay instead of heading back uphill and away from the port area of the city. Then they turned and seemed to follow the river inland. They had to meander in ways that sometimes took them away from the water, but Paddy always headed back.

Finally, Chadwick called a halt. He carefully set Georgina on her feet. He kept his arms around her so she couldn't run off while he tried to catch his breath. She was pretty light, but she was still a full grown woman.

"Paddy, where are we headed?" he asked.

Paddy had moved closer and was trying to get a glimpse of Miss Yelverton. It wasn't easy given how dark the night was.

"I think you can take the gag off now, sir," he said. "She doesn't look like she is going to scream, and I don't hear anyone behind us."

Chadwick listened carefully for any sound of following footsteps, but all he heard was water sloshing against the various boats that were docked along the quay. He looked at Georgina's face for signs of resistance, but she only stood quietly with her eyes closed, even as she leaned against his arm. He gently pulled the cravat down, but she still didn't show any sign of responding. He looked at Paddy as he asked again, "Where are we headed?"

"I am trying to find an empty boat so we can wait out the night. I think it's about midnight and since we can't go back to *The Citizen,* we need somewhere to go."

Chadwick nodded in agreement and then realized that it was too dark for anyone to see the gesture. "Sounds better than anything I could come up with," he said.

Paddy continued, "I think, or maybe I am hoping, Hastings and those bastards will think she ran away by herself and will be spending their time searching around that dump."

"Well, I am hoping the same thing. Look, I am going to take Miss Yelverton over to the building and stand there. It's even darker by the wall and will be harder for anyone to see us. You scout around and see if you can find a boat or dinghy for us to wait out the rest of the night. One with a tarp would be even better."

* * *

The night was long and uncomfortable. Eventually, his resourceful assistant found a small skiff that was deserted and, judging by the amount of trash and water in the bottom, had been so for quite some time. Chadwick sat on one bench, leaning against its side, trying to keep his boots out of the sludge at the bottom of the boat. Paddy handed Miss Yelverton in and Chadwick directed her to lie down on the bench. He bade her pull her bare feet up and try to tuck them under his coat. The air wasn't terribly cold, but he could only imagine how uncomfortable she must be. Still, she didn't talk, just silently followed his directions.

The thought crossed his mind that she might, in a quixotic gesture, try to return to Hastings, believing that would keep her father safe. He kept his hand on her shoulder, so that in the dark, if she tried to sneak out, he stop her. Now that he had found her, he wasn't going to risk losing her.

"Paddy, before you leave, try to drape that old piece of sail so we look like just some more trash."

He sent Paddy back to *The Citizen* to reassure Monsieur Vipond, the landlord, that they were returning, but, more importantly, so Paddy could return with food and information. They needed a safe place to keep Georgina Yelverton. Obviously, her wounds would raise questions with any law-abiding landlord. If Vilet thought his story about Dublin was fishy, how would he react to his explanation of how he had acquired a young woman with multiple bruises, a broken finger, and who knew what else wrong? It would be enough to land him in a cell for a long time. So he directed Paddy to ask the landlord where they could rent rooms for an extended stay, since it looked like they would be in Calais for a while.

Chadwick could see now why his initial plan to simply nab Miss Yelverton and ride to the coast to catch up with Captain Byrne was just so much romantic nonsense. Vilet was obviously going to be keeping track of them, and this poor girl was in no shape to go riding off, while he and Paddy hunted down an elusive smuggler. And that was another thing: she obviously had been abused badly. What little medical knowledge the Captain had acquired in the army did not equip him to handle female issues. Thinking about Vilet reminded him that he needed to report in to that office once a day.

Chadwick sighed deeply; too many problems and not enough answers. At least his charge could get some sleep. From the relaxing of the muscles in her shoulder under his hand, it seemed she was finally able to get some rest.

He shifted on the bench trying to get more comfortable while still keeping his boots from getting ruined in the muck. Then a new noise sounded in the dark and he jerked to attention. Above the sloshing of the water against the quay and the creak of the wooden boats, he heard footsteps, multiple pairs. It wasn't Paddy coming back.

He resisted the urge to push back the sail to see what was going on. From his position under the sail, he could just barely make out the reflection of torches on the oily water that surrounded the skiff. Now he could hear English-speaking voices, ones similar to those of the men he had heard in the tavern yard. Georgina stiffened under his hand, coming awake. He put his finger over her mouth, hoping it could be enough to keep her from calling out.

"How do you think she would have got this far?" one asked.

"Someone helped her," another voice snarled. "Someone opened the shed. She could not do that on her own."

After a pause for thought, the first voice said, "Only new face in the pub was that red-haired chap. Didn't say much, just drank a bit. And now that you mention it, didn't come back when he went to take a piss."

"Yeah, him. I'd bet good coin he took off with her."

"Why?"

"Good question, and when we find them, I will beat the answer out of him."

In the skiff, Chadwick could feel Georgina tense. He put his whole hand over her mouth but lightly, since he couldn't feel her making any other movement. When the footsteps finally moved off, he removed his hand.

"Nasty piece of work, that one," he whispered when he was positive they were gone.

"And now I have got you and your friend in trouble," she moaned.

"You have not done anything," Chadwick responded. "When we get someplace safe, I will explain everything. Right now, try to rest. We need to wait until dawn before moving on. I have a deep and profound hope that by then, my friend will be back with some food."

Hastings and company had moved off and they didn't seem to be circling back. However much the thought of crouching in the foul-smelling skiff for several more hours did not appeal to Chadwick, the alternative of finding a stone doorway in which to huddle was less alluring. He patted Georgina Yelverton's shoulder encouragingly and leaned against the side to wait for dawn.

He must have dozed off. A light tapping jerked him awake and he realized it was no longer pitch dark but gray. The dark scenery reminded him of yesterday morning when he had watched the sun rise in Vilet's office.

"Mr. Couture?" The Irishman's voice sounded next to him.

"Yes," he responded quietly. Pushing back the sail cautiously, he looked up into Paddy's anxious face. He hadn't realized how scared the lad must be, on his own in Calais. He wasn't all that confident himself, but as the one in charge he knew he had to look confident. He nodded reassuringly at Paddy and then glanced around quickly and saw it was still early enough that few people were about.

Chadwick stepped out of the skiff and stood stretching his spine, trying to get the knots out of his muscles and blood flowing to his numb feet. Miss Yelverton sat up but kept her feet up and out of the sludge at the bottom. She looked even worse than she had in the shed, her legs a mass of bruises and her hair filthy and knotted.

Paddy leaned over and held out his hands to her. "Here, miss, let me help you out."

Once Georgina Yelverton was standing on the pier, both men could get a better look at their new charge. Chadwick sighed. In her condition, there was no way she would not stand out in any crowd. Her feet were covered in muck up as far as he could see. Many people went about dirty, even barefoot, but he hadn't seen anyone who was that dirty wear a pristine gentleman's coat. He exchanged looks of dismay with Paddy.

"Do you have any food?"

The words were whispered but again shocked Chadwick. Here he was worried about how she looked and had forgotten she probably hadn't eaten a real meal in days. Before he could respond, Paddy opened a small bundle he had laid on the pier, revealing a small loaf and some cheese. He broke off pieces of bread and gave the girl small bits. "Not too fast, miss, or it won't be staying down for long," he said.

"Good man," Chadwick complimented him. "Any news from our landlord?"

Paddy nodded. "For whatever reason, and I think it was the fuss Vilet's men caused when they found we had left, Vipond has decided to help us out," he said. "I told him what you said about staying a few weeks and it seems his sister has rooms to let."

"Probably wants to keep any money in the family."

Paddy kept handing Miss Yelverton bread alternating with cheese, as if he was feeding a baby bird.

"We can go around as soon as the day really begins but how are we going to sneak her in?" he asked.

"Good point," Chadwick answered. He studied Miss Yelverton thoughtfully. He couldn't decide how to begin to make her incognito. Finally he said, "Dress. With a dress, the dirt won't be so noticeable."

"Where are you going to find a dress?" Paddy asked. "Not like we can take her to the high street and just buy one."

"Market for used clothes. Every city has them," Chadwick replied. "We need to find a place where you and Miss Yelverton can wait for a couple of hours while I go see about the rooms and a dress."

"How about a church?" Paddy suggested. "Worked good for meeting that chap back in Dublin. I saw one on my way here. We could sit in a dark place and just wait for you."

"Good idea," Chadwick responded. "A place of sanctuary."

He looked again at Miss Yelverton trying to assess her condition. How far could she walk? She seemed so fragile. Or maybe 'bruised' was a better term. Now that the food was gone, she seemed to sink into a fog, staring at the ground and totally ignoring her surroundings.

"Miss Yelverton?" he tried to get her attention. "Georgina?" He started to put a hand on her arm, but she flinched noticeably. Well, she wasn't totally unaware of her surroundings. He bent down to look into her face and attempt to get her to look at him. It was hard to tell if she understood him.

"Miss Yelverton," he repeated slowly and carefully, "we need to move to a safer location. How far can you walk, or do you need me to carry you?"

Slowly her eyes lifted but never quite reached beyond his chin. "I can walk," she said briefly. Her voice seemed rusty, as if not used much.

"Fine. But if you need help, let Paddy or me know."

"Are you going to gag me?"

"No, I am not," he said. "I am sorry about that, but I was worried you would scream and alert Hastings."

"Now that I am gone, he will likely kill my father. I can't stop him now, so I might as well go with you," she said miserably.

Chadwick did not want to stop in the middle of the quay to offer a long explanation. The sun was coming up and more people were about their business, casting questioning glances in their direction. He was worried someone might report their activities to Vilet. Since Georgina Yelverton was at least willing to move, they might as well get started looking for a suitable church. The Captain gestured to Paddy to lead the way. Miss Yelverton immediately staggered, belying her words about being able to walk. He stepped next to her and put his arm around her waist to support her. That seemed enough assurance to get her to move slowly.

Paddy started off up a small street leading immediately away from the quay and toward the center of the city. Most of the streets still lay in shadows cast by the two – and three – storied buildings on each side of the road. A few women could be seen sweeping their steps and setting off with market baskets, but the foot traffic was still mostly men. Chadwick worried that they would not know it if they inadvertently met up with Hastings, as they only knew how he sounded, not how he looked. And he knew a suitable disguise for Miss Yelverton was critical.

"Do you speak any French?" he asked quietly.

After a long pause, she responded, "Yes, some."

"Do you know we are in Calais?" he asked in French. She seemed so out of it, it was hard to tell what and how much she knew.

After another long pause, she again replied, "Yes, I know." But to his surprise, she answered in French. She limped badly, favoring her right side, and after a few blocks was gasping painfully. Just when Chadwick was about to ask Paddy to stop, Paddy slowed until he and Miss Yelverton came abreast.

"Here, sir," Paddy nodded to the building on their left. "On the other side of that building is a small church. I noticed it on my way down this morning. We can go down that alley to get to the front or maybe find a side door. Maybe there will be an early mass we can sit through," he added hopefully.

The alley did indeed lead to the front of the church, which proved not to be as small as Paddy first thought. 'Saint Anne of Calm Waters' read the sign out front. To their good fortune, a number of women and a few older men were making their way through the open front doors.

"Here, take Miss Yelverton and sit inside as long as you can without raising any questions," Chadwick whispered in English. "If you have to leave, try not to go where I cannot find you. Stick around this church. I will be back as soon as I can find some clothes for Miss Yelverton."

Paddy nodded to show he understood but said nothing out loud. He put his arm around Georgina's waist and helped her to slowly mount the steps. She seemed to go willingly enough, and Chadwick watched until they disappeared into the depths of the church. He turned and continued up the hill, keeping a lookout for a woman who was out shopping and looked kindly enough to give him some directions.

* * *

It must be close to noon, Chadwick thought, as he came into view of St. Anne of Calm Waters. The shadows had long since faded from the streets and the sun was almost directly overhead. The heat from the sun was welcome as the breeze off the quay never seemed to stop. The name of the church amused him. He surmised it must be a supplication by fishermen for tranquil seas where they might prosper. Chadwick hoped Paddy would send up a few prayers for the success of their assignment. Even Catholic prayers might help, he thought.

He had been successful finding a market that sold used clothes. But finding appropriate garments had proven to be harder than finding the market itself, until a kindly older woman had taken him in hand. She had pointed out the best merchants for skirts, the ones whose wares were not so full of holes as to be of little use. Then she took him to other tables where women's tops were sold separately. At home, all the women he knew, – well both of the women he knew well enough to know how they dressed, Marion and his sister – wore only one piece dresses. Fashion in Calais, especially for working women, was a bit different. He had picked up a shawl, as most also seemed to keep their heads covered. *That might be really useful*, he concluded.

Finally, he had found a cobbler where he bought a pair of wooden clogs. His friendly guide assured him that clogs were best for the streets of Calais and the muck that was so prevalent this season. He was beginning to think he should buy a pair for himself. Everywhere he looked the tradespeople were wearing clogs with soles thick enough to keep their feet out of the mud.

From the door of the church Chadwick surveyed the nave but could not spot Paddy's red head anywhere. He slowly paced the side aisles, looking into the few side chapels to see if his companions were among the old women lighting candles. After circling the nave twice, he had to admit they were not in the church itself. Tucking his package of clothes more tightly under his arm, Chadwick went out into the sunshine again.

From the top of the church steps, he surveyed the small court in front and what he could see of the streets that met at the square. There at the fountain stood a red-haired man. It wasn't until he was nearly on top of Paddy that he saw Miss Yelverton sitting on the base of the fountain, trailing her fingers in the water.

Paddy looked up at the sound of his footsteps.

"Ah, Mr. Couture!" he said. He didn't try to say anything more but from the expression on his face, he was clearly relieved to see Chadwick. Chadwick was relieved to see that Paddy was attempting to stay in character and remembered his name.

In French, the Captain apologized for taking so long. Then he asked if Paddy had identified any place Miss Yelverton could change.

To his surprise, it was she who answered, again in French.

"Yes, Mr. Couture. We think we have a place. There's a privy out back of the church. Tight, but I should be able to manage."

"Why are you out here?" Chadwick asked curiously.

Paddy pointed at her hand and said torturously, "Tied her finger."

"Tied?" Chadwick repeated. And then he saw that Paddy had tied the fingers on her hurt hand together and understood that they were using the water to try to alleviate the pain. She evidently had also tried to wash her face and neck, with varying degrees of success.

"Are you going to be able to dress yourself?" Chadwick asked. Women he knew generally needed a maid, and this was going to be especially tricky with a bound hand.

Georgina stood and held out her hands for the clothes.

"I may need help, but first let me see what I can do."

"Is there any place around this privy that I can wait in case you do need help?" Chadwick asked.

Paddy nodded to the church. "There is a door from inside the church leading to the privy. We can wait inside the church."

"Good. I do not want the priest thinking we are perverts lurking around the privy," Chadwick replied. "Miss Yelverton, come into the church as soon as you can."

She seemed to take forever. Chadwick was beginning to worry she had run back to Hastings and was about to go out to search for her, when Georgina came slowly into the church through the side door. Even in the dim light he could see she looked a little green. She carried the clogs in one hand, the other hanging uselessly down her side.

She sagged as he put his arm around her to lead her to a pew to sit.

"I kept hitting my hand. Not used to these clothes and it is really hard with only one hand." Her French was way and above better than Paddy's, he realized with relief. She was still incredibly dirty and smelly, but with the skirt and blouse on, she at least looked more like a street urchin than a runaway from a brothel.

"My coat?" he asked cautiously.

"Still outside," she gasped. "I put the shift down the privy."

"Good girl," he said approvingly. He looked at Paddy to ask him to retrieve the coat but Paddy was already to the door.

"As I was telling Paddy, I have rooms where we can go and regroup. It is not a terribly long walk, but I am worried about your leg."

"I will make it," she said with some stubbornness.

"Ah, Paddy, thank you for getting the coat. Now, a couple more things before we set out. Paddy, do you have a hat? That red hair is too noticeable. I heard Hastings or the bar man, refer to you last night by the color of your hair."

Paddy pulled a stocking cap out of his pocket and put it on.

"Oh, I see," said Chadwick. "Not quite up to the standards for an assistant to a merchant. We will have to see about replacing it first chance. Now, as we discussed, you follow with Miss Yelverton and I will lead to the new rooms our landlord was so obliging to locate for us."

"Not too obliging do you think, sir?" Paddy questioned.

"Maybe, but he doesn't know about Miss Yelverton and we plan to keep it that way. So even if Vilet comes by asking questions, he won't know anything. Speaking of whom, I need to drop by there this afternoon and report in. I don't want him sending out more men looking for me." He sighed tiredly, "Now, Paddy, you have any idea how to drape the shawl so Miss Yelverton's face is not recognizable?"

Chapter Seven: Of Bugs and Lice

While not on the same street as *The Citizen*, the rooms the landlord had recommended, were in the same neighborhood. And there was a personal connection, as his sister, Madame Fabre, owned the rooms and lived on the property. While they waited for Georgina to change into the market clothes that Chadwick had bought, he and Paddy had discussed the pros and cons of having rooms so handy to the tavern and the proprietors so closely connected. Landlord Vipond could easily report to Vilet on their activities. But he had proven to be helpful with information, for a fee, and didn't seem especially happy with Vilet's men drinking for free in his tavern.

"We have to hole up somewhere until we can find Captain Byrne's contact and get a message to him to pick us up. At least these rooms are a place we can tuck Miss Yelverton away until she heals. I don't want to return her to her father in the condition she is in right now," Chadwick said.

"Why do you think she doesn't talk much?" Paddy asked. "My sisters never shut up and Miss Yelverton hardly makes a sound."

"I am assured that is a result of what Hastings did to her. He certainly beat her and probably abused her in other ways. She will take some time to heal."

"That's for certain," Paddy growled. "I can't say I have ever been in a tavern where someone was selling the favors of a woman before. I mean one who didn't do that for a living. But no one seemed surprised, so I am thinking it must be common here."

Chadwick shook his head sadly. "God, I hope not. No woman should go through that. It's going to take quite a while before she trusts anyone again, if ever."

He thought about that conversation as they made their way to their new rooms. The streets were marginally cleaner in this area of Calais and there were a lot more trade-folk about. The rooms were not so close to the quay, where it was mostly sailors, soldiers and maritime activities; instead, this area had shops and a number of women going about their daily purchases.

The sight of them reminded him of his next hurdle. Miss Yelverton was filthy and probably covered in fleas and lice. She was going to need at least a bath. Providing a lady's bath was not an activity he had any experience with. If this was the army, he would have marched her to the river and told her to jump in. But she was not an army private he could order about. She was a lady who had been much abused. He needed female help, but where to get it? From his first impression of their new landlady, he didn't think Madame Fabre would be a person Georgina could look to for aid and comfort. In fact, she reminded him of the old witch he had met in Dublin where Madra Dubh had first hidden out. Did being a proprietress turn women into money-grubbing crones?

By the time they reached their new setting, Georgina was visibly fading. Paddy had his arm around her waist and probably was the only thing keeping her from collapsing onto the ground. Chadwick had tried to go slowly, but he had been worried someone would recognize her. Hastings probably had contacts in Calais he could call on for help. Chadwick was also concerned that a member of Vilet's network would see them with Georgina and wonder what a wine merchant was doing with a woman in her condition. He couldn't pass her off as a willing prostitute when she could barely keep her head up. He worried that one chink in their cover story could lead to the whole story falling apart. Vilet seemed to him to be a very shrewd character.

He definitely wasn't feeling the exhilaration Nathan Donnay exhibited when discussing his exploits in the field. All the ways this project could go wrong were just plain terrifying, as well as exhausting.

He had rented the two rooms for a month. The street door opened to a hallway with a narrow staircase on the left. Their rooms were on the second floor facing the back alley. A single door provided entry to the first room, where there was a fireplace for cooking and a table with mismatched but usable chairs. A pair of buckets, on the side of the fireplace, were evidently going to be the only supply of water. The sole source of natural light came from a window in the next room. The two rooms were connected by a doorway without a door. Chadwick surmised that the lack of privacy was going to be the least of their problems.

Paddy led Georgina to a chair and helped her sit. He looked at Chadwick inquiringly. Chadwick went to the next room and studied it. On the rope bed, there were now two thin mattresses. Sleeping arrangements were going to need some thought. Then he noticed his trunk tucked into the corner. Good. Vipond had remembered to send it over.

"Captain?"

Paddy's voice broke into his reverie. He glanced at Paddy. "Yes?"

"Remember that pretty maid at *The Citizen*?" he questioned. "Maybe we could hire her to help Miss Yelverton. You know, wash and such."

Chadwick's eyebrows shot up. "Paddy Cavanaugh, you have some brilliant ideas," he complimented. "But here's the problem. We are trying to keep Miss Yelverton's presence a secret, and there is nothing to stop the maid from telling the landlord. Good idea, though."

Paddy frowned thoughtfully. "How will the maid know who Miss Yelverton is?"

"You may be right. Go on and tell me what you are thinking," Chadwick encouraged. He noticed that Georgina had stopped staring at the floor and was studying Paddy with some interest. For some reason, she seemed less threatened by Paddy than Chadwick. He needed to think about why that might be. He pulled out a chair, sitting and gesturing to Paddy to do the same.

"Well, sir," Paddy continued earnestly, "she could be a tart we pulled off the street. Her French is good; all we need to do is give her a new name and she could pass for a local." After a moment's pause, he offered another possibility. "Remember how we told the landlord we were looking for my brother-in-law? Maybe Miss Yelverton could be my niece who my rat of a brother-in-law has been abusing. That would be consistent with the story we already told him, account for any issue of accent, and explain why we want to hide her from him," he finished triumphantly.

"Let me think a moment about this, but on the face of it, I like the second story a lot. Not for Vilet. I am afraid he has too many agents and could check things somehow. But it should work for Vipond, the maid, and probably that witch downstairs."

"Miss Yelverton, what do you think? Do you think you could bear being related to me, even if it is just a cover story?" Paddy looked at Georgina, who surprisingly was nodding in agreement.

She coughed and tried to clear her throat. Finally, she got out, "You seem a kind man." She paused as if her throat was rusty and words were something she hadn't used in some time. "Are you really going to take me home?"

Paddy nodded vigorously. "Yes, we are. Right, Captain? I mean, Monsieur Couture?" He looked at Chadwick expectantly.

It really was a perfect introduction for what Chadwick had wanted to tell her anyway. He decided to keep his story simple and not divulge the government connection. Who knew what could get back to Vilet?

"Miss Yelverton, we were hired by your father to investigate your kidnapping and to bring you home. Please believe me, we mean you no harm." She still would not look him in the eyes, but he could tell she was listening.

"However, we need to keep you hidden until we can make contact with our ride home. Hastings is still out there and probably looking for you." He paused and then said in his most sincere voice, "Hastings is here in Calais. He did not leave anyone in Dublin who could begin to threaten your father. I know because I met the only one left. That chap told us where to find the house you were first taken to and that he was the only one Hastings had left behind." A thought occurred to him.

"I bet you know exactly how many made up his original group. Can you tell me?" he asked.

"I tried to count them," she acknowledged. "I only saw six men."

"Smart girl," he complimented. "Did most come to Calais?"

She nodded tiredly. "Yes. I thought the whole group was larger and some had been left behind."

Chadwick felt a surge of satisfaction remembering the number who were killed or arrested in the Southampton raid last year. That probably took out most of Hastings' group.

"Monsieur, did you rent this furnished, sir?" Paddy broke into his musing.

"Yes, but some stuff seems to be missing." Chadwick looked around the room. "How are we going to heat water? And I know I told her we wanted some firewood. Those are some questionable looking mattresses, and there are no candles or blankets. She charged enough for this hovel."

"Oh, it's not so bad. It's fairly clean," Paddy said. "She's probably trying to see how much she can get away with. I'll go talk to her. Where do I find this landlady?"

Paddy stood. He had removed his hat and hung his coat on the nail by the door. He looked back at Georgina with concern. "She's not doing very well, sir."

Chadwick agreed with his assessment. The sooner they got a woman to help her clean up and find out if they needed a doctor, the better.

"Madame Fabre's rooms are on the first floor, but how are you going to talk to her?" Chadwick asked.

"Don't worry, this I can handle." He left the room. Chadwick could hear his footsteps descend and then a brisk knocking on a door downstairs. He left the hall door open, hoping to hear the exchange. Evidently Paddy was going to try charm first, because he could only hear a murmur of voices. He smiled at Georgina Yelverton, hoping to get her to respond with mutual amusement at Paddy's antics, but she had returned to staring at the floor.

"Miss Yelverton?" he asked, trying to get her attention. She looked so tense, ready to flinch, that he wanted to offer her some reassurance that she was safe.

"Miss Yelverton?" Finally, she glanced quickly up at him. She had remarkable eyes, even if they were half shrouded by the lank, greasy hair. Her big brown eyes, and they looked cautiously back at him and then dropped back to the floor.

"No one is going to hurt you here," he said softly. "We are going to get you help. But right now, we want to keep you hidden. I do not want the landlady to see you. I do not know yet whom we can trust. Will you please go to the next room and sit on my trunk in there so Paddy can get the things we need to stay here?"

He wanted to touch her hand and offer her a modicum of comfort, but the way she flinched every time he came near made him hesitate to go near her.

She nodded stiffly and stood, still clutching her bandaged hand to her chest protectively. He watched until she had moved out of sight into the next room and then stepped out into the hallway to see if he could tell how Paddy was progressing. To his surprise and delight, Paddy was navigating the narrow stairs with his arms full of utensils. He made his way into the room and dumped his haul onto the table. Chadwick noticed a large pot, fry pan, and cooking ladles. Paddy had also procured some cups and dishes. He grinned cheekily at Chadwick.

"She thinks my accent is adorable," he said. When Chadwick laughed, he added, "She is also going to bring some more blankets, probably after she hauls them off someone else's bed. I asked about a bath and there is one out back we are welcome to use but she was clear we have to haul the water ourselves. Pump is out back, so at least we don't have to wander the streets looking for the communal pump."

Chadwick stopped laughing. Hauling water was not a chore he was fond of. "Where's Miss Yelverton?"

"In the next room I did not want that shrew of a landlady to see her. Probably up the rent as well as turn us in."

"She's not so bad," Paddy returned. "I bet you didn't take the time to throw her some charm."

"You're probably right," Chadwick admitted. "I was in a rush."

"So which one of us is going to charm the maid from *The Citizen* into helping us and who is going to haul the water?" Paddy smirked at him.

Chadwick grinned back wryly at Paddy's sneaky side. "I think it is water duty for me," he said.

* * *

While Paddy was gone, Chadwick spent his time learning about the bathing facilities available to the renters of Madame Fabre's rooms as well as the dreary job of drawing water at the pump in the yard and then hauling the buckets upstairs. He wasn't thirty yet and thought of himself as strong enough, but after the second trip he found his arms aching. He also lugged upstairs the barrel that residents used for immersion bathing. From the looks of the barrel half covered by debris in the back yard, it seemed most residents made do with sponge baths. He was having new respect for his valet Thomas's work.

By then, Madame's son had arrived with an armload of wood. Miss Yelverton sat at the table and quietly watched him work, shuttling back and forth to the inner bedroom when young Fabre arrived. It seemed to take forever for the large pot to show any signs of heating up. Chadwick tried to estimate how long it would take for enough water for a bath to heat.

Finally she spoke, "Mr. Couture, maybe you could borrow another pot from the landlady?" Her voice was still low and rusty from disuse.

"Yes, I think you are right. One pot is not going to be enough."

"All this is so I can bathe?" she asked.

"Do you want to get clean?" he asked cautiously. That she was talking to him must be a good sign, right? However, he didn't want to spook or scare her any more than she was already. "Of course, I do. I think I am covered in fleas and other horrid things. I can't stand myself," her voice trailed off despondently.

Chadwick took one of the mugs Paddy had weaseled out of Madame Fabre and poured her some water.

"Miss Yelverton," Chadwick asked diffidently, "did Hastings do something to your throat? It sounds like-did he try to strangle you?" Her voice sounded so labored he felt there must be something physically wrong with it. He looked at her, but as usual she was back to staring at the floor, slowly scratching her hair.

She finally looked up at him. "Screaming," she said shortly.

He gave an inward groan when her comment about fleas and things finally sunk in. In the army, they had been rampant and he had gained a real hatred of little crawly bugs that could make your life miserable and were so hard to control.

"Better let me see your hair," he said grimly. "Washing may not be enough. I became too experienced with bugs in the army and the only way to finally get rid of lice is to shave the head."

As he stood there, waiting for her reply, a knock sounded and the door opened to reveal Paddy and the young maid from *The Citizen*. Paddy's arms were filled with packages. From the aroma, it had to be food. Chadwick noted with pleasure there was at least one bottle of wine. The maid gave him a big smile and entered the room. Her smile faded when she saw Georgina.

"Mon Dieu, what has happened to her, Monsieur Couture?" she gasped.

"Bad things, I am afraid, and that is why we need your help," Chadwick replied. He looked inquiringly at Paddy.

"Monsieur Couture, this is Marie who has come to help us. She had to finish some chores before the landlord would let her go and I had to pay him for her services. That is what took so long. That and picking up some food."

Paddy surveyed the room, apparently checking Chadwick's progress with his half of the chores. Chadwick decided to make a good natured report.

"As you can see, I brought up water and the wash barrel that Madame assures me is good enough for everyone else in this house and I got the fire going. It's going to take some time to heat all this water," he said.

Marie must have thought their conversation was strange with Paddy talking in English and Chadwick responding in French.

"I was just about to go down and ask Madame Fabre for another pot."

"Let me do that," Paddy said.

"Wait, monsieur," Marie interrupted. She had been standing near Georgina peering at her with great intent. "I need to go out to buy some different soap for these bugs and something soothing for all these bruises. When I return, go ask Madame for some of the water she probably has on the fire all day, as that would be hottest for us." She shook her head in some dismay. "Those monsters, or whoever is responsible, should be flogged."

After Chadwick handed her some coins, she slipped out of the room while Paddy laid some food out on the table. They ate a cold lunch while they waited for the maid to return.

"Paddy, did you make clear to Marie that we don't want Madame Fabre to know about Georgina?" Chadwick asked.

Paddy had loaded his bread with cheese and meat and was taking a huge mouthful, but nodded vigorously in response.

"In that case, when Marie comes back we should head over to the *hotel de ville* and report into Vilet." He turned to Georgina.

"You understand, Miss Yelverton, that we need to go out for a while, but we will be back. Marie is going to be here with you and I will tell Madame downstairs that no one is allowed up here. I don't believe anyone followed us here, but just in case."

"Do I need to go with you, sir?" Paddy asked.

"Yes, I think so, at least this first time. We want to look like good citizens who are being gracious about this hitch in our travel plans. Also, who knows what you may overhear while I am in with Vilet?"

"What if we don't come back? What will happen to Miss Yelverton?"

For once, Georgina's eyes looked up startled from the floor and stared at him in dismay. Chadwick willed himself to look back at her calmly.

"Miss Yelverton, are you listening?" At her nod he continued. "I am leaving money in my trunk. It's enough that you will be fine for some time, long enough for you to find a countryman to take you home."

"How am I going to do that?" she questioned slowly. Each word seemed to be painful.

"By going with Marie to *The Citizen* and asking the landlord to send a messenger to the ships down at the port to find someone going to Ireland. This is kind of hazy I know, but I heard a lot of Irish brogues down at the harbor last night. Once you are cleaned up, you will look like the lady you are, and you will have enough gold to pay your way. Do you think you could do that if you had to?" It wasn't a great plan, but it was the best he could do since they had not found Captain Byrne's contact yet.

"I guess…"

"We only plan on being gone an hour. But it could take longer. Do not do anything unless we aren't back by tomorrow night. I have no reason to think we will not be back-it is just good to have a backup plan," he tried to inject reassurance into his voice. Just like with new recruits before facing armed foes. Georgina nodded her understanding.

After Marie returned with her purchases, more water was retrieved from Madame's kitchen and the two men slipped out, hoping Madame believed that Marie had been brought in to help Chadwick bathe and serve as their all-purpose personal maid.

* * *

Upon their return, Chadwick sent Paddy in first to make sure Madame was not waiting for them by the stairs. He didn't feel up to answering any of her endless questions and the less she knew about their comings and goings, the better for all of them. Thankfully, all was quiet, and they made their way upstairs to their rooms unobserved. Marie answered their tap immediately, closing the door behind them.

Georgina still sat at the table. But, this time, she was wrapped in what looked like Chadwick's coat and a blanket that had been draped over her head. Bare feet were shoved into the wooden clogs he had bought. Her clothes, he observed, were slung over chairs near the fire. The bathing barrel was still full of water and he could see bugs floating on the top of the scummy water. He thought grimly it would take both him and Paddy to get the barrel downstairs to empty. Both women looked exhausted; Georgina, in particular looked as if she could hardly keep her head up.

The past few hours looked to have been hard on everyone. Chadwick opened the bottle of wine Paddy had brought earlier and poured everyone a measure, even Marie.

Paddy handed out the cups and then sat at the table.

"How are you, Miss Yelverton?" he asked with concern. "You look ..."

While Paddy searched for a word, Chadwick filled one in silently. She looked 'shattered.' He looked at Marie questioningly.

"Do I need to call in a physician?" Chadwick asked quietly.

"Not at the moment. She needs time to heal both in body and in mind," Marie offered.

She sipped her wine and leaned back in her chair.

"Her hair," she shook her head as she spoke, "was very hard. Finally, I had to cut it. I am sorry, Monsieur, I did the best I could, but it is not looking good. I had no scissors only a knife."

Chadwick looked over at Georgina.

"How are you feeling?" he asked, realizing she had not answered Paddy's question.

"Better," she replied. Her hands gripped the wine cup tightly.

Paddy reached over and gently raised the cup to her lips. "Here, lass, take a sip. It will help."

Again, Chadwick wondered why she didn't shrink from Paddy the way she retreated from him. It wasn't as though Paddy was that much younger than Chadwick; he was a grown man and his presence could be as threatening to a woman as his own.

Marie finished her wine and carefully placed the cup on the table.

"I must be off, monsieur. I have duties at *The Citizen* I must attend to."

"You have done excellent work here, it seems," Chadwick said. He reached in his pocket for some coins to tip her. It must have been generous, as she smiled gratefully.

"Shall I come by tomorrow?" she asked.

"Yes. We have to report to the police commissioner each day and I don't want to leave her alone." He had not even told Marie Georgina's name.

"Very good, sir. I have some free time in the afternoon. I will be here then."

"I say," Paddy interrupted. He had stood and was holding Marie's shawl for her. "Can you cook if I buy the fixings?" he asked. Chadwick could barely understand what Paddy was saying so garbled was his French but Marie didn't seem to have the same trouble.

She gave a trill of laughter.

"Cooking a stew would be much easier than this afternoon. I am pretty good. I have been studying with Madame at the inn. Be certain you buy garlic and onions."

As her footsteps retreated down the stairs, Chadwick thought she seemed to take all the good will out of the room with her, leaving those who remained depressed and tired. He divided the rest of the bottle between himself and Paddy and then turned to study Georgina.

"I know it hurts for you to talk," he said. At Paddy's questioning look, he said simply, "Strained vocal cords."

He looked at Georgina again and noticed that she was shivering.

"Miss Yelverton, let's move you closer to the fire. It will help warm you up. Paddy, can you find another blanket?" He moved Marie's empty chair close to the fire and turned to help her change places. When she stood, the blanket that had been draped over her head slipped down to her shoulders. Where there had been long greasy hair, there were now short tufts. Oh, dear. Marie had warned him the hair had been a problem.

Georgina pulled the blanket up over her head again before he could see much and huddled closer to the fire. Paddy added another blanket from one of the beds.

"Let's get this barrel out of here, shall we?" the Irishman said. "Then I thought I might walk over to *The Citizen* and see about getting us a hot meal."

"Good idea," Chadwick responded. "It's been a long day and I don't know about you, but I am hungry." Also, with Paddy gone for a bit, he might make some headway gaining Georgina's trust.

After Paddy left, Chadwick puttered around a bit, finding places for the items purchased earlier that day and putting Georgina's clothes away so they could pull the other chairs around the fire. Although it was late spring, he felt the air turning chilly. He thought it might be a result of being so close to the sea. Certainly the tang of salt in the air was still noticeable.

Finally he settled in a chair on the side of the fire furthest from Georgina and stretched out his legs. He looked forward to a decent night of uninterrupted sleep and stretched out, if not on the bed, at least before the fire.

* * *

"Monsieur?" The voice was so soft he thought he had imagined it.

"Monsieur!" The voice was slightly louder and finally cut through his exhausted haze. He sat up with a jerk when he realized he had dozed off and Miss Yelverton was trying to get his attention.

"Yes?" he said. "So sorry, I didn't realize how tired I am. What can I do for you?"

"I just wanted to know where I will be sleeping tonight?" she responded. "I only see two beds in there."

"Oh, not to worry. You will get one bed, and Paddy and I will toss a coin to see who gets the other and who gets the extra blanket and the floor."

"But I don't have anything to sleep in. Marie was kind enough to rinse out everything after she helped me bathe – but all my clothes are still wet." Her hand fluttered in a slight gesture indicating the clothes now draped on the wall pegs. "I have hope that we at least got most of the bugs." She sounded as tired as he felt.

"Let me look in my trunk. I think I have an extra shirt you can use, if the chaps who went through my luggage when we landed left me anything. Paddy said they helped themselves to at least one shirt."

Chadwick went to the other room to check his trunk and found that though his gear was no longer neatly folded, at least everything seemed to be there. He returned with a shirt.

"Here, put this on. You can sleep in it tonight. The rest will be dry by the morning, but we will have to see about getting you some other clothes. You must be getting pretty tired of my coat?" He tried to lighten the atmosphere with a little joke.

She did seem to try to smile. "It makes me feel sort of safe," she admitted.

"Really?" he asked. "My old coat?"

"Yes, a bit. It smells a bit of your soap, and a bit of clean air and so much better than anything else I have smelled recently."

"Miss Yelverton," he spoke cautiously. "I would really like to know what happened to you."

"No, not now," she said quickly. "I don't want to talk about it just yet. Maybe later."

He nodded in agreement. He felt too tired to be a good listener tonight.

"We will have plenty of time. We did not dream we would be able to find you so quickly, so our ride home won't be back for some time. And to further complicate things, we have to check in every day with the local police chief. He is supposedly checking my story and we can't leave Calais until he finishes. So we are stuck here in these two rooms for the duration."

"I guess you had better tell me your story also," she said.

"Tomorrow," he agreed. "Now that you are a bit more comfortable, we can spend all day telling stories and making plans."

"I do have another problem," she said carefully.

"Do you want me to have a doctor come by for you?" he asked equally carefully.

"A doctor for what?" she asked confused. Then a look of comprehension crossed her face. "Oh, for my hand?" She held out her hand for his inspection. Marie had bandaged it with a small piece of wood to keep the fingers straight. "I can't think a doctor could do any better. Marie said she had several little brothers who were always getting hurt."

"Well, that is good," Chadwick responded. "I hope it is giving you less pain. But I didn't mean your hand." His voice trailed off as he searched for the right words to bring up such a delicate matter with a young lady of breeding.

Georgina looked at him with some perplexity and then, finally, understanding crossed her face. "Women's issues. That is what you mean, right?" she asked. At his confirming nod she said to his relief, "No, no doctor is necessary right now. Marie says it's a matter of time and rest."

She took a breath and plowed on. "It's not that. This is rather stupid and entirely vain of me, but even without a mirror here, I know Marie couldn't do much with my hair. Her knife was rather dull and all she could do was hack it off. And I am grateful, I really am. At least the horrid bugs seem to be gone. She told me about getting a comb to use so I could make confident they don't come back."

She paused and seemed to need to catch her breath to find the right words for what she wanted to say. She had talked more in the last two minutes than the whole of the time since he had found her in the shed.

He tried to help her out. "Miss Yelverton, if it is in my power to help you, you only have to ask."

Instead of answering, she dropped the blanket from her head. He managed to keep himself from gasping out loud but he was confident the look of surprise must have crossed his face as her eyes dropped quickly and her face blushed furiously in embarrassment.

"Can you fix it?" she asked desperately.

What a strange girl! After all she had been through and suffered, she was embarrassed because her hair was …well, he wasn't quite sure what to call it. When Marie said it wasn't good, she wasn't joking. She had evidently tried to cut Georgina's hair down to several inches, she hadn't tried to shave her head. The shaved head was the standard in the army for lice and what he had expected to see here. But the young maid seemed to have made an effort to save Miss Yelverton some dignity. However, it was vastly uneven; in some places she had cut down to the scalp and in other places she had left tufts standing out.

He nodded firmly. "Yes, we can fix this or at least make it better. Again, something for tomorrow. Paddy has some sisters; maybe he has more experience with ladies' hair. But in the army, I got rather good at clipping other fellows' hair. We will sort it," he said reassuringly. "Ah, I think I hear Paddy returning now. Let's eat and go to bed and worry about such things as haircuts and stories tomorrow."

Blessedly, Paddy had brought more wine.

Chapter Eight: Transformations

C hadwick groaned as he rolled onto his back. It had been some time since he had slept rough, and the floor before the fireplace could be considered rough. Even with a couple of blankets and a pillow from one of the beds, it wasn't comfortable. But he had lost the coin toss and the floor was his for the night. Paddy had protested that Chadwick should have the bed but at last he had accepted that as associates, it was only fair that each take his turn on the floor. Chadwick rubbed his sore shoulder – the one that had borne most of his weight during the night and was now protesting the treatment. He had spent much of his army days in Dublin where, as a bachelor, he had been given space in the barracks and a bed of sorts. But he had slept on the ground during the occasional foray into the hinterlands to track down rebels. Was the ground softer than this floor? What he could remember of his time in Ireland with the army was endless days in the saddle and rounding up rebels, tasks that had been exhausting and stressful.

The floor creaked. Chadwick glanced around to see Paddy creeping out of the sleeping room with his pants and boots in his hands. The two nodded at each other without speaking. They both seemed to agree that Miss Yelverton should be left to sleep as long as possible. After he got his boots on, Paddy took a bucket and headed out. Chadwick pulled on his own clothes and started to build up the fire.

"Monsieur Couture?" Georgina called softly from the bedroom. "Are you dressed? Can I come out?"

"Yes, of course," Chadwick responded. He quickly finished tucking in his shirt and pulled on his vest. Neck cloths could wait.

Miss Yelverton emerged from the inner room still wrapped in his coat and wearing the wooden clogs. The bruises and welts on her legs looked even uglier today. She came to huddle from the morning chill by the fire. Paddy returned with the water and stood by the fire, rubbing his arms for warmth.

"Let me have the pot and some of that tea I bought yesterday," he said. "Madame has water boiling in the kitchen and said I could help myself."

While he was gone again, Chadwick sat studying Georgina's head. By the time Paddy returned, he had his shaving kit out and was stropping the razor.

"Don't you want to eat first, sir?" Paddy asked.

"Yes, let's lay out the food we have left from yesterday." Chadwick laid aside his razor. "I have to fix Miss Yelverton's hair. Marie isn't very skilled at hair dressing."

Paddy glanced at Georgina and nodded in agreement. He continued laying out what was left of the pigeon pie from their dinner, and the rest of the bread, cheese, and cold meat from his earlier shopping trip with a few apples whose origins mystified Chadwick. Paddy grinned at Georgina Yelverton.

"Well, at least she got rid of the bugs, eh miss? I am quite positive monsieur will fix you right up. He can do anything," he added reassuringly.

The young woman ran her hands through her cropped hair and grinned wryly. "Getting rid of those things has surely been a relief. And I always wondered what short hair would be like," she added bravely. "It takes forever to fix long hair."

She accepted a cup of tea from Paddy. "Thank you, this smells like heaven. I haven't had real tea in ages." She still spoke as if her throat hurt, but at least she was talking. Chadwick added honey to his mental shopping list. Didn't his nanny give him honey in tea for a sore throat?

Chadwick was watching how awkwardly Georgina was handling her cup. "I think I had better take a look at your finger also. How long ago was it broken?"

She grimaced for real. "At least a week. I am not really positive; the days were running together and all I wanted to do was sleep."

"Yes, that is quite understandable," he answered. He had heard somewhere that sleep was a way of avoiding painful experiences. "But we may not be able to straighten that finger out. And I am afraid whatever I do to help is going to be painful."

"Maybe we should take her to a real doctor," Paddy suggested hesitantly.

"Yes, I would feel more comfortable doing that. Although almost everyone who has been in the army has had to set some bones, I cannot say I've practiced my skills such as they are, on any ladies." The Captain paused and drank some tea. He toasted Paddy with his cup after his first sip.

"Miss Yelverton is correct. After all the wretched coffee we have had, this tastes like ambrosia." He turned back to study the young woman.

"Monsieur, you are making me uncomfortable," Georgina whispered.

"Forgive me. That was not my intention. I have an idea and am trying to work it through in my head." Chadwick turned to Paddy. "If I trim her hair down, way down, do you think she could pass for a boy or a young man?"

Now it was Paddy's turn to study Georgina. A look of amusement crossed her face and she almost smiled.

"How am I supposed to pass as a young man?" she asked. "I don't look like a boy."

"People mostly see what they expect to see," Chadwick explained. "If you present yourself as a young man, with the right clothes and mannerisms, then most people won't look deeper. If we do this right, you won't have to be holed up here but will be able to go out. We could even take you to a real doctor for that hand. But the mannerisms are important. Without mannish mannerisms, you would just appear to be a woman in boys' clothes."

"Speaking of hands, hers' might be a problem," Paddy said. "Even now they are rather soft for a young man's."

Georgina spread her good hand on the table and they all studied it. Her nails were broken and the cuticles had been chewed, but her hands were soft and had no calluses or other signs of work.

"A mama's boy?" Paddy suggested thoughtfully.

"We will worry about the doctor later," Chadwick said. "Only the doctor has to see her hands and maybe we can bribe him into silence. Just in general, it will be easier to explain her presence as a male."

When the other two nodded, he continued. "So, we will start with her hair. Then it it back to the clothes market for me to find appropriate garments. While I do that, Paddy, you will teach Miss Yelverton how to walk like a male?"

"I think I would feel safer dressed as a male," Georgina said thoughtfully. "Hastings is looking for a girl, so this should confuse him at least." Her eyes flashed and for a moment, Chadwick saw a glimpse of the beautiful woman in the portrait.

"Well, let us get on with this hair styling. We would be better off in the sleeping room; with the window, it is lighter. Sorry, but it is cooler." Chadwick picked up a chair and positioned it in front of the window.

"It is fine," she said. She followed him into the sleeping room and settled on the chair. He laid out his shaving gear on the near bed and, draped a sheet around her neck. With a comb, he divided her hair down the middle. Taking a section he began to razor the edges.

"I will try to be as gentle as possible, but my friend Nathan says my use of a razor is grating. Well, he says a few other things, most not very complimentary about my skills."

"You have a much lighter hand than Marie. Poor thing only had a dull knife," she answered. "I am not complaining; she did her best. So, you cut your friend's hair?" she asked.

"He is too cheap to pay a valet, and when he found out I did some cutting in the army he badgered me into doing his. He has naturally curly hair like yours."

"Like mine?" she questioned. Her hand shot up to touch her head.

"Watch out!" he exclaimed. "I am using a sharp razor. You don't want your other hand injured."

"No, no, of course not." Her good hand went back to holding the injured hand in her lap.

Paddy cleared away the food and then came in to watch the proceedings. As he watched Chadwick even out the edges and tufts fall to the floor, Paddy couldn't stop himself from commenting. "I say, that looks amazing. You know if we run out of money, you could do haircuts for food."

Chadwick could see Paddy's teasing relaxed Georgina and made her feel more comfortable. Maybe that was the difference between them: Paddy could make her smile, he didn't seem to be able to do that.

Finally Paddy went downstairs to Madame Fabre to see if she had a looking glass he could borrow. He came back with a small handheld one.

"Look, miss, it changes the whole aspect of your face!" he said excitedly. And in fact he was right. For convenience, Chadwick kept his own dark blond hair long enough to tie up in a queue. However, seeing how the new haircut changed Georgina's appearance, he would keep it in mind if he needed to do likewise.

Without the heavy weight of long tresses, Georgina's honey colored hair had proved to be rather curly. Chadwick had severely cut it to about two to three inches and then feathered the edges. He had been aiming for a cut called 'the Brutus' that he knew was becoming popular in London. Nathan Donnay had told him once that short styles were a protest started by some nobleman or another against the flour tax. Since then, many London men, especially those of the more fashionable set, had adopted the short style. The Brutus, however, was one of the shortest styles, with interesting edges framing the face. Now that the curls had taken over, Georgina Yelverton looked like someone had gone wild with a curling iron.

"My sisters would kill for those curls," Paddy said admiringly.

"Curls?" Georgina asked. "Where did they come from? My hair has never been curly."

"Has it ever been this short before?" Chadwick asked.

She studied herself in the mirror. "No, never this short. Are you suggesting my hair is normally this curly?"

"Evidently. I imagine the weight of the long hair pulled it straight," he explained. "I rather like it this way, even if it is my own work. It certainly came out much better than any of those chaps I worked on in the army," he said laughing.

"I like it, too," said Paddy. "And if she wants to go back to being a girl, all she needs to do is add a ribbon. Now with the proper hat, I think she can pass as a boy, but only one who hasn't started to shave yet."

Georgina had been running her unhurt hand through her hair with some glee. "Oh, my, this feels so good! No hair pins to stick me with. I don't have to worry about it falling down if I try to run or anything. I love it!"

Chadwick chuckled at her enthusiasm. Not too many women would be happy about losing their hair in such a manner. He had been afraid she would end up in tears, but thankfully she seemed able to see the bright side of her new hair style. And he found it rather attractive. Honey-gold curls lay all over her head, some framing her face. Without all the filthy hair hanging all over her face, he could now see her features better. She was still thinner than she should be, but at least her eyes were bright and looking about with curiosity instead of staring at the floor. Chadwick thought her eyes were the only feature that looked a bit out of place and overly large on her pixyish face. He averted his glance when he realized he was staring at her overlong. He remembered something he had forgotten.

"Did Marie give you any salve for those bruises on your legs and arms?" he asked.

"No, not really. She mainly had the soap for the hair. I don't think she was really prepared for me. She said she would try to bring something today."

"When I go out to the market, I will find an apothecary and see if I can purchase something to help heal them. I think we need to see about some boots, as well. Wooden clogs worn with skirts might be fine for a local girl, but I am supposed to be a wine merchant and a man of some means. Can't have you trailing me about like a poor street waif, now can we?"

"Paddy, where is the string that tied the food together? I need something to measure Miss Yelverton's foot."

Paddy handed him the string that had found its way into his pocket.

"Hold out your foot so I can figure out what size boots to buy." Chadwick pinched off a length of string to mark the length of her foot. He noted that her feet were also badly bruised and scraped and one had a rather deep cut across the fleshy part of the sole. Again, he marveled at how she had walked on those feet yesterday without any complaint. He added socks to his mental shopping list.

"Monsieur Couture," she said, "remember to buy Paddy a hat also. Yesterday you said his knit hat wasn't quite the thing for a man of means."

"Fancy you remembering that," he answered, surprised. "Yes, I must do that."

"Monsieur, there is something else."

Chadwick paused and looked at her inquiringly. Her face had flushed again.

Georgina seemed to be struggling with her thoughts. Finally she gasped, "I need some fabric to wrap...around...my ..."

"Ah, Captain, Miss Yelverton needs to have the figure of a boy," Paddy interjected. "That means..."

"Yes, Paddy, I understand," Chadwick cut him off. "I am glad you remembered. When I get to the market I will look for a length of cotton." He took his own hat from the hook by the door. "Paddy, try that on," he directed. "I need to know what size to get. I shall be quite the procurer today. Good thing that is my supposed job."

"You are supposed to tell me your story also." Georgina added, softly.

"You know, I will let Paddy entertain you with that story while I am gone. Just remember to keep your voices down. I wouldn't want Madame hearing anything she shouldn't."

* * *

Chadwick was feeling pretty good as he set off for his daily check-in with Commissioner Vilet. He had found the used clothes market and made his purchases unaided. He even bought himself and Paddy some slightly used shirts. The boots he found at the cobbler's seemed to fit Miss Yelverton reasonably well and hopefully, with the socks, she wouldn't limp so badly. Best of all, with the hat pulled over those riotous curls, she was starting to pass as a boy. She must have used the length of cotton he found to bind her breasts, as he now noticed she had the flat chest of a boy.

Paddy's instructions on walking like a male were coming along. Georgina already had very good posture, so it was mainly a matter of getting her to lengthen her stride and not mince along like a young lady.

The Captain had informed Madame Fabre that he had hired a young man to assist them and would of course pay extra for the new boarder.

The three of them decided that Georgina's first foray into public should be after dark. When Chadwick returned from checking in with Vilet, they would venture out to eat supper.

Now, he decided, their next objective would be to find Captain Byrne's contact. They needed to be able to contact Byrne to move up the time of their departure. At some point, Chadwick's cover story was going to fall apart and he really didn't want to be anywhere close when Vilet realized he had been lying to him.

Unlike yesterday, when he and Paddy had been forced to sit waiting for some time before being shown into Vilet's office, today Chadwick was shown immediately into the inner sanctum. Yesterday's check-in had taken less than a minute, when Vilet looked up from his paperwork and grunted that he would see him tomorrow. Today Vilet was gesturing to a chair and telling – no, was he *inviting,* Chadwick to be seated? Even more startling was Vilet's demeanor. Chadwick realized the grimace on the *Agent in Charge's* face was meant to be welcoming, but its effect on Chadwick was chilling. When a coffee tray was brought in, the situation bordered on bizarre.

Chadwick removed his hat respectfully and placed it carefully on a corner of the desk. He sat in the only available chair, crossed his legs casually, and tried to look totally innocent.

"Well, sir," he said. "This is a welcome change from our previous encounters. To what should I attribute the warm welcome? A busy man like you doesn't usually have time to take coffee with each of his bonded visitors," he added sardonically. He decided an innocent man would not necessarily worry about irritating a police commissioner, but would let his own irritation with his predicament show.

"True, true," Vilet answered airily. "By far, Monsieur Couture, you are more interesting than most of my visitors lately. Here, let me pour you some coffee." He handed Chadwick a cup and pushed the sugar bowl towards him.

Chadwick took the cup and helped himself to sugar. This man wanted something. Both his gut and his brain agreed on this. However, if he had proof of Chadwick's real identity, he would have immediately tossed him in jail and there would have been no coffee party. There was nothing to do except wait it out and see where this led. He leaned back in his chair and sipped.

"Excellent coffee, Commissioner," he said. "I haven't been too successful finding such a quality beverage in Calais, but I assume that is because I just haven't found the right seller."

"There are many fine coffee shops in Calais," Valet boasted. "I suspect you are not staying in the right area. Which reminds me, where exactly are you staying?"

"Since it seems we need to stay in Calais for some time, I decided to rent some rooms instead of just staying at an inn. Our host at *The Citizen* recommended us to his sister who lets rooms. We are staying with Madame Fabre. Not the fanciest of lodgings, but it will do. However," he continued, "if you know of a coffee shop near there, I would be glad of its direction. Paddy is an Irishman and prefers tea."

"Ah, yes, I am aware of Madame Fabre. She appears to be a worthy woman and probably won't cheat you much." Vilet scratched a note on one of the voluminous scraps that littered his desk. "How are you finding our fair city?"

That comment was so out of character for Vilet, that Chadwick almost dropped his coffee.

"Really, Monsieur Vilet," he responded, "we have not seen much of Calais at this point. Just finding lodgings and getting settled has taken most of our time. Would you like to point out some places of interest we should visit?"

For a few minutes, Vilet discussed some places with vistas or of historical import that interested visitors, as well as a winery he particularly liked. Chadwick could almost be lulled into thinking it was a conversation between two civilized men, not a police commissioner and a prisoner. Even though he wasn't behind bars, his movement was curtailed and to him, that meant prison.

"A winery this far north?" he asked mostly to keep the conversation going. He was beginning to suspect that Vilet had an agenda in mind, and whatever was on his agenda, was not going to be to his liking.

"Unfortunately, you won't have too much time to see these sights," Vilet said unexpectedly.

Chadwick's stomach gave a lurch. Vilet was getting to his agenda. "You are letting me go!" he said enthusiastically. He didn't really believe it, but thought he would try anyway.

"No, not yet, monsieur," Vilet said coldly. "But I think your presence would be of better use to French interests if you were in Boulogne."

"Whatever for?" Chadwick protested loudly. "I don't even want to be in Calais. I need to be heading south to Bordeaux to begin purchasing wine for my clients. You can't really expect me to kick up my heels in some backwater like Boulogne while you sort out paperwork?"

"Well, actually, yes, I can," Vilet responded smugly. "I have a task for which you seem perfectly suited."

"I don't work for you," Chadwick disputed hotly.

"And you have not proved that you do not work for the British government, either," Vilet shot back.

"That logic is just ridiculous," Chadwick remonstrated. "How can I prove something I am not? I have paperwork, which, by the way, you have on your desk, that proves who I am."

"That is correct," Vilet returned crisply. "And yet you arrived in the middle of the night, with an Irish assistant via a well-known smuggler. I find your so-called side trip to Dublin very suspect. And until I can verify your story, you are staying where I can keep an eye on you." He stood sharply. "Come with me," he ordered.

He strode out of the room and then waited in the hall for Chadwick to join him. Chadwick took a last gulp of coffee and grabbed his hat. Vilet had already charged down several halls and up a staircase, leaving Chadwick doubtful that he would be able to find his way back to the office. He thought they must be heading for the back of the building, probably overlooking a courtyard. Vilet finally threw open a door and marched through the room to a large window that reached from floor to ceiling. He opened the window and stepped out onto a balcony, gesturing for Chadwick to follow him.

As he had suspected, they were overlooking a quad. But the scene below was far from idyllic. Jeffrey had to swallow several times before the bile in his throat stopped rising.

"What in the name of all that is merciful has happened here?" he gasped in shock.

Eight bodies of men lay in various crumpled positions along one side of the courtyard. Blood, lots of blood, stained the ground beneath them. Across the square, soldiers were cleaning their rifles. Obviously, he had just missed the firing squad that ended the men's lives. Even as they stood there, Chadwick could see other men emerge from the buildings and begin to carry off the bodies.

He stared at Vilet in shock. "Why are you showing me this?" he demanded.

"Last night, one of our patrols found those men on the beach between Calais and Boulogne, not so far from where we picked you up. The men were well-dressed, with weapons. There was also some boat wreckage on the beach. It would seem their mode of escape failed them. You might not know, but last night the sea was rather rough with a big swell. I am told by my seamen-who ought to know-that it was not an opportune time to take to the seas. But seriously, do the British think we are stupid?"

"They were British? How did you know?" Chadwick asked.

"The smuggler they were trying to meet up with sent us word that he was to meet them. He was one of ours."

"And you shot them, just like that?"

"We are not uncivilized, Monsieur Couture," Vilet said indignantly. "There was a trial this morning. They had no defense," he added dismissively.

Chadwick watched as the last body was loaded onto a wheel barrow and taken away without much dignity. At least he didn't have to feign his shock. Any man would be shocked to be faced with such a scene. Now he needed to discover why Vilet had subjected him to it. This man was scary and he certainly had an agenda. So, since he knew offense to be the best defense, he decided to go on the offense.

"Monsieur Vilet, this is an abominable scene. I don't care if those men are British or French. I doubt they could have mounted a reasonable defense given the few hours they had. But, be that as it may, I fail to see what their deaths have to do with me.

"Yes, I arrived here via a smuggler. I had no other recourse but to hire a free trader. As you know, all legal shipping between France and Britain has stopped. But that is where the similarities end. I was hired by respectable people to carry out their commissions here in France. You have my paper-work and letters of introduction. I have given you my parole and reported to you as instructed.

"To be threatened in this manner is extremely offensive. Yes, I realize you have not threatened me in so many words, but I am not stupid. I understand what you are doing by showing me these poor souls and their unhappy ending. You are telling me in no uncertain terms, that I might end up the same way." Chadwick paused for breath. Had he been over the top in his speech? Had he laid it on too thickly?

"Then we understand each other," Vilet replied coolly. "Let us return to my office. I have a proposition for you." They retraced their steps in silence.

Once they were seated again, Chadwick immediately asked, "What proposition?"

"Before we get to that, I have some questions for you." He touched the side of the coffee pot and sighed when his hand came away cool. He picked up the pot and walked to the door. Chadwick saw him hand the pot to the soldier on duty with a grunt to "heat that up." Returning to his desk, he shuffled papers, obviously hunting for something.

Chadwick occupied himself by counting the number of papers Vilet looked at before he found the one he was searching for. At thirteen, an ominous number he thought, Vilet stopped. He looked at Chadwick with a steely gaze.

"I assume, Monsieur Couture, that you went to Dublin on a British ship?" the police commissioner asked unexpectedly.

"No, American," he answered cautiously. American seemed a safer choice.

"While you were on the ship, were you made aware of the English terms for various pieces of naval equipment?"

Of all the questions Vilet might have asked, this was the last topic Chadwick expected. So if he seemed confused, it would seem natural.

"Yes," he said slowly. "That is an unusual question."

Before he could continue, Vilet cut in. "What is your native language, English or French?"

That was tricky but he thought it best to stick with the cover story.

"French, although I understand my accent is not as 'French' as you might like it. I assume that is because of the influence of New Orleans and the island. There's quite a mixture of cultures there."

At this point, there was a welcome interruption when the private brought the coffee pot back. Vilet poured them both more coffee, to which Chadwick freely added sugar. Reheated coffee, in his experience, needed something to offset the burnt taste. He was rather pleased with the result. Whoever had charge of the kitchen had been pretty careful with Vilet's coffee and managed not to burn it. The chef probably feared facing a firing squad if he did, he thought sardonically.

"My compliments on the coffee," he offered. "It's very good."

Vilet nodded in acknowledgement but only sipped his coffee as he studied his list. "We, the French Army that is, have a problem and I have been asked to help."

"Do I understand that you think I might be of assistance in solving this problem?" Chadwick surmised.

"A little background, monsieur," Vilet said. "Am I correct in assuming that this is your first trip to France?" At Chadwick's nod, he continued. "Frenchmen are very proud, of their country, their culture and their language. They do not easily or willingly learn other languages."

Chadwick poured himself more coffee. Then he leaned back in his chair to see where this was going. Not to the firing squad just yet, he thought.

"In fact, I have heard that Bonaparte himself does not understand English and that there are very few Frenchmen who are fluent in English." He paused as if searching for words.

"Now here is the difficult part. Bonaparte is planning an invasion of England. That is no secret I am sharing with a person who might very well be an enemy agent. You can't keep something that big a secret. The when and where of the invasion is only in the head of the First Consul, and I am assured England will be very surprised. However, some very smart general or his aide, has realized that once the French Army gets to England, they will have no way to communicate with the populace."

"Well, that is ridiculous," Chadwick was almost laughing. It seemed so preposterous that they had no translators. "What did you do in Germany and Italy if Frenchmen do not want to learn other languages?"

"We have many people from Alsace-Lorraine who grow up learning both French and German and it is the same in the French Alps near Italy. We can use them as interpreters when we need them. No one seems to learn English willingly, and if so, they don't seem to know the military terms the army and navy need."

Chadwick swore out loud, "Damn me, Vilet, you want me to do translations for you?" he asked incredulously. He could hardly keep from laughing out loud at the irony of it.

"My proposition is a little more formal, monsieur." Vilet seemed taken back by Chadwick's obvious mirth. "Until I get your paperwork verified, I am going to attach you to a company of translators in Boulogne, under the leadership of Captain Cuvelier de Trie."

"I am not yours to order around like that," Chadwick protested.

"I can give you some choices," Vilet responded coldly. "First, firing squad. That saves me from paperwork. Second, cell downstairs. That doesn't solve the paperwork issue and it is not very comfortable, but no one will know where you are, so if you disappear down there, who will look for you? Or, go to Boulogne, translate some manuals for the army, and in a month or so, when the verification comes from Dublin, you can be on your way. Until then, the army can watch you and make certain you don't take off without permission and I don't have to waste my men's time following you around. And even better, I get some good will from the army without having to do anything but lend you to them."

Chadwick's mind was in a whirl. He obviously wasn't enamored with Vilet's first two choices. But how could he move to Boulogne when his return trip with Captain Barnes was supposed to be from Calais? He didn't want to leave Paddy and Georgina alone in Calais, but how could he take them along? Vilet's next words really tipped the scale.

Cheyne Row, Chelsea

"Ah, good, there you are," Nathan Donnay rose to his feet as his wife entered the room and greeted him with a smile and kiss.

"I didn't realize you were coming home early," Marion responded, settling herself on the loveseat by the fireplace. "I told Thornton to bring the tea tray in here." They were seated in the parlor in the house where they lived with her father, retired General Ambrose Coxe. Although not the most sophisticated of neighborhoods, the house in Chelsea offered easy access to the center of London where Donnay worked and a larger – than – normal garden for Marion.

Donnay sat beside his wife and rested his hand on her shoulder. "How is your back, – still aching?" he asked.

"Yes, it aches, but not too bad at the moment. Nanny Jean says it probably will ache from now until the babe finally makes an appearance," she sighed. "It certainly did the last time."

"I rather hope this time it will be one babe and not twins."

A quiet knock at the door heralded Thornton with the tea tray, followed by one of the new kitchen maids with a tray of sandwiches. "Afternoon, sir. We didn't expect you home so early. Sorry for the delay." Thornton began to arrange the tea pot and assorted items on the table in the window enclosure. "Do you prefer tea, sir, or something stronger?" he asked.

"Tea is fine for both of us." Nathan smiled at Marion. "Does everyone know my schedule so well that when I sneak off work early it is a notable event?"

"Well, this is unusually early for you," she looked at him closely. "What exactly are you doing home?"

"I have a letter I want you to read and give me your opinion on. Here, let me pour the tea while you read this." He rose, giving Marion a hand up off the couch. She was already showing a slight bump and he enjoyed imagining what she would look like when she was farther along. He pulled a packet out of his inner pocket and laid it on the table for her.

Marion immediately laid out the pages and began to read. Almost instantly she exclaimed with pleasure, "This is from Jeffrey! I have been wondering how he is." Then her face turned serious as she read further.

"Will there be anything else?" Thornton's voice interrupted Donnay as he stood studying his wife's face. He turned to the butler.

"If the General is available, you probably should ask him to join us."

"Very good, sir. He is in the garden." Thornton withdrew, taking the maid with him.

Donnay had poured two cups of tea by the time Marion got to the end of the first page, she rapidly turned to the second. "Oh, my," she said softly. "What has Jeffrey got himself into?"

Donnay sat in the other chair and started in on the sandwiches. "I did not have lunch," he explained.

Marion laid aside the pages and took a sip of tea. She grimaced when she realized she had forgotten the milk and sugar. As she stirred her cup thoughtfully, she asked Nathan, "When did you get this?"

"It came today in the diplomatic bag from Dublin. The date of the letter is a week ago, so I believe he will already be in France by now, or at least well on his way there."

"By himself?" Marion's voice rose a bit. "Isn't that dangerous?"

"Damn right it is dangerous," Donnay answered angrily. "What is Wickham thinking of? Jeffrey is a good man, but Wickham just sent him into a nest of vipers! Alone and without any support."

The door to the parlor from the hallway opened and an older gentleman entered the room. He stood ramrod straight, as he had always stood from the time he entered the army at sixteen. Now in his 60s, his military bearing was one of the first things people noticed about him. Today he was casually dressed with an open collar and his sleeves rolled up. Marion knew he had been tending the gardens, a favorite activity for both of them. When he wasn't at home, the General was at his desk in the Alien Office where he and Nathan worked compiling intelligence reports for the government.

Nathan rose politely and asked, "Tea, General?"

General Coxe pulled a chair over to the table and sat, "Yes, thanks. Thornton says you have a letter that is causing some concern."

Marion handed her father the letter without a word. As the General perused Chadwick's letter, she studied her husband. She had not seen him so angry since they had married. His gray eyes were stormy, and his usually full lips were a thin line of tension. He had run his hands through his dark hair, leaving him looking ruffled and unkempt.

Nathan pushed the tea-cup over to the General. Again, he had forgotten the milk, so Marion added some. "What do you think, Papa?" she asked as the General laid down the pages.

He drank half the cup before he answered. "Damn fools, both of them. Wickham for sending Chadwick off on such a stupid errand, and Chadwick for going." He shot a piercing glance at Nathan. "What do you think?" he demanded.

"Same," he answered shortly.

The General sighed deeply, "What I am going to tell you Marion, remains here. Nathan already knows this."

All Marion's life, the General, her brother in the diplomatic corps, and now her husband had worked in positions that demanded secrecy and confidentiality. She had proved her own ability to keep secrets, which was why the General trusted her now. She nodded her understanding back to him.

"We know something is going on in Calais. Top people in the government believe Napoleon is planning an invasion and the main work is going on there. We just sent some chaps over to investigate, six of them. I haven't heard anything back from them, but I really can't expect anything for another couple of weeks. If there is an invasion being planned at Calais, then Wickham just sent Chadwick into the middle of Napoleon's damn army. How could they be so stupid?" he ended angrily.

Donnay pushed his plate away from him and drew his tea-cup closer. "The question now is not their stupidity but what can be done about it," he said. He added more hot water to the tea pot and poured them all fresh cups.

Marion said flatly, "You are thinking of going after him, aren't you?"

"I am trying desperately to think of another way to help him out," Donnay said. He reached across the table and clasped her hand. "I know this is not a good time for me to leave you here. It is too much like the last time I had to leave you and I do not want to do it, but I can't think of what else to do."

"I suggest we wait until we hear back from my agents that I sent over," the General said. "There may be no reason for you to hie off to France right now." Then the General stood abruptly. "I am going back to deadheading my flowers while I think over this development. The least I will do is write Wickham and ask for more details and the name of the smuggler that took him over. Then we might be able to pinpoint where he landed." He drained his cup and headed out the door, leaving Marion and Nathan holding hands and looking at each other with concern.

Chapter Nine: Boulogne-Sur-Mer

"Leave your hat on," Chadwick directed quietly. "Most do in here." He saw her give a quick look around to verify his instructions and sank slowly onto the seat he had indicated. A public room in a tavern was not the best place for her first foray into Calais society as a boy, but they were all hungry and there was little time to spare if they were to move the next day to Boulogne-Sur-Mer as Vilet had directed.

The tavern was near their rooms and recommended by Madame Fabre. *Probably owned by another relative*, he thought sarcastically. At least it was dark, almost gloomy, with the majority of the light coming from the fireplace and candles on individual tables. He had chosen a table against the side wall and as far from other patrons as possible. However, at the rate the tables were filling up, they wouldn't be alone for long. He hoped that meant the food was decent.

Paddy arrived at the table carrying three mugs of beer. He took one and drank about half of the liquid before placing the remaining beer in front of 'George,' the name Miss Yelverton had suggested they call her. Evidently, she had been nicknamed George or Georgie at school, and so was used to answering to it. The three had not yet decided on a family name for Georgina. Chadwick took a full mug and swallowed a mouthful. Beer was not his favorite beverage, but tonight was not a time for being picky.

"What are they serving for dinner?" he asked.

"I think they said a meat stew," Paddy responded. "Sorry about drinking part of your beer, George, but they only have one sized mug, and my mam would not let the little ones drink that much beer at one time. Old habits, I guess you could say." Paddy was speaking in English but softly to try to avoid attention. In public, Chadwick and Miss Yelverton were careful to answer him in French, but switching back and forth led to some complicated conversations.

"Bread will be along also. That I understood very well."

Paddy glanced around to see if their neighbors were paying them any attention. The room was filled with working class men stopping off for a pint and something to eat to finish up their day, before trudging home. They seemed mostly exhausted men who were paying them no mind. Later, the crowd would likely be more rowdy.

"It doesn't make any difference if someone is listening to us," he quietly assured the others. "We are only following the directions given me by the police commissioner."

"Tell us again exactly what he said," Paddy directed.

"I already told you about those executions. Those poor men were found guilty before the sham trial he mentioned. He really emphasized that willingly going to Boulogne would go a long way to proving my patriotism. He also clearly said that if I did not readily agree, I could join those poor souls or rot in a cell. He also made it clear that if I really wanted him to believe I was a wine merchant and not a spy, I had better be prepared to join this company of translators in Boulogne. I think doing these translations is the easiest way to buy time and stay out of prison." Chadwick took another healthy swig of beer. Vilet's eyes were like a dead man's that never showed any expression, almost colorless and very cold. He was afraid that Vilet could see through his disguise putting his companions in even more danger.

Paddy said thoughtfully, "This doesn't sound so bad. We have to hang around here anyway and this gives you a cover. Why are you worried?"

"Vilet is a scary character. I am not assured I have convinced him with my story. And I have to report there tomorrow. On a positive note, he really did not give me the impression it was forever, but rather just until he verified my story with someone in Dublin." Chadwick grimaced and continued, "But I do not know whom he expects to check with or even if that someone will be able to verify anything."

Bowls of steaming stew arrived with a small loaf of bread for each of them.

"Are you going to eat all that bread, George?" Paddy asked hopefully.

"Yes," came the quick response. "You already had half my beer."

Chadwick hid a smile as the two bickered like siblings over the bread.

Finally, he said, "Paddy, please go get more. I want another bowl too. How about you?" He looked inquiringly at 'George'.

"I have had enough food," was the response. "But I am just not giving up my bread. I might want it later."

Paddy hailed the bar maid and passed along the request.

"So how are we going to do this move, and when?" he asked, bringing the conversation back to the issue at hand.

"We need to leave soon. In fact, Vilet instructed me to report to Boulogne tomorrow. It is too far to walk, so I will need to hire a horse. But we have not had time to look for Captain Byrne's man," Chadwick mused.

"Monsieur?" Georgina interrupted. "Tomorrow? What about us? Are you leaving us here?" She started coughing as if something was caught in her throat. Paddy whacked her on the back and pushed her mug to her so she could drink. By the time she got her breath back, refilled bowls of stew had arrived along with fresh tankards. She wiped her still streaming eyes on her sleeve but managed to glare at Chadwick, obviously for his anticipated desertion.

He had to admit as he studied her short hair, mostly covered by the hat and rumpled boy's clothes, and especially with the angry glare, she gave a good impression as a youth. He now realized she probably would have eaten in the kitchen if she was really a servant, but he didn't want to put her in such untested waters right now. Better to look like he favored boys than put her in danger. He wondered vaguely if they could pass her off as Paddy's brother. No, he thought, the language skills alone were too different.

"I do not want to split us up," he said seriously to both of them. "There are just too many ways we can lose each other and get into trouble. But I am not confident how best to proceed. I cannot afford to anger Vilet, so I think I need to report to Boulogne. But we have some leeway on how to accomplish that. Got any ideas?"

"The way I see it," Paddy started, "we could go together, set up rooms or a common meeting place, and since only you have to do translations, I would be free to wander about."

"You and I are free," Georgina interjected. At Paddy's raised eyebrow, she continued, "Do you think I want to be sitting around wondering what is happening? I should be able to help somehow. And my French is better than yours."

"After all the trouble we went through already…" Paddy started.

Chadwick cleared his throat and the conversation stopped. "Later. We will talk about helping later." He drained his mug and stood. "Let us go back and finish packing. I still do not even know how far it is to Boulogne."

* * *

Back at their rooms, the three sat around a small fire as they discussed and discarded various ideas. Chadwick noticed that his companions were definitely made anxious by this turn of events. Well, honestly, so was he.

"I keep going back to Paddy's belief that we not split up. I agree separating is a bad idea, so let's all of us prepare to go to Boulogne in the morning. Maybe at some future time, when we understand more about the situation we are in and how far Boulogne is from Calais, we can come up with a brilliant idea how to find Captain Byrne's contact.

"In truth, I have been finding it hard enough to play at being a wine merchant and now to become a French patriot and do translations for the enemy – I just do not know how I can do it.

Paddy asked curiously, "Didn't you say that was your job back in London?"

"Shush," Georgina said quickly. "Don't say anything about London here."

"Sorry," Paddy apologized.

"Actually, yes," Chadwick answered. Glad he wasn't the one who had to correct Paddy for speaking out of turn. "I'm not usually a field agent so this is pretty ironic, don't you think?"

"Yes, I do see the irony," Georgina smiled. "But this assignment may not be the worst thing that could happen. Maybe this time the best place to lie low would be with the people who might be looking for you?"

Both Chadwick and Paddy looked at her with approving smiles.

"I say, George, that's brilliant," said Paddy. "Hiding under their noses. I love it."

* * *

They were trying to decide how to tote their gear when pounding on the front door froze them all in their places. Madame must have answered the door, as they first heard heavy footsteps on the stairs, then more pounding, this time on their door. Chadwick flung it open. The man facing him wasn't tall but was solidly built with broad shoulders and well-muscled. Chadwick imagined he would be difficult to best in a one-on-one fight. He recognized the man as someone he had seen when he visited Vilet at the *hotel de ville*.

"Monsieur Vilet has directed we are to see you and your assistant to Boulogne," the man stated. "I have horses waiting downstairs, so don't be long," he added sharply.

Chadwick decided that no real answer was necessary, so he simply nodded his understanding of the order.

A slight tug at his sleeve and he turned to see Georgina standing anxiously at his elbow. "They don't know about me, do they?" she whispered.

He squeezed her shoulder quickly. "Do not worry, we will not be separated if I can help it. But remember what I said about how to find a boat to Ireland?"

She nodded.

"Good. Let us go see what is waiting for us downstairs."

Downstairs were two men, four horses, and one very vexed landlady.

"Monsieur Couture, what is the meaning of this?" She demanded. "What have you done, that you are being taken away by the police? I keep a clean house."

"Madame, please," he protested, "we have been asked to help the government. We are going to Boulogne for a few days to help with some translating. We will be back. In fact, I want to keep the rooms. We are going to need them when we finish in Boulogne." He fervently hoped that would be true.

"And who is this?" She had finally noticed Georgina. "You told me only the two of you were staying here?"

"If you remember, I did tell you I would be hiring a lad to help with chores," he said sharply. He judged that now was the time to act as a wealthy merchant would act. "You don't really expect us to continue to carry our own water, do you?"

"Madame, enough!" Vilet's man interceded sharply. "We need to be about our business. These mounts are for you two." He pointed at two horses, not the top of the line in Chadwick's opinion but not decrepit either. Both were equipped with saddlebags he noticed with relief. He didn't want to carry his extra shirts under his arms. He stuffed the shirts and shaving bag into one of the saddlebag and gestured to Georgina to fill the other side with her spare socks and shirt. He noticed with some amusement she was also stuffing the wooden shoes he bought her into the bag. *What did she need those for*, he wondered. Paddy had already finished stuffing his gear into his bags and seemed to be checking his horse's girth with some authority. Chadwick had assumed Paddy could ride, but that might not be true, he realized, as he had grown up a city lad and then been part of the infantry who walked everywhere. Paddy, however, seemed to know what he was doing and was preparing to mount.

Chadwick turned back to Madame Fabre.

"I am leaving my trunk upstairs, and I expect it to be there, intact, when I return," he said forcefully. "If you go through it, I will know." He thought about the skirts they had packed at the bottom for Georgina when she needed to be a girl again. Maybe they should have tossed them, but such thoughts were too late now.

He glanced around for Georgina to make sure she was nearby. She stood a little apart from their group but with such a look of fear and anxiety that it took him by surprise. Did she really think he might leave her?

At first, he had thought that she would ride behind Paddy, but his own horse appeared to be the sturdier of the two and better able to carry both of them. Georgina really had a slender figure, he noticed, and although he thought she could gain some weight it was possible she was naturally on the thin side. Her lack of womanly curves thankfully made her disguise easier to achieve. He was pleased that the clothes covered all the bruises and the hat most of her hair. Her thin face and prominent cheekbones made her eyes seem unusually large. But none of her features in his opinion were distinctly feminine, and if she continued to hold herself tall and walk as Paddy had taught her, he thought it would be really hard to see her as anything other than a boy.

Chadwick mounted quickly and then nudged the rather placid horse to where Georgina was standing. With the reins in his left hand, he reached across to her with his right.

"Take my hand, put your foot on my boot and get up behind me. Won't be the most comfortable ride, but it is better than running behind," he grinned in an effort to cheer her up.

She lifted her face to look at him as she reached up to take his hand. She grinned back. With a shock, he again recognized the relationship to the beautiful woman in the portrait. Her face radiated happiness. In the short time he had known her, he rarely saw her smile and it showed him a different side. She was stunning.

She grasped his hand, and using his boot as a stepping block, lifted herself with practiced ease up behind him. Obviously, Paddy wasn't the only one who had ridden before. "Thank you, Monsieur Couture," she said happily. "It's not the most comfortable of seats, but this is much better than walking." She added in a voice so low, he almost missed it, "And much better than being left behind."

If she had really been a boy, he would have squeezed her knee to give some sign of comfort, but that smile reminded him vividly that she was not a boy, and he didn't dare offer such an intimate gesture in case anyone noticed. The whole situation just seemed to spiral more and more into confusion and danger.

Vilet's men led them through the town and finally onto a fairly well-maintained road leading west. There were even road signs listing various towns and villages and the direction each lay in. It appeared that Boulogne was fairly close, as it too was listed on the road sign. But he still couldn't tell precisely how far away it was. Chadwick was worried that if they were too distant, they wouldn't be able to find Captain Byrne's contact to make their way back to Dublin.

The road was bustling with traffic. Chadwick could identify various farmers bringing produce or driving livestock to the city. Suddenly, with a jolt, he began to notice a fair number of military. He had been so focused on his assignment of retrieving Georgina that he had forgotten what Wickham had said about a possible invasion of England from these shores. Certainly, Vilet had suggested that possibility, but Chadwick had not really thought carefully about the information. He looked around carefully for more evidence.

Because of the traffic, they were finally forced to travel in single file with Vilet's man in the lead, followed by Chadwick with Georgina, then Paddy, and finally the other officer. Obviously, they were not under arrest. Vilet's men, while brusque, hardly bothered with them once they got to the main road west. He didn't want to loudly point out to his companions his conclusions about the number of military men they were passing, but it certainly would be odd if they did not talk at all. After all, he was supposed to be a merchant who had never been to this area before. How should he act? What would he be talking about?

"George?" he asked. He could feel her holding onto his coat trying to sit up and look the proper boy. "Lean in a moment. I need to talk to you." When she leaned against him, he was surprised at how comfortable it felt. He cleared his throat. "Did you notice all the military uniforms?"

"Um, yes," she whispered.

"Try to remember the different colors you are seeing," he directed quietly.

"Why?" she murmured.

"It will give me an idea how many regiments are here. London may have no idea how large this encampment is." He thought of the eight dead men he had seen in the *hotel de ville* de ville in Calais. If those were British agents as Vilet seemed to think, London might not be aware of what Napoleon had started here only twenty miles from the British coast. Then, with a sinking heart, he realized that he and Paddy might be the only operatives still alive to bring the tale home.

He kicked his horse to a faster walk to catch up to Vilet's man. "Pardon, but how far is Boulogne from Calais? Monsieur Vilet never really told me," he said.

The agent turned to glare at him. He grumbled, "About twenty miles, monsieur. We should be there a little after noon," he added grudgingly.

"And where in Boulogne did Monsieur Vilet tell you to take us?"

"Monsieur directed I was to take you to Captain Jean Cuvelier de Trie."

"And our quarters? Do you know where we will be billeted?"

"The Captain will show you," he answered curtly. He turned away from Chadwick. The conversation was over.

Vilet's man set a steady pace, not particularly aggressive, but he didn't stop for any breaks either. Chadwick wondered what the problem was. He obviously resented the guide duty, and seemed to want to get to Boulogne as soon as possible, He only interacted with Chadwick when he needed to give directions. Well, the disdain was mutual. Hopefully they would be rid of him soon.

As they put some distance between them and Calais, the road became less crowded and the Captain could ride next to Paddy. It seemed a good time to practice Paddy's French lessons, which at least passed the time. Chadwick used the passing farms and fields to point out various words for food and crops and then moved on to the people they were passing, pointing out the difference between officers and enlisted men, various transportation vehicles, and anything else he could think of that sounded innocuous but might be important in a report of enemy capability. Paddy was making good progress with nouns and simple verbs, but using the right tense was causing him problems and he often got the male and female endings confused causing some amusing mix-ups.

Chadwick's stomach was growling by the time the sun was high. He could still feel Georgina leaning against his back, but he realized she had not spoken a word or even moved, in some time.

"Paddy, is George asleep?" he asked.

"No, but he is looking a bit peaky, Monsieur Couture," he said. "I guess it can't be much further. Good thing, because we could all do with some food and drink."

"I am feeling pretty peckish myself," Chadwick responded. "George, can you get into the bag where my gear is? There is a canteen there."

"I am fine, sir," came the soft answer. "I will be glad to get off this horse though. It's been a long time since I have ridden and I am afraid I am really sore." Then even more quietly she added, "I really need to relieve myself."

Chadwick flinched inwardly at her words, remembering the bruises. After what she had been through, sitting astride a fat horse must be excruciating. To have to admit to needing to urinate must also have been humiliating to a young lady. He considered how a young boy might be treated.

"We will stop quickly at the next grove of trees. You jump off and just walk into the woods. When you return, Paddy will put you up so you can sit sideways. Do you think that will help?"

"Yes," came the quiet answer. "But, Monsieur Couture, don't you think it will look odd? I mean, giving me preference like that?"

"Maybe," he answered. "But we can just say you have never ridden a horse before and leave it at that."

He heard a deep sigh. Then she said, "I do not think I will be doing any jumping. My legs feel numb."

"Paddy will help you to the trees," he said. "It probably would look odd if I did."

He glanced at Paddy and said, "When we reach the trees, just toss me your reins, jump down and help George. I will keep our 'guides' occupied."

When they reached the spinny in question, Chadwick asked, "Ready?"

Paddy slid off his horse quickly and handed his reins up to Chadwick. Before Georgina could get her leg over the horse to dismount, Paddy had grabbed her by the waist, pulled her off, and was rushing her to the trees, grumbling, "You are more trouble than you are worth, lad. Now be quick about it." He stood at the edge of the wood, arms crossed obviously waiting for Georgina to reappear while giving her some privacy.

Chadwick watched his actions with some surprise. *Paddy Cavanaugh might have a future on the stage*, he thought with amusement.

"Monsieur Couture! What do you think you are doing?" This time it was the rear guard who had not spoken a word to them yet. "You can't just stop when you feel like it!" he protested.

"Do you think I want the lad peeing all over me," Chadwick growled back. "You have set a bruising pace without any breaks. We will stop here for a few minutes." He dismissed the rear guard and turned to give the lead man his most imperious glare.

Surprisingly, the lead guard gave a shrug and swung off his horse. He tied the reins loosely to a bush and headed to the trees.

Chadwick looked in panic at Paddy. Then he saw that the guard hadn't bothered going into the trees, just stood at the edge and relieved himself in the open. With some dismay he saw Paddy turn and follow the guard's lead. Chadwick found himself praying that Georgina would not emerge from the woods at this moment. As a gently bred young lady, she might faint at the sight of men relieving themselves in the open. As the complications of shepherding her around an unknown area filled with military bore in on him, Chadwick began to think he should have left her in Calais with Paddy.

"Monsieur," the quiet voice brought him out of his panicked reverie. He saw with relief that Paddy and Georgina were standing by the horses, waiting for him to notice them. He handed her the canteen for a drink of water and then Paddy tossed her up on the horse and they were off.

"That was interesting," he said dryly after Vilet's men moved ahead.

The only answer he got was a quiet chuckle.

"That was not funny. Suppose he had walked up on you?" he protested.

"I agree. But the look on your face was almost worth it," she said.

He wished he could see her face but no way was it possible for him to see behind himself. It sounded like she was smiling. That smile would have made all his worry worthwhile.

* * *

Captain Jean Guillaume-Antonine Cuvelier De Trie put the letter he had been reading on his desk, carefully placed his spectacles on top of it and smiled happily at Chadwick. To Chadwick, the Captain's office was remarkably similar to Vilet's office, having only basic furniture and bad lighting, but the atmosphere was very different. When Vilet's men had essentially dumped Chadwick, Paddy, and George on the Captain, he had greeted them civilly, directed Paddy and George to go to the mess hall for some food and took Chadwick to his office. There he offered him a chair and wine even before he had broken the seal on Vilet's letter.

"Commissioner Vilet recommends you to me for some translating work," he said in careful English.

Chadwick answered in French. He had decided that to play the part of a wine merchant, he needed to become the part.

"Pardon, Captain, but my conversational French is better than my speaking English. I come from that part of the Caribbean where French is the first language. I learned English and Spanish in New Orleans, where both are spoken."

"Perfect," the Captain replied with a smile. "My English is better understood in writing also."

"I hope Monsieur Vilet made clear I am only a merchant passing through. Unfortunately for me," he continued ruefully, "I came on a smuggling vessel from Dublin and Vilet is suspicious and that I am a British spy. Until he clears me with someone – he never said who – I am to stay in Calais or rather, now, Boulogne. I have to stay, as he kept my travel papers and letters of introduction."

"I know of Monsieur Vilet, but not through personal knowledge," Cuvelier responded. He poured more wine into Chadwick's glass. "I have heard he is a careful man and not one to be crossed. But your misfortune is my good fortune, Monsieur Couture. We, my company and I, have a little problem, and if you can help me with it, I will be very grateful. I cannot replace your travel papers. In fact, Vilet is pretty insistent that I guarantee you do not leave Boulogne. But I can make your life here fairly comfortable."

"Captain Cuvelier, I have nothing against comfort but I wanted to make certain you understood I may not be here for long. My assignment, why I am in France at all, is to purchase wine for my clients back in New Orleans and to that end I must continue on to Bordeaux."

"Monsieur!" Cuvelier cried. "You are nowhere near Bordeaux. How did you get so far afield?"

"It's a long story," Chadwick answered. "I detoured to Dublin to look up the relatives of one of my clients. He was worried they had not been able to flee France and wanted them to know they are welcome in New Orleans."

"Are your clients royalists?" Cuvelier exclaimed. "You must keep such connections quiet. There are still many who would do harm to those of the old regime."

"Ah, you are absolutely right," Chadwick answered, horrified at his own stupidity. When he fabricated his story, how had he not remembered that people fleeing the revolution were bound to be royalists who were still considered political anathema in France?

Aloud he continued, "At the time I took the assignment I didn't understand the political ramifications. No wonder Vilet is suspicious of me. I did not realize that such feelings were still so raw.

"By the time I got to Dublin, the damn British had annexed all of Ireland. I found the people I was looking for, but when it came time for me to leave, war had been declared again and there was no legal way to get to France. Desperate to get on with my duties, I hired a smuggler to drop me off. Foolishly, it never occurred to me that this might be seen as suspicious. The last few weeks have been trying to say the least." He sighed and sipped his wine. He saluted the Captain to show his appreciation for the quality of the wine.

Cuvelier De Trie was studying the letter again. "Vilet does say he is checking out your background, and he estimates I can only have your services for four to six weeks."

Chadwick inwardly groaned at the length of time, but at least now he had an idea of how long Vilet meant to keep him.

"Why, Monsieur Couture, does Vilet think you will be able to assist me with the translations?"

"When Vilet first interviewed me, he questioned my accent. I explained to him that what he heard as an accent that was 'off' was merely the way French is spoken where I come from. I grew up in a diverse society with many languages. Few of my acquaintances at home speak with perfect Parisian accents, since none of us went to school here. But it is my fluency in both French and English that enables me to do what I do. One needs enough English to conduct business. I think mine is a bit better than that, but I am more comfortable speaking French, as it is my native language."

"So you can speak and write both French and English?" the Captain asked excitedly.

"Yes, and some Spanish. I don't feel very confident that my Greek and Latin would hold up now, though," Chadwick responded. "Vilet seemed especially interested to learn I sailed on an American ship to Dublin. He wanted to know if I was acquainted with the English terms for naval equipment and gear."

"Are you?" The Captain, if possible, seemed even more animated.

"Yes, you know how long those cruises are. After we exhausted current events and other conversational gambits, the sailors thought it great fun to teach me some of the ins and outs of sailing a merchant ship," Chadwick answered cautiously.

"We have been directed by the First Consul himself to draw up a list of English naval terminology so that our men will be able to commandeer British ships when we invade," Captain Cuvelier explained. "Up to now, we have made no headway, as we have no one who has any experience with the British Navy. If you can help us, you, sir, are a gift from God on high."

"I was on an American ship," Chadwick said cautiously. A list of naval terms? That didn't sound too hard and was not something that would help the French unduly or mark him as a traitor. The casual reference to invasion, though, chilled his bones.

"English terms, my dear Monsieur Couture. America has not been free so long that the terms for sailing vessels have changed. I am assured the armaments on such ships are the same also."

"In that case, Captain, I feel positive that I would be able to provide such a list. As a citizen of France, although one from the Caribbean, I would be proud to help you with such a project."

"Excellent, excellent. I am deeply grateful that you have arrived at such a fortuitous time, monsieur." The grateful Captain started to pour more wine but Chadwick waved him off.

"Sorry, Captain," he said. "It has already been a long day and I would welcome a chance to clean up and rest. I have traveling with me my assistant, who I hired in Ireland and a young lad to run errands. Do you have a place where we can bunk while we are in Boulogne?"

While the Guide Interpreters, as Captain Cuvelier de Trie explained, had its own encampment outside of town, the actual work of translating was done in the very warehouse where Chadwick and he were talking. Since Chadwick and his entourage were not military, rooms at a tavern in town would be hired for them. The Captain had already sent his adjutant to find rooms and was just waiting for him to return.

"Until then, let me acquaint you with our operation," he said. They went into the body of the warehouse, where he showed Chadwick around and introduced him to several of the men working at the various long tables.

"This building was empty when the company was organized and General Berthier set us up here," the Captain explained.

"It's pretty dim with just those high windows for light," Chadwick noted. "What is it like when it rains?"

The Captain sighed even as he nodded. "There never seem to be enough candles, no matter how often I complain to the quartermaster," he said. "On good days, we can open that large sliding door." He gestured to the large door at the end of the building that was obviously for unloading goods brought by wagon.

"The tables are light enough that we can move them easily to follow the light. But you are right; it is a problem."

Chadwick almost chuckled out loud; different army, same problems. There was money for arms, but the support services were always shorted. He should be right at home here.

Chapter Ten: Boulogne

C hadwick closed and locked the door with a sigh of relief. In the end, Captain Cuvelier's lieutenant could not find them a room at a tavern; the town was too full of military who had taken all the available rooms for themselves. Lucky for Chadwick and his companions, the Lieutenant had found a woman willing to rent them a bedroom and small sitting area. The accommodations were better than their rooms in Calais and were further enhanced, in his opinion when he learned the widow was willing to provide breakfast and dinner. Since the French Army was paying for the accommodations in return for his translating, Chadwick thought he had gained the better part of the deal.

He sagged tiredly into an upholstered chair in front of the small fireplace. The two small rooms were on the top floor of a home that faced the street. He had noticed that the street was mainly residential, which he hoped would make it quiet, as the bedroom and the smaller of the two rooms overlooked the street. The bedroom was so small that the double bed with a trundle took up most of the floor space. He and Paddy would have to take turns dressing as there was not enough room for both of them to move about. At least George had a bed and a door to close when she dressed.

The other room, facing the rear of the house was marginally larger. There were, however, only two chairs by the fireplace. A small table with a couple of stools made up the rest of the furnishings.

Georgina was curled up in one chair, wrapped in a blanket. She admitted that she couldn't seem to get warm. He put more wood on the fire and then grabbed the half empty wine bottle their landlady had thoughtfully shared with them over dinner. He poured healthy portions into both glasses.

"Drink some wine," he advised. "It will help you warm up."

She sipped cautiously. "I think I am just reacting to everything that has happened in the past couple of days: you and Paddy finding me, me turning into a boy, and the terror of being found out by the French. I should have more sympathy for those women who are always chattering on about their 'nerves.' How do *you* stay so calm?" she asked.

Chadwick surveyed her anxiously. She had been amazingly calm ever since he had dragged her out of the dung-infested hut Hastings had locked her in. He was surprised that she had not broken down into hysterics before now. But what, he wondered, would he do with a female who was having an attack of 'nerves'? Maybe enough wine would put her to sleep and she would be better by tomorrow. He hastily refilled her glass to the brim.

"Stop, stop!" she almost laughed. "My teeth are chattering and I might spill some. That would be a shame, as we don't know if Paddy is bringing anymore."

The day had not been as stressful for Paddy as he did not have to maintain a disguise, but could simply be himself. To Chadwick's admiration, the lad still had plenty of energy. After dinner with their landlady, he asked if it would be all right for him to go investigate the town. Since this seemed to be a perfectly rational activity for a man of Paddy's age, Chadwick acquiesced and gave him some money for beer.

"Keep your ears open to any bits about what is going on here in Boulogne," Chadwick advised him. Now, rather than play the spy, he sincerely hoped Paddy would think to bring back more wine. After today, he felt like he could drink a bottle by himself.

"How was dinner in the kitchen?" he asked Georgina.

"Surprisingly good," she responded. "The cook was busy serving, so I just sat with the stable chap and ate. Not much conversation going on. He didn't take off his hat, so I didn't either. And yours?"

"I felt like I was back in Vilet's office with the number of questions our gracious landlady threw at me. That rat Paddy pretended he couldn't understand her accent," he chuckled.

Georgina put her wine down and snuggled deeper into the blanket. Chadwick added more wood to the fire. She finally stopped shivering so much.

"What did you have for your dinner?" he asked for something to say.

"*Lapin* stew with some amazing bread."

"We had the same – with a bunch of side dishes." He poked at the fire some more to make sure it caught the new wood. He leaned back, stretching his legs to the fire and then pulling them back quickly when he realized there wasn't enough space. If he ever built his own home, he promised himself, there would be plenty of room to stretch out.

"It is just remarkable what that cook can do with some vegetables. If we stay here long enough maybe you can put on some weight," he said without thinking. He cringed and glanced at her to see her reaction. No gentleman commented on a lady's figure.

"I am so sorry..." he started.

"Don't worry," she said evenly. "I know I have lost weight. Between the fear and everything that happened...I just couldn't keep much down."

She seemed fairly calm and not sleepy. He studied her thoughtfully. The days had been so chaotic that he had never heard her side of the story. Maybe now was a good time.

"Can you tell me how Hastings managed to kidnap you?" Chadwick encouraged. He didn't know how much new information he would get from her, but he still had unanswered questions. He hoped she might be able to shed some light on them.

"I have talked to the coachman and your brother, but they didn't seem to know very much, other than that you seemed to disappear into thin air."

"I am not convinced there is a lot to tell," she began hesitantly. "I was shopping, well, just to pick up a bonnet. I had a note saying it was ready and when I got to the shop, they claimed no such thing. I mean, really! Why would they send me a note if it wasn't finished?" She paused and sipped her wine. She settled the blanket again and continued.

"The day had started badly. To get to the haberdashery, I had to have this fight with my brother. Have you met him? He can be such a prig. He insisted I take the carriage when everyone knows it is faster to walk from our house and perfectly safe to do so. Well, it used to be perfectly safe..." Her voice trailed off despondently.

The fire was the only light source in the room. It was now totally dark outside and Chadwick had drawn the curtains some time before. He studied the shadows that drifted across Georgina's face, mixing with expressions of pain and sadness.

"Then what happened?" he prompted.

"I walked out onto the street searching for the carriage. It was not anywhere to be seen. I got to the corner and was looking, when this rough-looking man came up to me and said the carriage was on the side street. I turned to say something to Mary, but she had tripped and fallen. Before I could get to her, this man had my arm and was forcing me into a carriage. Someone else tied me up and blindfolded me." She sighed deeply. He could see her hands clench at the memory.

"The one good thing is that they didn't take Mary at the same time. Every day I would say a prayer of thanksgiving that she was safe at home, as they probably would have treated her even worse than they treated me, and that was badly."

She paused to take another sip of wine. "Did you see her when you went to my house?" she asked.

Chadwick glanced at the fire, trying to find a way to give Georgina the bad news. When Paddy had filled her in on their side of the story, he must have skipped the maid's death. He felt that Georgina was still very fragile, but he could think of no way to avoid telling her Mary's fate. He leaned forward and took her hands trying to be careful of the splint on her left hand.

"I am really sorry, Georgina, but Mary did not survive the kidnapping."

"What do you mean? I saw her trip and fall myself," she insisted, confused.

"Yes, she fell. But she did not trip. Someone knifed her, causing so much confusion so that no one would notice when Hastings grabbed you."

He tightened his grip on her good hand. "It was very quick. She didn't suffer."

He could see the moment the realization that her friend was dead hit her. The large eyes filled with tears, the blood drained from her face, and she seemed to crumple from inside. In an instant, she had flung herself into his arms and was sobbing uncontrollably into his chest. He settled her on his lap, put his arms around her thin body, and let her give herself over to her emotions. It had been a long time since he had sat holding his sister and trying to comfort her over some catastrophe. He never could think of the right words to say then, either, so he just sat as he did now, patting her back while she cried herself out.

* * *

The fire had burned down to embers and Chadwick had finished both glasses of wine by the time Paddy returned.

"Where's George?" Paddy asked.

"In the trundle bed," Chadwick replied. "He fell asleep by the fire, so I just put him to bed in his clothes." Paddy had the right of it, referring to Georgina as a male so they wouldn't slip up when it was important.

"What did you find out?" he asked.

"Lively night life, what with all the soldiers and military types," he laughed. "I saw more fights in one block than I normally see in a week at home."

He plunked a bottle of wine on the table. "Shall I open this?" he asked.

At Chadwick's enthusiastic nod, he started on the cork. "All anyone is talking about is the invasion, but I couldn't really understand much beyond a few words, so I didn't get real stuff like dates and all."

"Could you get any idea how big this town is?" Chadwick asked. It seemed odd to him that the French would stage an invasion from a backwater. But when they rode in yesterday, Boulogne had not seemed very city-like. Admittedly, Vilet's men had ridden straight to the warehouse and essentially dumped them, so he hadn't seen much at all. He doubted that Paddy had seen much in the dark, either. He poked the fire up as Paddy served the wine and sank into the chair Georgina had previously sat in.

After her outpouring of grief, she had remained silent for a long time and then fell asleep still in his arms. She had not made the slightest move to separate herself from him. He hoped he had been able to offer her some comfort. After he had felt her drift off, he had moved her carefully to the trundle bed. She had woken briefly and squeezed his hand when he had smoothed her hair away from her face. Then she drifted off again.

"I couldn't tell too much, but I have to say, no one tried to stop me from wandering about," Paddy broke into his thoughts. "I would have thought that if they were worried about spies, they would have more guards going about checking papers."

"That *is* odd," Chadwick said thoughtfully. "I assume there must be a port here somewhere. Maybe they guard that better. We'll have to try to look around more tomorrow."

"About tomorrow, sir," Paddy said cautiously.

Paddy's tone had changed and seemed to signal that he had something he considered important.

"What do you think George and I should be doing while you are doing that translating?" he asked. "I know we should find out what we can about this invasion but we also need to be getting George back home, and to do that we have to get hold of Captain Byrne."

"I was worried you were going to bring up planning," Chadwick said wryly. "I haven't had much time to think."

He gave Paddy a brief account of his conversation with Miss Yelverton and how much the news of her maid's death had shaken her.

"I really want her to stay here tomorrow and rest. She has not had any real rest since we found her and she needs to be more comfortable in her disguise. I doubt, too, whether her feet have really healed. At least here there won't be any problem with latrines," he added.

"The landlady might think it odd if she sees George just lazing about," Paddy remarked.

"Good point," Chadwick agreed. "Then I guess he had better have some light chores. After all, we just got here. And maybe he can do the reading I am assigning him."

"Are we teaching him to read?"

"Hmm," Chadwick mused. "How about part of his duty is to help you improve your French?"

"That's better. I think that might even be believable."

Paddy drank some wine and gazed at the fire for some time before speaking again.

"Sir, I feel like we are in a bit of a situation," he began.

When he paused, Chadwick gave an encouraging motion with his wine. "Go on, Paddy, get it out. What is bothering you? It is probably the same thing that is bothering me."

Paddy ruffled his hair in such a frustrated gesture that Chadwick almost laughed out loud. Finally, he said, "Nothing has gone right since we landed, sir. We are essentially prisoners, we don't really have a way to get home and we have lost our papers. Trying to find Captain Byrne's contact back in Calais will be like finding a needle in a haystack. What are we going to do? Do you have any idea?" His voice almost broke on the last question.

Chadwick sometimes forgot that Paddy was not very old, had never traveled, and yes, they were in a situation that could scare anyone silly. How did he expect a young, inexperienced fellow to react? He really missed Nathan Donnay. Nathan was always calm and focused. How the devil did the man do it? He tried to picture Nathan in a crisis. How did he always appear so controlled?

"But Paddy," Chadwick protested, "a lot has gone right. Let me list the things that I think have gone our way. Tell me if you don't agree.

"First, we got to Calais in one piece. Yes, we missed making the contact and Vilet is suspicious, but we are still at-large and he is focused on me, not you. Second, we have Miss Yelverton, and that really was our goal all along. She is safe with us. Third, we have an opportunity to gather some information that would be of real help to our government." At number three, Chadwick ran out of ideas. He ended quietly with, "I agree we have problems, but I refuse to think that they are insolvable."

A motion to his side caught Chadwick's attention. He watched Georgina slip into the room and make her way to the fireplace. She sat quietly on the floor, leaning against Paddy's chair facing Chadwick but able to easily see Paddy, as well.

She glanced at both of them. "If you are going to be making plans, I think I should be part of this discussion," she said firmly.

"I am sorry we woke you. We did not mean to," Chadwick said. "You should be resting more than you have been."

"I will, I promise. But I cannot agree with you, Paddy, that nothing has gone right. I want you both to know, I need to tell both of you how grateful I am that you found me and rescued me. Paddy, do you know what those men were planning on doing to me?" Her voice almost cracked on the last word and Chadwick could hear the terror she had been holding in.

Paddy reached down and patted her shoulder. "Yes, George, I think we have a very good idea what was going on. No need to give us the details." He sighed and took a gulp of wine. "I didn't mean finding you, when I said nothing has gone right. I guess I am just worried we are going to get stuck here with no way out. I am not used to such responsibilities; I am just a simple soldier."

Chadwick grinned, remembering some of Paddy's quick responses in what were tight spots. "I don't think you are a 'simple' soldier, Paddy. You are showing a lot of initiative on this trip. I am assured I would have stumbled over myself and landed in gaol by now without you," he said. "But this is a good time to reevaluate our situation and how to go forward."

"What do you mean, forward?" Paddy asked.

"I bet he is thinking about what kind of information we need to gather to take back home," Georgina said unexpectedly. "And now we are going to figure out how to get that information."

She grinned triumphantly at Paddy, then grabbed his wine glass and took a big gulp. "That's for drinking my beer last night," she smirked.

Chadwick immediately started to protest, trying to sound firm, while speaking quietly so no one could overhear them. "No 'we' about it. You are *not* going to be involved. It's too dangerous."

"Of course I am," she returned blithely. "You have to go translate. Paddy and I can wander the streets and no one will look askance at us – just a young man and his retainer. Besides, by the time you get off your duties, it will be dark. How will you reconnoiter?"

Chadwick took a deep breath, ready to refute her logic, when Paddy interrupted.

"I think, sir, that George might have a good point. By myself, I might look suspicious, but who brings a lad along on a dangerous mission? Besides, you know his French is much better than mine. He will understand conversations I might miss."

Yesterday, having seen Georgina in daylight made him realize that she would never pass for a lowly servant. She just carried herself too well. She would have to be some merchants' offspring, maybe someone who wanted training. Yes, 'retainer' was a good word to describe her position. He laughed to himself, realizing he sounded like a school master taking his charges to the continent. Now that he thought about it, that was sort of what he was doing.

"The two of you are ganging up on me," he sighed. "Why don't you both go to bed, and let me think on it?"

Paddy stood, stretching up to his full height. He tossed off his wine and then grinned at Chadwick. "You just want the rest of the wine."

* * *

The next morning, the three companions stood in front of their rooming house and tried to decide the best route to the warehouse where Chadwick was due to take up translating duties. Jeffrey wanted Paddy and George to accompany him to his worksite so they would always know where to find him. But how to get there? The landlady had given them at least three possible ways, which only served to confuse them all. All Chadwick could clearly remember from yesterday was that the warehouse was near the water and the rooms they were in now were on some kind of a hill. Some spy! He thought with frustration, getting lost outside his rooming house. Before he could ask Paddy what he thought, a cheerful voice hailed them.

"Monsieur Couture!" Cuvelier's young lieutenant from yesterday hurried up the slope of the street. "I was just coming to escort you. The Captain wanted to be assured you did not get lost." His enthusiasm was engaging. "It is easy to get lost in this town. It is not large but it is tricky with the Upper Town and the Lower Town and lots of twisty streets."

The friendly officer removed his hat and bowed properly to Chadwick. He looked at Paddy and George. "I don't think we were properly introduced yesterday," he continued. "I am Lieutenant Jean Poulin."

"Ah, Lieutenant, well met. I really wasn't confident how to find my way back to the warehouse. We were going to head to the river and hope something looked familiar."

Chadwick shook the young man's hand. "May I introduce my associate, Patrick Cavanaugh, from Dublin? He is Irish, learning French and the wine trade at the same time. He is not too fluent just yet, but understands more than you might think."

Paddy and the brash young Lieutenant shook hands. Chadwick noted with interest they were both about the same age.

"This is George. We hired the lad in Calais to help us out but especially to help Paddy with his French."

Poulin even shook George's hand. To Chadwick's relief, he seemed to accept her without questioning Chadwick's explanation. On George's part, she said nothing except "Good morning" and stood slightly to the side of Paddy like a good retainer.

The Lieutenant led them through the maze of streets, ever downward until they reached a medieval wall.

"They say this wall was built on Roman ruins." Poulin had kept up a running commentary on the various sights they passed and never seemed to run out of things to discuss. Chadwick decided that he might be a good source of information. That is, if he knew anything that would be useful. For the time being, his guided tour of Boulogne was proving to be very valuable.

"There are three sections of the town. The Old Town, where your rooms are, was built on the Roman ruins. During the Medieval times, they put up a wall around the Old Town that incorporates part of a castle and some towers. I always say, you can tell you are in Old Town when you get breathless from climbing up from the Lower Town," he grinned cheekily at Chadwick. "Wait, Monsieur Couture, until you see the stairs."

"Stairs? We didn't use any stairs yesterday to get to the rooms."

"We were in a carriage, monsieur. These stairs are not for horses. Yesterday we took the long way around the town; this is a more direct way, but only for pedestrians."

Sure enough, when they reached the wall and could see the Lower Town laid out beneath them, they saw a long length of stairs, zig-zagging down the hillside. Poulin stopped at the top of the stairs to continue his monologue about the town. He was pointing out the warehouse where the translating company was stationed when Chadwick's gaze was caught by another sight. He glanced at Paddy and George to see if they also had spotted what grabbed his attention. George was looking back at him, huge eyes open in recognition of what they were seeing. Paddy just stared.

Chadwick cleared his throat, preparing to interrupt the Lieutenant's discourse.

"Excuse me, Lieutenant," he said cautiously. "Those boats, over there," he pointed to the river. "For the invasion?"

"Oh, yes," Poulin answered confidently. "Isn't that some sight? The ship builders are moving right along. Boulogne is a major fishing port, but the fishermen have had to move to make way for all this." He waved an arm to encompass the massive ship-building efforts that had stunned his audience into silence.

"We should be moving along. The Captain will be looking for us." He blithely led them to the top of the stairs. "Watch your step now; the steps can be slippery in the morning."

Besides being careful not to slip, they had to dodge vendors balancing baskets of vegetables and bread, a milk maid carrying empty pails on a yoke, and various other tradesmen going about their business. When they finally reached the Lower Town, the number of military men increased. Chadwick followed what he quickly noted was the local practice of letting them have the right of way. At one particularly busy intersection, they had to flatten themselves against a building while several mounted officers nonchalantly rode down the street with total indifference for anyone else in the area. Chadwick was just glad it wasn't his boots splattered with horse dung.

The warehouse that was their destination proved to be near the river. The Lieutenant had guided them on a different route from the day before, but Chadwick could see how using the stairs between the Upper and Lower towns was quicker and more direct.

Captain Cuvelier greeted him enthusiastically. "Monsieur Couture," he cried when Chadwick finally made it to his office. "I am so glad you are here. How are your accommodations? Are they satisfactory?" After the usual greetings, handshakes, and assurances that the rooms were more than adequate, Chadwick stepped aside to talk to Paddy and George.

"When I see you later, Paddy, I expect you to know at least five new words and their proper use," he said. "Return in the afternoon so we can go back together. Do not get lost," he cautioned.

He watched as the two joined the crowds in the streets. When they were lost to sight, he turned back to Cuvelier.

"So, Captain, how can I help you?"

As it turned out, the Captain really needed help. As he explained to Chadwick, the French did not generally feel the need to learn languages of other countries. This was true even of the ones that they conquered. There were a number of citizens who spoke two languages but they usually lived on the French border of Germany or Italy. Since there was no land border with England, fewer spoke English and those who did generally used it only for social occasions. The Captain had had a hard time finding anyone who could translate technical terms for military use.

He handed Chadwick a stack of papers with lists of terms. After a quick scan, Chadwick could tell they were generally terms identifying items aboard a naval ship, armaments, and other military items. He could make quick work of them, but was that a good thing? He had decided that they needed to stay in Boulogne until he had a handle on the threatened invasion.

"Captain, what will these lists be used for?" he asked.

"The generals assume we will be taking over a number of British war ships during the invasion. Our men need to be able to give orders to the existing crews so they can understand the commands."

"Rather a big assumption that the crews will be willing to take orders."

"I am assured the alternative to not taking orders will be more unpleasant," Captain Cuvelier answered cheerfully. "Can you work on these lists?"

Chadwick nodded cautiously. He had an idea that would draw this project out indefinitely. "How about pictures?" he asked.

Cuvelier looked confused. "Pictures?"

"Yes, I doubt that many of the men on British war ships are literate. Also, they might pretend to not know what our man means, even if he has learned the English word for say a…" he glanced at the paper and selected a word at random, "howitzer. If there was a picture, the Englishman couldn't say he didn't understand. Additionally, it will be easier to teach our side what the item should look like."

Once he had articulated the idea out loud, he immediately thought of a reason it was not particularly useful. Having just fought your way onto a vessel, you could not very well whip out a booklet from your back pocket to look up words. Oh, well, he only needed the Captain to buy the idea. It didn't have to be realistic.

"Let me think about it," the Captain responded. "Pictures could be very useful. Can you draw them?"

"I can handle simple outlines. For more elaborate items, that young chap, George, has some sketching skills." After all, wasn't sketching *de rigueur* for all properly brought-up young women? He only hoped she had paid attention during lessons.

Captain Cuvelier proved to be remarkably appreciative of Chadwick's efforts. At regular intervals, he had coffee served, and when Paddy and George did not come back for lunch, he insisted that Chadwick accompany him to his favorite tavern where he picked up the bill.

The Captain spent most of his time teaching basic English words to various groups that came and went throughout the day. Chadwick wondered how the Captain could contain his frustration with these unwilling students. They were obviously ordered to be there and paid little attention to the lesson. Chadwick heard one group laughing as they went out, saying that the only words they really needed to know pertained to women and how to order wine. He laughed to himself as he thought of them finding out what the same wine they paid pennies for in France cost in England.

The afternoon wore on as he studied his lists of terms and decided which would benefit from having a sketch attached to it. He needed to ask Paddy for help with some of the more obscure naval terms. The lad should know them from the years he had spent with Byrne. He made a short list to take home to discuss with Paddy.

But by the end of the afternoon, Paddy and George still had not made an appearance and Chadwick was beginning to become concerned. Cuvelier came over to thank him and make sure he would be back in the morning. As they shook hands, Chadwick mentioned that he was just waiting for his associates, who were supposed to meet him for the return journey to their lodgings.

"I have not seen Monsieur Cavanaugh, but your young assistant is over there by the outside door," the Captain said.

Chadwick could now see George just inside the door, pressed against the wall in the shadows. He shrugged into his coat quickly and strode over. ...

"George," he anxiously surveyed her pale face. "What is wrong and where is Paddy?"

She seemed to have difficulty catching her breath.

"He's here, Jeffrey. Here in Boulogne!" She answered in a harsh whisper, similar to the way her voice had sounded when he first found her. She must be getting more comfortable with him if she called him by his Christian name… or so shocked she wasn't aware of what she was doing. At least she was still speaking French. Another part of him realized he really liked the way she pronounced his name in French. It had a nice ring.

Her hand reached out and clutched his sleeve, bringing him back to the present.

Chadwick gave a quick look around to see if Cuvelier was observing them, but the Captain had gone into his office and seemed to be shutting down for the day. Jeffrey took George's arm and led her to a sheltered spot by the side of the warehouse. Not the best smelling place but at least not in the chaos of the afternoon activity in the area.

"Who, George? Who are you speaking about?"

"Hastings!" she all but spat out his name. "We saw him riding a horse down the street like he owned it."

Chapter Eleven: Boulogne

"Did he see you?" he demanded.

"I don't know," she gasped. "I don't think so." Chadwick could see her large eyes were awash in tears that she was only just keeping from pouring out. "Paddy sent me here to find you while he followed him."

He put his hand on her shoulder to offer some comfort and that seemed to break the dam. She started sobbing and practically threw herself into his arms. Although his instinct was to hold her tightly, he forced himself to grab her arms to keep her at a proper distance just as the door to the warehouse opened. Captain Cuvelier de Trie stepped out. He raised his eyebrows inquiringly as he looked at Chadwick.

"Trouble?" he asked as he nodded at George.

Chadwick forced a grimace. "Homesick," he said shortly, trying to sound exasperated instead of concerned. "I'll take him back to the rooms and make him get a good night's sleep." He patted George on the shoulder and went to stand near the Captain.

George faced the wall and Chadwick could hear that she was desperately trying to conquer her fears and get her emotions under control. He stepped back to hand her his handkerchief. "Here, lad. Get a grip. Wash your face. You don't want to walk about the streets like that. Someone would think I beat you."

"Children," the Captain said sympathetically. "First time away from home? It can be hard, if I remember rightly. I didn't much like getting sent to school."

Chadwick watched George walk to the public fountain and dip the handkerchief in the water and wipe her face. He turned back to the Captain with a shrug.

"Maybe I hired him too quickly. Vilet had ordered me to Boulogne the next day and I didn't have time to check references. The landlady knew the family and until now he seemed fine." He paused as he watched George come slowly back to them. He noticed with approval that her stride was still in character, even if her eyes were red.

"I will give him a few more days before I send him home. Maybe he will settle down."

George had reached them and stood forlornly at his side clutching the sodden cloth. "Please forgive me, Monsieur Couture. I don't know what came over me. I am fine, it won't happen again," the words came out rapidly. Even as distressed as she was, her French still sounded perfect to his ears.

"It's all right, lad," he responded. "Let's go get some dinner."

He turned to the Captain and offered his hand again. "Good night again, Captain. I will see you in the morning."

"As will I. Good evening to you, sir. Good work today."

"Thank you, Captain." Chadwick and George turned away and started to retrace their route of the morning.

"Where did you see Hastings?" he asked her quietly. At her confusion, he asked another question. "Upper or Lower Town? Was it on any of the streets we walked this morning?"

"Oh, no, sir. It was closer to the river."

"Good. Then you don't think we need to avoid any of the streets we took to get here?" They were at the steps leading to the Upper Town. Although there was no reason to think Hastings could identify him, he didn't want to meet the man just then. There was too much of a possibility that he might recognize George in such close quarters.

"He was on horseback," she said quietly. "I am sorry I was so shocked that I froze and then just fell apart."

"What did Paddy do?" Judging by the way she was having so much trouble talking coherently, Chadwick thought she was still in shock. He stepped up the pace to reach their rooms more quickly, hoping she would feel safer inside.

"Paddy was wonderful," she gasped. Her breath seemed to be coming in pants. Then he realized she was having trouble keeping up.

"Wait, don't talk until we get to the top," he ordered.

When they finally reached the top, she practically bent over trying to catch her breath. He waited until she could breathe easily. As she straightened up, he took a good look at her face. She looked to him to be too pale. Damn, he kept forgetting the trauma she had been through and now she had spent the day tramping around when she should have been resting.

He started towards the rooms at a much slower pace. Now that he was watching her carefully, he noticed she was limping badly but trying to cover it up. He flashed back to the condition of her feet and realized they could not have healed in that short a time. Another wave of guilt hit him as he appreciated the extent to which he had forgotten her physical condition.

"Just a bit farther now and we will get you off your feet," he said. "They must be bothering you a lot."

She nodded miserably. "I won't mind sitting down, but I expect I have some duties I need to finish."

"Don't worry, I will let it be known you have twisted your ankle and are incapacitated." She hobbled a few more steps until he couldn't take it any longer.

"Look this is not going to be classy, but..." and he grabbed her left arm, bent it, and put his shoulder under her arm. He hoisted her up so that her head dangled down on his back while he steadied her with an arm across her legs.

She grunted and started to protest, "Monsieur...I can make it..."

"Shut up, George." He was surprised at how light she was. He would have preferred to carry her in his arms, but he was pretty confident that would cause more interest than he was willing to risk right now. In a short time, they were at the house. Unfortunately, their landlady was on the steps gossiping with a neighbor when they arrived.

"Monsieur, what has happened?" she gasped.

"Twisted ankle," Chadwick managed to reply. "Could you open the door?"

At the top of the stairs, he set George down carefully and opened the door to their room. With his help, she limped into the room and slumped into the chair by the fireplace, closing her eyes in relief and resting her head against the back of the chair. Chadwick thought with appreciation that George had picked the chair that had its back to the doorway so Madame could not see her face. He was also impressed that she had managed to keep her hat on while hanging upside down his back. Even now she also did not remove it.

"Do you need me to send for a doctor, monsieur?" the landlady asked from the doorway.

Chadwick pulled off one of George's boots and pretended to prod the foot. George gave a fairly realistic moan.

"No, Madame. I believe it is not broken only badly wrenched. If it was broken, he would be screaming." He looked up in time to see George looking askance at him. He shook his head slightly to keep her from screaming and said rapidly, "We will soak it and wrap it up. He will be fine."

"Then you will want some hot water," the landlady insisted. "Your other man is not here?" Obviously, she wasn't going to carry it up, Chadwick thought sardonically.

"I sent him on an errand before this one took a fall. I will come down in a few minutes for the water. Do you have any balm that could keep the swelling down?"

She raised her eyebrows at him. "That will be extra."

"Of course, Madame."

By the time he returned with a pail of hot water, balm, and a pot of tea, George had taken off her boots and socks and rolled up her pants. At that point exhaustion must have set in; she still wore her outside coat and hat. In fact, she seemed asleep and barely moved when he closed the door.

"George, I am putting your feet in hot water," he warned. The only response was a moan of approval as the warm water covered her feet. He poured a cup of tea and set it on the small table next to her chair.

"Lean forward, let's take off the coat. I think it is warm enough inside."

She leaned so that he could remove the coat and finally opened her eyes. She pulled off her hat and dropped it on the floor. Finally, she ran her fingers through the short curls making them even more riotous.

"I am such a mess," she moaned. "I can hardly walk fast enough to keep up with you and my feet are so bruised I can't think about anything else."

She wrapped her hands around the tea cup and breathed its scent deeply. "I wasn't always this way."

"I know," he sympathized. "I am sorry I haven't been making it any easier for you. You seem so fit, I keep forgetting what a bad time you have just gone through."

He leaned back in his chair and sipped his own tea. He glanced at the fireplace and noticed with relief that someone had cleaned out last night's ashes and set fresh kindling in place. Weather in France was as changeable as in England, reminding him of the saying that you could experience a year's worth of weather in one day. He quickly lit the fire and the room started to warm.

He laid a cloth across his knees and reached for one of Georgina's feet. "Let me see how bad the damage is," he said. She must have been dozing as, at his words, she jerked up.

"No, no, it's fine! I can take care of them. I will put the balm on them."

"Peace, please, George," he said sternly. "Let me see your feet. Think of me as your commanding officer. I need to know what condition my men are in. And you don't want your feet to become inflamed or infected."

"Commanding officer?" she almost chuckled. "And I thought you were a wine merchant."

He grimaced as he grasped her ankle and raised the foot to his lap. "I do seem to get my roles confused sometimes," he admitted. "Right now, I am a medic." He frowned as he surveyed the bottom of her foot. It was a mass of bruises, with several blisters and one openly weeping cut. He gently took the other foot out of the water and found it to be in a similar condition. He sighed deeply.

"You are right. You are a bit of a mess." He replaced both feet in the bucket.

"Drink your tea while I see what Madame can give us in the way of some bandages." He refilled her cup before he left to consult with their landlady.

He returned to find Georgina sitting with one foot in the bucket and the other leg folded so she could peer at the bottom. She was frowning unhappily.

She glanced up at him.

"How am I going to pose as a boy if I cannot get around?" she asked quietly.

"Even boys get hurt and sprain things, you know. I remember a number of days spent in bed because I hurt some part or the other. Don't worry about it. I brought more water." He set another steaming bucket at her feet then laid the bandages and cloths on the small table. He pushed the first bucket slightly to the side and then returned to his chair.

"Put your feet back in that. I want to make certain they are clean before we bandage them. How did you ever get through today walking on those cobblestones?" he asked.

She shrugged. "By the end of the day, I have to admit I could not really think of anything else." She replaced her feet with a low sound of pleasure. "That does feel good," she admitted.

"Well, this part is going to sting. I need to wash them and the soap looks a little harsh."

"I can do that," she argued.

"Just sit there. We have gone through this before. It is the commanding officer's responsibility to look after his men," Chadwick said in his most proper voice. He hoped she got the fact he was quoting his own former commanding officer.

"By washing their feet?" she asked sardonically.

"No, this is a first," he responded. He grinned at her suddenly. "But this trip has been full of firsts, so just sit back and let's get this over with."

He took one foot and carefully soaped it, trying hard not to cause her any more distress, although by her grimace he could tell it wasn't much fun. He worked quickly, dunking the soaped foot into the first bucket and then back into the hot water.

"If you have never done this before, how do you know what to do?" she grunted.

"I had to deal with some nasty wounds when I was in the army. Medics never seemed to be around when you needed them."

"Where?" she gasped as he dealt with her second foot. Obviously she wanted to keep the conversation going to distract herself from his scouring.

"I was stationed in Ireland during the uprising. I hated it, so I sold out and found other work." Both feet were now soaking in the hot water while he retrieved the balm and bandages.

He looked at her with interest. He wondered if he had ever really looked at her before. She sat there in her boys' clothing, soaking her feet in a bucket without any of the histrionics he imagined a female of her class would normally pitch. What had happened to her over the past few weeks must be so far from her realm of experience. He wondered with amazement how she was managing to hold it together. There was strength in that thin frame, he realized.

"How old are you, George?" he asked. Since she had finished school, he assumed she was in her late teens, but he really knew very little about her.

Mostly only what others, her father and brother, had told him, and it wasn't much. Surprisingly, he found he wanted to know more.

"I am almost twenty-three," she said to his surprise. With her short hair and boyish clothes, she looked so much younger, fifteen or sixteen. "I stayed longer at school than my friends when my mother died. Since I was in mourning, I could at least help out with the younger girls while I continued my studies."

He thought again of the traumatic experiences she had gone through, and yet here she sat, seemingly calm and anxious to keep up her disguise. He had to admit she was really good at her disguise. Other than the one teary breakdown at the warehouse, she had stayed in character and had not once slipped up and used English. She probably would make a better spy than he would.

"Where did you learn your French?" he asked.

"I always had French governesses and then the French teacher at school was very good." She smiled at a memory. "I got a prize once for being able to go the longest without speaking English; I lasted almost a week."

"I wonder if my sister would benefit from school," he speculated. "She doesn't seem to like staying at home with our step-mother."

"Step-mother probably doesn't like her much, either," Georgina murmured.

"What do you mean?" he asked.

"Step-daughters always make step-mothers look older than they want to look. Or they take attention away from them or something. It never seems to be a good relationship. My mother and Walter never got along either," she said.

As he thought about what she said, Chadwick smeared the balm on his fingers and started to work the lotion into her foot, trying to avoid the cut that ran across the sole. It didn't look deep enough to need to be sewn shut, for which he was grateful, as there was little skin to overlap for stitches. He glanced at her face to find her eyes now half-shut.

"Does this pain you?" he asked.

"No," she responded quietly. "It feels fine, better than fine, really. Thank you for doing this."

He ran his fingers under her toes and worked the balm in between them. Then he rubbed the balm into each toe, sliding his thumb from the base to the tip. Glancing at her face to see if she was being truthful that he wasn't hurting her, he saw that although her eyes were closed, her brows were forming a small frown. Was she in pain? He worked the balm into the arch and ankle. No, that pain didn't seem to cause the frown as it smoothed when he stopped the massage and started wrapping the foot.

But her cheeks seemed flushed. Oh no, he hoped she was not getting a fever. But he noticed the flush faded as he padded the bottom of the foot with a folded cloth held in place with a bandage. He picked up the other foot.

"How come you are not married?" he asked, more to keep the conversation going than because he cared about the answer.

"Lack of opportunity, I suppose. I was in school, then my mother died, and now this." She gave a deep sigh and her eyes opened. "Now I guess I won't be marrying anyone once they hear about this disaster. Everyone will assume I am a ruined woman. I hope my father provides for me. I do not look forward to keeping house for that idiot brother of mine."

"About that brother," Chadwick began. He continued to rub her foot as he thought about how he wanted to phrase his question. "I met him, you know, when I was investigating in Dublin."

"Charming, isn't he?" she responded, the sarcasm plain in her voice.

He grinned back at her; his fingers were working their way down each toe. "He did seem to think well of himself."

Her feet were like refined pieces of sculpture. Shocked, he suddenly found himself wondering about the rest of her body. Was it as delicately formed? He must have seen a great deal of her the night he found her, but he couldn't remember anything. Keeping his hand on her ankle, he leaned back and looked into her face.

"He certainly has an affinity for fashion statements if his waistcoat is indicative of his usual attire," Chadwick joked. "I only had one interaction with him so I cannot say I know him well. He seemed concerned." He really did not want to tell her how shocked and unable to function her father had seemed. She probably wouldn't be too happy about how her brother had taken charge. "He came by the Castle a lot to discover any news. Well, I can't blame him for the visiting," he added thoughtfully. "It must have been a very frustrating situation for both men."

"Well, it must be the first time in his life he was inquisitive about me," she said. "All my life, all I remember from him is either 'go away' or 'why don't you just disappear'?"

"You are an adult now, so presumably his attitude is different. To me, he seemed very concerned for your safety, as when he ordered you to take the carriage instead of walking."

Chadwick studied her foot to see how much bandaging he should put on. At least this foot did not have any open cuts. He still padded the sole before wrapping the bandage around it. "We'll soak your feet again tomorrow after you spend a day laying around resting," he told her. "This foot has a nasty cut that could go bad easily. I want to keep an eye on it."

He also had to admit how reluctant he was to end their intimate time together. He took a deep breath.

"Now, tell me about seeing Hastings and in what direction Paddy took off. If he is not back soon, I may have to go searching."

She gasped guiltily. "Oh, my," she said in a panic. "I almost forgot about him. You made my feet feel so much better."

"Just tell me what happened," he said calmly.

"Paddy thought we should investigate the port area, so we headed to the river after we left you. We decided we should look like travelers out for a stroll and not try to investigate or get too close to anything we were told not to look at."

Chadwick nodded in agreement. He had no idea how he would get anyone released if they got arrested.

"Oddly enough, the French do not seem to be keeping the boatbuilding a secret. Honestly, it is hard to see how they could, the construction is everywhere. Everywhere..." her voice faded off as she thought about what she had seen.

"And?" he prompted.

"Well, Paddy didn't want us to get caught gawking, so we kept going up the bluff. Now mind you, all this time I was teaching him French words. I wonder if he learned anything. Anyway, up the hill there are some more buildings that look really new. We couldn't get too close to them, but they looked important."

A knock at the door heralded the voice of their landlady.

"Monsieur Couture, dinner is served!"

Chadwick stood and rolled down his shirt sleeves before donning his jacket. Madame set a proper table and he didn't want to shock her by showing up in his shirt sleeves. He looked down at Georgina. "I will have some food sent up, just stay in the chair and look pathetic."

"That I can do."

He grabbed the two buckets and went out the door only to smack into Paddy.

"Evening, sir. Did I make it back in time for dinner?" Paddy asked cheekily. "I really hope so. I am famished."

"Good timing on your part. I am just going down now," Chadwick said. "Here, take one of these buckets with you when you come down."

Dinner seemed interminable; Madame was starved for conversation, or maybe for an audience. But the food was good, with some dishes bordering on excellent. It was hard to miss Paddy's enthusiasm for the pork loin, and Jeffrey thought the fish sauce particularly tasty. Madame seemed especially generous with the wine. Chadwick began to wonder if she had some ulterior motive. Was she reporting on them to someone like Vilet? He made a point of keeping the conversation general, but after deflecting a few of her more personal questions, he began to talk about his need to get to Bordeaux to fulfill his commissions.

* * *

"That was the best meal on this trip," Paddy swore as he pulled a chair up to the fireplace. "I think I want to marry the cook."

Georgina, who had been dozing by the fire as Chadwick had directed, came fully awake and demanded to know what Paddy was talking about. Paddy described some of the dishes with enthusiasm.

"Oh, my tray had some of them also. You are right, the food was delicious. I ate so much, I dozed off in front of the fire, just like my papa," she laughed.

Chadwick nodded in agreement. "It was pretty amazing. I got the impression from Captain Cuvelier that the meals would be much more basic. Certainly not the feast she put on tonight. Very odd, don't you think?"

Paddy looked at him in astonishment and started to laugh. Then Georgina started to chuckle also.

"What? What am I missing?" he demanded.

Paddy continued to guffaw, but Georgina looked at him seriously.

"Do you not have any idea how women react to you?"

Chadwick could feel the flush start up his neck.

"Well, I know they don't run screaming away," he said stiffly.

Paddy snickered and interjected, "George, you should have seen her. Dress cut down to here, hung on his every word and the disappointment when we left together to come upstairs...I think from now on it will be bread and water for us."

"Oh come on, Paddy," he protested. "It was not that obvious. Was it?"

"I feel sorry for her," Georgina said. "She is a widow and probably lonesome, and along comes this," she gestured to Chadwick, "totally acceptable man. Now she is probably furious and feeling rejected. I bet we get tossed out tomorrow," she added with a grin at Paddy.

Chadwick looked at them incredulously.

"You can't be serious," he began and then thought back to the dinner. Oh, no. He had been so caught up with thoughts of their own situation, Georgina's feet, and what news Paddy had of Hastings that he had completely overlooked Madame's attempts at flirtation. She had been asking some rather personal questions.

He sighed deeply and looked at his companions. "What now?"

Paddy shrugged and shook his head.

"Drop the name of your betrothed back in New Orleans," George said.

"Do you think that will help?" he asked.

"Probably not, but what else can you do?"

"I will see tomorrow if the Captain can find us other quarters," he said in a flat voice. What else could go wrong? An infatuated landlady was as bad as one spying on them. It was dangerous either way. He groaned internally and said, "Paddy, tell me what you learned today. George told me her side, so start with seeing Hastings; we can go back to the shipbuilding later."

Paddy proved to be quite an observer and storyteller. Chadwick figured that the lad had spent about three hours trailing Hastings and he took almost a third of that to retell the tale. It proved to be quite the epic, at least from Paddy's point of view.

It had been obvious to Paddy that George's feet were giving her grief and he had been about to call off their wanderings when a party of horsemen trotted down the street, shoving the pedestrians out of the way. He had not recognized anyone of course, but George's reaction, – however much she tried to remain calm – had alerted him. He had pulled George into a doorway and stood in front of her as the men rode by. Once she had identified one of the riders as Hastings, he immediately sent George to find 'Monsieur Couture' and set off after the horsemen.

Although it was late afternoon, the sun was still bright, so Paddy had to keep fairly far behind them to avoid being noticed. Ironically, he found the fresh feces of the horses to be rather helpful. Generally, the streets were cleaned quickly of horse dung, but today, clean up behind Hastings' party wasn't that swift, and enough was left behind to allow Paddy to follow them to an inn at the edges of town.

"I found them on the side of town, George, where we saw the new buildings on the bluff."

"Not where we stopped for lunch?" she asked.

"No, but near there. This one looked more hoity-toity. But the ostler was pretty horse-proud when I finally got him to chat. It seems Napoleon stays at the inn when he is in town and this chap really likes taking care of his nag although he had some fancy name for him which I didn't understand."

"Paddy, how did you get him to talk to you?" Chadwick asked surprised. "Could he speak English?"

"No, sir, but George here has been working hard on my words. I have enough French, to admire a horse and ask the name of a tavern. And the name Napoleon is the same in both languages, right?"

"That is pretty simplistic, Paddy. Don't you think that someone with a pronounced accent asking questions about horses would get attention?" "Of course it would," Paddy replied reasonably. "I told him I was an Irish sailor that got left here and I was looking for some work until I could find a ship home."

"That's true, monsieur," Georgina interrupted. "We worked on the story all morning in case Paddy had to ask questions or give an account of himself."

"The chap was clear that there were no jobs, but the tavern's name is *La Vielle Alliance* and I followed Hastings right to it. In fact, I saw his horse in the stable waiting to be attended to. After that, I just hung around a bit to see if they were going to leave, but it looked like they were there for the night."

"When you say 'they,' how many do you mean?"

Paddy frowned in thought. "About ten."

"Was Hastings the leader? Did they wear uniforms?"

"No, I would not say Hastings was the leader. Another chap, thin face with beaky nose, had the lead as they rode down the street. But Hastings was at his side and they were chatting like old friends."

Paddy looked at Georgina again. "Uniforms?" he asked.

"No, I don't think so," she responded. "Well, maybe not real uniforms, but their coats were all sort of dull green and identical. Maybe they are volunteers who got their own outfits together," she suggested.

"Sorry, sir, there was too much street noise to hear anything."

Paddy's face lit up as he remembered something. "Wait, the ostler at the stable did make a joke – at least I think it was a joke – that I sounded like the bunch that just came in. So maybe they were Irish, come to volunteer or something."

"Or something is right," Chadwick agreed.

Chapter Twelve: Boulogne

Chadwick lit the kindling in the fireplace and watched to make sure it caught. It had been a long, dreary, rainy day and his head ached from poring over documents all day in a dim room with inadequate lighting. The smell of the cheap candles didn't help, either. Dinner tonight had been far different than the night before with only soup and bread offered. He had been relieved when Madame Traver had not made an appearance, leaving only Paddy and him to eat rapidly and retire as soon as possible to their rooms.

The weather had continued to cool and with the rain, the rooms seemed damp. He added a small log to the kindling. The fireplace was so small it barely heated the sitting area much less the bedroom. He estimated he could fit only two pieces of wood in it at a time. The servants, whose rooms he surmised Madame was renting out, must spend some cold winters up here if it was this chilly in late spring.

Chadwick sank in 'his' chair. There had been some unspoken agreement that of the two chairs with backs, one chair was for him. No one even tried to sit in it that he could see. This expedition might be falling apart in his opinion, but his two companions seemed to have confidence in him as a leader. He sighed as and surveyed Paddy and George sitting across from him.

As per his orders, Georgina had spent the day resting with her feet up, but he thought she might still be in pain. He had noticed that although she was wide awake, there were small lines by her mouth making her face seem drawn and pale. The expression seemed to support his supposition. He reminded himself to recheck her feet.

Paddy sat with his head resting on the back of his chair. He looked and acted exhausted. There had been a quiet squabble over who got the other good chair, a discussion that Georgina won by the simple expediency of announcing that she had sat in the chair all day and needed a change. Then she plopped herself on the floor between the two chairs facing the fireplace. He poured some wine for each from the bottle he had liberated from the dinner table. "Well, George, did you find anything to do today?" he asked.

She shook her head slowly. "No, not really. I did peek around downstairs to see if Madame had any books, but I didn't find anything to read." She stretched her bandaged feet to the fire and sighed. "There are really only so many naps you can take to pass the time. I spent most of the day just thinking."

"Poor you," Paddy groused. "I get to run all over town and risk my neck…"

"Paddy!" Chadwick interrupted sharply. "That's not called for."

"Oh, don't worry, sir, I am just teasing." He turned to Georgina, who was looking amused. "You know that, right?" Paddy asked her.

"Of course I do," she responded. "And if he wasn't teasing, I wouldn't blame him. I felt pretty guilty sitting around all day and not doing anything constructive. I did spend some time sketching."

Chadwick looked at her with pleased surprise. He hadn't known for sure that she could sketch but if she could, it would help him gain the trust of Captain Cuvelier. Admittedly, he should not be surprised. His sister had informed him that all proper young ladies were given instruction in sketching and sometimes painting with water colors. "You'll have to show me after we hear Paddy's report. We didn't discuss much over dinner, as I was afraid Madame might be lurking around, but I have an idea how your sketching might help with the translating."

"Madame Traver didn't join you?" she asked.

Paddy chuckled as Chadwick said, "No thankfully. Just Paddy and myself at the table." He could see his two companions exchange conspiratorial grins. Georgina turned an innocent gaze at him.

"All I had for dinner was soup and bread. The stable lad brought it up. What did you get for dinner?" she asked.

Paddy laughed outright. "The same. She must be really angry at him."

"Oh, please," Chadwick groaned. "We have a lot more problems than whether the landlady likes me or not."

"Sorry to correct you sir, but it could be a real problem. You know the old truism: nothing like a woman scorned, or something like that," Paddy said seriously. "We don't really want her taking too much of an interest in us, either. When I think of the things my sisters would get up to if they thought a fellow wasn't treating them right…Well, it's enough to curl your hair." He took a sip of wine and asked, "Did you ask the translating chap you are working for if there was another place we could stay?"

Chadwick groaned, "Nothing else available. I didn't have much time to talk to him; he was very busy with messengers coming and going. Rather top-level messengers it looked to me, there was lots of braid and stuff on their uniforms." His voice trailed off in thought as he sipped his own glass.

Georgina cleared her throat, catching his attention. He looked at her inquisitively.

"Better get Paddy's story before he falls asleep in the chair," she prompted.

"Oh, right, Paddy, look alive. Tell us what you found today," he prompted. Paddy's glass was empty and his eyes were closed. He nudged Paddy's foot with his own boot. "Wakey, wakey."

Paddy shook his head, trying to wake up. "Right, yes, it was a long day." He looked sadly into his empty glass and glanced hopefully at the bottle, but it, too, was empty. With a sigh, he rubbed the sides of his face, trying to get his thoughts in order. "As you remember, George, I walked monsieur to the warehouse. We decided I should get the lay of the town. We saw most of it yesterday, as your feet can no doubt still feel, but there are certainly parts we might need to know better. Also while I was wandering about, Captain thought if I could get an idea of the size of the scheme that is going on here, it would be a good thing. And, of course, I should do this while not looking as if I was doing anything suspicious."

"Of course," Georgina answered seriously. "I am positive no one would recognize you with that red hair."

Paddy grimaced. "No doubt that hair is going to get me in trouble some-time, but monsieur bought me a hat remember? I pulled it down low so little of the red was sticking out."

"Good," she nodded approvingly. "Go on, what did you do all day?"

"I walked. I walked the Upper Town, I walked the Lower Town and I walked the port. Why do you think I am so tired?"

"And?" Chadwick prompted.

"It's smallish. It's cramped. Prices for food are ridiculous and the army is everywhere." Paddy stood and stretched his back. He then put another log on the fire and returned to his seat. "Since I was in the Lower Town by the warehouse, I started there. This is a port town, so most of the lower area, near the quay supports the port. There are warehouses along the street you are on and more by the quay. There are many shops selling marine or shipping supplies and a huge number of taverns. Because that part of the town follows the flow of the river, I don't think there is a straight street anywhere."

Chadwick said thoughtfully, "It's an old town. I am pretty confident that England claimed it when this part of France was English some centuries ago. It is not the closest to England however – that would be Calais. So why all the activity? All of it devoted to the invasion?" he asked.

Paddy nodded. "There is no doubt it is an invasion force. There seems to be no secret. And really when you think of it, how could you keep it a secret? If you could see the port, you would see what I mean. Remember yesterday, from the stairs, we all saw boats along the docks?"

Georgina nodded. "Yes, there were a lot of boats there. Some were finished and some were not. Were those the boats to take the soldiers to England?"

"I think so," Paddy responded. "And from the way they were pounding away, I would say they are in a hurry to get ready."

"What do you mean? Where did you see all of this work going on?"

"After I walked around the Lower Town, I started on the port side. Now that is a large space. I would estimate the port is easily the size of the town. It stretches up and down the river and on both sides of the river," Paddy explained. "Everywhere you look, there is construction mainly of these flat sort of boats. I think they must take the finished ones somewhere, as all I could see were boats under construction."

"Did no one stop you or ask what you were doing?" Chadwick asked in concern.

Paddy shook his head. "As far as I could see, no one paid me any mind. I wandered about, but I tried not to stay and gawk. I tried to look as if I had a destination, like I was supposed to be there."

"Good man," Chadwick approved. A thought occurred to him. "How do you think we can make an estimate of the number of boats?"

"I bet you could get a good idea of the size of the army simply by asking your translator captain," Georgina spoke up suddenly. "Then all we need to know is how many soldiers are supposed to fit on a boat."

"Good idea, George," Paddy said approvingly, while Chadwick nodded thoughtfully. If he could get that information, their ability to relay reliable information would take a big step forward. But again, that brought him back to their biggest hurdle.

"How are we going to get back to England with this information?" he mused out loud. "Well, we can think about that tomorrow. Anything else about the town you discovered, Paddy?"

"I spent so much time on the port that I didn't spend much time on the Upper Town. I did notice a huge castle that seems to be used by the army, with lots of military types wandering about there. There is an old wall around the Upper Town, but you know that from using the steps that go down one side of the wall. I guess most people live on this hill, lots of houses and people moving about. But again, military types at all the taverns and food places."

"Good work, Paddy," Chadwick commended. "Best go off to bed; you look all in. We can talk more tomorrow. I'll bank the fire before turning in." He sat for a time, thinking about what Paddy had reported before turning to Georgina, who was still sitting on the floor. "Have a seat," he gestured to the chair Paddy had vacated. "Let's see how those feet are doing."

"I wondered when you would get to me," she smiled. "You never seem to forget anything." She sat in the chair and stretched her feet out.

"I know you had to make some trips to the back yard," he said. "How did you keep these bandages so clean?"

"I wore those wooden clogs you bought me. Without backs, they are a lot easier to slip on than the boots." She nodded to the door where the clogs were neatly lined up by the door with her boots. "I made certain I limped a lot in case anyone was watching."

Chadwick grinned as he retrieved the balm from the fireplace mantle. He started to unwrap the bandages. "You are quite the actress," he noted. "But how do you really feel? I want an honest answer. What do you think you are up for doing? It is not going to help any of us if you think you are up to more than you really are."

"Honestly better," she said.

Chadwick studied her now bandage free feet, picking each one up to view the heel and bottom. "Well, they look better, but the bruises and blisters are still there," he noted. "How are the rest of your bruises progressing?" He held one delicate ankle and began to apply the balm, starting at the toes and smoothing the cream slowly down each toe.

Georgina gave a small jerk when his fingers reached the sole of her foot.

"Sorry, did that hurt?" he asked anxiously. "The cut is on the other foot."

"No, it just surprised me," she said.

Chadwick glanced at her face again to see she was not biting her lips. "Are you positive this isn't hurting?"

"No, monsieur, it feels rather good. I was just surprised. I thought it would hurt but it didn't."

"While we are in private like this, I think you could call me Jeffrey, monsieur seems so formal." He realized he wanted to hear her say his name again in the French way. He liked the way she said it. Before she could reply, he said, "Tell me what you thought about all day. You said you didn't have anything to do but think."

To his surprise, her face flushed with spots of red. After a moment, she replied, "I was thinking about how we are going to get home, I mean Dublin or seriously, any place that is not Boulogne or Calais."

Chadwick carefully put down one foot and started his ministrations on the other carefully avoiding the cut on the sole of her foot. He noticed that the flush on her cheeks faded as she talked. "Did you come up with any ideas?" he asked.

"I have a couple of ideas; I am not confident how viable they are."

"Tell me, please. They cannot be any crazier than the ones I have come up with lately," he prompted.

"First of all, nothing can happen for a couple of days while I am laid up," she started.

"Why not?" he asked. "Paddy and I are still mobile."

"Well, my plans involved me," she responded. "I thought that while I am laid up, it might not be a good time for Paddy to wander about on his own. I know his language is getting better but that red hair is so recognizable and we both heard Hastings refer to 'the red-haired' chap that night in the boat. Also, he has wandered around the port two days in a row, and even if it seems no one is watching, we cannot be sure. So it might be time for him to lay low and out of sight, or at least we should think about dying his hair."

Jeffrey was impressed with her thinking. It underscored his concerns about Paddy wandering about on his own. "Yes, I agree that what I have been asking him to do is pretty dangerous." While he mused about the issue, he recognized he was still holding her foot although he had already massaged in the balm. For the second time, he really did not want to let go of her foot. He sat, pretending to have forgotten about her foot, and yet his thumb still massaged the tender part under her ankle.

"The bandage," she said softly.

"Oh, right," he said regretfully. "Any other ideas?"

"Yes," she said determinedly. "Paddy has no papers, and I have no papers. What is to keep us from going through the taverns in Calais looking for someone to take us home? You, I think, are too memorable. Someone will report you to Vilet if you leave Boulogne, but either Paddy or I could do it, especially now that we know Hastings is here and not in Calais.

"Remember how you told me if I got stuck to go to the tavern keeper of *The Citizen* and ask him for help?" she continued. "I think I should do that, line up a boat going somewhere, and then send Paddy back for you."

Chadwick was amazed at the simplicity of the idea and appalled at the thought of her wandering the taverns in Calais, knowing how rough those places could be.

"I rather thought that since both of us are Irish and therefore not at war with France, we might be looked at more compassionately. Of course, we can't prove anything without papers, but smugglers aren't so choosy if you have money, right?" she added hopefully.

"You know, George, that might be a brilliant idea. Let me sleep on it and the three of us will discuss it in more detail tomorrow." He looked at the wine bottle hopefully, but it was still empty. "Let me get these boots off and then I would like to see your sketches, please," he said.

When it came to his boots, he really did miss his valet. David Thomas would have helped pull the footwear off and then take them away for cleaning and polishing. Here, he struggled to get the snug-fitting boots off and he had no supplies to keep them in good condition. As he started the nightly fight to get the boots off, Georgina grabbed the boot from her sitting position and gave a mighty pull. It went so much easier.

"Is this a knife?" she asked. She had his right boot in her hands, the one that had a sheaf for a knife specially fitted.

"Yes, I cannot carry a sword at Vilet's orders but I didn't want to be without any weapon. The knife is so low in the boot you can't see the handle, but I can still get it out quickly if I have to."

"I am envious," she said smiling. "I don't have any place to hide a knife but it would have been so useful." She laid the boot aside and helped him get the other off. "Here are my sketches."

Somehow she had acquired some materials from Madame Traver, but obviously not of good quality. The little scraps of paper she handed him were simple pencil drawings, but they were all of the boats and boat-building that she had seen the previous day.

"I thought we could use them as proof that there was actual building going on and what the boats looked like," she had said with innocent pride. "For when we get back to Dublin."

Chadwick hated to deflate her pride in her initiative. "Miss Yelverton," he began hesitantly. "I am so sorry, these are really good." And, in fact, her sketching was quite talented. Not as good as his sister's sketches, but then even Marion and Nathan thought his sister showed an unusual amount of natural talent. Georgina showed an attention to detail that made her pictures very real to life. "But we cannot keep something like these around."

She looked at him with light slowly dawning in her eyes. "Oh, I am so stupid. Of course, we can't. If someone like Vilet saw them they would use them as proof that we were spies. I cannot believe that I could forget something so obvious." She grabbed the sketches from his hands and threw them into the fire before he could say anything. They watched them disintegrate into ashes in silence.

"I had an idea about your sketching even before you did those," Chadwick said. "I want Captain Cuvelier to think well of us and send a positive report back to Vilet. It seemed to me that some of the terms I am translating would be clearer if there was a sketch to go with it. According to my sister, all young ladies receive lessons in sketching, so I thought you might be able to do some for me." Another idea occurred to him. "This also might require you to take a closer look at some boats so you could sketch the item." He looked at her inquiringly.

Georgina nodded vigorously. "I would be glad to help. But how do you see this working out? Do I come to the warehouse with you or would it be better if I work here?"

They spent some time discussing pros and cons of her working at the warehouse. Then she brought up another issue: "If I am a male retainer to help Paddy get around, how do we explain my ability to draw?"

"Lots of young men draw," Chadwick replied. "I don't myself but lots of fellows at university would wander about with sketch books, looking 'interesting'."

Georgina laughed softly. "Yes, I have seen some of those 'interesting' types. Between their bad sketches and their bad poetry, you have to hope they grow up soon. I guess I will just have to be a shy, intellectual type who is rude enough to never take his hat off."

Chadwick nodded, "I think at least you will have to work at warehouse for part of a day but it is dim and my desk is off in a corner. I will ask Captain Cuvelier tomorrow if he is interested."

"If I had real drawing paper and pencils, I would do some sketches of the harbor that look like just that, a sketch of the harbor, say, at sunset. If I added a boat or two, it would only make it realistic right?"

"Right!"

* * *

Paddy wasn't particularly happy the next day to find his activities curtailed but he seemed to understand the necessity of not drawing any more attention to himself. He agreed that people did identify him by his hair and, although no one seemed suspicious yet, that could change, especially with Hastings in the area. Chadwick left him with a few errands that included buying George some real drawing paper and laying in several bottles of wine. He hoped that those errands would keep Paddy in the Upper Town and with his hat on, inconspicuous.

Captain Cuvelier now proved to be in favor of the idea of adding some sketches to the definitions of the naval terms Chadwick was working on.

"You mean the young chap that was in tears the other day with homesickness can draw?" he asked. "So you didn't send him home?"

"He sketches surprisingly well," Chadwick responded. "However, he really wrenched his ankle the other day and is somewhat hobbled for a few more days. I would rather see him working on this project than lying about our rooms idle." After a moment he added, "No, I am not sending him home; he is getting over it, I think. Less moody, last night at least."

They agreed that Chadwick would get George to do some drawings for the Captain to approve.

"He might need to see the items we are describing," Chadwick said cautiously. "In fact, I have a couple of items I need to see. I don't understand from just the list what the blasted thing is. Remember, I learned most of these terms in English, not French. Maybe George and I can check out a boat with a real sailor together?"

"I think I can arrange that," the Captain replied approvingly. "I might even come with you. I am not familiar with most of the terms so it would be good for me to learn them also. After all, you are not going to be here forever."

"No," Chadwick agreed. "I hope Vilet gets my papers approved soon. I have clients waiting for goods that I am already late on delivering."

"I am looking into getting more help," Cuvelier said unexpectedly. "There is a new unit of volunteers from Ireland and I am hoping some of them can read and have some knowledge of French. That would help with translating and teaching."

Chadwick thought over the Captain's words all morning while he worked. There couldn't be too many Irish units, and if this was a new one just forming, he felt sure that Hastings would be part of it. By the end of the day, he was more tired from the endless whirl of his thoughts and fruitless planning than any work he had done. He hurried back to their lodgings to share and discuss the latest news. But the need to get Georgina and Paddy out of harm's way lay heaviest on his mind.

His junior colleagues seemed to have had a good day, judging by their cheerful countenances when he came in. But before they could gather for an exchange of information and a planning session, there was dinner with Madame Traver to get through. Madame was icy and gave Chadwick the cold shoulder, although she deigned to speak to Paddy. Not that her attitude bothered him overly much. He spent much of the meal wondering what the effects would be if he just announced that they would eat at the local tavern from now on. She probably would toss them into the street, and Lieutenant Poulin had been pretty clear they were lucky to get these rooms at all. He worried that if she was so focused on him, she might also look at his companions closely. He really had hoped to stay unobtrusively at Boulogne for a few days while they worked out their transportation back to Ireland. Madame Traver's offended feelings made him nervous. As Paddy had said, a woman scorned could be a bad enemy.

Finally dinner was over and they could retreat to their rooms. Obviously, Georgina's dinner had not taken as long as she was ensconced by the fire with her sketch pad on her lap. Looking over her shoulder, Chadwick could see she was intent on producing a picture of a block and tackle.

"Paddy gave me some ideas about items to start with," she explained. "I find it rather hard to sketch from a description. I am probably going to need to see the stuff you have in mind. I thought you could just use this to show the Captain what I could do."

"That is not bad, not bad at all," he said admiringly.

Paddy shrugged off his jacket and pulled a stool up to the fireplace. "That was one awful dinner," he said. "How are we going to avoid that tomorrow?"

"I have a couple of ideas, but I have to say, Paddy, you did first-rate down there. It looked like she found the mixture of French and English charming. Honestly, you looked like you had used different cutlery your whole life. Good job!" Chadwick complimented. "Are you positive you were never on the stage?"

Paddy grinned triumphantly and said, "I just followed you, sir. I was just so glad there were no peas," he laughed. "I wasn't sure how to eat those."

Chadwick settled gratefully in his chair. He didn't have to worry right now about which mask to wear. "Tell me about your day, and George, tell me how your feet are progressing," he directed. "Before we decide what to do about Madame Traver, I need more information."

"What kind of information?" Georgina asked.

"First and foremost is your physical condition and what you are capable of doing. Something came to my attention today that makes me think we need to be able to move on a moment's notice. I think our time here in Boulogne is even more limited than I originally thought."

Chadwick then told them about the conversation with Captain Cuvelier de Trie about the newly formed Irish unit and how the Captain hoped to recruit more English-speaking translators. He then shared his assumption that the unit was the same one Paddy and George had seen Hastings with and followed to the tavern.

"How God awful it will be if Hastings ends up at the translation warehouse with me?" he ended with.

"At least of the three of us, Hastings doesn't know what you look like. If he does show up, just do that icy look you do when you want to intimidate someone."

"I do not," he protested.

Both Paddy and Georgina laughed and said at the same time in both English and French, "Yes, you do!"

During his account, Georgina had unwrapped her feet. "Look," she said, "they are pretty good. Mostly healed, and that long cut is scabbed over. With a bit of thick padding, I can get by just fine."

Chadwick gently grasped the foot in question and studied it thoughtfully. "It definitely looks better, no doubt about that. I think the longer we can give you to totally heal, the better. Keep the bandages off for the night. I think the air might dry out those blisters better. Of course, cover up your feet when you go out back." As much as he wanted to, he hesitated to rub the balm into her feet in front of Paddy. For some reason, it seemed to him too intimate a task for the young man to watch. George seemed to understand.

"If you hand me the balm, I will rub some in before I go to bed," she said.

"Paddy, how did your day go?"

"As per your orders, I didn't do much, sir. I did go out to buy George his drawing supplies, but I only walked around the Upper Town and I kept my hat on."

"Did you notice any place we can get horses around here?" Paddy shook his head in response. "In that case, that is the first thing I need you to do tomorrow. Find a stable and hire two horses for the day after tomorrow." When both Paddy and George looked at him startled, he said, "Here is what I have in mind."

Although he was pretty confident George had already discussed with Paddy her idea of going to Calais to look for transportation and by-passing Captain Byrne's contact, he went over the plan again, laying out the pros and cons as they had swirled around his head all day. No way was he going to let Georgina wander around Calais alone, so sending Paddy with her seemed the only option. He tried to emphasize how Hastings' presence threatened even more their precarious safety, if he so much as suspected he had seen Paddy before especially on the night George disappeared. By the time he ended, both his colleagues were sober and thoughtful.

Paddy spoke first. "Just so I am clear, tomorrow first thing, I go out and find two horses to take me and George to Calais. Once we get there, we start with the innkeeper from *The 'Citizen'* and try to find a boat to take us to … where, Ireland?"

"Pretty much anywhere but here," Chadwick responded. "But, yes, start with Ireland or Dublin. Although I would prefer to get to London, I think that would be too dangerous. I am positive Vilet is watching for anyone trying to get to England. Maybe head for one of the Channel Islands where we can get a boat to Cornwall or some such place."

"Do you think we can use the rooms you already paid for?" Georgina asked.

They spent the rest of the evening discussing details, including where they should start their search and what taverns to visit. Finally Georgina asked, "How do you think we can get information back to you so you know when and how to join us?"

That problem seemed to stymie all of them. Finally they admitted defeat and Paddy and George went to their respective beds. As Chadwick banked the fire for the night, he sat with his head in his hands. Events seem to be unfolding faster than ever and he felt so unprepared. He suddenly felt a light hand on his shoulder. He looked up to see warm brown eyes gazing at him in concern.

"Jeffrey," she said softly. "You can't take the weight of the world on your shoulders."

He reached up and interlocked his fingers with hers. Her skin was soft, but her grip was strong. They looked at each for a few moments. "It's hard not to worry. I couldn't bear it if something happened to you."

She nodded and sat in the other chair extending her foot. "I didn't put the balm on my feet. Would you do it?"

Cheyne Row, Chelsea

"Marion! Nathan! Where are you?" Marion could hear the General's voice even as the front door closed behind him. It was anxious in a way she rarely heard. She rushed to throw open the door to the breakfast room where she was reviewing the menus for the week.

"Here, Papa. I am here. What has happened? You sound upset."

"Is Nathan with you?" the General demanded.

"No, he is upstairs reconsidering plans for the nursery again. The baby is not due for months, but he acts like it is tomorrow."

The General turned abruptly from her to the butler, Thornton, who was standing in the hallway as if waiting for orders. "Thornton, would you ask Donnay to join us? I need him immediately."

At once, Thornton started for the stairs while the General stepped into his study. He reappeared almost immediately carrying a bottle of brandy. Knowing her father would not tell her whatever was happening until Nathan arrived, Marion busied herself with selecting glasses from the side board and setting them on the table. The breakfast room was light and sunny today, but Marion thought that whatever the General had to say would bring a dark cloud of worry with it. She sat in her previous chair, put her menus to the side, and poured herself another cup of tea while she waited for her husband to join them.

The General had finished a half glass of brandy by the time she heard Nathan's steps moving rapidly down the stairs. From the hallway, she could hear him speaking: "General Coxe, what has happened? Thornton says there has been trouble." He wheeled into the room and grasped the General's hand. He looked in surprise at the brandy on the table. General Coxe was not known for early libations.

Marion met his questioning gaze and shook her head. She didn't know what had upset her father so much.

"Father, sit down and tell us what has happened."

The General's hand shook as he poured himself more brandy and filled Nathan's glass. "This is bad," he said. "I just got a report this morning from a smuggler source. He had just come from Calais."

"Calais?" Nathan said sharply. "Has this to do with Jeffrey?"

"Not directly I think, but I don't know for certain that it does not pertain to him. Sit and let me tell you what I do know."

Nathan took a seat to the left of Marion and took her hand. Although she could still sip her tea with her right hand, she had lost all taste for the beverage. She did see Thornton glance in the room, note the brandy bottle, and then slip out, closing the door. For years he had been the General's bat man in the army and even now, he always had the General's interests at heart.

Marion glanced back at her father, who was sitting and staring at his glass.

"Good God, man," Nathan exploded, "what has happened? Don't keep us in suspense."

"The General shook his head, getting his thoughts together. "Captain Byrne showed up in my office this morning. Turns out he is the smuggler that took Jeffrey to Calais. He does business along the coast and sometimes does the odd job for us. I had hired him to take my agents to France."

"If he came here personally, it is bad news."

"Yes, it's bad, but not about Jeffrey," the General said. "The news Byrne brought me is about my group I sent over to find out about the build-up of forces on the coast. He says the men never got out of the surf before the French picked them up. There was a trial for show and they were all shot. All of them." The General's voice trailed off. "I knew all of them," he said wretchedly. "I sent them to their deaths."

"That is terrible, Father," Marion murmured.

"Where did Byrne get his information?" Nathan demanded. "How can he be sure?"

"His contact was so distressed, he rowed himself out to his boat to report. The French were evidently not keeping it a secret. He said the news was all over Calais' maybe as a warning to other would-be spies."

"I can understand that you are upset about the deaths but you were in the army for years. Why is this so different for you?" Marion asked.

"This seems so much more personal. These men all volunteered for a mission I put together. You may not remember, but a couple of the men came here to play cards and socialize. We even had them to dinner." He took another gulp of brandy. "And then, too, I am getting old and after what happened with the Madra Dubh here in this house, I think I am too personally involved."

Nathan leaned forward, grabbed the bottle, and splashed more brandy into his own glass. "Any news of Jeffrey after the Captain dropped him off?" he asked. "I am worried about him. He doesn't have much field experience. And honestly, his ability to lie convincingly is pretty poor. This news only increases my concern."

General Coxe shook his head. "I asked Byrne if he had any news but his contact had only a rumor. And that is rather old news. He said that Vilet, the bastard in charge of northern France's security, has been asking a lot of questions about an American wine merchant."

"That's it?" Nathan asked. "What makes Byrne think that is Jeffrey?"

"I gather Jeffrey discussed his cover story at length with Byrne who helped him with some of the holes. Jeffrey was traveling as a wine merchant. Didn't he tell you that in the letter?"

Marion said thoughtfully, "He never came out and said wine, just used the word merchant. But trying to pass as a wine merchant in northern France makes no sense, does it?" She looked at her husband to see him gazing wistfully back at her. "What are you thinking?" she asked. "Oh Nathan," she sighed immediately understanding his mood.

Nathan dropped her hand and reached out to surround her shoulders with his arm and kiss her temple. "You know me better than I know myself," he answered. "Yes, I think I need to go to Calais and bring back our wayward friend."

Chapter Thirteen: Stepping Lightly

C hadwick took the stairs to the Lower City the next morning with more enthusiasm than he had felt recently.

Neither he nor Georgina had spoken as he had rubbed the balm into her feet last night, but he had sensed his growing attraction to her was being reciprocated. After he had finished, she had gone to her pallet with a quiet 'Good night,' leaving him to bank the fire and seek his own bed. He thought he would lie awake and think about their escape route, but he found himself distracted by the memory of warm brown eyes and strawberry-blond curls topping a sweet smile. Then it was morning, Paddy was stoking up the fire to heat water, and they needed to begin to put their plan into action.

He had no time alone with Georgina before he needed to leave for the warehouse, but her smile-full of promise and just plain happiness-sent him off with hope. That lasted until he walked into the warehouse and realized that they might already be too late. A man fitting Hastings' description stood with Captain Cuvelier at his desk, discussing the papers Chadwick had been working on.

"No, Captain," the man was saying with the soft lilt so dominant in Dublin. "I am not your man for naval items. I have spent my life on dry land and am better for it."

As Chadwick joined them, Captain Cuvelier made the introductions. "Monsieur Couture, may I make known to you Lieutenant Hastings, who has just come from Dublin to join our cause?"

Hastings stood about a head shorter than Chadwick. He had an average body but the thick thighs of a horseman. His posture, however, was such that Chadwick wondered if that was how he tried to intimidate others. It was not the kind of posture drilled into a military man, but the assertive stance that says to the world, 'Do not make the mistake of judging me a less dangerous man because of my lack of height.' From the advantage of his six plus inches,

Chadwick could see that although Hastings kept his brown hair trimmed close to his head, it was thinning. What struck him most, were Hastings' eyes, icy pale blue with colorless lashes. They were surveying Chadwick with interest and some emotion that was hard to place.

Chadwick was so busy studying Georgina's kidnapper that he almost missed how Captain Cuvelier introduced him.

"Monsieur Couture is a purchasing agent for clients in New Orleans and has agreed to help us do some translating while he is in this part of France." Chadwick noticed with interest that he left out any mention of Vilet and that Chadwick had also just come from Ireland.

The men bowed and murmured politely. Chadwick noticed immediately that Hastings had all the trappings of a gentleman, using proper English, easy with the social niceties, and even his bow seemed natural to the man. Because of his brutal actions, Chadwick had never imagined Hastings to be of the upper class. He would have to rethink his attitude towards the man. Hastings was obviously ruthless, but the civilized veneer, with the exception of his eyes, certainly masked it well. Chadwick had to keep reminding himself that the man was a lot more dangerous than he appeared. This was the man who had splintered off from the United Irishman insurgency because the group was not aggressive enough. This was the man who would kidnap children to further his cause, who had sent his own wife into danger and subsequent death to further his cause. He was not to be trifled with or judged less dangerous because he had decided to join Napoleon. And his French was damn good.

"My man saw a group of riders wearing green jackets in town recently," Chadwick said, nodded to Hastings' coat. "Is that the company of Irishmen that Captain Cuvelier has been telling me about?" he asked.

"Probably," Hastings answered. He looked at Captain Cuvelier. "Do you know of any other Irish here?"

Cuvelier shook his head. "There are a number of Irish mixed in with the regular troops, but I only know of one Irish company posted in Boulogne. I have been looking for translating help for some time; believe me I would know if there was a source of English speakers I could tap." He grinned happily. "But now that I have you two, even for a short time, we should make good progress."

"I heard Captain Hastings saying he hadn't much experience with naval items. Shall I continue with that project then?" Chadwick asked the Captain.

When he nodded agreement, he continued, "I brought some sketches to show you. Maybe when you finish showing Captain Hastings around, we could chat about how to incorporate them into the booklet?"

"Excellent. Excellent. I will return shortly." Cuvelier looked happier than Chadwick had ever seen him. He surmised that the Captain really took his work seriously and was frustrated by the lack of progress caused by the shortage of educated personnel.

Chadwick sat at his table, grateful that the sun was shining today and that they wouldn't need the noisome candles. He reorganized his papers and sat for a few moments, getting his thoughts in order. Meeting Hastings like that had been a shock. He felt he should have been more prepared, especially after yesterday, when Cuvelier had mentioned he was trying to recruit more help.

"Monsieur?" Lieutenant Poulin's welcome voice interrupted his thoughts. "Coffee?" Chadwick accepted with gusto. Coffee was just the thing to give him time to ponder how to put his part of the plan into action. He needed to get Cuvelier to give him, and maybe George, permits to visit the ships so they could get close enough to evaluate the threat they posed to Britain. When he reported back to London, he wanted as much information as he could garner to present.

Chadwick rose and followed Poulin to the urn just brought in by an aide. As he added sugar to the brew, he asked the young lieutenant as casually as he could, what other projects Captain Cuvelier might have for them.

"A large number of newspapers just arrived from London," was the surprising reply. "I am confident he will want us to drop everything and scour them as soon as possible for any military or political items."

"How did they get here?" Chadwick asked in surprise.

"Same way you did," Poulin answered. "Smuggler to Calais."

Thoughtfully, he took his coffee back to his desk. Georgina's scheme suddenly gained traction. If there were so many smugglers slipping in and out of Calais, surely there was one that could get her to safety. He fingered the earring in his pocket. Georgina's well-being had suddenly become very important to him.

He could send the relevant information about the invasion back to the government with her. Even if he couldn't go with her, Paddy would. All she had to do was get to London and to Nathan. *Nathan would take care of the rest,* he thought with relief.

* * *

Captain Cuvelier De Trie received the passes late in the morning so it wasn't until after the mid-day break that he and Chadwick left for the port. That had allowed enough time for a messenger to be sent asking George to join them. Chadwick would have been happier to leave her out of the expedition but he had already said too much to Cuvelier about how seeing the actual boats would improve the sketches. The best he could do was to tell Georgina to meet them at the bottom of the steps to the Lower Town, well away from the warehouse and Hastings' presence.

Hastings had been cordial, maybe too cordial, in his interactions with Chadwick. He asked a few questions about supplies but mainly seemed to want to chat about the newspaper articles he was supposed to be translating. He would work for a few minutes and then draw Chadwick's attention to some subject and ask his opinion on the topic. After a short time, Jeffrey suspected it was just a way for Hastings to find out about his political leanings. He played up his fictitious background about being from the Americas and played ignorant with most of the topics Hastings raised. He was relieved when Cuvelier arrived with the passes and they arranged to meet at the bottom of the stairs for an afternoon on the quay inspecting landing craft.

George was waiting for them at the bottom of the steps, with Paddy next to her wearing his hat pulled down low. Although Paddy was not included in the port tour, Chadwick was glad to see the lad had accompanied George to the quay. With all the sailors and soldiers flooding the town, even a young man might be at risk alone on these streets. Now, when Jeffrey looked at Georgina, he could only see her as the vibrant woman with the delicate feet. He anxiously wondered why any other man would not see what he saw when he looked at her. Did dressing her as a young man only make her more vulnerable to discovery?

But when he looked more closely, he realized that George was carrying off her disguise with aplomb. Dressed as a young man wearing boots with a sketch pad tucked under one arm, she leaned casually against a brick wall, perfectly imitating any number of sons of society. He could see several pencils sticking out of a pocket. As Chadwick and Captain Cuvelier approached, George finished sharpening one with a small pen knife. Jeffrey wondered briefly where that had come from.

"Monsieur!" Paddy's cheerful voice sailed over the various noises of the quay. "We are here as you directed," he announced in English.

Chadwick could see, but not hear, as George murmured to Paddy.

"We are here," Paddy declaimed again, this time in stilted French. *What game were these two playing?* Chadwick wondered. Paddy's French was better than that.

But Cuvelier didn't know about Paddy's emerging language abilities. He laughed and said, "Good for you, lad, learning the language. I see your young helper has been giving you lessons. Keep at it!"

"Yes, sir," Paddy answered slowly in French.

"Thank you for making sure George found the right place to meet me," Chadwick said in English. As they parted ways, George tried to hand Paddy the pocket knife.

Paddy shot off the gesture, saying, "Keep it, lad, for the afternoon. You may need to sharpen more pencils."

With a salute to Chadwick, Paddy headed back up the stairs to the Upper Town.

Captain Cuvelier then led his small party up the quay to a part of the river Chadwick had not seen before. From George's interested expression, he assumed she had not, either. Once they turned a bend in the river, they came to a blockade of fence and gates guarded by armed soldiers who carefully checked Captain Cuvelier's papers before allowing them to pass. Once through, Chadwick was aghast to see all manner of boats and barges under various stages of construction as far as he could see. If he had thought the regular quay had more than the normal amount of construction, he was seriously misguided. Preparation for this invasion was indeed massive.

"*Mon Dieu!*" George whispered, her eyes round in astonishment. "So many!"

"Yes, my young friend, it is an amazing sight, isn't it?" Captain Cuvelier asked with satisfaction. "Only Napoleon could make such an immense undertaking happen." He surveyed with understandable pride the crowded dock area with the many boats tied to the piers jutting out into the river.

Chadwick glanced around trying to cover up his dismay at the evidence of a serious invasion plan laid out before him.

"I hardly know where to begin, Captain," he said hesitantly. "Can you give me an idea what we are looking at?"

"With pleasure, monsieur," the Captain responded happily. For the next hour, he expounded on the four types of invasion ships: the three-masted, twelve-gun prame; the two-masted *chaloupe canniere*; the bateau canniere gunboat; and the sixty-foot peniche with its two howitzers. Chadwick listened intently, trying to hold on to the information without making notes. He could see George also trying to keep up. The Captain might have been assigned to a desk and dry translations, but he obviously loved – and was impressed by – the invasion fleet. The whole idea had so captured his imagination that he couldn't wait to impress Chadwick with his knowledge.

"I do not understand, Captain," Chadwick finally interrupted. "What are all those boats under construction out in the regular quay? Why aren't they here where there is some protection from prying eyes?"

"Unfortunately, monsieur, there is not enough room." He gestured to the craft before them. "These are undergoing the final phases. The ones out in the other quay are just the skeletons, the foundations. At a certain point, the crafts are brought back here for finishing. Not too many people besides the workmen get to look back here."

"I am very honored that I was considered trustworthy enough to see this glorious sight," Chadwick responded more than half truthfully. "It is beyond amazing. Can I ask some questions?"

Captain Cuvelier nodded so he continued. "My first question has nothing to do with translating, but just because I am so amazed. How many craft do you think are here?"

"I have heard that our dear Consul has ordered two thousand boats to be available. Not all, of course, will carry men; there must be some for shipping horses, equipment, cannons, and so forth. Not all of them are being built here. I hear they plan to requisition fishing vessels, private yachts, and anything else the military might find."

Chadwick did some math in his head: Two thousand boats, each holding about seventy-five men would mean an invasion fleet of close to 150,000 men. Britain had no standing army that could repel an assault of that magnitude. It would be a slaughter. He wondered how many questions he could ask before the Captain got suspicious, but he really wanted to verify that Napoleon had such an army ready to invade.

"I have only been in Boulogne a short time, and while I have seen military men in the streets, I haven't seen anywhere near the number of men that will fill these ships. Is the First Consul bringing them from somewhere else?" he asked.

"Oh, you haven't been out to the camp yet," the Captain answered blithely. "There are almost 80,000 men camped out there. They rotate who can visit the town so the town is not overrun. I imagine that General Napoleon will show up one day soon with the rest of the men and announce that they are off. Then everyone will jump into these boats and who knows? Maybe my music will be played in London?"

Chadwick was shocked to his core. Was it possible that they were that close to the start of the invasion? It did seem that many of these boats were finished except for the loading of the guns. Where was Napoleon getting the armaments? Even one thousand boats with twelve howitzers each was an astronomical amount of iron work. Could France produce that much? He glanced over at George to see if she was following the conversation.

He saw with pride that George was sitting on a barrel, hat pulled low, doing general sketches of the nearest craft. She was doing exactly what he had asked of her, trying not to draw attention to herself while quietly putting as much on paper as possible. Even if they left all the sketches with Cuvelier, she should remember enough about the boats to replicate the drawings for the government in London.

She was working on a full-page sketch done in broad strokes showing the general design and layout of the craft. Several smaller, more detailed sketches filled the margins. Captain Cuvelier had moved to stand at George's shoulder and seemed to be following her work intently. Since he was throwing a shadow over her work, George couldn't ignore his interest. She tilted her sketch pad toward him and started showing him various aspects of her work.

"Make sure you get the detail about that piece there," Cuvelier pointed out something to George. Chadwick followed his pointing finger to see what they were looking at. It proved to be a howitzer.

He turned to his own work and the sailor who had been assigned to answer his questions.

"What is that used for?" Chadwick asked, pointing at a random object. The man didn't seem to mind, no matter how simple his questions were. Chadwick thought he probably enjoyed the break in the routine. He made copious notes so he would look busy and intent on his job.

As Chadwick looked around the marina, he noticed there seemed to be two types of ships. What had the Captain called them? Prame, the sailor reminded him. The longer ships had three masts and places for more than ten guns. The smaller boats were flatter, with lower sides than he was used to seeing on ships on rivers. The sailor told him they were called peniches. Well, that made sense since 'peniche' translated into 'barge' in English. He didn't think he had ever seen barges on the Channel. Personally, he wouldn't want to be on a peniche when a storm kicked up which was often, even in summer.

"Captain Cuvelier, when we finish with these craft, do you think we will have covered most of what you need?" he asked. "In other words, how much detail will be essential to the average sailor?" He didn't think that in the heat of battle anyone was going to have time to consult a pamphlet to find the proper word for an instrument.

"Good question, monsieur. I want to be as complete as possible but you are right, we need to balance need against too much detail," Cuvelier replied. "We probably should visit a larger ship to make certain we have all the basics covered." He sighed and said, "We will need another pass to do that. This endless paper work is just that, endless."

Chadwick laughed to himself about the Captain's grumbling. *Same issue, same garbage, no matter the army*, he agreed to himself.

* * *

"How are your feet after all that walking today?" Chadwick asked George as they sat in a tavern lingering over their beer. Chadwick couldn't stand the thought of another meal in their landlady's presence, so he had briskly told her they would be taking their evening meals at a local tavern from now on. From the furious look on her face, he sincerely hoped his stay in Boulogne would soon be over. But once Paddy and George left for Calais, he would be on his own. He wondered grimly how he would fare with the aggressive widow without his young chaperones. She would probably poison him if he ate at her table again. Maybe he could bunk with Poulin? He doubted even the widow would be brave enough to follow him into the army camp.

"My feet are pretty good," George responded. "I was worried that the amount of walking would set me back, but, except for the one cut, I hardly felt anything at all. I did put on both pairs of socks, so I had a lot of padding. Where did Paddy go? He hot-footed it out of here as soon as he finished eating."

"Since you are hoping to start at first light tomorrow, I asked him to go double-check that the horses will be ready that early," he answered. "I may have also given him some coins to have a few drinks around and see if he hears anything of interest." To himself, he admitted that the last part was so that he could have a few hours alone with Georgina. Who knew when he would see her again?

She topped up their glasses with the beer pitchers the server had left on their table and grinned at him, saying, "I could develop a taste for beer. It's not bad at all."

Chadwick laughed with her. "I can see you now, hiding a keg of beer in the basement with the wine bottles, all for your personal pleasure."

George sobered quickly. "We have never talked about going home," she said quietly. "I am pretty anxious about that. My reputation is going to be beyond redemption. I doubt anyone will receive me now."

Jeffrey wanted nothing so much as to take her hands to comfort her but even in the dark pub he didn't dare. He stretched out his long legs and pressed his right leg to her left under the table. She didn't flinch or move away but returned the pressure while studying his face.

"I have been wondering if I should return to Dublin," she said quietly.

Chadwick returned her gaze while thinking over her words.

"Do you feel well enough to walk about so we can talk?" he asked. "As dark as this place is, I am thinking we would be safer talking outside as we move about."

She nodded, immediately stood, and drained her mug. Chadwick threw some coins on the table and led the way out of the tavern.

While they had been eating, the sun had set and now the streets were clothed in gloomy shadows. There was still enough light to wander about but full dark would not be long in coming.

"Any special direction?" she asked.

"Let us see if we can find the wall of the castle that overlooks the river." He did a full circle in the street trying to get his bearings. "I thought I saw some greenery; there may be a park out there."

George laughed and pointed off to the left. "The castle is that way," she said. "Paddy took me around a bit in the morning so I could get the lay of the land so to speak. You can feel the land slope ever so slightly down and next thing you know the castle is between you and the cliff that leads to the Lower Town. I doubt we can see much in the dark except ships' lights."

To avoid acting on the impulse to take her arm and be close to her as they strolled, he clasped his hands behind his back.

"Lead on, then. You obviously know the way better than I do. I do not think anyone is following us, but try to keep a sharp eye out just in case."

She obviously knew what he was talking about, since she immediately turned to walk backwards while still chatting in the animated way young people have.

"Did you see how closely Captain Cuvelier de Trie studied my drawings? He seemed to really like them." Her enthusiasm was infectious. "He said he thought I had real talent." She turned to walk normally.

Chadwick had to laugh when she fell into step with him. Her enthusiasm for Cuvelier's compliments seemed to be real, not feigned, while she scanned the shadows for followers. "Anything?" he asked quietly.

"No, but I will turn again soon to see if I spot anything."

"I did notice the good Captain was pretty complimentary about your art. I have found him to be a man of his word. I do not think he was giving you false accolades. He told me earlier that he writes music and hopes to have his work produced in Paris someday. I think he must recognize you as a fellow artist," he said out loud.

"My father always liked my work, but he *has* to: he's my father! Not too many people outside the family have seen it."

They continued discussing art for several blocks until they both felt positive they were not being followed. The streets were not deserted by any means, but the folks they passed walked with purpose and did not dawdle, workers making their way home or men heading to a tavern for a drink. George did not identify any suspicious figures behind them and they finally emerged from the twisting streets to a small park on one side of the castle. Paddy had identified the castle as being a military building. While there were lots of lights on in the windows, few figures wandered about.

"Everyone is probably still at dinner," George guessed. "During the day, we didn't see many people in this little bit of greenery. Why do you suppose that is?"

"Hard to say in the dark, but since there are so few trees and I seem to be walking on fallen fruit from the few that are here, maybe this used to be the kitchen gardens. The military have no use for fine cuisine, so it could have been left to grow over," Chadwick suggested. "Anyway, look at the river. Even if all you can see are the ships' lights, it really is beautiful."

They stood in silence for a few minutes, leaning on the wall and admiring the lights that seemed to dance, presumably movement caused by waves rocking the ships. Finally, Jeffrey tried to look at Georgina's face. But it had fallen full dark and as close to each other as they were standing, he could see only the lighter shadow of her skin. He carefully reached out and found her wrist. He circled it with his thumb and forefinger, thinking how her wrists were as delicate as her ankles.

"It's going to be hard to leave you tomorrow," she said quietly.

"It's going to be hard to stay here and watch you leave," he responded. "I hate even the idea of separating. I hate it for several reasons, but mostly because I am worried something will happen to you and I won't be able to help."

He pulled gently on her wrist and she came willingly into his arms. He rested his cheek on the top of her head.

"I can hear your heart," she whispered. "It's beating so fast, like you're running a race."

"In some ways I feel like I am, or maybe *we* are. A race to get back home before Hastings sees you or Vilet doesn't get confirmation of my papers."

He ran his hand up and down her spine and in the process pulled her even closer. She made no move to pull away; instead, her arms went around his waist. When her chest pressed against his chest, he realized he wished he could feel her unbound breasts. So many regrets.

"I have been giving a great deal of thought about whether to go back to Dublin. I do not want to go," she murmured.

"No listen," he said. "I agree with you. I do not think Dublin is the place for you. But we need to follow the plan for you and Paddy to go to Calais. It's a good plan and I think, in our situation, the only one with a chance of working. But once you get to Calais, I want you to board the first boat that takes you out of Calais. It would be best if there was one that would drop you in London, but that's not likely. Anywhere in Britain will do. Then get yourself to my friends, Nathan and Marion Donnay, in Chelsea, Thirteen Cheyne Row. Please remember that. They will take care of you and get the information we've gathered to those who need to see it."

She obediently repeated that address after him. "But what about you?" she asked horrified. "You are supposed to come with us."

"Right now, I am much more concerned about getting you out of harm's way. Once I am convinced you and Paddy are safely away, I can disappear somehow and meet you in London."

He was glad he sounded much more confident than he felt. Although he had no intention of falling into Vilet's grip, getting Georgina and Paddy to safety with the information about the invasion fleet was more important than his personal well-being.

"No," she said flatly. "I won't go without you. If it weren't for you, I would still be in that pig sty, being sold like a piece."

Chadwick's lips covered hers, muffling her words.

Chapter Fourteen: Destination Calais

D awn was just breaking the next morning, as Chadwick stood on the steps of Madame Traver's house waiting for Paddy to bring up the hired horses. Night lifted slowly and the streets were still deserted. Even the soil men had gone to their beds. Jeffrey imagined that soon the maids unlucky enough to have the responsibility of lighting the fires would be dragging themselves out of bed.

He heard the clops of the horses' hoofs before he could see them. When Paddy finally emerged from the gloom, Jeffrey was able to inspect the horses his aide had chosen. His military eye assured him that while they wouldn't win a derby or even a beauty contest, they looked sturdy enough to make Calais by noon. Paddy dismounted and started to tighten the girth on George's horse.

While he waited for Georgina to show up, Chadwick replayed the events of the night before in his mind. She had kissed him back, several times. They had stayed in the park looking at the lights. She had felt so right in his arms. She was just the right size. Since she was not wearing a corset in her boys' clothes, he could just feel her bound breasts against his chest, and it was a feeling he wanted to repeat soon, without the binding. What a time to realize he had feelings for this woman, just when he had to send her off on a mission thwart with danger.

Of course, by the time they had returned to the rooms, Paddy had been there waiting. He had looked at them carefully but wisely said nothing. Their feelings seemed too new to share with anyone, even a close companion like Paddy.

They spent some time going over the plan once more, including how Paddy would contact Chadwick when they had a boat lined up. Jeffrey reiterated his orders, over their objections that they leave as soon as they possibly could. He would join them if possible but if not, he would follow them. They were to make for Marion and Nathan Donnay in Chelsea and have Nathan give their information to the Alien Office. He made both memorize the address. They put nothing in writing and George left whatever sketches she had with Jeffrey. He would trickle them to Captain Cuvelier as if George was still working on them in the rooms.

Paddy had wandered off to bed, but Jeffrey and Georgina had stayed up until the small hours of the morning holding on to each other and talking softly.

Even as he sighed with regret that the evening had not lasted longer, Georgina stepped out of the house behind him and gave him a warm smile full of hope and promise. He gave her arm a quick squeeze of encouragement and they went down the steps to meet Paddy. Chadwick couldn't help but notice that her smile had turned to a glum expression shared by Paddy, mirrored his own sense of impending calamity.

Separating his little group seemed so intrinsically wrong and would make them even more vulnerable. But if he stayed behind in Boulogne, it would give the others more time to find a boat out of Calais. After all, he was the only one under suspicion. As many times as they reconsidered their plan, unhappily they couldn't come up with a better one.

Leaving Georgina proved even harder than he had thought it would be. He now realized that he had found a woman of spirit and courage who he could admire as well as love. Marion Coxe had taught him that he really didn't want a clingy beauty who had only her looks to offer. Georgina had proven she was brave and was willing to contribute to the well-being of all of them. She had a temper, but she did not have the narcissistic attitude of so many of the socialites he had met in London.

Conversation was sparse this morning as the actuality of splitting their group became real. Chadwick cupped his hands to give Georgina a step up into the saddle and then just stood there gazing up at her, holding her hand.

"I do not even have a talisman to give you," she said sadly.

"I do not need a talisman to remember you," he replied.

He remembered the earring in his pocket. "But I do have a talisman," he said as he pulled the bauble from his pocket and held it up for her to see.

"Where did you get that?" she asked in amazement.

"Dublin, when we found the house Hastings had kept you in."

"And you kept it all this time?"

"I was going to return it to you, but I forgot. Anyway, now I have a talisman. But you're pretty memorable all on your own."

Paddy nudged his horse closer and leaned down to shake Chadwick's hand.

"Don't worry, Captain, I promise I will take care. She's too precious to lose now," he said quietly. "Come on, George, let's get this over with."

With a final squeeze, Chadwick stepped back and George and Paddy urged their mounts to move.

Jeffrey stood watching them ride away until he remembered something Marion had said half in jest. 'It is bad luck to watch someone out of sight.' True or not, he would not bring bad luck on their heads so he turned at the last minute so he didn't see them turn the corner and George's last sad little wave.

He did look up in time to see a curtain in an upstairs window twitch closed.

* * *

Chadwick was already at his desk poring over his notes from the trip to the quay when Hastings made his entrance. And it was quite an entrance. He seemed full of bonhomie, stopping to chat at various desks, back-slapping and telling jokes. Raucous laughter followed his progression around the warehouse. Chadwick noticed that he helped himself to the coffee urn before entering Cuvelier's office. It was some time before Hastings emerged and made a bee line for Chadwick's desk. Chadwick wondered if he hadn't been the object of Hastings wanderings all along.

"What news, monsieur?" he asked as he hitched a hip on the corner of the desk. "Did you and the young assistant enjoy your trip to the quay yesterday? Quite a sight, isn't it?"

Chadwick wondered with dismay how he knew George had accompanied them to the quay; maybe Captain Cuvelier had mentioned it. "Yes, it is beyond impressive the effort that is being expended here," he tried to keep his voice calm. What was Hastings playing at? "So you have seen the construction?"

"Of course," Hastings replied importantly. "When I first got here, I was given a complete tour." He straightened and turned as if to move off to his worktable.

"I guess you didn't get the tour. Oh, yes, you were sent by Vilet here. Maybe they don't trust you," he said slyly. "By the way, where is your young assistant today? Will he be joining us here in the warehouse?"

Chadwick went back to reading his notes, saying briefly, "That's right, and as soon as he verifies my credentials, I will be on my way south to conduct the business I was sent here to do." He chose to ignore the pointed questions about George and sincerely hoped that was to be the end of the conversation. He had no time or patience for Hastings' prodding exchange.

But it was not to be. All morning, Hastings continued to read parts of the newspaper out loud, urging Chadwick to give his opinion on the topic. The constant interruptions did nothing to either improve his humor or assuage his increasing anxiety over Paddy and Georgina.

When the midday break came, Cuvelier asked Chadwick to accompany him and Lieutenant Poulin to a local tavern for food. Unfortunately, Hastings joined their group and spent the entire meal either boasting of his exploits – some sexual, some just abuses of others – or making snide comments at Chadwick's expense. Cuvelier looked uncomfortable but did nothing to stop Hastings. Chadwick finally stopped responding to Hastings jibes about his 'colonial' background and accent, retreating first to polite nods and then to silence.

The meal seemed to take forever, but finally the Captain called a halt and said they still had work to do. On the walk back to the warehouse both the Captain and Poulin were unusually quiet while Hastings filled the air with blather. The demeanor of either man did not do anything to allay Chadwick's anxiety or help keep his mind occupied. Something was happening, and if Hastings was this happy, it couldn't be good.

At the warehouse, the sight of some horses and green-jacketed men at the door seemed to increase Hasting's rather manic posture.

"Oh excellent, they are back early!" he exclaimed. "Chadwick, I have such a surprise for you!"

Chadwick glanced rapidly at Captain Cuvelier 's face and found him grimacing in distaste. "What is happening here, Captain?" he demanded.

Cuvelier did not answer but turned his face away, at which gesture Chadwick pushed his way through the green jackets and into the warehouse. The scene before him struck him speechless.

George was sitting on a chair with her hands tied before her. Her face was white with fear and her eyes were huge. She was not looking at him, but at a body lying on the floor, a body that appeared to Chadwick to have been just dumped on the floor. Paddy must have given them some fight from the way his face was a swollen mess, both eyes blackening. His nose must be broken too. As Chadwick looked at the men lounging in the doorway, he saw that several of them who were smirking also sported bruises and contusions. He knelt at Paddy's side trying to evaluate his condition. No matter where he touched him, it was bound to hurt.

"They wouldn't stop hitting him, even after he was down," Georgina gasped. "It was horrible. They just laughed."

Chadwick spun around to face Captain Cuvelier. "What is the meaning of this outrage?" he practically snarled. "This man has done nothing to warrant this abuse."

Although Cuvelier was standing nearer, it was Hastings who answered.

"Well, now, we don't know that he is so innocent, do we?" he practically purred. "He was sneaking out of town before dawn even. Looks to me like he and your other 'assistant' were trying to get away."

"And why shouldn't he take George home?" Chadwick demanded. "I am the one Vilet sent here; they work for me. No one said Paddy was under orders to stay here."

"Well, Monsieur Couture, your whole story smells to high heaven and when the Captain here was made aware that your assistants were sneaking out of town, he asked that a few of my fellows bring them back," Hastings answered blithely.

"Captain," Chadwick protested, "this is outrageous! Vilet never made clear to me that Paddy was under the same restrictions as myself. And even if he had, such a beating was not warranted."

He turned back to Paddy and rolled him on to his back. "I have to get him back to our rooms so I can call a doctor to attend him." He started to loosen Paddy's coat and shirt to see if he had any wounds that were not easily visible.

"Monsieur," George's voice was a little less strained, "untie me so I can help you with Paddy."

"No," Hastings cut in sharply, "the brat stays tied. He kicked a few of my men and will remain trussed up until we get to the bottom of this mystery."

Ignoring him, Chadwick stood and quickly cut George's bonds with his pocket knife. "And what do you think he can do with all your brave fearless men around?" he asked sarcastically. "Kick his way out of here? All he wanted was to go home."

Chadwick surveyed the warehouse. All work had stopped, and every eye was focused on the dramatic scenario being played out by the entrance; the room was filled with green jacketed men staring intimidatingly at him. Paddy must have put up a hell of a fight. But getting out of here was impossible. Even if he had had his sword, there were too many men for him to take on. Captain Cuvelier and Lieutenant Poulin stood off to the side. Their expressions were hard to read. He wondered what their position in this situation was. Who was in charge? Time to find out. He walked over to the Captain and stood looking him in the face. Interesting how short the Captain was when he wasn't behind a desk.

"Captain," he demanded, "what is this man's authority here that he is allowed to kidnap my people, beat one of them senseless, and drag them back here? Why are you allowing this?"

Now, Chadwick could easily read the Captain's expression; he saw unease coupled with indecision.

"Lieutenant Hastings has information that you are not the man you present yourself as," he said slowly. "He seems to think you are an English spy."

"Me?" Chadwick exclaimed. "And on what is he basing that accusation?" he demanded angrily. "No, wait, that discussion can wait. I insist that you send for a physician to attend my man. And I want to move him. They had no business beating him so, and dumping him on the floor."

"I had every right," Hastings announced. "That man is a spy."

"And what are you basing that accusation on?" Chadwick returned.

"I remember him from Dublin," Hastings said surprisingly. "And in Dublin, he wore a red coat, an army coat. He definitely wasn't a merchant's assistant. And I intend to get to the bottom of why he is here."

"Well, your men have certainly put a stop to that plan, since he is senseless and can't answer any questions now, can he?" Chadwick asked sardonically.

While Hastings was announcing Paddy's duplicity, Chadwick noticed Cuvelier call one of his men over and give him some directions. Chadwick couldn't really understand all that was said, but he did hear the word 'physician' so it would seem the Captain was at least getting Paddy some aid. He looked over to Paddy's body on the floor. George now hovered over him, patting him somewhat uselessly on the shoulder.

"Where can I put him?" he asked the Captain. "He obviously is not running away, and I am not leaving him on the floor. I don't believe these allegations. He has become a friend and I want him treated as such."

Finally, Captain Cuvelier seemed to come to a resolution. "Enough, Lieutenant Hastings," he said firmly. "Your men have seen that we cannot question the young man at this time, so let us see to his injuries and hope he doesn't die on us before we settle this situation."

He turned to Lieutenant Poulin and directed, "Find a table and put it against the back wall, out of the way. Put him there with a guard, one of our men, not theirs. They seem too ready with their fists, Lieutenant Hastings. I want you to keep them under control while in this place."

'Thank you Captain," Chadwick said gratefully.

Getting Paddy care was his first priority and now it seemed he would have some time to think. This situation just seemed to be getting more complicated. He turned to Poulin. "Lieutenant, would you help me carry him to the table?" he asked. "He is rather tall, and I don't want to drop him."

Paddy groaned as they tried to settle him on the table. George, with her hat down low, stood at the head of the table looking deeply distressed. From somewhere she had found a cloth and was wiping Paddy's face of blood.

"Try to keep him from waking up," Chadwick said softly. "He will be in pain and we have nothing to give him until the doctor gets here." And then even more softly, "He can't answer questions if he is unconscious."

George's nod of understanding was almost imperceptible.

"And you, are you also hurt, young man, besides the bruise I see on your face?" Cuvelier 's voice startled Chadwick. He hadn't realized he had followed them across the warehouse floor. Now he looked closely at George's face and realized that she, too, bore evidence of Hastings' men's brutality.

Before Jeffrey could ask his own questions, George answered the Captain.

"Thankfully no, sir." Her voice was low and respectful and she kept her eyes on Paddy, not looking at anyone directly. "They took it out on Paddy," her voice caught. "It was awful."

The Captain moved off, probably to try to bring some organization to the chaos that had disrupted his work area.

Lieutenant Poulin however, still stood by the table gazing down at Paddy with a sordid and fascinated revulsion.

"It's hard to tell what this man even looked like," he said with dismay.

"Have you ever been in battle?" Chadwick asked.

"No, monsieur, but I take your point."

"Let's get his coat off him before he wakes up. Do you think anything is broken?" Chadwick asked Poulin. The Lieutenant shrugged in response but put his arms under Paddy's shoulders to lift him so Jeffrey could remove his coat. Thankfully it was looser than a more fashionable coat would have been, but still it was a struggle. Paddy was a big man and heavier than one might think. Finally, George managed to get hold of a cuff and tug the sleeve off. Paddy moaned but didn't wake up.

Chadwick ran his hand down the arm, breathing a sigh of relief when he did not feel any bones jutting out. "Let's do the other side," he said. "Should be easier."

Soon Paddy was lying there in his shirt and pants. Chadwick couldn't find any obviously broken bones, but he feared his friend's ribs had taken the brunt of the beating. Paddy's breathing was stressed, as if each movement hurt something inside.

Movement among the soldiers in the doorway signaled the arrival of the physician. He was a small man, clothed in black with even a black neck cloth, and carried a black case. He moved with decision and purpose in their direction.

"Oh my God, he looks like an undertaker," George whispered.

Chadwick noticed that while some of the men had gone back to work, Hastings stood close to the table, watching each action carefully. What did he think was going to happen? Paddy was obviously not going to jump up and run off.

Jeffrey tried to think carefully about what accusations Hastings had leveled. He had said he had seen Paddy in Dublin wearing a red uniform. He could fit that into his story by saying he had hired Paddy in Dublin when he was cashiered out. He couldn't let Hastings' claim of spying stand. The French would shoot him immediately. Somehow, he needed to convince Captain Cuvelier to continue to believe his cover story. Should he insist that they send for Vilet to buy them time? Chadwick wasn't worried about Hastings calling him a spy, but he supposed it was possible their paths had crossed when he was stationed there during the 'disruptions'. It was possible, but unlikely or Hastings would have blurted it out already. He didn't seem the type to have much patience. He would just have to stick with his original story and call Hastings' bluff if he tried to label him a spy.

While the doctor made his examination of Paddy, Jeffrey tried to study Georgina's face to see how she was holding up. Again, her resilience and bravery impressed him. She was still wearing her hat and kept her head down, but he could see she was unusually pale. She watched the doctor's movements carefully as if she would jump in and protect Paddy somehow if she needed to. Her only comments had been whispered asides to Jeffrey, which meant no one would notice that her voice wasn't as low-pitched as a young man's usually was. He took a deep breath, stood aside, and waited for the physician to finish his examination.

Finally he was done. He straightened, spent some time putting his coat on and adjusting his cuffs. Jeffrey tried to contain his anxiety but it wasn't easy. Evidently it wasn't easy for George either.

"Sir?" she prodded quietly. "Will he recover?"

"That is quite a beating this young man took," the healer replied. "His nose is broken, obviously. However, I can find no other broken bones in his face, although the swelling makes it very difficult to be exact. I think his ribs bore the brunt. They seem to be bruised and there may be some that are broken. That is why his breathing is so labored. His legs and arms, while badly bruised, are not broken. His left hand is definitely broken. I will send my assistant to set that." He paused and stood studying Paddy.

"Can't you set it now, while he is unconscious?" Chadwick asked. "He is going to be in so much pain as it is."

"Why are you worried about a dirty spy?" Hastings snarled.

"He is not a spy and he is my assistant," Chadwick responded angrily. "Your actions have been outrageous."

Before he could continue, the physician interrupted, "Gentlemen, I am not finished."

He paused to make sure they were listening; he obviously liked an audience.

"As I said, my assistant will set his hand. I am needed at another place and he does well enough in bone splintering. However, I am more concerned about this young man's head. While I cannot find any broken bones to speak of, I think he is badly concussed and must not be moved for a number of days." He looked at Chadwick as the one most likely to understand and do something about his directions.

"Have this young person," he gestured at George, "keep cool cloths continuously on his face and neck. Ice would be better, but that is in scare supply right now. It would be best if he is kept unconscious, so he doesn't move around too much." He turned and started rummaging in his black bag finally emerging with a bottle which he handed to Chadwick.

"Laudanum," he said shortly. "Several drops in some water should do it. Don't worry about feeding him, but keep trying to drip water into his mouth."

Now he was looking at George. "Maybe with a spoon."

Sometime during his instructions, Cuvelier had rejoined them. "This is not a hospital, Doctor. I can't have that man lying here for days, interrupting our work."

"Moving him will probably kill him," the doctor replied shortly. "Figure it out yourselves. I am needed elsewhere."

He turned to face Chadwick directly, "If you care about this young man, you will move him as little as possible and follow my directions. I will check back later."

He stalked out as briskly as he had arrived leaving Chadwick, Captain Cuvelier and Hastings facing each other over Paddy's inert form.

"He can't stay here," the Captain started.

"He has to stay here," Chadwick responded.

"The spy isn't going anywhere but prison," Hastings practically shouted. "And he stays here until he wakes up and can be judged or dies there."

"From the looks of it," Captain Cuvelier returned, "death is a good possibility but he is distracting my men from their work. He needs to be someplace where he can be properly nursed."

"He belongs in a prison more like," Hastings growled.

"If we can't move him, I can't take him back to our rooms. That is all up hill and we are on the second floor."

When the Captain moved to interrupt him, Chadwick held up a hand gesturing for patience.

"Wait," he said, "I have a suggestion." When Cuvelier nodded, he continued. "This warehouse has a lot of room. We could make up a pallet for him in the corner and rig some kind of temporary screen so that he is not a distraction. Then if you insist on guarding him, although in his condition I can't see the bother, your men can just stay outside the door."

He looked at Cuvelier anxiously. He needed time for Paddy to heal. Paddy had gone into this adventure willingly and had been an enormous help. Although he really wished he could grab Georgina and run, he knew he couldn't live with himself if he just dumped the lad here. The longer they stayed, the more the noose tightened and the more likely it became they would discover George's identity. He looked at her to see if she could give him some sense of her feelings on the situation. She was looking at him steadily.

"We need supplies, monsieur, if I am to care for him," she said calmly. "Captain Cuvelier, can I be allowed to go to our lodgings and get blankets and such? I don't see anything here that will be much help."

"Another reason he doesn't belong here, but Monsieur Couture, your suggestion is reasonable."

When Hastings threw his arms up in exasperation, Cuvelier addressed him. "And what, Lieutenant Hastings, do *you* want to do?"

For the first time since Chadwick had met him, Captain Cuvelier sounded angry. "You come here with this tale of spies and such and expect me to execute a man on your say so. Then you beat him to within an inch of his life and now you want to drag him off to prison. Why? What use is that but his certain death?"

Hastings stood aggressively with his arms crossed and an enraged expression on his face. He obviously did not like being thwarted. Chadwick wondered idly if his face got any redder, if he would explode from anger. It was such an inappropriate and ridiculous thought that he wished he could share it with Georgina. Another glance in her direction showed her to be staring at Hastings with such revulsion that Jeffrey realized she had seen him in his manic stage before. That was probably where the bruises he originally saw on her came from.

"Captain Cuvelier please," he said "can we care for our friend and try to settle the matter of spying later? The man isn't even conscious."

The Captain nodded in agreement. "Yes, one step at a time. Give him a few days to recover and then we will see where we are."

"You are making a mistake in trusting this man," Hastings pointed at Chadwick. "They are probably working together."

"Enough, Lieutenant," Cuvelier talked over Hastings' sputtering. "I have made my decision. He stays here and his friends can nurse him until he is conscious and we will take the next step."

He turned his back on Hastings and addressed George. "Go to your lodgings and get supplies. We really have nothing here to work with."

"Thank you, Captain, for your humanity," Chadwick said. "Can we wait until George gets back before moving him?" Chadwick asked. Cuvelier De Trie nodded and moved off in the direction of his office.

"George, we need to discuss supplies."

Ignoring Hastings, the two started to move off when Jeffrey realized Poulin was still with them.

"Excuse me, monsieur, but can I help?" he asked, to Chadwick's surprise. "I like Monsieur Cavanaugh. We have spent some evenings drinking and I have been helping him with his French. I hate seeing what they did to him and what they might do again. If it is acceptable, I will accompany your young assistant George to the lodgings so there is no interference."

Chadwick felt, rather than heard, George's sigh of relief. Yes, walking back to the lodgings by herself after this horrible day would take a lot of strength. And, while she no doubt was brave, he was glad not to have to ask her to make the trip alone.

"Lieutenant, that is very good of you. Yes, please go with George. I don't trust those men any more than you do, so obviously I feel I need to stay here." He handed George a handful of coins. "If you think of anything you need to purchase, go ahead and get what you need. Oh and if you can get me a clean shirt, I would greatly appreciate it."

She took the coins, nodded at his directions and then made certain Poulin was behind her. Jeffrey had heard her ask Poulin about the possibility of ice. He felt a wave of relief that she could handle nursing Paddy.

Poulin and George exited the warehouse, leaving Chadwick sitting by Paddy's side, his hand on Paddy's arm, wondering how they were going to come out of this increasingly complicated situation.

Chapter Fifteen: Trial by Error

Chadwick woke with a jerk. What was it? He raised his head from his arms and looked about cautiously. He was sitting at the side of Paddy's pallet and remembered putting his head on his arms. He didn't mean to fall asleep, just to rest his eyes but exhaustion had won over good intentions.

Something in the warehouse had changed, startling him into total awareness.

There was only the one low lantern in the corner where Paddy lay, leaving the rest of the space in darkness ranging from pitch black to varying degrees of gray. He could see no movement, no figures heading towards them. As agreed, Hastings' men had stayed outside. No real hardship for them in this weather but he worried they might still try to creep in and cause trouble.

Only he and Paddy remained in the warehouse. Poulin had walked George back to the lodgings for the night. She had wanted to stay and nurse Paddy, but there was little to do except apply damp compresses until Paddy regained consciousness. It would, he hoped, give her a chance to relax. She was really marvelous at acting like a young man. No one seemed to look at her twice. But her constant vigilance over her disguise must take a toll.

Chadwick was grateful that Paddy had not been conscious for the bone setting that afternoon. It had been ugly enough watching. The poor lad was going to be in a world of pain when he did come to. Jeffrey patted his pocket to make sure the laudanum bottle was still there. Paddy would probably need every drop. He surveyed the warehouse for any other movement and then decided to try to drip more water on to Paddy's chapped lips.

A light tap on his arm brought his attention back to Paddy.

"Captain," Paddy's hoarse whisper reached him.

"Shush," Chadwick replied rapidly and just as quietly. "Don't talk. You have been badly hurt. We are in the warehouse. I will explain more in a minute. Let me make certain we are alone."

Taking the lantern, Jeffrey walked the edges of the warehouse, then checked between the desks, stopping often to listen but hearing nothing. Finally, he returned to Paddy. He realized then, it must have been Paddy tapping him on his arm that had awakened him.

"Can you drink?" he asked.

When Paddy nodded, Chadwick helped him raise his head and sip from the mug of water he had kept at the ready. But after a few drops, Paddy began to gag and tried to turn to the side as he started to retch. Chadwick moved the bucket into position, grateful the doctor's assistant had warned him what to expect with a concussed head: vomiting, pain and, probably, memory loss. Finally, Paddy stopped gagging. There seemed to be nothing to come up. That had probably happened at the time of the beating.

Chadwick held the young Irishman's head up so he could rinse his mouth and take another sip of water.

"How bad is it?" Chadwick asked. He was going to pretend his assistant was not seriously hurt.

"Bad. But where is George?" Paddy gasped.

"Don't worry, she is safe. I have laudanum for you. Let me put some in the water."

"No, wait. That stuff will knock me out," Paddy waved his good hand weakly. "First tell me what happened. Last I remember, I was on the ground and that group was kicking me." Paddy ground his words out slowly, each one a painful reminder of his beating. "I don't remember anything until waking up just now. Who were...?"

"Hastings' men," Chadwick answered. "He claims he saw you in Dublin in the King's uniform and therefore you are a spy and should be shot. He is trying to convince Cuvelier to haul you up on espionage charges before Vilet. He claims you and George were trying to get away. George, by the way, is supposed to be your assistant."

Paddy groaned. "God damn hair. He must have recognized my hair somehow."

"That is what I think too and he is making the rest of the story up in order to find George."

"Why haven't you taken her and run?"

"As soon as you can stand, I plan on doing just that." Chadwick surveyed his assistant soberly. "I can't leave you like this, Paddy, and still live with myself. I am going to try to hold off disaster until we three can go together."

"You are a fool, Captain. You will both get killed," Paddy told him soberly.

"I certainly do not intend for that to happen. I have a plan, or part of one. A lot of it does rely on you." Chadwick put his hand on Paddy's shoulder keeping him still while he whispered his plan, or at least the part of it that pertained to Paddy.

"How long do you think you can keep me in a laudanum haze?" the young man finally asked.

"I am not positive. But at least for a couple of days."

"I don't have a problem with that," Paddy agreed. "My head throbs now so bad I wish I could rip it off."

"I hope to keep giving you enough so that you do not really wake up. In the day-time, we will probably have to drip it in with a cloth. Just keep swallowing and don't open your eyes unless I say so."

"My hand…"

"Bastards stomped it and broke a bunch of bones. But that and a couple of ribs seem to be the only things broken. It is mostly your head that took the worst of the beating."

"Sure feels like it," Paddy sighed. "But Captain, if this plan goes bad, you've got to take George and go as far and as fast as you can."

"I understand what you are saying," Chadwick replied softly. That was one decision he did not want to make, and he knew he would put it off as long as possible.

"Just play your part and stay unconscious as long as you can. George will be here in the morning to sit with you. Now, drink this and go back to sleep."

* * *

"How is he?" Georgina's low voice woke Chadwick the next morning. Damn, he couldn't seem to stay awake. To his delight, she handed him a cup of coffee.

He stood, trying to stretch out the muscles that ached from sleeping in an awkward position all night. He sipped the dark beverage. It bore little resemblance to the coffee his valet brewed, but at least it was hot and likely to keep him awake for some time.

Georgina stood at his shoulder, both hands clasping her mug. She raised the cup in a slight salute. He noticed that her broken finger was still at an awkward angle but the splint and bandages were much reduced. "The coffee is courtesy of Lieutenant Poulin. He was waiting for me outside Madame Travers' this morning. He really is a good man."

He nodded at her hand. "How is the finger?"

"It is doing fine. Honestly sometimes I even forget about it. He is so much worse." She gestured at Paddy. They stood quietly studying Paddy.

When Chadwick was reasonably sure no one was overtly trying to overhear, he quietly filled her in on his middle-of-the night conversation with Paddy and their decision to keep Paddy drugged so whatever trial or hearing Hastings thought up would have to be put off.

"Can we confuse the physician when he comes by?" she asked softly.

Chadwick shrugged. "I hope so. But, honestly, it is Cuvelier who will make any important decisions."

They talked a few more minutes about how to drip water into Paddy's mouth while he was unconscious and then Chadwick saw Captain Cuvelier making his way to them from his office, Lieutenant Poulin in tow.

"Ah, Captain," he said. "I was just coming to you to tell you there is no change just yet. He was restless during the night, but I gave him more laudanum and he has been as you see him since."

Again, all stood surveying Paddy in silence.

Finally the Captain spoke, "Good, as long as he is unconscious, maybe we can get some work done around here without these constant interruptions."

Chadwick wanted to retort that it wasn't him but Hastings who was causing the interruptions but from the warning look on Poulin's face, he thought maybe correcting the Captain right now was not a good thing. He decided instead to offer a peace gesture.

"Since I have George, here, to watch and nurse Paddy, I might as well work on those translations," he said. "I want to go back to the lodgings, get a clean shirt and shave and then I will return and see what I can finish."

Captain Cuvelier looked surprised but pleased with Chadwick's plan.

"Thank you," he responded. "That would be very helpful. I assume when the young man finally wakes up, Lieutenant Hastings will insist on continuing with his accusations and that will disrupt our work all over again."

Chadwick nodded in agreement. "Yes, I am confident you are right on both accounts. Especially since I will have to accompany Paddy and see about his defense."

He paused and tried to evaluate how sympathetic the Captain might be. From the look on his face, not very, but then his warehouse and work had been disrupted and that obviously was his first concern. "Captain, do you have any idea what Hastings has in mind?"

Cuvelier turned from studying Paddy to frowning at Chadwick. "What do you mean, have in mind?" He asked. "He has been pretty clear he thinks your chap there is an English spy and should be shot. I think if you had not been here, that would have happened already."

"I was thinking along the same lines, but if it was that simple, surely his men would have 'accidently' shot Paddy when they kidnapped him in the first place," Chadwick said thoughtfully. He had a different thought, that Hastings was looking for another kind of information, and it terrified him that Georgina was hiding in plain sight. He did not want to think how soon Hastings might spot her.

"I keep feeling there is something more involved, but I can't see what it is. They brought Paddy back here for a reason. It seems to me there is some information Paddy has or Hastings *thinks* he has. Some reason for an interrogation." Chadwick hoped he was sowing some seeds of doubt in Cuvelier's mind about Hastings' motives.

Poulin at least seemed receptive.

"I see what you mean, monsieur," he agreed. "He has said he wants to ask Paddy questions when he wakes up. But if not about spying, what could he mean?"

"I do wonder that myself. Since I do not believe Paddy is a spy, I keep wondering what Hastings thinks he knows." There was no answer from either of the Frenchmen, so Jeffrey sighed.

"George, any questions before I go to the lodgings?" He asked.

George, as had been her practice, kept her head down even now.

"No, sir," she said. "I have the laudanum and fresh water. Do you think you will be long?" She sounded a bit anxious. He couldn't blame her, surrounded as she was with soldiers and trying to protect an unconscious man.

"Lieutenant Hastings might return before you do."

"I asked him not to come here today," Cuvelier said unexpectedly. "Too much disruption, and unless the young man wakes up, no need. He doesn't work the way you do, monsieur."

The senior translator moved off, leaving Chadwick and Poulin with George.

Poulin glanced after his superior to make sure he wasn't in hearing.

"Very unfortunate events, monsieur," he said. "Captain doesn't like Hastings, but he can't ignore his accusations. Especially since Vilet hasn't verified your papers. However, he likes you and is impressed by the work you have done for him. I don't think he can make up his mind. Hastings' accusations have just enough veracity to make them possible, but until he has more proof or Vilet verifies your papers, he told me, it is hard for him to know what to do."

Chadwick nodded gratefully for the information.

"Thank you, Lieutenant," he said. "I will think on what you said and see if I can find a way to allay his fears."

"I know he said he was writing to Vilet this morning with details of Hastings' accusation and asking him to send him any information he might have," Poulin added casually.

George's and Jeffrey's eyes met in shock.

Whatever Vilet could say might prove to be another new and very unwelcome wrinkle in an already complicated situation.

The rest of the day passed quietly enough. Hastings' men made regular trips into the warehouse to check on Paddy. Chadwick thought to ask them how Paddy was supposed to slip away in his condition, but then thought better of having any interaction with the men. They gave every appearance of being the fuse for a powder keg and would use any excuse for an explosion of violence. George stood back whenever they made an entrance but Jeffrey noticed she never really left Paddy's side when he would be alone with Hastings' men. After one such visit, she made her way across the room to Jeffrey's desk, which was set somewhat apart from the other work tables.

"Monsieur Couture," she whispered when she got close to him, "what is going to happen when the warehouse closes down for the day?"

Chadwick had been wondering the same thing.

"They never once came inside last night. Hastings must have ordered them to watch for Paddy to wake up," he said. "It seems clear that they are not going to kill Paddy while he is unconscious. I think Hastings wants information about Miss Yelverton."

"Oh, so the spy thing is a cover?"

Chadwick judged it to be safe to fill George in on the thoughts that had been roiling in his mind all day. "I think he recognized Paddy from the night we found you," he said quietly. "Hastings would never have been in Dublin Castle, so he could never have seen Paddy in his uniform. That story is just garbage."

Georgina expelled a soft breath and said, "You think he is still looking for me."

"I think he is an opportunist. He recognized Paddy and realized that he might find you again. But he hasn't put all the parts together yet, and he doesn't know where I fit in."

"If he wasn't so excited yesterday, he might have looked at me closer and then, where would we be?" she asked.

"I am hoping that we will get away before that happens. We need Paddy to wake up later to see how he is and whether he can be moved yet."

Georgina shifted so that she stood with her back to the room, making it even harder for someone to overhear her. "Even if he is aware, I doubt he will be able to walk. He will be stiff from lying on that pallet. Can you carry him?" she asked intently.

Chadwick looked over at the still form and gave her question serious thought. Paddy was almost as tall as he and fully formed. Chadwick thought that he, himself, was reasonably fit, but it had been some time since any serious physical exertion had been part of his life. Could he lift someone who was almost his exact size?

"Maybe not," he admitted.

Georgina nodded in agreement.

"Here's what we should do," she began. "We limit the laudanum so that he can regain his senses tonight. Then we can get him up and walk him around to evaluate his condition. Then we can make better plans."

Chadwick realized gratefully, yet again, that she had a good brain. He wasn't totally responsible for any escape plan; Georgina also could offer ideas and proposals that were viable. In other words Georgina was a real working partner.

Even as he was nodding in agreement, he could see over her shoulder, Poulin approaching.

"I am leaving soon," the Lieutenant said. "Do you want me to escort Monsieur George to your rooms?"

"Thank you, Lieutenant," Chadwick responded, "but he is staying here tonight. Honestly, I am concerned by the number of times Hastings' men have come in here to check. If they come in during the night and cause trouble, at least I have George to send for help."

Poulin frowned in concern. "How often have they come in?" he asked.

"Every hour or so."

"That often?" Poulin asked thoughtfully. "Hastings must have told them to send for him if Paddy woke up." He looked over the warehouse where the other translators were packing up, obviously ending their work day. He glanced at Paddy and then back at Chadwick.

"I will stay tonight also," he said firmly.

"I am not sure that is necessary," Chadwick replied carefully. "I can send George to get you if they cause any nonsense."

"I do have a commitment this evening," Poulin said. "But it is nothing that should not be cancelled. Paddy's life is more important."

Chadwick had been studying the doors.

"Lieutenant, consider this idea," he said. "Lock us in. We can bar that small back door from the inside. You lock the main door. We should be fine. They can't get in and we can't get out if they watch both doors."

Poulin looked at him in surprise. "You are comfortable doing that?"

"Yes," Chadwick said. "Paddy isn't going anywhere in his condition. The locked doors will keep Hastings out, at least until you arrive in the morning. We will be safe enough."

It wasn't the most comfortable night he had ever spent but since he got to spend it almost alone with Georgina, it was one of the best.

Before Poulin locked the main door, Georgina had retrieved some blankets from their lodging and some food from the local tavern. The long hours of the night seemed to race by as they talked quietly or simply sat with their arms around each other.

Unfortunately, for their plans, Paddy never woke up.

"We must have given him too much laudanum in the first place," Chadwick surmised.

"His pulse is still steady and his breathing is also. I guess we just have to wait for him to wake up," Georgina sighed. "Do we put him back under when he does wake?"

"Let's see how he does and then decide."

"Look at his face," she said. "It looks like his whole face is going to be black and blue, but at least a bit of the swelling seems to be going down."

Chadwick pulled her back into his arms. He had no real idea what was going to happen the next day, but he feared he was headed for a French prison cell. Tonight could be the last time he would be with her. He couldn't be unhappy that Paddy was taking his time waking up. It meant that he could spend more time with Georgina, stroking her soft curls, kissing her lips, and listening to her soft gasps of pleasure. Sometime during the night, he finally got the binding off her breasts and they proved to be as full and pleasurable as he had imagined. Even though he desired her and George seemed willing, he knew this wasn't the time or place. She deserved so much better than dusty blankets on a warehouse floor.

In the end, they dozed on those dusty blankets with him spooned around her, his arm holding her close while they waited for the dawn.

As luck would have it, it was dawn when a groan from Paddy brought Chadwick awake. He groaned himself when he realized he had to leave Georgina's warm body and see if, in fact, his young aide was really coming to. Neither man woke Georgina, so Jeffrey carefully covered her with the blanket and crept over to the pallet where the young Irishman lay. He seemed to be in some distress by the way his head shook back and forth and his body moved restlessly. Then his eyes fluttered. The gloom was lifting in the warehouse and Chadwick could see Paddy's bruised face with some clarity. The night had gone so quickly.

"Jesus, what happened to me?" Paddy moaned.

"Do you remember anything?" The doctor had mentioned that concussed people often had memory loss.

"No, did someone take a pipe to me?"

"Rather," Chadwick replied. He gave Paddy a sketchy summary of the past forty-eight hours and warned him that they were in real danger that Hastings would return and attempt to finger Paddy as a spy.

"So I have been unconscious all this time?" he asked.

"Trying to give you some time to heal and keep you from having to answer questions. I don't think it has been enough time for you, though," Chadwick said.

He grimaced as he surveyed Paddy's swollen and bruised face. "How do your ribs feel?"

Paddy gave a small shrug. "Not really sure how I feel until I try to get up."

"Are you ready for that?" At Paddy's short nod, Chadwick put his arm under his shoulder and slowly helped him into a sitting position.

By now Georgina was awake and had positioned herself at Paddy's other side to help lever him up.

"Um, George," Chadwick murmured. "He doesn't have any pants on."

"I won't look," she promised grimly. "You need me if you are not going to drop him on the floor."

She studiously looked at the wall as they both heaved to get the beaten man to his feet. Paddy proved to be very wobbly as he tried a few steps.

"Damn," Chadwick hissed. "George…"

The turning of a key in the lock sounded like a cannon shot and the front door opened. Poulin, followed immediately by Hastings and Captain Cuvelier poured in. Chadwick, Paddy, and George froze.

"Excellent!" Hastings shouted. "The spy is awake. I was beginning to think there was something mysterious about his condition."

Then Jeffrey realized that George didn't have her hat on or her breast bands. In the sudden daylight there was no way she didn't look like the beautiful woman she was.

Hastings gave a shout of triumph. "See Captain, they are not what they appear to be. That woman, pretending to be a boy, is Georgina Yelverton from Dublin. Her father has been searching for her since she ran away. These men spirited her away from her father's arms and took ship for France. I have been following them and I have a letter from her father commissioning me to search for her."

Jeffrey glanced at Georgina's face to see her staring at Hastings. Her lips were thin with anger. There was no fear on her face, just disgust and revulsion.

"Kidnappers?" Cuvelier asked shaking his head in confusion. "You said spies."

"Captain," Lieutenant Poulin interjected, "may I suggest we let Monsieur Couture tend to his friend and then we can sit and hear both sides."

At his Captain's nod, Poulin moved to take George's position at Paddy's side.

"I hope your story is a good one monsieur," he said softly. "This looks like a God awful mess and my good Captain hates a mess."

* * *

As he helped Paddy into Cuvelier s office, Chadwick tried to study the Captain's expression. But it was intentionally neutral and told him nothing. He arranged a chair against the wall so Paddy could lean against the wall. He was far from well, but Chadwick could see he was desperately trying to stay awake and involved. George had given him another drop or two of laudanum, hoping to dull the pain without putting him to sleep.

Paddy closed his eyes, but Chadwick could see his good hand clench and unclench as he tried to deal with the agony in his head. He put a hand on the young man's shoulder.

"Let me do the talking," he said.

George took the chair next to Paddy. Chadwick thought with some satisfaction that Hastings was going to have to explain why she was not greeting her 'rescuer' with any enthusiasm and seemed not just content, but determined, to stay at Paddy's side.

Poulin brought in more chairs, arranging them in front of the desk, although he didn't choose one for himself, but instead stood with arms crossed by the door.

Chadwick grabbed a chair and placed it between his friends and the Captain's desk. He was now also positioned between Hastings and Georgina. He stretched out his legs and crossed his arms and studied Hastings. He could count on one hand the times he had met the man, but each time his demeanor seemed to be bordering on manic. Even now, he could hardly sit still, shifting constantly. He crossed and re-crossed his legs almost constantly.

With Hastings was another man, maybe an officer in Hastings' unit as they wore the same uniform, but Chadwick could not see any insignia of rank. No one introduced him or, to Chadwick's dismay, questioned his right to attend the meeting. He stood against the wall with his arms crossed, almost mirroring Poulin's stance. To Chadwick, the man looked more like hired muscle than any military officer, with a face that bore the results of numerous fights, oversized hands, and small angry eyes.

Cuvelier cleared his throat. "Lieutenant Hastings, you may begin," he said politely.

Hastings immediately jumped to his feet and began pacing, even in the small space left by the chairs. He repeated his accusations that Chadwick and Paddy were kidnappers who took Miss Yelverton from her home in Dublin and he, Hastings, had been asked by her distraught father to bring her home. Words spewed out without pause, so Chadwick could not interrupt with any questions or point out the gaping holes in his story. It was still impossible to tell from his expression if any of Hastings statements made an impression on Cuvelier.

Then Hastings threw in the accusation that Paddy was a spy because he saw him in Dublin in a red uniform.

"A moment, Captain," Cuvelier finally interrupted. "What say you about all this?" He gestured for Chadwick to take the floor when Hastings started shouting.

"Are you serious? Haven't you been listening? The man is a kidnapper, an abuser of gently raised young women. You saw the condition she was in this morning. You cannot take anything he says seriously."

Then Cuvelier was on his feet. "Sit down, Lieutenant Hastings," he ordered. "I will hear what he has to say. You have made grave accusations against him and his assistant. You have even physically attacked the young man. Monsieur Couture deserves the right to refute your allegations."

Chadwick remained seated, trying to look calm and confident and pondering how best to make his case and how much of the truth to tell. He had to assume that admitting he was a British citizen would not be in anyone's interest, but his original cover story might still work. However, with all Hastings remonstrations and protests, he couldn't really get a word in. Finally, Hastings slammed a letter down on the desk.

In the sudden quiet, the Captain picked up the missive and began to read. He scowled as he read but then silently handed the letter to Chadwick.

The message wasn't long, only a couple of sentences dated almost a month ago. It told the reader that the bearer of the letter, one Lieutenant James Hastings, was directed to find the missing daughter of the undersigned. She was believed to be in the company of Monsieur Couture, a merchant from New Orleans, and a Paddy Cavanaugh, his assistant, having disappeared from Dublin with them and believed to have taken a ship to France. The letter was signed by Walter Yelverton.

Chadwick read it through a second time. From the gasp in his ear, Georgina had obviously been reading it over his shoulder. He glanced at her face to see if she had finished it. Then he passed it back to Cuvelier.

"The timing of this is all wrong," he said. "The Lieutenant has been in this county too long to have brought this note with him from Dublin. Additionally, how do we know it is Mr. Yelverton's writing?" he asked.

Hastings again began to bluster but the Captain cut him off. "Enough," he told him. "I will get to the bottom of this." The Captain handed the sheet to Georgina. "Mademoiselle?" He asked. "Do you recognize the writing?"

George took her time studying the document despite the blustering of Hastings and his constant dialogue. Finally, she handed it back.

"Honestly I am not positive, Captain," she said with what Chadwick thought was admirable composure. "My father usually does not write his own letters but has his secretary pen them. So, I find it strange that he wrote out the whole letter."

Hastings took real umbrage with her comments, saying, "Given the delicacy of the content, I would find it strange if he dictated such a missive."

"I mention it, Captain," Georgina spoke louder in order to be heard over Hastings, "because even when I was at school, he dictated his letters to me.

What that means is that I can't really tell you what his hand looks like," she protested. "I have not seen much of it, so I cannot say this is his writing."

"Captain, can I say…?" Chadwick began when Hastings interrupted him again.

"There is nothing you can say," Hastings practically screamed. "The girl is mine! They sent me after her and now I have found her!" Suddenly he charged around Jeffrey and grabbed Georgina by the arm. The other man moved for the first time, pulling a pistol, which he aimed at Georgina. Chadwick, Poulin, and Cuvelier froze.

"As you can see, gentlemen," Hastings sneered, "I will be taking her with me. Any movement on your part and it is not you who will be shot, but Miss Yelverton. Now, move from the door, Poulin. You are not part of this and I would rather not have to hurt you."

Hastings jerked Georgina to his side and started dragging her, protesting, to the door. She looked pleadingly at Chadwick. Jeffrey was frantically study-ing the distances trying to decide if he should tackle Hastings' assistant with the gun before he shot Georgina or jump Hastings.

Before he could make a move, an explosion behind Chadwick caused everyone in the room to jump. George gave a startled scream and jerked even harder in Hastings' hold. Hastings' man suddenly slumped to the floor. Hastings also jumped, giving his associate a surprised and then dismayed glance.

Georgina pulled again and then gave Hastings' shin a stout kick with her wooden clogs. Although she couldn't break free, it was just enough to draw Hastings attention away from Chadwick.

Chadwick pulled the knife from his boot and charged Hastings. He slammed his shoulder into the man's chest and thrust his knife into the top of Hastings' thigh, trying for the major artery there.

Chapter Sixteen: Where Now?

"I never killed a man before with a knife!" Chadwick admitted. His hand shook visibly as he tried to grasp the cup of coffee Georgina was attempting to hand him. Finally, she wrapped her hands around his so he could sip the beverage.

"Well, we are not confident he is dead yet," she said calmly.

"Should be," interjected Paddy softly. "That was a good thrust, sir. You gave a good impression of a man who knew what you were about." Paddy still leaned against the wall with his eyes closed, obviously in pain.

"I have never ever, been that angry."

The three sat alone in Captain Cuvelier's office. Hastings had been removed by his men in hopes of getting him to a physician before he bled out. Chadwick agreed with Paddy that that was probably a futile effort. He might never have used a knife on a man before, but his time in the army had taught him the more vulnerable parts of the body and the most effective way to kill a man quietly. One did not forget such training.

He studied his assistant anxiously. If possible, Paddy was even more ashen than before. "When did you have a chance to load the pistol?" Chadwick asked Paddy. "Or, more to the point, how did you do that with one hand?"

"George loaded it," was his surprising answer.

"She knows how to load a pistol?" Jeffrey asked incredulously.

"She does now," was Paddy's laconic reply.

"That was a damn good shot, even if it did scare the bejesus out of me," Chadwick remarked. "You have many hidden skills."

Paddy opened his eyes a slit and gave a small wry smile. "A lot of my skills are thanks to my seafaring days with Captain Byrne. He made certain his crew was well-trained." He rested his head against the wall again and closed his eyes. Chadwick assumed the explosion of the pistol in the small office had intensified the lad's headache. The young man was obviously suffering but still managed to not complain or moan out loud.

George, who had disappeared a moment before, was back. She seemed to be allowed to move about the warehouse easily, while Jeffrey and Paddy had been clearly ordered to stay put. She carried a damp cloth, which she put on the back of Paddy's neck.

"How are you?" she asked quietly.

Before Paddy could reply, Lieutenant Poulin came back into the office and sat in one of the vacant chairs. "He's dead," he said shortly. "One of his men just came back to say he didn't make it to the surgeon's. They want your head, monsieur. What are we going to do?"

"Where's the Captain?" Chadwick asked.

"The Captain isn't feeling well and had to go to his lodgings. He left me in charge," Poulin said blandly. "Here's the situation as I see it: You just killed a lieutenant of the French army—scum that he may have been, And Paddy here, killed one of his men. There is a crowd of men outside the door who want to see you both hanged. Commissioner Vilet is expected here momentarily, and *you* have no papers."

Chadwick sat very still in his chair and thought furiously. It was odd that Poulin seemed to be in charge.

"Lieutenant Poulin," he said. "I understand we have little time, but I would like to reassure you that Miss Yelverton is the victim in this matter."

"Oh, I can see that from the way she reacted to Hastings. There was no pleasure and gratitude about being 'saved' by that piece of garbage. I can also see she is not frightened of you."

Chadwick pulled the small portrait from his pocket. "This is what her father gave to me when I met with him. Not a letter."

"So, Hastings was the real kidnapper," Poulin said thoughtfully. "Why?"

"That I don't know. But I hope to get back to Dublin to find out."

"Not going to Bordeaux?"

"Soon, but I need to take Miss Yelverton home. I can't just shove her on a boat—especially since there is no legal way for her return."

"It's going to be even more complicated if you aren't gone by the time Vilet gets here," Poulin warned. "I was hoping that you had a plan already in place."

Chadwick sighed, "It has been difficult without papers to get anywhere. That was why Paddy and George were heading to Calais, to find us transport back to Dublin."

Chadwick hoped that his cover story was holding. He was not to admit at this point that he really was British. Poulin seemed to be sympathetic, but Jeffrey knew he was still a French soldier whose first loyalty was to his country.

"But we need to leave and leave quickly. Is that what I understand you to be saying?" he asked Poulin.

The French lieutenant nodded in agreement, but it was George who interjected, "Can we get to Calais by boat?"

"Boat is the best bet, but I do not know where to suggest you go to find one," Poulin replied ruefully. "I am not from this area and really don't know much about it. I have heard that since the navy started building the landing craft here, all the free traders have left. As you found, some of them have started to use Calais, but most seem to have found other ports or deserted beaches."

Chadwick leaned forward to shake Poulin's hand.

"Lieutenant, you are an honest and a good man. I think that how we leave Boulogne is up to us. You shouldn't be involved in anything that will get you in more trouble."

"It is not just me," Poulin replied. "Captain Cuvelier took to his sick bed so he can honestly say he did not know anything. He feels awful that he sent for Vilet and made your situation even more precarious. Whatever his suspicions are, they are just that, suspicions."

"Well, I did kill Hastings in front of him."

"A justified action in my opinion," came the firm answer. The Lieutenant stood and Chadwick stood with him.

"I think I will go now to Hastings' commanding officer and give him the bad news. I will need to take some of the men with me to show me where they are billeted. I will assure everyone you are locked in this office."

"What about the back door?" George asked, referring to the door she had been using to get to the public well.

"The last time I checked, the idiots were all out front arguing about who was going to be lieutenant now. Do they really elect their officers?"

"Who knows?" Chadwick answered. "But if it keeps them occupied, it is all for the best. If you can keep them out front for a few more minutes, we will be out of your hair by the time you get back. Obviously the less you know, the better."

Poulin nodded. He went and shook Paddy's hand. "I will miss our chats, my friend," he said. "Be safe." And he slipped quietly out the door.

Chadwick surveyed his companions. Paddy was dressed, but looked half-dead. Jeffrey would probably have to support him and hope he just looked drunk if anyone noticed. Georgina was once again in her young man disguise. "Where is your hat?" he asked her.

George gasped. "On the floor by the pallet. I will grab it on the way out."

"Good enough," Chadwick tried to smile encouragingly. George gave him a wavering smile in return, but Paddy's eyes were shut.

"Time to go, my friend."

Jeffrey snatched the miniature of Georgina from the desk and shoved it back into his pocket. He reached an arm around Paddy and helped him to his feet.

"You are going to pretend to be suffering from a hard night at the taverns, Paddy. Keep your eyes shut if you need to; I will lead. George, follow us, but try to not appear to be with us. If anyone follows us, they will be looking for three people. I want to appear to be just two. However, do not lose sight of us. We are heading for the docks and I hope, some kind of boat."

George nodded and led the way out the office door.

Paddy gasped in pain when they stepped into the sunlight. Chadwick pulled Paddy's hat down so that the brim covered his eyes. The young man took a deep breath and tried to step out, but he obviously was in too much pain to walk on his own. Jeffrey pulled Paddy's arm over his shoulders and wrapped his own arm around his waist. They moved slowly down the alley that bordered the warehouse.

"Where are we going?" Paddy gasped.

"To the waterfront. Where else would we find a boat?"

Chadwick's plan – which wasn't much of a plan he admitted to himself – revolved around getting to the quay, locating a place to stash Paddy and George, and finding a boat. From something Poulin had said, he realized that there was another reason the smugglers had vacated Boulogne: the British Navy was patrolling the Channel, and had been for a number of years. They were keeping the French Navy bottled up. No smuggler would want to tangle with them. Maybe, they wouldn't need to get totally across the Channel; if they made it part of the way they could get picked up by a British ship. It was totally worth a gamble.

It seemed to take hours to get to the quay. Since Chadwick stayed in alleys and out of main thoroughfares whenever he could, it might have taken hours. All the time, he berated Paddy out loud for being so stupid and drinking so much the night before. Occasionally, they had to stop so Paddy could rest and try to regain what little strength he had. George would use those opportunities to catch up and exchange information.

Paddy's condition didn't seem to cause much comment, at least any that Chadwick could hear. George hadn't heard much, either, although she did notice various eye rolls and sneers. Chadwick was pretty confident that at times the poor chap had been unconscious, especially when his body slumped heavily. But somehow his feet kept moving, and they trudged along.

"Monsieur," George's quiet voice called. Chadwick stopped and let her draw even with them. "There! That tavern looks adequate, don't you think?"

Chadwick looked to where she was nodding and saw a building that seemed to be held up by the surrounding buildings. An ill-fitting door was propped open with a keg upon which an equally ill-looking character sat sharpening his knife. He looked up when they paused in front of him.

"What the hell happened to him?" he barked, gesturing at Paddy.

"Pissed off the wrong soldiers. But he gave as good as he got," Chadwick replied. He assumed there would be no love lost between locals and the soldiers, and from the man's snort of laughter it seemed he agreed.

Chadwick continued inside, hoping they could find refuge here for a short time. He was exhausted from propping up Paddy and needed some time to think about their next moves. They all needed some food.

He braced Paddy in the darkest corner he could find. While Jeffrey stretched his back and surveyed the place, George slipped onto a stool next to Paddy.

"How are you doing, Paddy?" she asked.

Paddy didn't really answer, only groaned in reply and patted her with his good hand. "Any water, George?" he croaked.

"Not in this place; maybe small beer. I will go ask," Chadwick said.

The man from the keg had wandered in and made for the plank resting on two other barrels that passed for a bar. He tied a dirty cloth around his waist and looked at them expectantly. "What?" he barked at them.

"Three beers and maybe some information," Chadwick held a coin up in his fingers.

The man's eyes glistened greedily.

"Don't get too greedy; those soldiers took about everything I had," Jeffrey warned.

"Don't see any bruises on you," the man said pointedly.

"I had to buy them off from killing my friend," Chadwick replied. He hoped the man believed him. He did not intend to get this far only to be killed for the few coins he had left.

"I got beer, not positive about information, especially if you are running from the authorities."

Chadwick took two beers over to Paddy and George; he returned for his own.

"I need to get my friend out of town. I thought I might hire a boat. Do you have any ideas where I might find someone interested in a fast boat ride away from here?"

"And where do you think you might be going to?" the man asked.

"Hamburg would be best," Chadwick said cautiously.

"Let me think on it."

"Do you have anything to eat?"

"Nay, but send your lad down the alley. Mistress back there usually has an extra loaf of bread she can sell you." He slouched out his back door calling for Henri.

George was back with the bread before the man returned. When he did return, he was followed by a small boy who didn't look more than six years old to Jeffrey. Amazingly, he left the child to tend the bar. But such customers who wandered in and found the bar tended by such a youngster did not seem at all surprised. Chadwick assumed it must be a common occurrence for the barman to slip off in the daytime.

The next time the barman reappeared, he was accompanied by another man whose visage made the barman look almost angelic.

"This is François," he said to Chadwick as he jerked a finger at his companion. "He has a boat."

Jeffrey studied the newcomer. There was absolutely nothing about the man to inspire confidence or help him believe that the man might help them. He was dirty, and Chadwick could smell him from where he sat. But he wouldn't judge him on the odor.

"What kind of boat?" he finally asked.

"One that floats," came the snarky reply from the barman.

"Jeffrey..." said George hesitantly from behind him.

Georgina's voice reinforced Chadwick's own feeling of unease. He stood suddenly.

"Thank you gentlemen, I am sorry for the inconvenience, but we will look elsewhere for transportation. Here's for your trouble." He made to hand the barman a few coins when Francois spoke.

"You are not going to find it in time, monsieur," he said. In spite of his looks, he sounded almost educated. "Even coming this short distance, I saw green jackets up and down the quay asking questions. They are obviously looking for someone and you and that chap are the only non-locals I've seen around here in days. You may not want my help, but you need it. You have few other options."

Chadwick turned and looked at Paddy and George. Paddy was still slumped over the table, resting his head on his arms, his eyes closed, obviously trying not to show how much pain he was in. George looked steadily back at Jeffrey but her lips were thin in an effort to conceal how concerned she was for the situation in which they found themselves.

"Boxed in," she said finally.

Chadwick turned back to the boat captain. "I ask you again, monsieur, how big is this boat? Can it take us to Hamburg?"

"No, not Hamburg," came the swift reply. "But I am willing to go the other way, to the Channel Islands. We won't meet as much of the British Navy going west."

"It will fit all of us?" Chadwick asked.

"Should. But I don't have much in the way of supplies on board. You had best pick up some food and drink if you expect to eat."

Suddenly the door flew open and the young Henri, who had been sitting out front on the keg came running in. "Papa, they are coming!" he yelled.

François nodded at the barman and jerked his finger at Chadwick. "Come, we go to the cellar." Without ado, he grabbed Paddy's arm and together they hustled him behind the bar, where the owner was now holding up a trap door.

"Jump," he ordered. "It is a short drop and we don't have time for the stairs."

The owner dropped the door as soon as George tumbled through.

Crouching in the darkness, it was easy to hear the boots of the searching soldiers. Their voices were as clear as if they were standing next to them. Chadwick cringed as he heard an exact description of himself, George, and Paddy, followed by the offer of a reward. He couldn't see Georgina in the dark, but suddenly her hand found his. He squeezed it back, hoping it gave her some comfort.

It seemed to take forever for the soldiers to leave. Finally Chadwick realized they weren't leaving. They had settled down with drinks and seemed to be making themselves quite comfortable.

The situation became clearer when new footsteps were heard overhead. The soldiers all scrambled to their feet. Obviously, they had been waiting for someone. The new voice was not someone Chadwick had been expecting.

"They were seen coming in here," Vilet was saying.

"As I told your men, monsieur," the barman replied, "they came in and went out the back door when they heard your men were looking for them. That is all I know. I will say that unlike your men, they paid for their drinks."

The hatch door over their heads creaked and Chadwick realized the barman must be standing on it.

"You should be paying people to drink this swill, not charging for it," Vilet said repressively.

"Here, you men! Go out the back door and search every house," he then ordered. "Look for cellars and attics, too. They can't have gone far if the Irishman is as beat up as I hear. The rest of you continue down the quay. Be certain you search every alley you see."

The men groaned as Vilet gave them their orders. It was now the middle of the afternoon as far as Jeffrey could estimate, and they must have been searching for hours already. He could hear the men file out.

"If I find you are not telling me the truth, you will meet the same fate as the ones we are searching for," Vilet threatened.

"What did they do?" the barman asked curiously.

"Killed a soldier."

"Really, who did that? The one so beat up he can't walk, or the pansy-waist one who looks like he never gets his hands dirty?"

"Doesn't matter," Vilet growled. "They were both there, so they are both guilty." Chadwick could hear him slam his mug down on the plank bar and stomp out. "That stuff is enough to make you puke."

When all was quiet in the tavern, François grabbed Chadwick by the shoulder. Could everyone see in the dark cellar but him?

He whispered, "We will stay here until nightfall."

It was just as well Jeffrey thought. Neither he nor Georgina had had much sleep the night before, and Paddy could use all the rest he could get. So he pulled on her arm until she sat by his side, their thighs touching. He could feel when she slipped into sleep and her head dropped onto his shoulder.

The creak of the hatch door opening woke Chadwick from the light doze into which he had fallen. Sentry sleep, they had called it in the army. He looked up to see the barman peering down at them.

"Time to go," he said rather cheerily, to Chadwick's disgust.

Francois was the first out of the hole. He seemed to have had a lot of experience with this particular hideaway. The Frenchman leaned back to help Paddy who was definitely rocky on his feet. Chadwick and George followed, although it took a few minutes to get the blood flowing to Jeffrey's legs which were numb from sitting too long in one position.

Once back in the dingy tavern, Jeffrey could see no drinkers. The front door was shut.

At his questioning look, the barman said, "I don't make enough money serving that swill to keep body and soul together. If I close the place down while Francois and I take a little trip, I doubt anyone will even notice." He turned to lead them out the back door and Chadwick saw he now carried a backpack that he hoped had some food in it.

Chadwick didn't want to mention that Vilet seemed to be a man who would notice anything out of the ordinary, such as a tavern that was closed when it should be open. He needed these men to get them out of Boulogne. He was thankful that they hadn't turned them in when they had the chance, but he sure did not trust them, either.

As they filed out the back door to a narrow and dank alley, Chadwick fell back to whisper to George, "Where is the pistol?"

She didn't respond, only patted her pocket.

If he thought he had seen most of the back streets of Boulogne before, he was mistaken. With Francois in the lead, they twisted and turned between increasingly ramshackle buildings as the evening gloom went from dusk to total dark. Finally, they emerged at the edge of town. At their backs, they could see the lights of the quay, where work continued on the invasion fleet. But they appeared to be heading into the marshes. *What better place to get rid of a few bodies,* he thought. Yet neither man tried to get behind them and the Frenchmen took turns helping prop up Paddy.

After slogging along a barely discernable path for a fairly short time, they found that the path abruptly ended. To Chadwick's amazement, there was a small boat floating in some open water. By Francois' lantern, it appeared large enough to fit all five of them. Jeffrey could see a single mast.

Paddy spoke for the first time in hours.

"Oars?" he asked. "Where are the oars?"

"They're in there," Francois said.

"With all of us rowing, how long before we reach the Channel?" Chadwick asked. He was well aware a long trip by boat was out of the question, since they had not brought any supplies.

"Change of plans," the barman unexpectedly said.

Chadwick felt, rather than saw, George move to a place where she would have direct line of fire at the barman or Francois, although she didn't yet have the pistol in her hand yet. Was it too early to reach for his knife?

"What change?" he demanded.

"We are not going with you," Francois said.

"That was the deal," Chadwick growled.

"Look, it's a good boat. Just give us the money and it's all yours."

"How am I going to handle that by myself?"

"You can row," came the disinterested answer. "You are a big healthy chap. Once in the river, the current will take you to the Channel."

"If we even make it that far, then what?"

"Put up the sail."

"Jeffrey, we are safer without them," George interjected.

"I don't know how to sail a boat," he hissed back.

Paddy, who had been resting by leaning against the side of the boat, pushed himself upright. "But I do," he said. "I might not be much help in the actual manning, but I can tell you what needs to be done."

Francois shifted uneasily. "We stole this boat last week from the yard where they were putting on the finishing touches," he said. "Now they are looking for it. We can't keep it here long."

George unexpectedly let out a burst of laughter. "You are trying to sell us stolen property so we take it away and you don't get arrested! And for this, you expect us to pay you?" She gave another chortle. "You have a lot of nerve."

Francois looked offended. "We are doing you a favor!" he exclaimed. "You need a boat, we have a boat. We need to get rid of the boat, you want to get out of Boulogne. How doesn't this benefit everyone?" he protested.

George just shook her head. "I can help you row," she said to Chadwick.

"Any supplies on the boat?" he asked Francois.

The barman unexpectedly handed over the pack he had been carrying. "Some bread and hard tack. All I could grab."

Chadwick reached into his pocket and pulled out a few coins from his greatly diminished hoard. "Half the help gets half the payment," he groused.

Francois grabbed the coins and started to push Paddy into the boat.

"Hurry up, it won't be long before they start to search this part of the river bank and you only have the night to get far away. You can't go wrong if you keep rowing away from those lights on the quay."

Francoise jumped into the boat and started to set the oars into the row-locks. "Getting out of the marsh will be the hardest part. I wasn't lying about the current heading out to the Channel. Then it's all about steering, and the chap," he gestured at Paddy, "will be able to do that. I am not convinced your other fellow will be much help."

Chadwick sighed as he looked over his companions. Just when things couldn't get worse, they managed to.

"How do I find the river in the dark? Got an answer for that too?" he asked sardonically.

"Actually, yes," Francois replied. "The boat is already pointed in the right direction. Just do not make any turns into the marsh. It's not far. We didn't have time to properly hide her yesterday," he admitted. "Now get in and we will push you off with our good wishes." He sounded pretty self-satisfied, like a man who had managed to solve a sticky problem with little harm to himself.

"I get the lantern too," Chadwick demanded.

The barman grumbled but finally handed the lantern to George, who blew it out and stored it under a seat.

To Chadwick's surprise, the two scoundrels stepped into the water and gave them a substantial push into the center of the open water.

George and Paddy sat in the back by the rudder. Jeffrey took up the oars. They were much larger than the ones he had handled in his university days – much more awkward too. The boat tipped a bit as George moved forward and settled next to him. She grabbed the handle of one of the oars. Her hands looked so small, but she managed to dip the oar, providing a forward thrust. Maybe this would work if he could match his strokes to hers. At least it was worth trying until they got to the river.

It wasn't long before he could feel blisters from the rough wood of the oar.

"Hold up a moment," he said to George. He pulled out his shirt and, using his knife, cut stripes from the tail. "Here, wrap these around your hands," he directed.

"Thank you," she said gratefully. "Yet again, I am shown how unprepared I am for real life." She took a few moments to wrap her hands. While she was doing that, he took the time to remove his coat, cut more strips, and wrap his own hands.

When they took up the oars again, she asked, "How far do you think to the river?"

"I really have no idea. It is so dark, I suppose we might be going in circles."

From the back of the boat came Paddy's disembodied voice. "Have a little more faith, Captain," Paddy said from his position by the rudder. "I can get my eyes open enough to know I have been faithful to the direction Francois pointed us in. I don't know when we will get there, but I see enough of the lights of the quay to be certain of our direction." He paused and Jeffrey could hear him struggle to breathe. "The air seems a bit different. Can you smell it?"

Chadwick took a few deep breaths and then shook his head. Nothing seemed changed to him. But realizing no one could see him, he said, "Not really."

George, however, seemed to smell a difference. "Yes, it smells a bit fresher."

Paddy said with satisfaction, "Fresh water means the river is near."

Yet, making the turn onto the river caused its own problems when the current suddenly took over the momentum of the boat and swiftly pushed it along, almost swamping them in the process. Finally, they righted. Without the need for him to row, Chadwick took over handling the rudder as Paddy's strength gave out and he slumped against the side. The young Irishman assured him there was no need to try to raise the sail, only keep the craft to the middle of the river. He delegated George to the bow to look for any hazards, although it was more likely that anything she saw would be too late to avoid.

"Captain," Paddy murmured. "you know we can't get to England in this boat. It's too small and the sides are too low. The Channel is probably going to be too rough for us to get anywhere. I think this is intended for rivers."

Chadwick nodded thoughtfully. "I am hoping we can get far enough to find the navy. Admiral Cornwallis is supposed to be blockading the French ports. At least that was what it said in the last report I read after war was declared again."

He looked over the small craft with its one mast. To him, it looked more like a pleasure yacht than anything that could be used in an invasion.

"How do you think we can best do that?" he asked Paddy.

"I am going to give you a lesson in raising sails and tacking. I hope we will stay afloat long enough to find a ship. Honestly, Captain, I don't have a good feeling about this."

Jeffrey realized that Paddy's face was now a white blur in the darkness. Dawn must be coming. "Try to rest a bit," he said. "I have this feeling I will recognize the Channel when we get there and will wake you."

"The smell of the water will change again," Paddy murmured as he closed his eyes gratefully.

Dawn was just breaking when they arrived at the Channel, taking them all by surprise. Chadwick had expected at least one fort with guns protecting the river entrance, but it seemed the French had put all their energy into manning forts down the river that surrounded the city. He simply felt relieved that something was working in their favor. The relief was short-lived as he noticed the grayness of day break was not from lack of sun but from the denseness of the clouds. He gently nudged Paddy awake and gestured at the clouds.

Paddy sighed, "Rain and lots of it by the looks of those clouds. Waves look high, also."

George had joined them at the rear of the boat and started handing them the hardtack and break. "Better eat this before we are water-logged," she said.

Chadwick took a piece of tack. "Paddy, let's get this lesson started," he said as he stood. "George, I think we should light the lantern just in hopes someone sees it."

The lesson went about as well as he expected it would go. Exhausted, he finally got the sail up and the boat skimming along to the west. That was not the direction in which he wanted to go. England was north and he assumed the fleet was in the middle of the Channel. West took them too close to the French coast, but at least it was away from Boulogne.

The storm overtook them in a few hours and Paddy judged it time to take in the sail. Once again, they had to fight with the wind; now, the rain made it even harder. Finally, the sail was lowered and the momentum of the craft slowed but did not stop. The rain increased so much that soon they were all soaked and shivering.

"We need to get out farther into the Channel," Chadwick told Paddy.

Paddy shook his head, "I doubt we can do that, Captain. I think we just need to ride out this storm. Trying to turn this boat now will probably swamp her."

Chadwick surveyed the waves breaking over the bow with dismay. "Can we run into shore?"

"Same problem. We can't turn without taking on too much water."

Chadwick turned to George who was snugged up against his side. He needed both arms to struggle with the rudder, but he leaned in to place a quick kiss on her wet forehead. She was staring off in the distance. "Look!"

Chelsea

"Dry clothes, Mr. Donnay?" Shaking his head, Nathan handed Thornton his soaked overcoat and his sodden hat.

Before he could form his question, Thornton answered it. "The Mistress is in the parlor, sir."

Following the butler's nod, Nathan pushed open the door to the parlor.

Marion must have heard Thornton's voice, as she was just standing up when he came into the room. He noticed approvingly that her chair had been pulled up close to the fire. As he knew all too well the weather was miserable outside and he was glad to see she was not exerting herself but resting. She put her book on the side table, and stood, holding out her hand while the other hand pressed against her back.

"Nathan!" She exclaimed. Before she could say more, he reached her and pulled her into his arms. After soundly kissing her, he pushed her gently back into the chair. Kneeling at her feet, he put his arms around her now nonexistent waist and pressed his ear against her stomach. "We are fine, Nathan," she reassured her still silent husband. She stroked his damp hair pushing the curls away from his face. "Ah Nathan," she said sadly, "you did not find him, did you?"

With his ear still pressed to her stomach, Nathan said, "I can just hear his heart beat. Has he been kicking much?"

"Not as much as I suspect he will. He does like to get active when I try to rest. Feels funny." She started to massage the nape of Nathan's neck. "Tell me, Nathan, what happened in France?"

Reluctantly Nathan stood, his shoulders slumped in defeat. Marion stood also and rang the bell that summoned Thornton. The butler must have been on the other side of the door, he responded so quickly. "Please Thornton, pour Mr. Donnay some brandy, and then bring up a tea tray. Something substantial to eat. Maybe some of the beef we had last night, in sandwiches, with Cook's special mustard?"

By the time Marion finished speaking, Thornton had handed Nathan a glass almost three quarters full of brandy. "Yes, Mistress," he responded. "I am sure Cook has just the thing." And he disappeared as quickly as a he had arrived.

By the time he returned with the tray, Nathan had added some fuel to the fire and pulled the love seat over to face the fire. He also placed the low tea table in position so Marion was well placed to pour tea and keep her feet warm. He joined her on the small couch, pulling her close. 'Where's the General?" He asked. "He should hear this."

"My father has taken Charlotte for a trip to Salisbury to look at the old standing stones there. They are expected back tomorrow," she said with a smile.

"Charlotte?" Nathan's asked incredulously. "Seriously? When did this start?"

"For some time evidently," Marion answered. "She told me they became comfortable with each other when she was nursing him after the kidnapping. But," she said firmly, "we will discuss this later." Her voice held a finality that she was not willing to wait any longer for information about his trip.

Nathan glanced at Thornton who was standing at attention just like the soldier he used to be. He wasn't meeting Nathan's stare but he also didn't seem to be going anywhere willingly. "I guess you had better hear this also, Thornton," Nathan said. "I know you think pretty highly of Captain Chadwick."

"Yes, sir," Thornton responded. "He's a good man."

Nathan reached for a sandwich when Marion's hand grasped his wrist. "Talk first, eat after," she demanded. Her patience was obviously at an end.

Releasing his hold on the first fresh food he had had in days, Nathan studied his wife. "As you know, I left here and headed to Dover to catch a smuggler's boat or something to Calais," he began. He glossed over the trip crossing the Channel to France. It had not been pleasant but it was nothing out of the usual. "Once the boat got close to Calais, it began to get interesting. The French have a lot of coastal schooners gadding about so it made getting in rather sticky. We tacked east until we found a dark beach. It took a while to find a road and then a horse but it is amazing what gold will buy."

"So you did not try the beach those unfortunate men got picked up on?" Marion asked. She started to pour Nathan tea but Thornton got there first with the brandy bottle.

Nodding his thanks, Donnay continued. "Calais has not changed much since the last time I was there. So I sort of knew my way about. I was not sure where to start my search so I went to the hotel de ville and asked if anyone fitting Jeffrey's description had been noticed."

Both Marion and Thornton gave gasps of astonishment at such audacity. "My God, Nathan, what were you thinking?" Marion exclaimed.

Nathan sipped his brandy before continuing. "I was thinking that was the easiest way of getting information and that my own papers were actually good and not forgeries," he responded calmly."

"What reason would you give for asking about Jeffrey?"

"I was going to be a possible client who wanted to hire him. For all the good it did me, though, it was wasted effort. No one I talked to claimed to know anything. However, as I was leaving, one chap, who looked like he had been though at least one of Napoleon's campaigns, suggested I check out a tavern, called *The Citizen*. Said the food there was pretty good, and the beds were clean. Turns out he was right."

Jeffrey had stayed at the tavern and interviewed the landlord and some servants. The landlord informed him Chadwick had taken rooms with the landlord's sister. "And this is where it gets interesting. She said he hired a boy. However, the maid at *The Citizen* says it is a girl."

"Girl or boy?" Marion mused. "They cannot tell the difference?" she smirked.

"It depends on who you talk to. The landlady said boy or young man to do errands. But the person, I believe, is the maid from the inn who helped her bathe and said definitely a young woman. But a female, who had been beaten and abused. She also said the female had been covered in lice, like she had been in a stable or something. They had to cut her hair off. Strawberry blonde, the maid said she was."

"Jeffrey's letter did not give a description of the woman who was kidnapped and he was searching for. Can we assume that he found her?"

"Jeffrey was always a soft touch, so it could be anyone in need. But I do not think this was just anyone. I think it was Miss Yelverton. It also makes sense, to me, that if he found her, he would try to adjust her appearance so no one would recognize her. After all, we know Hastings is in the area, surely he would be furious, especially if Jeff snuck her out from under his nose. I think, we can assume Hastings would be looking for her. Poor Jeffrey, being hunted by two foes." Thornton cleared his throat. Donnay looked at him expectantly. "Speak up, man. What is the question?" he asked.

"Yes, sir. Where you able to ascertain how far behind them you were?"

"Ah, Thornton. You have just identified the crux of the issue. I appeared too long behind them to catch up. The landlady knew they had been sent to Boulogne, and that there had been a guard to take them there. But Jeffrey had left behind his travel trunk, so I cannot believe he thought he was going for a long time. But she had no idea where, in Boulogne, they were being sent. Even though I was very close to my retrieval date, I went to Boulogne."

"Why did you do that?" Marion asked in exasperation. "You had so little information to go on."

"I actually found where the Irishmen who volunteered for Napoleon's army were billeted. I hung out in the tavern for a couple of nights but I heard nothing. I had to leave or miss my trip home. I landed in Dover two days ago." Having finished his tale, Donnay reached for the sandwiches and started eating.

Marion sighed and exchanged a disheartened glance with Thornton. "What happens now?" she asked.

Nathan shook his head and shrugged helplessly. "I do not know what else we can do until we get more news from Jeffrey, Wickham, or even that smuggler captain. I am hoping one of them sends word.

"Oh, I almost forgot, I did leave word at Dover to send word, to Cornwallis and the Channel fleet, to watch for Jeffrey if he tried to make a Channel crossing, and needed help."

Chapter Seventeen: Any Port in a Storm

The three of them strained their eyes to see what George had glimpsed. "What did you see?" Chadwick asked.

"Something that was darker than its surroundings. I want to believe it was a ship."

"Paddy, can you and George hold the rudder? I want to get that lantern up higher on the mast if possible. The waves are so high no one could see it where it is."

"Go," Paddy gasped and reached for the rudder. George took Chadwick's spot and they both hung onto the steering rod. It was obvious they wouldn't be able to hold it for long. Chadwick struggled to the front of the craft to find the lantern George had hung. It was out. Well, what did he expect with all this water? He couldn't think of anything else he could use as a signal, except for his shirt. After too long spent fumbling, he managed to get the shirt off and tied to the mast. He returned, to the back of the boat, exhausted and wearing only his jacket, and took his seat.

"Lantern was out," he said shortly.

Paddy looked half dead but nodded as he said, "I think the ship George saw was heading east. We need to turn the boat."

"How can we do that without a sail?" This time it was George asking.

"Very slowly move the rudder, just a little bit at a time. I am not positive it will work, but we're out of options," Paddy responded.

They no sooner tried to change course when a huge wave crashed against the side of the bow.

"Jeffrey, I can't swim," Georgina said. Her voice sounded so soft to him but she probably was screaming.

"Don't worry, I can."

Time seemed to stand still as they struggled with the rudder and the endless waves. If they were making any progress, Chadwick couldn't tell. He had lost feeling in his hands from the cold. He could feel George shivering un-controllably beside him. Paddy seemed to be unconscious again. He almost envied him; if they drowned, Paddy wouldn't notice. The boat now was so low in the water, he doubted anyone could see them, much less get to them in time. A final giant wave swamped the boat without further ado.

Chadwick threw his arms around Georgina as they were swept overboard. He kicked furiously as the water pulled them under. Breaking the surface, he could see the boat had turned completely over. Struggling with George in one arm, he tried to grab some part of the craft to keep them from going under again. The cold was unbelievable.

* * *

"Were you trying to kill yourselves?" The deep bass voice seemed to come from the bright light shining in Chadwick's eyes. He blinked rapidly, trying to focus enough to see the speaker.

"George?" he croaked. His throat was sore; in fact, almost every part of him hurt.

"I am here, Jeffrey," came the welcome response.

He felt rather than saw her move nearer to him and take his hand. He sighed in relief. "What happened?"

"Something close to a miracle," she said. "We got rescued by one of the ships on the blockade. A naval ship, just like you had hoped."

Chadwick finally managed to get his salt-encrusted eyes open. When they finally decided to focus, he could see Georgina's face, definitely with some bruises she didn't have before, and a strange man peering at him from behind her shoulder.

"I am First Officer Peter McClain of the HMS Emmett. You are one lucky son of a. Sorry miss, we don't get many women on board and we tend to get casual with our manners."

"Of course," Georgina said softly. "Jeffrey, this ship is too small to have a doctor. How do you feel? Is anything broken? You were unconscious a long time," she ended miserably.

After another internal review, Chadwick decided he was more bruised than seriously damaged. "I think I am still in one piece," he managed.

"Can you give me a hand to get up, Lieutenant?" he asked. Then he realized he was naked. Someone had even removed his breeches. He grasped the blanket to make sure he was decently covered.

McClain helped him sit up on the narrow cot. Chadwick could see a small port hole over the bed; the sky outside was still gray and cloudy. The cabin was tiny by any standards and with the three of them in it, was very crowded. But this seemed to be the First Officer's cabin.

"These are my quarters," McClain then affirmed. "As Miss Yelverton said, this is a small ship, no lock-ups. Captain has questions for you. I will let him know you are awake."

Jeffrey looked at Georgina in surprise. 'Prisoners?" he asked.

She shrugged. "No papers," was the curt response.

"Paddy?"

The Lieutenant answered before George could.

"He's in another cabin. He hasn't regained consciousness. Miss Yelverton told us he already had a bad beating and was concussed. As I said, we don't have a doctor, just a bone setter. He is with him now, but I doubt there is much he can do."

He pulled open the door. "There is a marine on guard out here," he said. "I will return shortly with the Captain."

"Is there any water?"

Georgina poured a mug and held it out to him. Then seeing how unsteady his hands were, she steadied it while he drank. It reminded him of how he shook after he killed Hastings.

"The last I remember," he said, "is being washed overboard and trying to reach the boat. What do you remember?"

George sat on the edge of the cot and studied him with serious eyes.

"Oh, Jeffrey, it was awful." She shuddered remembering. "Somehow you managed to get hold of the boat and push me back up on it. I think it was at that point you passed out. I held on to you by the arm as long as I could. Just when I felt you slipping, this boat came out of nowhere. They already had

Paddy and they just pulled us in and rowed back to this ship like it was a normal everyday practice. The waves were crashing over the bow, but the sailors never seemed fazed by it. I was so scared, I guess I screamed, and everyone knew right away I was a woman. They have been very polite to me, and since they are British, I told them everything."

She paused, chewing her lip thoughtfully, and said, "But I don't think they believe me."

"How long was I unconscious?" Jeffrey asked.

"While it seemed forever, I suppose it was not terribly long," was the welcome reply. "We've been on the ship a couple of hours. Long enough for the Captain to ask me questions."

Suddenly the door flew open and Lieutenant McClain hurried back in.

"I was not supposed to leave you alone together," he said rapidly. At George's surprised look, he went on, "Captain doesn't want you conferring on your stories. So miss, would you mind stepping out while I get the Captain?"

Georgina rolled her eyes but rose willingly enough.

"I will go check on Paddy," she said to Chadwick. "I am really worried about him."

Jeffrey was left alone to look around the cabin. He had never been on a warship before but he had some understanding of their construction. As he studied the tiny cabin, he noticed how every space was cleverly fitted to hold the few personal items even the second-in-command could bring on board. He knew the thin walls would be removed when a ship went into actions so that the whole deck became a gun deck. In fact, if he wasn't mistaken, most of the outside wall around the small porthole was a large flap used by the sailors to thrust the cannon through to shoot at the enemy. Upon closer inspection, he could see the hinges for the flap and where there was a hook to hold it open. He felt sure that everything on this ship had multiple uses.

He looked around for his clothes and found his pants and jacket neatly hanging on some hooks on the temporary wall. Since the trousers were dry, he put them on. But the jacket was still soaked. He felt presumptuous to hunt around the Lieutenant's gear for a shirt, so he decided to wait until McClain came back to ask him for one. He didn't have to wait long.

"Captain Wright will see you now," the Lieutenant said, holding the door open. "Miss Yelverton said your name is Chadwick. True?" he asked.

"Yes, very true," Jeffrey answered. "My full name is Captain Jeffrey Chadwick of the Alien Office."

"Yes, Miss Yelverton did say that," was the noncommittal response.

"Uh, Lieutenant," Jeffrey said. "Do you have an extra shirt I can borrow or maybe my own is still usable? I hate to meet your captain looking worse than I need to. My jacket is completely soaked."

The Lieutenant grimaced. "I have one, but it's not very clean. We have been on station a long time and getting wash done is rather a problem. But if you can stand it, it is yours to wear."

The Lieutenant rooted around in a small trunk under the bed and came up with a rumpled shirt. Chadwick accepted it gratefully, although it was tight across the shoulders and short in the sleeves; and the Lieutenant was right – it was – not too clean. He put it on. Since most sailors went barefoot, he felt comfortable leaving his waterlogged boots in the corner and followed McClain the short distance along the narrow hallway to the Captain's quarters.

The Captain's cabin was the width of the vessel but hardly impressive in appearance. Like the Lieutenant's quarters, it had lots of fittings and bolts for storage but only contained a narrow bed, a small table, and two chairs. At least two cannons were stashed along the side walls. Georgina sat on the edge of the bed, looking tired and serious.

The Captain stood when Chadwick and McClain entered.

"Mr. Chadwick, if that is your real name?" he asked.

Chadwick bowed slightly and said, "My full name and title is Captain Jeffrey Chadwick of the Alien Office."

"Sit there," Captain Wright pointed at the one empty chair. Jeffrey sat gratefully. His legs were still weak and rubbery. His whole body ached. Lieutenant McClain leaned against the door. It looked like a position he was very used to.

"So Miss Yelverton said that was your name," Captain Wright started. "But have you any proof? Oh, and miss, if you want to stay, not a word out of you. I want to see if your stories match. Understand?" The Captain sounded rather sharp but then he obviously was used to being obeyed. Georgina nodded solemnly.

Then she asked, "Can I just tell him about our friend?"

"How is Paddy?" Chadwick asked quickly, even before the Captain nodded agreement.

"The same," she said. "I am concerned that if he wakes we have no laudanum to give him if he is in pain."

"Don't worry," the Captain said. "I keep it in here for emergencies."

He turned to Chadwick. "Let's hear your story."

Chadwick couldn't help but sigh. Logically, he knew he couldn't be expected to be believed but he was bone-tired and hungry. He knew he wasn't at his best. But at least now he could tell the total truth and not have to worry about his cover story.

"Could I have some water, sir?" he asked.

At the Captain's nod, the Lieutenant stepped outside and they could hear him holler for someone named Bradley. Shortly, he stepped back into the cabin carrying a tall mug with a frothy head. He set the mug in front of Chadwick saying, "Small beer. Water is not so good right now."

Jeffrey had never had a beer that tasted so good. He quickly drained half the mug and had to make himself stop. This might be a long interrogation.

* * *

"Let me repeat what I think you said and see if I understand this rather fantastical account."

Jeffrey had a clear view of George sitting on the edge of the bed. At the Captain's words, seemingly disbelieving him, her shoulders drooped while her right hand massaged her left hand anxiously. He noticed the bandage on her broken finger was missing, probably lost in the Channel. He wanted to put his arms around her and tell her not to give up yet. Technically they were safe, and the Captain hadn't definitively accused them of lying.

"So, it all starts with Miss Yelverton here," the Captain nodded at George, "being kidnapped off a major shopping street in Dublin during the day time. You," now he nodded at Chadwick, "working for some shady organization I have never heard of, are assigned to find her. You follow her to France, Calais to be exact, where you are dropped off by a friendly smuggler. There, miraculously, you find her within twenty-four hours and stage a rescue. Then you get stuck and are forced to work for the French Army as a translator."

The Captain stopped talking and scrubbed his face with his hands.

Chadwick could see his eyes were red rimmed probably from lack of sleep. When he looked closely, he noticed the Captain was much younger then he had previously thought. Being in charge of a ship carried a lot of responsibility, and with the weather and the stress of the blockade, it must age a man.

"Peter, tell Bradley to bring a pitcher of beer and more mugs," the Captain ordered. "I am becoming thirsty just trying to repeat this tale."

After the requested beverage arrived, the Captain continued.

"Then amazingly, the original kidnapper shows up wearing a French uniform and is assigned to the translator company. He recognizes your companion, the red-haired chap, and in the process of trying to get his hands back on Miss Yelverton, he beats him senseless. Which is probably why he is still unconscious right now."

He paused and drank more beer.

"When the kidnapper tries to get you all arrested and hanged for spying, you attack the chap with a knife and kill him. Then you make a daring escape with the help of two lowlifes you just happen to come across, and—I really love this part—with only a young woman to help, manage to row your way to the Channel. Then in the middle of one of the worst storms I have seen out here – and I have been here for several years – we just happen to see a white flag and rescue you as your boat is about to go under."

Chadwick flinched from the sarcasm in the Captain's voice as he finished the recitation. Georgina stood up as if she was about to refute the Captain's attitude, if not his words. But, when Jeffrey shook his head, she sat down, obviously frustrated.

"Um, Captain," Jeffrey began, "I realize when you phrase our story like that, it does sound fantastical. But there is more."

"Oh, please," the Captain said with a grandiose wave of his hand, "by all means, continue. I have nothing else to do today but be entertained by your Shahrazad-like story."

Jeffrey took a deep breath and plunged on. He needed Captain Wright to believe their story and help them get to London as soon as possible. When he had left London, not that long ago, there had not been any verification of the invasion, only rumors. He now had visual proof—but he had to get it to the Alien Office in London.

"We not only saw, but *studied* the craft that are being built in Boulogne for the invasion. Napoleon doesn't just have his army there; he has about 2,000 seafaring vessels almost built and ready."

The Captain's mug went down on the table with a crash! "What?" he bellowed.

"Napoleon's invasion fleet," Chadwick repeated. "It is not just a figment of someone's imagination. It's there in Boulogne, being built. Hell, it is practically finished and ready to push off."

"Why the hell, didn't you say this before?" the Captain demanded.

"I did not exactly have time," Chadwick protested. "I was trying to fit it in."

The Captain turned to Georgina Yelverton. "You did not say anything about invasion ships," he said accusingly.

"You didn't exactly give me much time, either," she snapped back. "You are in such a hurry to find us guilty of something—but of what, I have no idea!"

Chadwick grinned at her. He knew she was exhausted, her clothes and hair stiff with salt, and probably starving, yet she was still full of spark. She was magnificent.

As soon as the Captain turned back to him, Chadwick started talking. He realized that he probably should have started with the landing craft; obviously that would be the part of interest to a naval man. So he explained how Captain Cuvelier De Trie had been interested in having sketches to explain certain items whose names didn't really translate easily.

"He took us on a tour of the area where most of the craft are being constructed. Miss Yelverton was included in the visit." He almost stumbled over her real name, he was so comfortable now calling her George.

"Since she has some skill at sketching, I was using her ability to gain Cuvelier's trust. Before we left, we destroyed all her sketches of the crafts so they could not be used against us as evidence if we were picked up. However, she assures me she can replicate them if necessary."

Captain Wright now looked more awake than ever. He cast an interested glance in George's direction and motioned to Chadwick to keep talking. He even topped up Jeffrey's mug of beer.

Jeffrey motioned George over to the table. "Captain, do you have some paper and a pencil?" he asked. "Miss Yelverton, can you do rough sketches as I describe the different craft we saw?"

George nodded and said, "I remember three main types of craft."

The Captain produced the needed materials and even sharpened the pencil for George. Chadwick finished his beer and then proceeded to dredge his memory for details.

"Prames, about one hundred feet long, three masted, fitted with twelve guns. Next size down is the Chaloupe Canniere, with two masts to be used principally as troop carriers." Without pause he continued. "They are supposed to carry 200 men and equipment. The smallest is the Peniche with only two howitzers. With what they requisitioned of local boats, Napoleon is planning for over 2,000 vessels."

As he rattled on, George kept up with simple drafts of each craft. The two sailors watched her fingers intently.

Chadwick finished with, "The craft you saved us from was supposedly stolen from the marina where the finished boats are stored. I am not a seaman, obviously by the difficulty we found ourselves in. Paddy has experience on ships in this area. He was not particularly impressed by the boat. He said at some point that the sides were too low for the Channel conditions."

"He is absolutely right," Lieutenant McClain put in. "We barely saw it, it was so low in the water, even accounting for the amount of water you must have taken on. We only saw from the shirt that you were in trouble."

"Given that we were probably a French boat, why did you come to get us?" Chadwick asked.

"As one of the smaller craft in the blockade, our standing orders are to stay inshore and stop or disrupt local shipping to try to get information about the invasion fleet. Occasionally, we drop off agents or pick them up," he added.

"Given how bad the storm was, I am very thankful that you came for us," Chadwick said gratefully. "Especially since you probably thought we were French smugglers." He couldn't imagine anyone else being out in that storm.

"*That* storm?" scoffed Lieutenant McClain. "That was hardly worth writing home about. Most storms are much longer and the waves a lot higher." He put heavy emphasis on the word 'lot.' "The men hardly broke a sweat," he grinned.

"Seemed very different from our angle," Chadwick said.

"I was persuaded we were not going to last any longer," George agreed.

"It wasn't as simple as the Lieutenant makes out," Captain Wright cut in. "I understand, Peter, you want to make the men look good. But, in truth, I would not have normally sent out the side boat under those circumstances. The sea was pretty rough."

Chadwick saw the two other men exchange glances and then the Captain nodded.

"Yes, tell him. I feel confident he is the man mentioned," he said cryptically.

"Admiral Cornwallis sent out an order to the fleet recently," Lieutenant McClain said. "It commanded the fleet to be on the lookout for an agent of the Alien Office named Jeffrey Chadwick who fits your description. It said you disappeared in France and probably would be accompanied by a red-haired man and maybe a young woman. The main part was that, should we come across you, you should be offered any assistance you might need."

Chadwick sat back stunned. How would the Admiral know he was in trouble and trying to make his way across the Channel?

"Do you have any idea what caused him to send such a command?" he asked. "Only my home office in Dublin even knew I was going to Calais."

Then he remembered his last letter to Nathan. Damn, he thought gratefully, somehow *Nathan put it all together and got me help when I needed it. The man is a miracle worker.*

Out loud he said, "No, wait, I understand. If the request came from the Alien Office, Mr. Wickham in Dublin must have asked for assistance."

"What exactly does this Alien Office do?" Captain Wright asked.

"It is no secret," Chadwick said. "Today, the purpose is to keep track of possible insurrectionists. I understand the office started as a place where all those fleeing from the terror in France a few years ago had to register. Then it expanded to prevent uprisings against the government. In Dublin, we are supposed to track the United Irishmen who are trying to encourage Napoleon to invade through Ireland."

"If your office tracks insurrectionists, how did you get involved in my kidnapping?" George asked curiously.

"Mr. Wickham didn't have any other agents with any field experience," he said with a shrug. "At first, we didn't know who was responsible for the kidnapping, only that your father has political connections so it seemed likely there was a political connection. However, even though Hastings was deeply involved with the insurrectionists, it seems he was doing it for money. He probably needed money to finance his trip to France to volunteer for the army. He was the major figure behind a case last year trying to stop the Act of Union. Thankfully my office was able to stop him at that time."

"That's where Pitt made Ireland part of Great Britain?" Lieutenant asked. At Jeffrey's questioning look, he shrugged. "We don't get much in way of news out here and sometimes I miss events."

"How long have you been here?" George asked.

"Going on three years," the Captain replied. "Since the mutiny in 1797, they are pretty hesitant about letting us ashore. But they are going to have to let us in soon for refurbishment. We need more work than my carpenter can fix out here."

Silence fell over the cabin. George and Jeffrey sat pondering their good fortune. Finally luck had turned in their favor. He thought the Captain and Lieutenant might be pondering their next moves.

"May I ask, Captain, if you are Captain John Wesley Wright?"

"As it happens, yes. Why do you ask?"

"I just thought the name was familiar from files I have read about the blockade."

"Your office is doing more than just spying on rebels if you have been reading those files," the Captain said with some asperity.

Chadwick shrugged noncommittally. "What happens now, Captain?" he asked.

"Food," was the short reply. "We need to vacate my cabin so the men can set up for dinner. It's the only room large enough for my officers to sit together for a meal. We can just squeeze the two of you in." He turned to address George. "Miss Yelverton, as the only female on the boat, I have to ask you not to wander off by yourself. If you would, please keep to your cabin as much as possible."

George nodded in acknowledgement. "Can I attend to our colleague?" she asked.

"Yes, of course. He is in the cabin next to yours anyway. Anything you need, just tell our medic Russell to get it."

Chadwick stood, as they were obviously being dismissed. "Captain, I meant, how soon before we can get to land?"

Captain Wright sighed. "I know what you are asking. I do not have an exact answer for you. I have to send a note to Admiral Cornwallis to update him and ask permission to leave the blockade. It's going to be some days before we get an answer, I am afraid."

"In that case, we will both go and check on our colleague. Will someone get us for dinner? I have to admit I am famished."

"Don't expect too much," Lieutenant McClain warned. "Our supplies are getting low, and our cook isn't the greatest in the best of times." He grinned at them. "But I will find you in time."

Paddy was in a space even smaller than the cabin to which Jeffrey was assigned. There was really only room for one person, since the cot took up all the space. The medic, Jeffrey assumed it was Russell, joined them in the narrow hall to give them an update.

"I think he is starting to wake, as he is getting restless and tossing about. I think he is better off unconscious so I plan to get some laudanum from the Captain."

George told him how they had used laudanum to keep Paddy unconscious after the beating. She ended by saying, "I am worried about giving him too much."

"What condition was he in when you found him?" Chadwick asked.

"I wasn't there, sir, but the fellows told me he was delirious. He was trying to tell someone to take down the sail."

Suddenly Paddy shouted, "Jeffrey, take down the fucking sail!"

George darted to the cot and tackled Paddy before he could get up. Chadwick squeezed in and pushed Paddy back into a prone position.

"Take it easy, I got the sail down. It's down. It's down." He kept repeating himself until Paddy calmed down.

"What do you think, George? Do we drug him or not?" he asked.

"Let's just stay here and try to keep him calm. Maybe he will wake up and can tell us how much pain he is in. Then we can decide." She seemed to realize she was making medical decisions without consulting the one medic available. She looked at the medic, Russell, questioningly.

"If you are staying with him, miss, then that sounds good to me. I got other duties…"

"Of course," George said. "He is our friend and we will stay here. If I need anything, where do I find you?"

"Just tell anyone to get me. They all know where my berth is."

George and Jeffrey settled in for an extended wait. Paddy seemed to have slipped into a more natural sleep although he was still restless and tossed about enough that Chadwick had to hold the young man down a few times. Once McClain passed by and handed Jeffrey half a loaf of extremely crusty bread.

"I can't believe how grateful I am to get something I wouldn't normally think twice about throwing away," he said as he broke the bread into smaller pieces.

As George laughed at him, he continued, "You can't bite into this thing. It will break your teeth. No wonder sailors have so few teeth." He handed her a chunk.

"No, you eat it," she said surprisingly. "I got fed this morning before you came to."

"We will have to take turns eating dinner," he said. "I don't think we can leave him alone."

In the end, George sat with Paddy instead of joining the officers for a meal. She insisted she would be too uncomfortable being the only female at the table and asked that he just bring her a plate.

McClain was right about the food. If he wasn't so hungry, he would have had a hard time eating the salted fish—never one of his favorites—the boiled potatoes, with identifiable rot spots not cut out, or the tasteless beans. George looked as dismayed as he felt with the plate he brought her, but when he left, she was bravely forking it down. One thing the Lieutenant forgot to mention was that the Captain kept a surprisingly decent wine and generously served it to his officers. It made an otherwise disgusting dinner palatable.

As soon as it was polite, Jeffrey made his way back to Paddy's cabin, carrying a mug of wine which he handed to George. To his relief, Paddy was awake although obviously still in pain. He moved the invalid's feet so he could squeeze onto the cot.

"I am really glad to see you, old boy," he said. "You seem to be taking your good old time waking up."

"I guess, I am too, although my head feels like it is going to burst," the young Irishman replied. George wrung out a cloth in the bucket of water at her feet and reapplied it to Paddy's head. "How did we get here?" he asked.

The story of their near-miraculous retrieval was retold in an abbreviated version. Paddy was having trouble following the story, leading Chadwick to believe his head injury had been aggravated.

"I think his head has been reinjured," George said. "I suggest you get the laudanum from the Captain and we give him just enough to help him bear the pain." Since that was what Chadwick was also thinking, he willingly retraced his steps to the Captain's cabin.

Returning, he asked George to wait in her cabin while he checked Paddy over to make certain he had no new broken bones or other injuries from being thrown overboard. Paddy had no memory of the capsizing of their boat. Other than that, he didn't seem to have sustained any new injuries other than scrapes and bruises.

"You really are a mess," Chadwick sympathized. He placed a wet cloth on a particularly large bruise over Paddy's already battered ribs. "I think it will be some time before you are on your feet again. But then the Captain tells me it will be some time before we reach land anyway."

Paddy mumbled something that sounded remarkably like wishing he had gone down with the boat. Chadwick promptly dosed him with the drug and waited for him to drift off to sleep.

"Is he sleeping?" George asked from the door.

"Not naturally," Jeffrey answered. "I feel bad for the condition that he is in."

"Me too," George agreed. "After all, he took that beating so those men wouldn't find me."

"Maybe, but I rather feel like they just wanted to hurt someone. Some men are like that." He stood stretching his spine but careful not to stand too upright; the ceiling was well under his height, requiring him to walk hunched over. He moved into the narrow hallway which was slightly higher. Since no one was around, he wrapped an arm around George's shoulders and pulled her close.

"How do you want to split up the watch on Paddy tonight?" he asked.

George put her arms around his waist bringing him even closer to her. "The walls are pretty thin, aren't they?"

"Yes, they are," Chadwick agreed, wondering where this was going.

"We should be able to hear him from my cabin, wouldn't you say?"

Jeffrey was much more interested in nuzzling her neck than in doing anything more than grunt agreement. When she reached up and pulled him down for a deep kiss, he totally forgot what they had been talking about. He deepened the kiss, pushing her against the flimsy wall.

To his profound disappointment, she pulled back. He dropped his hands but remained pressed against her waiting. "Jeffrey, the door opens out."

He pulled back a fraction, confused by her comment.

"I can't pull you in with me, because I can't open the door," she explained.

Jeffrey grinned widely as he realized her intent. He stepped back pulling her with him. After they stepped into the mate's cabin, George pulled the door firmly closed.

Chapter Eighteen: Walmer Castle

Captain Wright's jolly boat ran up on the shingles of the beach and came to an abrupt stop. The men in the bow jumped into the water and tugged the boat higher up the beach while the rest of the sailors shipped their oars in preparation for landing. When the boat was secured, Captain Wright followed his men into the knee-deep water and onto the shore.

Chadwick, who had been sitting in the rear of the boat with Georgina, stood to follow the Captain's example. Now he understood why Lieutenant McClain had told him to carry his boots, not wear them. Georgina, whose wooden clogs had been lost when their boat was swamped, was barefoot. She sat wrapped in a blanket over her shirts and pants.

"If you would hand the young lady to me, sir, I will carry her to the beach." The coxswain stood in the water at the bow, his arms outstretched.

"This water is damn cold. Sorry for the language, Miss."

"Thank you." Chadwick, who had intended to carry Georgina himself, instead swept her up in his arms and handed her off to the sailor. Both coxswain and Chadwick made it to the beach in time for Jeffrey to don his boots before the Captain signaled to follow his path over the dunes. Jeffrey knew they were headed to Walmer Castle but to his frustration, he did not know why. Wright had been closed-mouthed about their purpose.

The sand turned to rocks, making walking treacherous for anyone without shoes or the hardened feet of a sailor. Chadwick, grateful for the opportunity to touch Georgina for any reason, picked her up and carried her to a steep staircase at the bottom of the bluff.

"Jeffrey, you can put me down, I can walk these," she whispered.

"What if I don't want to?" he murmured back.

"How far to the Castle?" she questioned a sailor walking next to them.

"Not too far, Miss," answered the same sailor who had carried her over the waves to the beach. "But after we get up this piece, we'll have to walk a long wall around to the entrance on the other side. I was thinking, sir, it might be a long haul for you to carry her that far. We are glad to help."

Chadwick wasn't happy about handing George off to a bunch of sailors who hadn't seen a woman in a few years. However, he was honest enough to realize he couldn't easily carry her by himself up the rock stairs to the top of the bluff and then around the wall of the castle. At least not at the pace the Captain was setting.

He nodded at the coxswain, "Thanks. After seeing those steps, you are right. I will need help."

He stopped and put George on her feet. He carefully wrapped the blanket around her so she was almost swaddled like an infant. No one could grope her through that. The coxswain grinned at him, nodding approvingly at the now-bundled George.

"Good thought, that, sir. Now we can hand her off to others and make better time." He swooped her up and then trotted swiftly after the Captain.

Chadwick couldn't understand the sudden hurry.

They had been a week making their way to the Kent coast from France. The week for Jeffrey had been one of absolute joy, as each night was spent with George in the tiny cabin, learning all the mysteries of her body and how to use them to please her. Just remembering how he had studied and touched the smooth planes of her skin by the light of a tiny candle rocked him so, jolting him to turn his thoughts elsewhere.

He watched carefully as Georgina was handed among the sailors during the trek up the cliff. He was so focused on her progress among the men that he didn't notice that Captain Wright had dropped by to walk next to him until the leader spoke.

"Good. It looks like Pitt is here. See the flag of the Lord Warden of the Cinque Ports?" Wright gestured to the flag flying briskly from the top of the largest tower. "That means Pitt is here. Even though he is no longer prime minister, he is still in charge of defense of the nation. I want him to hear your story first."

By now, the whole group had reached the top of the palisades. The sailors were all laughing as they stood George on her feet. It seemed there had been a competition as to who could carry her the longest without panting. When she pointed at two of the men, Captain Wright tossed them some coins.

"That was the fastest I have even mounted those stairs," he joked. "Nothing like a bit of a contest to get them moving. This way," he said, leading them along the castle wall.

Cleverly hidden in the wall was a small door, held open by a red-jacketed marine. Once through, Chadwick could see at least six more armed marines guarding the entrance and watching the newcomers carefully.

"Welcome, Captain Wright," said a marine lieutenant standing off to the side. Chadwick hadn't noticed him at first.

"Sorry about the welcome party. Can't be too careful these days."

"Not at all, Lieutenant," Wright responded. "I see Mr. Pitt is here."

"Yes, sir, he wants you to join him as soon as possible."

"Lieutenant Moore, may I introduce my companions? Captain Jeffrey Chadwick of the Alien Office and Miss Yelverton of Dublin. This is Lieutenant Moore, one of Mr. Pitt's aides. Shall we go?"

Having quickly dealt with the introductions, Wright gestured for Chadwick and Georgina to follow him as the coxswain took the rest of the men in another direction.

"We'll go around to the bridge at the front. If we went in one of these side doors, it would take almost as long wandering about the halls and tunnels. This place is quite massive," he said.

"How old is the castle?" George asked.

Wright looked at the marine for validation and then said, "I have heard that it was here before Henry VIII. It is different from other castles, as most of the buildings are circular. The central tower is round, and is surrounded by round bastions. The outside walls are circular and also include bastions, but of course they are much larger."

"Militarily it is quite brilliant to build a fortress of so many round spaces; there are no blind corners for the enemy to make use of," the marine officer added. "However, for those inside, it makes for lots of corridors and lots of steps."

Walking over the grass had been fine for Georgina's feet, but once they reached the cobblestone bridge, Jeffrey picked her up again. He didn't release her until they reached the entrance hallway of the castle. Captain Wright didn't even pause as he immediately made for one of the corridors branching off the main atrium.

"Is Mr. Pitt in the library?" Wright asked the Lieutenant.

"I can't meet Mr. Pitt looking like this," Georgina exclaimed in horror. "I don't even have shoes!"

Captain Wright paused and looked back at her in frustration.

"This is a bachelor household. We can't offer you a gown at the moment, and Mr. Pitt is waiting."

Chadwick stood with his arm around Georgina, sympathetic to her dismay. He, too, was inappropriately garbed to meet a man of Pitt's stature. But at least he still had his boots, even if they were cracked and water-stained. Once he got back to London, Jeffrey told himself, he would immediately replace them with new boots.

"Captain, can you give Mr. Pitt the report that I wrote up? While he is reading that, we can cast about for something more appropriate for Miss Yelverton to wear. Surely we can send into the local village?" he asked.

"We are not quite just an entirely bachelor establishment, Captain Wright," the Lieutenant interjected. "Mr. Pitt's niece has joined us. Perhaps you know her, Lady Hester Stanhope?"

"Oh, I wasn't aware," Wright nodded reluctantly. "Yes, I guess I can give Pitt the report while you figure out some clothes. But don't take too long. Mr. Pitt is a brisk reader and will finish the report in little time. Then he will want a verbal report," he warned. He turned to address the Lieutenant when the footsteps warned them of an approaching figure.

"Wright!" the man exclaimed. "Just the person we wanted to see!"

"Well met, General," Wright responded. "I have some important news." He introduced Chadwick and George to the newcomer who proved to be none other than General Edward Smith. His name had figured largely at the Alien Office as he collected information running his own men-often his nephews-into France and Germany.

"Looks like you and Miss Yelverton have quite a story to tell," he said eyeing their bedraggled state.

"We do, sir," George interjected firmly. "But I cannot meet Mr. Pitt in this state."

Before she could continue, Smith nodded and said, "Of course. Let's find you something more in keeping with your status, and perhaps a bath."

He looked at the man who had been following him. Dressed all in black, he was the first non-military man Jeffrey and Georgina had seen since they arrived in Britain.

"This is Fallon, Mr. Pitt's butler. Fallon, could you help them out?"

"Certainly, sir. But Mr. Pitt expressed the desire to see Captain Wright as soon as he landed."

"We'll take him to see Mr. Pitt, Fallon," Smith said. "You see what you can do with our guests."

As Wright turned to go with Smith and Moore, Chadwick handed the Captain his carefully worded report. Wright took the papers and followed the two army men down the long blue corridor on the left. Fallon stood for a few moments, studying Jeffrey and Georgina silently. He seemed to come to some decision, then gestured to the corridor on the right.

"If you please to follow me?"

* * *

Fallon was as good as his word. He conducted the couple to a sitting room where they were served tea and sandwiches while, he assured them, baths were being heated.

Chadwick had not realized how hungry he was until faced with a pile of freshly made ham and chicken sandwiches. There were salads, one of cucumber, another of beetroot, with goat cheese served as sides. After a week of the really dreary food on the Emmet, Jeffrey was not surprised to see George tucking into the food without any ladylike reservations. Together they demolished the sandwiches and salads, and then the lemon cake that followed. By the time Chadwick added several cups of tea to the feast, he was feeling himself. The two lovers agreed it was the best food they had eaten in ages.

"As bad as army food is, that slop the navy serves up is worse," Chadwick told Georgina. "I cannot understand how they stand it."

"It was pretty awful," she agreed. "We have to get Paddy off as soon as possible. Eating that food isn't going to help him get better."

"As soon as we finish reporting to Mr. Pitt, I will talk to Captain about having Paddy brought to shore," he assured her.

In spite of the fact that Lieutenant Moore had claimed Walmer was no longer a totally male preserve, Chadwick was relieved when a young maid tapped at the door.

"If you have finished, miss, will come with me?" she asked. "I have your bath ready and Lady Stanhope is seeing to a proper dress for you."

"For real?" George asked happily. "A bath? What richness!" She gave Jeffrey a quick kiss and jumped up to follow the young maid. Chadwick smiled, noticing that even in her enthusiasm Georgina kept the old blanket draped around her like a cloak.

No sooner had the females left than an older man, dressed in black, stood in the doorway. He bowed.

"Captain Chadwick, I am General Smith's man, Boyle," he introduced himself. "He asked me to help you get sorted. If you would come this way, sir?"

"With pleasure," Chadwick answered sincerely.

* * *

Jeffrey was still fumbling with his cravat when Boyle showed him to a room that was furnished with only a few chairs and couches.

"If you will step in here, sir," Boyle said opening a door. "This is the waiting room. When Mr. Pitt is ready, he will send for you."

As with most rooms in Walmer Castle, this one had a rounded side made up of windows. Chadwick assumed they were now in one of the bastions overlooking the ocean. Georgina stood in the window area staring at the gun-powder gray sea that was becoming angry with deepening waves breaking on the shore. *There must be a storm brewing farther out to sea,* he thought. He could see the *Emmet* rocking at her anchor and hoped Paddy was lulled into sleep by the motion.

He looked back at Georgina. She looked lovely to his eyes. Her hair was still damp, but he loved the way it curled widely around her face. This was the first time he had seen her in a real dress. While he loved how it softened her, it was overly large for her spare frame and Jeffrey found he missed how her trousers showed off her legs. Then he noticed how her arms were crossed over her body, with each hand squeezing the opposite arm. She looked like she was freezing.

Georgina turned when he drew close, her anxious expression becoming a slight smile.

"Why so sad?" he asked taking her into his arms. "We made it back, relatively in one piece."

"Yes we did," she agreed quietly, laying her head on his shoulder. "But that's just it. Our adventure is over."

"And?" he said questioningly.

"I know it was dangerous, but crazy as it seems, it was the best time of my life. And, honestly, I am afraid of what might happen next." She sighed. "I met Lady Stanhope and all she could talk about was how happy I must be to be going home to Dublin and seeing my family."

"Well, that isn't quite the plan," Jeffrey replied calmly.

"I am worried they will separate us," she offered anxiously. "I am not quite of age. I could be sent back and there is nothing you could do."

Chadwick pressed his lips against hers softly. Then he stepped back and, still holding her hands, knelt on one knee.

"Will you marry me?" he asked.

"Jeffrey…"

The door swung open. Wright entered the room followed by a thin man walking with a cane.

"Ah, Captain, we seem to be interrupting," the stranger said. A third figure, General Smith, followed the two men.

Chadwick rose to his feet. In spite of Georgina's tugging, he wouldn't release her hands. She had gone absolutely beet red and was staring out the window trying to get control of her emotions. It occurred to him that she might be so embarrassed that she would just flee and never give him the answer he wanted.

"Gentlemen, a moment if you please?" he addressed their audience. "Miss Yelverton was just about to tell me something important." He raised one of her hands and kissed her fingers.

"Please, George?"

"Yes, of course, I will," she murmured out of the side of her mouth, still staring out the window.

A glance over his shoulder showed that while the three men had retreated out of the waiting room, they had left the door open. He grinned at Georgina and found her returning his smile wholeheartedly.

He bent to kiss her thoroughly and then said, "Come on, let's go give our report. We will figure out the rest later."

Fingers entwined, the couple went through the open door into Mr. Pitt's office and library. Book shelves covered each wall and a large desk was stationed under a large bay window overlooking the sea. The three men were arranged in chairs flanking the fireplace. There was an empty couch to which, upon a gesture from Captain Wright, Chadwick led Georgina.

After introductions were made, Mr. Pitt began, "Well, Captain Chadwick, I have read your report. It is a very detailed and well-written document. But I guess what we want to know first is, are congratulations in order?"

"They are indeed, sir," Chadwick said spoke happily. He sat, still gripping Georgina's hand while congratulations were offered and Pitt sent for port and brandy to toast the couple.

"Now, to business," Pitt said. "I meant what I said about your report. It is one of the better ones to come across my desk. And by the way, I do indeed know your supervisor, Mr. Wickham. In fact, I was the one who sent him to Dublin to start the Alien Office there."

"Mr. Wickham is most insistent on complete, well-written reports. I learned a lot from him. Probably more than from my tutors in Oxford."

"Well, consequently, I don't have many questions. What you have written corroborates the information I've received from other sources. But yours is the latest. And honestly, since you are British, your report will carry weight when I ask Parliament for money. But, so I am certain I have a complete sense of what went on and why, I do want to hear the whole story from you and Miss Yelverton."

It took some time, what with the refilling of glasses with brandy and ratafia for George, and the two of them telling the same story from different perspectives. As they talked about the different types of vessels they had seen, George stood at Pitt's side to point to the different sketches she had made. Then Wright and General Smith discussed the seaworthiness of the various ships. As Chadwick had found out, some of the smaller ones had sides too low to take the waves in the Channel; others, Smith thought, might not be able to withstand the weight of the various cannons or howitzers planned for them.

Finally, Mr. Pitt folded up the papers. This seemed to be a signal for the discussion to end. Everyone fell silent.

"Whether the ships will do what Napoleon wants is not of real importance right now. First and foremost is the fact that England is not prepared for an invasion and I must convince Parliament and the military types in London that we have to do more. I am going to spend a few days working up my ideas for coastal preparation and for raising and training troops. Then I will go to London to begin discussions."

There was a pause as everyone waited for him to continue. He sat, sipping his brandy, clearly marshaling his thoughts.

"Captain Wright, take a few days before you return to your station. I don't think I need you in London. However, that could change. General Smith, I shall want you with me."

Finally, he turned to Jeffrey. "Chadwick, I will need you to be available to testify if needed. What are your plans now?" Pitt asked.

"Miss Yelverton and Paddy have been through a lot. I want to take them to London to stay with my friends, the Donnays, who live in Chelsea with General Ambrose Coxe."

Pitt and Smith nodded, with Pitt adding, "Yes, he's a good man."

It seemed to Jeffrey, the man knew everyone.

"I want to make sure that Paddy recovers fully. I owe him a lot," Chadwick continued. "And of course, we need to contact Mr. Yelverton and let him know his daughter is safe."

"I can help you with that," Pitt said. "If you give me a letter, I will see that it goes in the official pouches to London and then on to Dublin. That will be faster than any other method."

"Thank you, sir," George replied. "I will make sure I write a letter immediately."

"You are welcome to stay here a few days while you get on your feet. I understand you have lost all your luggage..."

Chadwick could see Pitt's eyes involuntarily go to George's dress.

"That looks like one of Hester's garments. She is a tall woman," he added. "We'll have to do something about your wardrobe."

"That's very kind of you Mr. Pitt," Jeffrey responded. "Besides having to get appropriate gear, it is going to take me a little time to get Paddy organized and fit to travel."

"Is there anything else we can help you with?" Smith asked courteously.

George was shaking her head and murmuring polite assurances that they had done a lot for them already, when a thought popped into Jeffrey's mind.

"Yes, there is, sir, now that you ask. Mr. Pitt, how do I get a special license?"

* * *

The carriage finally creaked to a stop. Chadwick grinned at his companions and then jumped out before the driver had lowered the steps. He turned back and held up his arms to Georgina, who had appeared in the opening. Grasping her by the waist, he swung her to the ground.

"Are you in a hurry, Captain?" Paddy's Irish brogue, always thicker when he was tired or feeling stressed, was evident. He grasped Chadwick's shoulder for balance and lowered himself gingerly. While the lad was still very pale, Chadwick noticed that his bruises were fading. Paddy's hand was still in splints, but he was breathing more easily. Thankfully, he was recovered enough to tease Chadwick about their errand.

"Well, yes, I am rather in a hurry," Jeffrey answered happily. "I may not get another chance to tie the knot with George. She could change her mind."

They both turned to admire Georgina. She was standing in the center of the archway with her back to them. Canterbury Cathedral formed a magnificent backdrop but Jeffrey had only eyes for the woman who had captured his heart. She turned to him, her face alight with amazement.

"I have never seen a more magnificent church! I expected it to be big but this is truly massive. Are we really getting married here?"

Chadwick laughed at her astonishment. "Yes, we are," he answered heartily.

At that moment, another carriage pulled up and began to dislodge travelers. Captain Wright was the first to emerge, Lieutenant McClain was second. They both offered hands to help Lady Stanhope down. She was followed by General Smith. After general greetings and questioning of how their travel had been, the small group started to make their way to the Cathedral.

"Wait, wait!" Lady Stanhope called to the driver. "I forgot something!"

It was Lieutenant McClain who retrieved the bouquet of flowers from the carriage. He presented them to Georgina with a bow.

"Fallon remembered what we all forgot, that a beautiful bride should have beautiful flowers," he said gravely. "He rushed after us with them. I am so glad Lady Stanhope heard him. Fallon would never forgive us is we forgot them."

"Oh look, they match my dress," George noted happily. "That was so kind of him."

General Smith shook the letter he had been consulting. "The Archbishop writes that he will meet us at the door to the southwest transept. That would be the door over there." He gestured to what seemed to be the middle of the massive cathedral. Even as he spoke, the huge doors opened slowly and an elderly gentleman in clerical vestments appeared in the doorway. "Ah, there he is now," the General said.

Their small group, led by General Smith and Captain Wright, followed by Lady Stanhope arm in arm with Georgina, went to greet the Archbishop. Behind them Chadwick and McClain walked with Paddy more slowly.

"At least we are going faster, Paddy, than that last day in Boulogne," Chadwick remarked. "And today you are walking on your own."

Paddy shook his head. "Ah, Captain, you know I don't remember all that. I think I must have been unconscious and you carried me."

"Part of the time, I think you might have been."

They reached the doorway and the waiting clergyman. He warmly welcomed them and led them into the Cathedral.

"I thought our little group would be lost in this place if we used the main altar, so I have arranged for the ceremony to be in one of the side chapels, St Anslem's. If you would follow me, it is just here on the right."

The little chapel was lit with several branches of candles and scented by fresh flowers on the altar. Chadwick was surprised to discover that St. Anslem's wasn't empty there was a small number of people already in attendance.

The Archbishop, noticing his glance, said "Some people just love weddings. They really are happy occasions."

He directed Chadwick and Paddy to stand at the altar railing, leaving Georgina and Lady Stanhope at the rear. The rest of their party had joined the other onlookers while the Archbishop took his place on the altar. He signaled for Georgina to approach.

Once George dropped her stole, Chadwick could hear a murmur of approval of her appearance. The simple dress she wore was a gift from Lady Stanhope. But Jeffrey knew it had taken a joint effort to finish it in time. Even he had been conscripted into spending an evening stitching some of the side seams so the one seamstress in the house could concentrate on the sleeves and neckline details. The end result, a gown made of pink silk, featured a high waist, a scoop neckline bordered with lace, long sleeves with rows of buttons, all of which showed off George's slim figure to perfection. Her hair was a riot of curls through which someone had threaded a ribbon matching her dress. But it was her flushed happy face as she walked the short aisle toward him that gave Jeffrey the most satisfaction and the certainty that this was the right move for him.

* * *

Jeffrey balanced the wine bottle and two glasses in his left hand while he fumbled with the lock on the door with his right. Maybe he should have drunk a little less at the wedding luncheon, but the toasts kept coming and etiquette required he respond in kind. Door successfully locked, he carefully found a place on the dresser for the wine and turned to look at his bride.

Georgina was gazing out the window. She seemed to sense her husband's gaze and turned to smile at him happily. As he joined her at the window, Jeffrey gave heartfelt thanks that George wasn't afraid of him physically and had even enjoyed the few times they had been together on the boat. Now that they were married, he was looking forward to years of conjugal bliss. Just hearing that ridiculous term in his head made him snort with laughter.

"What, what's funny?" she asked.

Putting her arm around his waist, she snugged up against him.

"Look at the Cathedral, Jeffrey. Even at night and in the dark it is magnificent."

They gazed out the window for a time. There were a few candles in the church that seemed to wander about the nave. But now, with the sun fully set, only the outline of the dark mass was visible against the darkening sky.

Jeffrey had booked a couple of nights in a room in the inn where they had had the wedding luncheon. Now that he had reported to the authorities about the invasion and Pitt was taking an active role in defending against it, he did not feel as anxious to reach London as he had. They deserved a few days of respite and the town of Canterbury seemed to be the place to rest.

He pulled her into his arms and pressed a kiss on her lips while he closed the drapes with his free hand.

He twisted the ribbon from her hair slowly.

"Do you want me to go wander about while you get ready for bed?" he asked softly. "I am sorry you don't have a maid to help you."

George looked up at him with mischief in her eyes.

"I have you," she smirked. "It seems to me you were pretty helpful getting me undressed before. I imagine you can make yourself useful tonight."

Jeffrey could feel himself hardening in anticipation of helping her.

"It has been a long week," he mused while he studied the neckline of her pink frock. "Lady Stanhope made quite the formidable chaperone."

She held up her arms and gestured to him to start on the buttons that ran from wrist to elbow.

"Jeffrey," to his ears, she absolutely purred. "Please start with the sleeves. There are so many buttons and at an awkward angle for me to reach."

It took a full glass of wine before he had managed all of the cloth covered buttons. George had an attack of the giggles watching him struggle, finally finishing up a few he had missed when he gave up and dropped to his knees to take off her shoes. Stockings and garters followed. As he slowly peeled the silk stockings off, he pressed kisses behind her knees and down her calves to her ankles.

"Jeffrey," she said shakily. "If you keep that up, I am going to be a puddle on the floor."

A quick glance at her face and all his teasing stopped. He rose quickly and turned her so he could easily reach the back of her dress and the lacings there. He gently pushed the dress off her shoulders and down her frame so it pooled on the floor. Wearing only her chemise and corset, she stepped out of the dress. She bent to pick up the frock, but he beat her to it.

"Remember, I am playing the lady's maid tonight," he said huskily. "Sit here, and drink this."

He led her to the bed and handed her a glass of wine to sip while he laid her wedding dress over the chair in the corner. His clothes and boots swiftly followed. Soon he was sitting with his bride on the bed in his shirt and trousers.

"Are you going to leave the candles burning?" she asked quietly.

"Yes, you are beautiful and I want to see you." He put his wine aside and made swift work of the corset lacing. He took his shirt off, laid her down, and proceeded to slide her chemise off, following its progress with his lips. As her breasts became visible, he stopped to marvel at their perfection. By the time she was nude, he was in agony with need and she was gasping.

"Jeffrey, how long do I have to wait? Lady Stanhope is not here," George's voice came in pants as she clutched his hair.

Chadwick was torn between laughter and need as he rose over her. "No she's not. It is just us," he groaned.

Chapter Nineteen: End of the Day

It was late in the day when the carriage reached the outskirts of London. "Do you want to continue on to Chelsea or stop somewhere and arrive in the morning? It has been a long day," Chadwick asked George.

Secretly he hoped she would pick the second option so he could have another night with her alone, but it seemed only fair to let her pick. His own desire must have been pretty clear, at least to Paddy, given the grin on his face. Thankfully, Paddy didn't add any teasing only smiled and then closed his eyes again. Chadwick studied his friend thoughtfully. Although his bruises were fading, he was not regaining his strength as fast as Jeffrey had hoped and he tired easily. Chadwick needed to find Paddy a place to recuperate without the constant traveling.

Meanwhile to his disappointment, George had decided to finish the trip. "Let's finish this. It's not all that much longer, right? I am tired of traveling and would like to stay in one place for a couple of days. We are staying with Nathan for some time, right?"

"Yes, at least for several nights, probably longer."

As he spoke, he raised the window shade and leaned out. "We want to keep going to get to Chelsea tonight," he called to the driver. "How long do you think it will be?"

"Did you hear him?" he asked George. "He says only a couple of hours."

"Good. This carriage is by far the best mode we have traveled by on this trip! But I am ready for a nice chair in front of a fire and a good cup of tea," she responded. "Now, shall we get back to our original topic? How long are we staying with your friends?"

"I gave up my London rooms when I moved to Dublin. It's going to take some time to find a place for us and make the trip to Ireland to see your father."

As he spoke, Chadwick held George's hand and idly toyed with the ring on her finger. "Second stop in London is the jeweler's to get you a ring of your own."

"I think the second stop better be a *modiste* as I only have my wedding dress and the one Lady Stanhope lent me." To his amusement, she chuckled.

"My father would be appalled to think I was going about in a second hand dress."

Jeffrey laughed, too. "Probably he would be more appalled if he saw you last week. I must say, I thought the trousers looked particularly attractive even if I bought them myself. I certainly have become quite the shopper in the used clothing market."

He turned his head so he could smell her hair.

"But you make even a used dress look amazing."

"Jeffrey, do not embarrass Paddy," she said chidingly.

"Speaking of Paddy," Paddy cut in with his eyes still closed, "Do you know of somewhere I can stop over? I don't think I can continue on to Dublin without a break."

Jeffrey leaned forward and placed his hand on his assistant's knee. "I am not dumping you anywhere," he said. "You are coming to Chelsea with us. Nathan said he had a room for you to use."

Paddy looked relieved. "But, sir, I don't want to inconvenience you or your friends."

"It is not an inconvenience," Jeffrey said emphatically. "I owe you, we both owe you. You saved us on more than one occasion; I didn't dump you in Boulogne and I am not dumping you now."

"Neither of us are, Paddy," Georgina added. "You treated me better than my own brother has."

Paddy nodded shortly but Jeffrey could see his shoulders relaxed. "I am sorry I took so long to tell you. I had some things on my mind, but I should have realized you would be worried. Wherever George and I end up, please know you are welcome." He turned to George and saw his own guilt reflected on her face. They had both neglected Paddy recently, indulging in their own happiness. He made a resolve to be more aware of his assistant's condition. After all it was as a result of his, Chadwick's, decisions.

He welcomed George's voice. "I meant to ask you, did you tell anyone else about the wedding? You didn't write any more letters that I don't know about?" she asked.

"I wrote to your father but that was when we first landed. Mr. Pitt sent it via diplomatic bag for me. I did not mention marriage only that you were safe and we would be stopping in London before going on to Dublin," he responded. "When I wrote Nathan, I told him when we would be arriving. I had to tell him we were married in Canterbury. If I had not mentioned it, we might find ourselves in different room!"

"When do you think my father will get the letter?" she asked.

"We have been about two weeks between Walmer and getting married. I expect he got the letter about a week ago. He will even have time to rush to London." He tried to read her face but the increasing gloom in the carriage made it difficult to see her exact expression. "Are you anxious about seeing him?"

"Actually, yes, I am," she said seriously. "I know you had a special license from the Archbishop of Canterbury and Mr. Pitt said it was legal, but I am not quite twenty-three and I am afraid he will want our marriage annulled."

"Honestly, George, I rather doubt that he would want you to have to face Dublin society unwed! But besides that, he seemed to really care about you. I am confident he will come around when he sees how happy you are, and realizes you were not forced into anything."

"I was far from forced into anything," she agreed wholeheartedly.

"Me either!" He squeezed her hand since with Paddy present he couldn't show her how happy he was.

The rest of the trip passed as Chadwick pointed out London landmarks and regaled her with stories about them. As they approached Chelsea, George started to carefully adjust her new hat. Just before they left Canterbury, they had wandered the streets admiring the medieval architecture, as well as various shop windows. In one establishment, Jeffrey had found a bonnet with a rolled brim that he thought charming with her short curls. He instantly insisted on buying it for her.

"I like your hair cut short like this," Jeffrey said as George carefully adjusted her new headgear. He was glad to see that his selection had proven to be right. In the light of the street lamps, he could see her cheeks were rosy and her eyes were bright. Short curls escaped the bonnet and edged her face in a charming manner.

Before she could ask, he said, "You look perfect."

* * *

Chadwick had visited the Chelsea home of Marion and Nathan Donnay any number of times in the past, but only once had he been upstairs to the family's sleeping quarters. On that occasion, there had been so much chaos that he had not had time to really notice anything. Now he saw that, while not particularly spacious, the rooms were well laid out and very comfortable. He slipped out while George was still sleeping and made his way downstairs to the breakfast room. Blessedly, there was hot coffee available and Nathan was reading the paper. General Coxe also sat at the table, reading his correspondence.

"Well, you are a sight for sore eyes," Nathan said. "I can tell you, I was glad to get your letter last week saying you got to Walmer Castle."

"'Morning General Coxe," Chadwick addressed the older man as he poured coffee.

"You were not nearly as glad as I was to get there," he said to Nathan. "It has been quite a trip."

He sighed gratefully as he sipped the coffee. It tasted like a little bit of heaven after all the other beverages he had had to endure over the past few months.

"Egads, this is good. Nothing like it in Dublin. The French say they drink coffee but they brew it differently."

"I know your trip was more exciting than just wandering about and tasting different beverages," Nathan said caustically. "While the ladies are still in bed, how about giving me a run-down of what you have actually been up to? Oh and by the way, your lady is quite something. But is she always so quiet?"

General Coxe had been finishing his toast while the two friends chatted. Now he looked at them and said, "Speaking of Miss Yelverton – no I mean Mistress Chadwick – I just received a note from her father. He has arrived in London."

"That was quick," said Nathan. "You only wrote to him last week."

"General, you wrote to Mr. Yelverton?" Chadwick inquired. "I did not realize. I know Mr. Pitt wrote, probably the day we got to Walmer Castle."

"As soon as we got word at the Office you had been picked up, I wrote. I was not sure whose message would get to him first but I assumed he would be anxious and it appears I was right. From this note, you can see he is in some state to see his daughter," the General replied. "He intends to call on us today, within the next hour or so. I believe he is accompanied by his son."

The General passed the letter he had been reading to Jeffrey who scanned it and sent it on to Nathan. Nathan tossed the paper onto the table, stood and drained his cup.

"I will go and warn Marion. When he finds out the rescuer married the victim, we might have a situation on our hands. I am positive she will want to be prepared."

"Prepared for what?" A light female voice asked from the doorway. Marion stood in the doorway, one hand on the doorknob. She was turned partially, evidently speaking to someone in the hall behind her.

Jeffrey saw her in profile first. She was huge. Theoretically, he knew she was pregnant. But he didn't have much experience with pregnant women. How could they get so large and still move?

"Jeffrey! How lovely to see you."

She strode into the room and gave him both of her hands. He could see that she must have noticed his initial reaction, as her green eyes were dancing with amusement. Thornton entered the room behind her with fresh coffee and a plate of eggs and ham steak for him.

As they all took their seats again, Nathan gave her the information that Mr. Yelverton would be arriving soon and that he didn't know about Jeffrey's recent marriage to his daughter. Marion seemed to take it all in stride. After a few instructions to Thornton for the cook, she seconded her husband's request for information about Jeffrey's recent adventures.

Nathan was waving around his coffee cup and demanding details about Hastings' death when George tried to slip into the room. Since the men rose at her entrance and Thornton was holding the door open with a grand gesture, there was no way she could avoid being noticed. Although he realized he was biased, Chadwick thought she looked particularly lovely this morning.

The green dress, one he assumed borrowed from Marion, showed her coloring to advantage. Her strawberry-blond curls were still a riot framing her face.

She smiled at everyone and thanked Marion in particular for her hospitality and for the dresses that had been left in the room.

Before she was able to sit down, however, they all heard a loud thumping on the front door. Loud enough, that is, that they could hear it clearly in the breakfast room at the back of the house.

"George, prepare yourself," Chadwick warned quickly. "I think your father is here."

George went unusually pale, her startled eyes focusing on Jeffrey's face. By the time he got an arm around her for support, Thornton was opening the door and announcing Mr. Yelverton's presence. Georgina's father had obviously not waited in the drawing room as requested, but had followed Thornton to the breakfast room and was peering over his shoulder. Once he spotted his daughter, he pushed Thornton aside and pulled her into his arms.

"Thank God, you're all right," he said softly. "I have been so worried."

Jeffrey was close enough to see that the elder man had choked up and tears were starting to run down his face.

"We both have been worried."

Chadwick had not noticed the second man following Yelverton into the room. George's brother stood there looking somewhat embarrassed by his father's outward display of emotion.

George took a step back while her father searched for his handkerchief to mop his face. She also seemed frozen by her father's display of sentiment.

To Chadwick's relief, Marion interceded. "Georgina, why don't you take your father to the drawing room for a more private reunion?" she suggested.

"No, no I am fine," Mr. Yelverton said as he wiped his eyes. "I can see she is just fine. But I want to know how she ended up in here in London with strangers."

"Then, please, sit down," Marion, said. She directed Thornton to bring more coffee and after finding out that Mr. Yelverton had skipped breakfast in his hurry to be reunited with his daughter, more food. Chadwick grinned to himself about Marion's ability to organize a situation when an elbow caught him in the ribs.

"Isn't she something?" Nathan smirked. "What an officer she would have made."

"From the looks of her, she is about to produce her own army," Jeffrey murmured back. "When is she due?"

"Not entirely confident of the date," was the smiling response from the proud papa. "But soon."

Chadwick saw the General glance around the table to make sure everyone was seated and had coffee or food. Jeffrey sat between Nathan on his left, George on his right. The elder Yelverton sat to George's other side, while the brother and Marion sat across the table from her. The General cleared his throat to get everyone's attention.

"Captain Chadwick, I think it's time you gave us the whole story from the beginning. I still have questions about this unsavory business. I have correspondence from Wickham asking me to investigate what I can from this end," the General directed. "Mr. Yelverton, I should explain," he continued, "I work in the same office as Mr. Wickham, only in the London branch of the Alien Office."

"Why can't Wickham do his own investigation once we get back to Dublin?" George's father asked.

"Nathan and I have information about the situation in France that Mr. Wickham is not privy to. Although I know that Captain Chadwick has already made a report to the appropriate authority, I will also be making a report to Mr. Grenville on the Privy Council in London. As you know, they report directly to the Prime Minister."

"I don't understand. What has all this reporting got to do with my sister's kidnapping?" the younger Yelverton protested.

The General gave him a look that would have had any officer in his command quaking in his boots.

"Not the kidnapping per se, but who the kidnapper was," the General answered shortly. "We will start at the beginning and maybe the connections will become clear. Marion, are you ready?"

Chadwick noticed with surprise that Marion now had pen, ink and paper spread before her on the table. Evidently, Nathan had delegated notetaking to her. That was a good thing, as Donnay's notes were usually indecipherable.

"Very well, General," Chadwick said. "Shall we do this in chronological order? If so, I think the story should start with the kidnapping."

He waited for the General to nod agreement then looked directly at George. "Would you start the tale, since the kidnapping took place before I arrived in Dublin?"

And so it went. First George related the horror of the day when Hastings grabbed her off the street. Then her father and brother talked about receiving the ransom demand and the tense time after they had paid the money when Georgina was not returned. Just as Chadwick began detailing his first interview with Vilet, General Coxe called for a break.

"Let us reconvene in the drawing room in about half an hour," he said.

As they all stood and stretched, Chadwick noticed that Nathan moved quickly to Marion's side and put his hand on her back and massaged her gently. He turned to find Georgina's brother pulling on her arm and trying to compel her out of the room.

"I have some questions for you," he was bleating.

George didn't look so much concerned as angry as she tried to pull her arm out of his grasp.

"Hold up, Yelverton," Chadwick said.

"This is not your business, Chadwick," her brother answered shortly. "This is family."

"Since that is my wife you are manhandling, I think this is totally my business," Jeffrey replied and grabbed his arm. Freed, George moved away quickly from her brother.

Over her brother's expositions of fury and dismay, he could hear her saying to her father, "Yes, we were married by special license by the Archbishop of Canterbury Cathedral. General Smith and Lady Stanhope, Mr. Pitt's niece, stood witness for us. It is all perfectly legal and I am very happy about it."

While it seemed her father wasn't going to raise the roof, her brother seemed to be angry enough for both.

"After all she has put us through, she has the nerve to just announce her marriage to this man, this agent..." Walter Yelverton seemed to lose his power of speech at that point—which was a good thing in Chadwick's view as the General cleared his throat again. It was not a happy sound. Jeffrey and

Nathan exchanged glances. They had seen the General in command form at work. It was never pleasant for the recipient of his displeasure.

"Mr. Yelverton, Senior," he said icily. "Please take your son to the drawing room and give him some time to control his temper. We will reconvene shortly and discuss the rest of the story. Later, you can talk with Captain Chadwick and discuss his credentials, but I can tell you right now, he is above reproach."

He paused until he spotted Thornton in the hall. "Thornton, show these gentlemen to the drawing room," he barked and strode out of the room without a backward glance.

* * *

The General cleared his throat again, and this time even Walter Yelverton took notice. They were all sitting in the drawing room at the front of the house. Most houses, Chadwick knew, now had their formal drawing room on the upper floor. The General had personally decorated this house and he kept the public rooms on the ground floor. Unconventional, but more comfortable than most other homes he had been a guest in.

Nathan was standing at the drum table in the window with writing paraphernalia spread before him. Obviously, he was taking over the note-taking. Chairs and one love seat formed a semi-circle around the fire place. None of the gentlemen sat until Marion and George came in. The General indicated the most comfortable chair for Marion and then invited the rest to arrange themselves as they saw fit. Jeffrey grabbed George's hand and led her to the love seat. Her brother frowned angrily at his maneuver but Chadwick ignored him. Her father, rather oddly, seemed to have fallen back into the abstracted demeanor he had shown in Dublin when Chadwick first met him. He avoided eye contact and stared intently into the cold fire place.

"Captain," the General said, "would you continue? I believe you had just been picked up and taken to the office of this Vilet."

The story went quickly until Jeffrey started to detail the condition in which he had found George. Marion's gasp of sympathy was audible and she reached over to grasp Georgina's hand.

Almost immediately, the brother interrupted, demanding to know if she had been 'Abused.'

Before Chadwick could jump to George's defense, Marion angrily asked what business it was of his. Across all the voices came one Chadwick didn't immediately recognize.

"Shut Up!" The elder Yelverton had come to himself and was speaking directly to his son. "And stay that way," he thundered.

"That's the father I remember," George whispered to him.

Yelverton moderated his voice, but kept speaking directly to his son, "There is something very, very odd, very havey-cavy about this situation and I think you know more than you are letting on. You treat me like a doddering old man who has lost his sense, but I still see things. I will have some questions for you when we have heard this tale to the end."

When the younger Yelverton tried to protest, the elder replied.

"Enough," he barked. "Please, Chadwick, continue," he said in a calmer tone.

Just when Georgina had finished describing their rescue in the Channel by Captain Wright, Thornton pulled back the pocket doors separating the drawing and dining rooms and announced luncheon was ready.

"Buffet style as you requested, madam."

They all stood in preparation for moving to the dining room. Nathan stretched his fingers, trying to work out the cramps. He grinned ruefully at Chadwick.

"This note taking is much your style than mine," he said.

"Nathan, Jeffrey, a moment if you please," the General asked. When the rest had filtered to the next room, he led them to the library across the hall.

"This won't take long, will it, sir?" Nathan asked. "That scurvy brother will likely steal all the best bits before we get back."

"Knowing my daughter, I am positive she hid all the good 'bits' for you in the kitchen," the General returned. "But I did want to talk about the brother. I don't want to discuss anything sensitive in front of him. I agree with the elder Yelverton: there is something off about his attitude."

Chadwick breathed a sigh of relief. He thought his reaction to the younger Yelverton was just his own.

"I also wanted to mention, those men you saw shot, Chadwick? Those were my men who I had sent there."

The General sighed deeply. He looked deeply grieved. "Their deaths will always be on my conscience. But what I wanted to say, was this: You managed to do what they had been sent to do, gather information about the invasion and rescue Miss Yelverton in addition. I am deeply impressed by your actions."

Nathan clapped Chadwick on the shoulder.

"I agree, old man," he said. "Damned impressive. I really was worried for you after I got that letter. You must have written it before you left Dublin. Marion and I both agreed I should slip over there to look for you myself."

"You did?" Jeffrey asked in surprise. "When was that?"

"I believe I got to Calais after you took off to Boulogne. I found the tavern where you stayed—the landlord remembered you, but he didn't know where you had gone to. I poked around for a few days, waiting, but then too many people seemed too interested in me, so I hopped it back home. I did leave a note with the naval blockade to be on the lookout for you. I couldn't think what else to do that might be helpful."

"That was pretty dangerous, Nat," Chadwick said. He was deeply affected by the efforts of his friend. "Vilet is no fool. If he had caught you, you might have ended up in front of a firing squad like our colleagues. That note, though, was really helpful. Captain Wright was primed to believe my story because of it. It made getting to England much easier than I would have believed possible. Thank you," he added sincerely. "In fact, now that I think about it, he might not have bothered to try to pick us up if he hadn't been watching for people trying to get out of France."

"Nathan!" Marion's call from the drawing room quickly brought all three men to the drawing room. The sight before their eyes froze all of them into inaction for a moment. The two Yelverton men were in the middle of the room with Thornton in between trying to separate them. Chadwick and Donnay each grabbed a Yelverton and tried to help Thornton. The elder Yelverton seemed to have his hands on his son's neck, while the younger man struggled to break his father's grasp. The General finally broke the impasse by whacking the younger Yelverton brutally in the back of the knees with his walking stick. He sank like a bag of rocks.

Nathan dragged him to a chair while the General demanded, "What the hell is going on?" of the elder man.

"That piece of shit..." Yelverton choked on his words, even as he wiped his face with his handkerchief.

Jeffrey helped his new father-in-law to a chair as far from his son as possible. He got him a glass of brandy. Glances at George showed that she and Marion were huddled by the fireplace, as far away from the action in the middle of the floor as possible, he noted with satisfaction. Before the General could repeat his question, George said, "It would appear that Walter had more to do with my kidnapping than we previously realized."

She sounded extremely calm but looking closer at her eyes, Jeffrey realized she was so furious she was shaking and it was Marion, by clutching George's hands, who was helping her hold it together.

"Explain," he snapped at the elder Yelverton.

George's father carefully placed his empty glass on a nearby table and then began to explain how, as soon as the other men had left the room, Walter had started demanding of Georgina confirmation that Hastings was dead.

"He seemed so stunned by the news, so I asked him why? What did the man mean to him? And you know what he says?" Yelverton was outraged. "He said, 'Hastings owes me money'."

"How did they even know one another?" Chadwick asked, confused.

"Exactly," George snapped. "What would they have to do with one another but my kidnapping?"

"I didn't get that far in my thinking," Yelverton continued. "So I asked him, 'What do you mean, he owes you money? It's more likely, given your gambling habits, that you owe him money. Guess that hit close to home, but when Georgina...'"

"I flat out accused him of selling me to pay his gambling debts," she interrupted. She left Marion's side and walked over to Chadwick to lay a hand on his arm. George looked into her husband's face with such hurt and disbelief that he ached for her.

"He started babbling about how the plan had gone wrong and Hastings was supposed to give me back after the ransom was paid and some other stuff about how sorry he is that it didn't work out."

"But look, it did work out!" her brother protested. "You are here, and you're fine. Everything's…"

Before he could go further, Chadwick crossed the room and silenced him with a brisk uppercut to the jaw that knocked him right out.

"Mr. Yelverton," Chadwick said adjusting his cuffs and pretending his knuckles did not ache, "you had better get him out of here before I give him the beating he deserves."

"Jeffrey," Nathan's dry voice cut into his red haze of anger. "you forget, we just pulled Mr. Yelverton off his son's neck. I don't think he wants to take him anywhere."

Chadwick turned to find George at his side, wrapping her arms around his arm.

"Is your hand all right?" she asked anxiously. "Should I get a cool cloth?"

The General handed a glass of brandy to Jeffrey and then one to George.

"Drink up," he urged. "It has been quite a day of revelations." He refilled Mr. Yelverton's glass and then poured more for himself and Donnay.

"What about me?" Marion asked. "I could use something too."

Nathan laughed as he hugged her. "Thornton, please pour my wife a dash of brandy. You are right, sir, it has been some day, and we haven't even had lunch yet."

Walter Yelverton groaned and sat up. Before he could open his mouth, his father announced, "I am cutting you off. You are a stain, a mockery of a son. Get out of my life. I will leave enough money with our solicitors for you to get to Canada, but what happens to you after that, I don't care."

"You can't…"

"I can," the elder man said. Turning to General Coxe, he asked, "Would your man see him out?"

Before the General could respond, Donnay and Thornton grabbed George's brother and marched him to the door. Thornton handed him his hat and opened the door.

George sank into a chair beside her father. She sipped her brandy and then said, "I can't believe it. How could he do such a thing? I know we weren't overly fond of one another but I thought that had to do with our having different mothers. Even still…" her voice wandered off sadly.

Her father reached over and patted her hand. "I bear responsibility for him. I knew he was keeping bad company. But when your mother died, I just lost heart. It was easier to just stay in my office grieving."

He sighed and then seemed to address the rest of the occupants of the room. "Recently, the gambling got so bad he had to come to me to pay off his debts. I did it because he promised no more. He must have lied."

"I guess we will never really know how he met Hastings," Donnay said.

"My judgement of Hastings is that he was a creature of opportunity," Chadwick responded. "Like when he recognized Paddy in Boulogne. He didn't know him from Dublin, but he connected him with George's disappearance in Calais and he went looking. He knew from Walter that Mr. Yelverton had someone hunting for her. It might have been the same with him," he gestured with his head to the door. "Hastings saw him as a way to get money; he didn't realize his father had cut off his funds."

"Demanding a ransom for Georgina was rather inventive as well as audacious. And then Hastings figured he could get more by dragging her off to France, where he wanted to go anyway," Donnay continued theorizing. "How could he ever think something so complicated would work out?"

"As I said, he was an opportunist. I can't believe he ever had a complete plan – just kept playing it as it went along," Jeffrey mused.

"Well, I am glad that is all sorted," Marion stood rubbing her back. "Maybe at dinner we can hear about the wedding. I never met anyone else married by special license and at Canterbury Cathedral no less. But now I am going to rest." She smiled at her guests as she started for the door. By the time she got there, Nathan was holding it open and saying he would see her upstairs.

* * *

Chadwick re-crossed his legs. He was in the drawing room, pretending to read while George and her father conferred alone in the library. The General had wandered off after luncheon, probably to write reports. Marion and Nathan never reappeared, and he was left to his own devices while waiting for his bride.

He had spent some time visiting with Paddy. Tucked up in a small room on the top floor, Paddy did not seem noticeably better but he said the service was far and above anything the Navy offered. "Better looking too," he added in his old manner.

Jeffrey was making a mental note to ask Marion to send for a physician to check over his assistant when a quietly dressed woman knocked at the door. "Paddy," she said with a soft Irish lilt to her voice, "I've brought the doctor to look at your broken head." She noticed Chadwick standing by the bed and gave him a short bob. "Afternoon, Captain. I'm Mistress Riley and this is Doctor Melton. He's come to check over Paddy. Mistress Donnay and I thought he still looked peaky."

Chadwick was pleased his friends were taking such good care of Paddy. After assuring Paddy he would check on him later, he made his way back to the drawing room, where he prepared to continue to wait for George and her father to finish their reunion.

He really could not blame them for taking so much time. Mr. Yelverton had been hit with two major bombshells today, his daughter's marriage and his son's criminal activity. He wondered how George felt about her brother being sent to Canada rather than prison.

The library door opened. George emerged, solemn-faced, her eyes red rimmed as if she had been crying. When she saw Jeffrey hovering in the doorway to the drawing room, she smiled and suddenly all was right. Her father walked heavily and slowly. Sadness seemed to seep out of his pores.

He asked Thornton for his hat and said to Chadwick, "It's been a full day, Captain. If it is acceptable, I will return tomorrow, and we can discuss marriage portions and those kinds of details."

He turned to Georgina, gave her an affectionate hug, and kissed her brow. "I am so sorry this happened to you, my dear. However, I can see that you have found your feet and what looks like a good man in the bargain." He shook Chadwick's hand and went out the door.

"Where's he going?" Jeffrey asked.

"To his club. He won't have to meet up with Walter if he goes there."

Jeffrey pulled her to sit with him on the love seat.

She put her head on his shoulder and said, "I have never seen my father like that."

Chadwick made a questioning sound.

"He was so sad about Walter, but he really seemed to want to make it up to me. He talked a lot about his finances and how he is going to reorder them and cut Walter out. He will explain that to you tomorrow. Also, he thinks we would be better off setting up somewhere besides Dublin. He agrees with you that society might not be welcoming. I don't really care where we live as long as I am with you. I don't have any real connections to Dublin."

He picked up her hand and started to play with her wedding ring again. "Did I ever tell you my mother came from Boston?" he asked.

* * *

Dear Reader

If you enjoyed reading *Facing Enemies* and spending some time in 1803, I hope you will spend a moment and leave a review on Amazon. Even a few sentences would be much appreciated. Review here: *Facing Enemies.*

As an author, I can only improve with your feedback. Reviews also have a major impact on how books are sold. They affect the way books are displayed on Amazon. They affect readers' choices, as some 85% of us read the reviews before making a purchase on Amazon. I know I do. Other sites—places like the Fussy Librarian and Bookbub—require a certain number of reviews before an author is even allowed to advertise.

Your willingness to write a review can make a huge difference.

I can be reached through my webpage Maryanntrail.com or at my Facebook page, Mary Ann Trail, Writer.

Thank you,
Mary Ann

What to read next?

The Enemies Collection

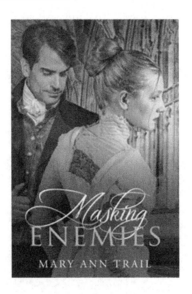

An innocent woman. A rascally dropout. Can they survive mortal danger and mutual loathing to find love?

The Cotswolds, 1803. Frederica Chadwick longs to fill her sketchbook with the beauty of the wide world. So when given the opportunity to tour England's magnificent antiquities, the aspiring artist jumps at the chance. Despite her efforts to ignore a disreputable traveling companion, fate soon reveals its dangerous hand.

After failing out of Oxford, Clive Dering is determined to distance himself from his father's rage. But when his sightseeing trip suffers one mysterious accident after another, he fears he won't survive his time away. And after a kidnapping attempt leaves him stranded with the pretty but vexing Frederica, he's sure his poor luck can't get any worse.

With only each other to lean on, the bad blood between Frederica and

Clive now boils with tender passion. But with ruthless adversaries hunting them down, their newfound chemistry may not be enough to keep them alive.

Can Frederica and Clive escape an insidious plot and chart a happy future?

Masking Enemies is part of the captivating Enemies historical romance series. If you like strong heroines, roguish heroes, and rich period details, then you'll adore Mary Ann Trail's page-turning novel.

Get *Masking Enemies* to explore love and adventure in the English countryside today!

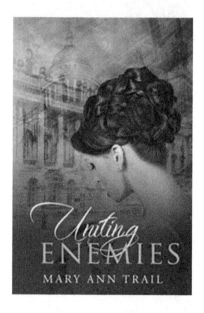

A determined woman. An angry man. London is dangerous but so is love.

England, 1801, as negotiations for the unification of England and Ireland grow heated, Marion Coxe and her family are the focus of a militant anti-unification group.

Fleeing to her father's home in London, she soon finds her heart in peril: caught between a fresh, new love and her old. With her soul pulled in two directions, a terrorist attack could destroy both her life and her love.

Will fighting for a happier future put her entire family in grave danger?

Each title in the Enemies series can be read as a standalone but *Uniting Enemies* is the first chronologically.

Some Notes

By 1803, England and France had been in and out of war for a good part of the previous century. In *Facing Enemies*, war had broken out in 1793 and would continue until 1815 with a brief pause in 1802.

Ireland, while a satellite of Britain - suffered under harsh England restrictions – leading to various resistance groups. The largest group was the United Irishmen, a group that lead an unsuccessful uprising in 1796. The Madra Dubh - a major player in the first book in this series, Uniting Enemies, however, is a complete figment of my imagination.

Alien Office

The Alien Office was a real government agency and I have tried to depict them as faithful to what I learned while researching it. The 18th century version of MI6, The Alien Office is the collected information on immigrants (usually French), kept track of various groups that preached against the government (usually through reports of members), and encouraged neighbors to say something if they saw something. (Someone actually did turn in Wadsworth and Coleridge as suspicious for their habit of walking on the beach in Somerset). Unfortunately, I could not find out how their information was organized as most of the records were destroyed during a fire. My description of the cross indexing books is based on a few examples from the Alien Office in Dublin that are still in existence.

Guide Interpreters

This company certainly existed and their purpose was as stated in the book, to translate military terms into French. My source for this information, Nicolay, stated the French really did not learn other languages easily. I was constantly amazed the detail in planning Napoleon, and his generals, put into their campaigns. However, because so many of the top naval commanders were killed during the revolution, Napoleon's naval advisors were not so experienced, hence the badly designed boats and the issue of the tides.

Historical Characters

The Guide Interpreters was led by Captain Jean-Guillaume-Antoine Cuvelier de Trie. After his military career, he became a playwright. There is no record that his plays ever opened in London, he was a notable success in France, where he is credited with a large number of productions.

While the actions of the Captain in the book are purely a figment of my imagination, I did want to properly credit his name. Use of titles during this time were problematic. I received the following advice from a French consultant:

> In the eighteenth century, presuming the man did not have a noble title he would be referred to by his first patronyme, so as Cuvilier. If he had a title it would be Trie. This would change by the late 19th and early 20th when it would be whole name, unless the speaker wanted to maliciously emphasize the person's non-noble birth.

Several other characters in *Facing Enemies* are based on historically real people.

William Wickham: William Wickham served his country during the latter part of the 18th century as a spymaster. He was posted to Switzerland and directed to ferment insurrections in France putting the royalists back into power. In the late 1790's he transferred to London, accepting the mandate to organize and lead the Alien Office. Although he was not particularly well known, most of the information about France, Napoleon and events in Europe affecting England's long term wars there, came through his hands.

Cornwallis brothers. Yes, those brothers who lost the colonies. After America won its independence, both continued to serve their country admirably in very respectable capacities.

Captain John Wesley Wright: Naval commander who patrolled the coast of France transferring agents until his capture and death in a French prison in 1805.

Mr. Pitt and Lady Stanhope are well known figures of the era.

Selected References

Barthélemy, P. (1825). *History of Boulogne-sur-Mer: From Julisus Ceaser to the year 1825*. Boulogne-sur-Mer: Griset.

Deacon, R., (1980). *A History of the British Secret Service*. Chicago: Academy Chicago Publishers.

Nicolay, F. B. (1848). *Napoleon at the Boulogne Camp*. Reprinted by Wentworth Press, 2016.

Pocock, T. (2002). *The Terror Before Trafalgar: Nelson, Napoleon and the Secret War*. London, John Murray.

Made in the USA
Las Vegas, NV
18 October 2022

57625761R00164